The Edge of Desire

Enter the World of Stephanie Laurens

The Bastion Club Novels*
See members list on pages vi-vii

#1 THE LADY CHOSEN • #2 A GENTLEMAN'S HONOR
#3 A LADY OF HIS OWN • #4 A FINE PASSION
#5 TO DISTRACTION • #6 BEYOND SEDUCTION
CAPTAIN JACK'S WOMAN (*prequel*)

The Cynster Novels

WHERE THE HEART LEADS • THE TASTE OF INNOCENCE
WHAT PRICE LOVE? • THE TRUTH ABOUT LOVE
THE IDEAL BRIDE • THE PERFECT LOVER
THE PROMISE IN A KISS • ON A WICKED DAWN
ON A WILD NIGHT • ALL ABOUT PASSION
ALL ABOUT LOVE • A SECRET LOVE
A ROGUE'S PROPOSAL • SCANDAL'S BRIDE
A RAKE'S VOW • DEVIL'S BRIDE

Also Available the Anthologies

IT HAPPENED ONE NIGHT • HERO, COME BACK
SECRETS OF A PERFECT NIGHT • SCOTTISH BRIDES

STEPHANIE LAURENS

The Edge of Desire

A BASTION CLUB NOVEL

AVON

An Imprint of HarperCollinsPublishers

AVON BOOKS
An Imprint of HarperCollins*Publishers*
10 East 53rd Street
New York, New York 10022-5299

The Edge of Desire

The Bastion Club

"a last bastion against the matchmakers of the ton"

MEMBERS

Christian Allardyce,
Marquess of Dearne

#2 ~~*Anthony Blake,*~~
~~*Viscount Torrington*~~

Alicia
"Carrington"
Pevensey

#5 ~~*Jocelyn Deverell,*~~
~~*Viscount Paignton*~~

Phoebe
Malleson

*Please see page ii for a list of previous

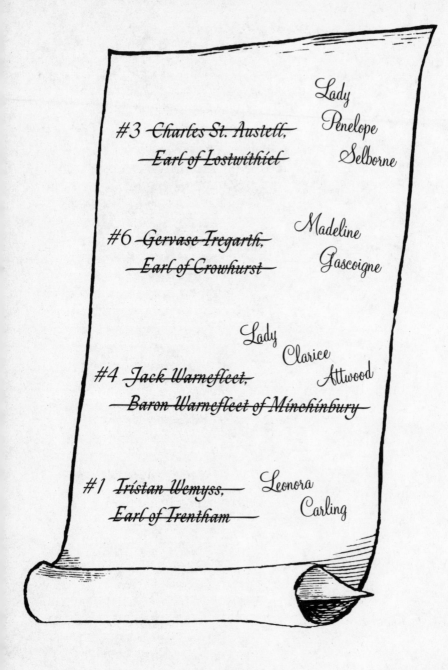

#3 ~~Charles St. Austell,~~
~~Earl of Lostwithiel~~ Lady Penelope Selborne

#6 ~~Gervase Tregarth,~~
~~Earl of Crowhurst~~ Madeline Gascoigne

#4 ~~Jack Warnefleet,~~
~~Baron Warnefleet of Minchinbury~~ Lady Clarice Attwood

#1 ~~Tristan Wemyss,~~
~~Earl of Trentham~~ Leonora Carling

titles in the Bastion Club series.

Chapter 1

August 1816
London

He should make her wait.

Thoughts and wild conjecture roiling in his head, Christian Michael Allardyce, 6th Marquess of Dearne, slowly descended the stairs of the Bastion Club. He'd been nursing a brandy and his despondency in the library when Gasthorpe, the club's majordomo, had appeared with a note.

A note summoning him to face his past.

That past awaited him in the front parlor, the room he and the club's other six owners—all ex-members of one of the more secret and select arms of His Majesty's services who had established the club as their bolt hole against the importuning ladies of the ton—had stipulated as the only room in which ladies were to be permitted. In the months since the club's opening, that rule had, incident by incident, fallen by the wayside, but Gasthorpe had rightly shown this particular lady into the formal front parlor.

He really should make her wait.

She'd said she would, twelve years ago, but then another had come along, and while he'd been buried deep in Napoleon's Europe, she'd lightly thrown aside her promise to him, and fallen in love with and married a Mr. George Randall.

She was now Lady Letitia Randall.

Instead of the Marchioness of Dearne.

Deep in his heart, where nothing and no one any longer touched, he still felt betrayed.

She'd been Lady Letitia Randall for eight years. Although he'd returned to England ten months ago, and he and she moved in the same, very small circle, they'd exchanged not one word. They hadn't even exchanged nods. Even that was too much to expect of him, given their past. She seemed to understand that; coolly detached, haughtily distant, as if he and she had never been close—never been lovers—she'd studiously kept her distance.

Until now.

Christian—

I need your help. There's no one else I can turn to.

L.

That was all the words her note had contained, yet between them those bare words spoke volumes.

His feet continued steadily down the treads. He should make her wait, yet he couldn't imagine what had brought her there. Nor could he imagine why his staff at Allardyce House in Grosvenor Square had divulged his whereabouts. His butler, Percival, was a paragon of his calling; nothing short of a force of nature would have induced him to disobey his master's express orders.

Then again, the lady presently occupying the front parlor had qualified as such from her earliest years.

Stepping off the last tread, he studied the parlor door. It was closed. He could turn around and retreat, and let her wait for at least ten minutes. Even fifteen. The desperation in her plea guaranteed she would wait. Not meekly—meek wasn't in her repertoire—but she would grit her teeth and remain until he deigned to see her.

Some part of him wanted to hurt her—as she'd hurt him,

as he still hurt. Despite the years, the wound was raw; it still bled.

The faint elusive scent of jasmine drew him to the door.

It was curiosity, he told himself, that had him reaching for the handle. Not the incredible, irresistible attraction that had from the first drawn them together—that even after twelve years of neglect and eight years of disillusion still arced across a crowded ballroom.

And made him ache.

Opening the door, steeling himself, he went in.

The first surprise was her weeds. He paused in the doorway, rapidly assessing.

Seated in one of the armchairs flanking the small hearth, the chair facing the door, she was clothed in unrelieved funereal black, dull and . . . On any other lady it would have looked somber. On her . . . even fully veiled as she was, the depressing hue did nothing to dim her vitality. It screamed in every line of her svelte form, a humming, thrumming energy, harnessed to some degree but forever in danger of escaping—exploding; she only had to move a gloved hand to instantly attract and fix any man's attention.

Certainly his.

She demonstrated; raising both hands, long slender palms and delicate fingers encased in fine black pigskin, she gripped the edge of the black veil and lifted it, setting it back over her piled hair.

So he could see her face.

Finely drawn features, a pair of ruby lips sculpted by a master, the lower lush and full and tempting. Large, almond-shaped eyes, their color an infinitely changeable medley of greens and golds, set above high, chiseled cheekbones. Lush dark lashes, a straight, patrician nose, all set in a oval of perfect porcelain skin.

The catalog of her features didn't do her face justice; it was the epitome of feminine aristocratic beauty not solely because of its composition but also because of her animation. In repose her face was serenely beautiful; awake, her expressions were startlingly vivid.

That afternoon, however, her expression was . . . contained.

He frowned. Stepping into the room, he closed the door. "Your father?"

He'd assumed the full mourning signified that her father, the Earl of Nunchance, had passed on. But if the head of the House of Vaux had died, the ton would have been abuzz with the news. Not only had he heard not a whisper, but Letitia's face, naturally pale, held no hint of sorrow; if anything, she seemed to be reining in her temper.

Not her father, then. Regardless of the familial disruptions that were commonplace among the Vaux, she was sincerely fond of her eccentric sire.

Her perfectly arched dark brows drew down, a slight frown that informed him he was being slow-witted.

"No. Not Papa."

The sound of her voice rocked him. He'd forgotten how long it had been since he'd heard it. Low-toned, with just the faintest natural rasp, it was a voice that evoked visions of sin.

Regardless, today those tones carried a certain tension. She drew in a tight breath, then bluntly stated, "Randall has been murdered."

As if saying the words had released her from some spell, she finally met his eyes. Hers sparked with undisguised temper. "Randall was beaten to death in his study last night. The servants found him this morning—and the idiot runners have fixed on Justin as the murderer."

He blinked. "I see." Moving into the room, slowly, to give himself time to dissect her news, he sank into the armchair facing hers across the hearth. Lord Justin Vaux was her younger brother. She was presently twenty-eight, nearly twenty-nine, making Justin twenty-six. Brother and sister were close, always had been. "And what does Justin say?"

"That's just it—we can't find him to ask. But rather than

do so, the authorities have fixed on him as the most convenient scapegoat. They are, no doubt, organizing a hue and cry as we speak." Letitia bit off the words, her tone acid. Now she'd got over the most difficult hurdle—getting Christian to speak with her—she felt able to concentrate on the matter at hand.

Which was definitely better than concentrating on him.

Watching him stroll, ineffably graceful, across the room toward her—allowing herself to—had been a mistake. All that harnessed power condensed into one male—a male no one with functioning eyes would rate as anything less than dangerous—was a phenomenon guaranteed to distract any living, breathing woman. Her most of all. Yet today she needed to reach past the glamour and deal with the man.

His expression was rarely informative, so did little to soften the hard angles of his face, the edged cheekbones, the long planes of his cheeks, the austere set of his features—large gray eyes set under a broad brow, straight brown brows, surprisingly thick lashes, thin chiseled lips, and the strong prow of his nose. His squared chin bore witness to the stubbornness he usually hid beneath a cloak of easy charm.

To him, charm and grace had always come easily, something she, being a Vaux and therefore attuned to all the nuances of appearance, had always appreciated.

Still did; if anything, the effect he had on her, on her senses, was more pronounced than she recalled. She knew very well just how deeply she still loved him, but she'd forgotten what it felt like, forgotten all the physical manifestations that came with that soul-deep connection.

She hadn't been this close to him for twelve long years. Her decision to keep her distance when he'd reappeared among the ton had clearly been wise; even with a good six feet separating them, she could feel her rib cage tightening, enough to affect her breathing.

Enough to make her feel just a touch giddy. To have her nerves stretching in telltale anticipation.

An anticipation that would never be fulfilled.

Not now.

Not after she'd married Randall.

His gray gaze had shifted from her; now it returned, focused and intent. "Why did the authorities fix on Justin? Was he there?"

Relief glimmered; that he was asking questions boded well. "Apparently he called on Randall last night. Randall's stupid butler, who thoroughly disapproves of all Vaux, Justin in particular, was only too happy to point his finger. But you know as well as I do that, all appearances to the contrary, Justin would never kill anyone."

Christian caught her eye, read therein both her temper and her worry. Her anxiety. "You don't believe he would. I might not believe he would. That doesn't mean he didn't."

Baiting a Vaux was a dangerous pastime, but this time she didn't bite back.

Which told him how deeply worried she was.

And despite the histrionics that were her Vaux heritage—the family weren't known as "the vile-tempered Vaux" without cause—she wasn't a female who worried unduly.

Which explained why she was there, appealing to him.

To the man she knew him to be.

One who had never been able to refuse her anything. Not even his heart.

She'd held his gaze steadily. Now she simply asked, in her low, raspy—seductive—voice, "Will you help?"

He looked into her eyes, and realized she didn't, in fact, know how he would answer. Didn't know how deeply in thrall to her he still was. Which meant . . .

He arched a brow. "How much is my help worth to you?"

She blinked, then searched his face, his eyes; hers narrowed. After a pregnant pause during which she assessed and considered his true meaning, she replied, "You know perfectly well I'll do anything—*anything*—to clear Justin's name."

Absolute decision, total commitment, rang in her tone.

He inclined his head. "Very well."

He heard himself urbanely agree; he hadn't known he would, certainly hadn't thought what he might ask of her in return. Wasn't even sure of his motives in pressing such a bargain on her, but "anything" gave him a wide field.

Revenge of a sort for all the years of hurt might yet be his.

At the thought, he stirred, whether in discomfort or anticipation not even he could say. "Tell me what happened—the sequence of events leading to Randall's death as you know it."

Letitia hesitated, then gathered the black reticule that had sat throughout in her lap. "Come to the house." Rising, she reached up and flipped down her veil. "It'll be easier to explain there."

She'd thought it would be easier—having places and things to point out to distract him—but having him by her side again kept her nerves in a state of perpetual reactiveness. Ready to respond to any touch, however slight, to luxuriate in the steady warmth that radiated from his large body, luring her closer.

Gritting mental teeth, she pointed to the spot on the study floor of the house in South Audley Street where she'd been informed her late husband had lain. "You can see the blood-stain."

The spot in question lay between the fireplace and the large desk.

She wasn't particularly squeamish, but the sight of the reddish-brown stain had her gorge rising. No matter what she'd felt for Randall, no man should die as he had, brutally bashed to death with the poker from his own fireplace.

Christian shifted closer, looking down at the stain. "Which way was he facing—toward the fire or the desk?"

He felt like a flame down one side of her body. She frowned. "I don't know. They didn't tell me. And they wouldn't let me in here to see—they said it was too . . . gory."

She raised her head, fought to concentrate on what they were discussing—struggled not to close her eyes and let her other senses stretch. She'd forgotten how tall he was, how large—forgotten he was one of the few men in the ton who towered over her, who could make her feel enclosed, shielded . . . protected. That wasn't why she'd turned to him, but at that moment she could not but be grateful for his size, his nearness, for the reminder of virile life in the presence of stark death.

"They've taken away the poker." Drawing in a tight breath, she turned and waved at the table by one of the armchairs flanking the hearth. "And they've cleared the table—there were two glasses on it, so I've been told. Brandy in both."

"Tell me what you know. When last did you see him?"

The question gave her something to focus on. "Last night. I went to dinner at the Martindales', then on to a soiree at Cumberland House. I returned rather late. Randall had stayed in—he sometimes did when he had business to attend to. He waylaid me in the hall and asked me in here. He wanted to discuss . . ." She paused, then continued, knowing her voice, hardening, would give away her temper. ". . . a family matter."

She and Randall had been married for eight years, but there'd been no children. With any luck, Christian would imagine that had been the subject of their discussion, the subject she'd so delicately refrained from mentioning.

His gaze on her face, Christian knew—just knew—that she was hoping to lead him up some garden path. Declining to follow, he made a mental note to return to the subject of her late night discussion with her husband at some later point. For now . . . "Discussion?" With a Vaux involved, "discussion" could encompass verbal warfare.

"We had a row." Face darkening, she continued, "I don't know how long it went for, but I eventually swept out"—a gesture indicated the force of her sweeping, something Christian could imagine with ease—"and left him here."

"So you argued. Loudly."

She nodded.

He let his gaze travel the room, then looked back at her. "No broken vases? Ornaments flung about?"

She folded her arms beneath her breasts, haughtily lifted her chin. "It wasn't that sort of argument."

A cold argument, then, one without heat or passion. For her, with her husband, that struck him as odd.

He looked away, again scanning the room. In reality looking away from her so he wouldn't focus on her breasts. Breasts he knew—or had, at one time, known well. Hauling his mind from salacious images from the past—all the more potent for being memory rather than imagination—took more effort than he cared to contemplate. He shifted. "So you left Randall here, hale and whole, and then what? What next did you know of this?"

"Nothing at all until my dresser came rushing in this morning to tell me about the body." She turned away from the bloodstain.

He moved with her, alongside her, as she glided to the window overlooking the street; she halted before it.

"By the time I dressed and got downstairs, the butler—he's an officious little scourge by the name of Mellon—had taken it upon himself to summon the authorities, who assigned an investigator from Bow Street—a weasely, narrow-minded man whose only concern is to close the case as soon as possible regardless of the truth."

She fell silent, but before he could frame his next question, she volunteered, "One other thing my dresser babbled—she was in a complete tizzy—was that this morning the door to the study was locked, with the key on the floor some way inside. Mellon and the footmen tried to force the door but couldn't." They both turned to consider the door, a heavy, inches-thick oak panel with a lock of similar ilk. "Luckily, someone in the household can pick locks. That was how they got in . . . and found him."

Quitting her side, he prowled toward the door; his senses

remained distracted, but his intellect was engaged. "How far inside? Guess from what she babbled."

"A few yards, not more. That's what it sounded like."

He was standing staring at the floor, absorbing the implications of the key being in that spot, when a girl appeared in the doorway. Looking up, he met her eyes, then glanced up at her hair and smiled. "Hermione."

"Lord Dearne." She bobbed a curtsy. "I didn't know if you would remember me."

He let his smile turn charming, as if he hadn't forgotten the scrap who'd been all of four when he'd last seen her. Luckily, her hair was a telling feature; in common with, as far as he'd ever heard, all those born to the house of Vaux, she possessed luxuriant dark locks that, despite their darkness, could never be described as anything other than red. With that, combined with the evidence of her features, a softer, milder version of Letitia's, placing her hadn't been difficult.

Her attention shifting to her older sister, Hermione advanced into the room. Christian noted she didn't look at the bloodstain; her focus was Letitia.

He glanced at Letitia; she was looking down, mind elsewhere. She was patently undisturbed by Hermione joining them.

Glancing at him, Letitia continued, "That's really all I know of my own knowledge. What I gathered from the investigator—"

"No." He held up a staying hand. "Don't tell me. I want to hear it from him, direct."

She narrowed her eyes at him. "Without my interpretations?"

He suppressed a grin. "Without your appellations."

She humphed, a sound Vaux females had down to an art, then looked at Hermione. "Are you all right?"

Hermione blinked. "Of course. I was wondering about you."

Letitia shrugged. "Once Justin turns up, and the fools who call themselves the authorities admit it wasn't him and start looking for the real murderer, I'll be fine."

Christian inwardly blinked. No sarcasm ran beneath her words—with a Vaux, one never needed to guess—yet she'd just lost a husband of eight years in shocking circumstances. . . .

He studied her; she was looking at Hermione, but there was nothing in either woman's attitude beyond sisterly comfort. While Hermione was presently a less intense version of Letitia, she'd no doubt grow into her dramatic powers in time. Both sisters seemed at ease with each other, the only real difference being in age, and the suggestion of care, of viewing Hermione as a person she needed to protect and watch over, that colored Letitia's eyes.

He recognized the emotion. Realized he knew it all too well. He stirred. "If you'll summon the butler—Mellon, was it?—I'd like to speak with him."

Interrogate him. He needed to focus on the matter at hand, rather than let his Jezebel play on his sympathies, however unconsciously.

Letitia crossed to the bellpull and tugged; the alacrity with which the summons was answered had her smiling cynically—and exchanging a look with Christian. Obviously Randall's staff found his presence noteworthy, enough to hover close.

Despite that, Mellon dutifully fixed his gaze on her, ignoring Christian. "You rang, ma'am?"

"Indeed, Mellon. Lord Dearne"—she waved at Christian—"has some questions he'd like to ask you. Please answer as best you can."

Mellon reluctantly turned to Christian, who smiled easily, charming as ever.

She could have warned him; Mellon turned rigidly frosty.

Christian saw, but chose to ignore the man's reaction. "You've been Mr. Randall's butler for . . . how long?"

"Twelve years, my lord."

Long before Letitia's marriage to Randall; Christian glanced at her, but all he could detect in her face, her stance, was a species of resigned indifference toward Mellon. She didn't like the man, but had let him remain as head of her household staff; he had to wonder why. He returned his gaze to the butler. "How did you get on with your late master?"

Mellon puffed out his chest. "It's a—" He broke off, blinked, then his chin firmed. "It's been a pleasure working for Mr. Randall, my lord."

"And the rest of the staff?"

"Feel the same, my lord. None of the staff had any problems with the master." Mellon's eyes shifted toward Letitia but stopped before he made contact.

The man's antagonism was obvious; Christian wondered at its cause. The Letitia he knew was invariably kind to the lower orders; the impulse was bred into her, all but instinctive, not something she could readily change. There had to be some other reason behind Mellon's patent dislike of her.

"Very well." He let his voice relax. "If you could tell me what, to your certain knowledge, drawing solely from your own observations, happened last night. Start from the point where Lady Randall returned home."

Mellon primmed his lips like an old woman, but was only too ready to oblige. "The mistress came in and the master asked to speak with her. Here, in the study. They closed the door, so I don't know what was said, but there was a great to-do." His gaze flashed to Letitia, then returned to a point beyond Christian's right shoulder. "We could hear her ladyship ranting and raving, as she's wont to do."

Ah. There we have it. Devoted to his master, Mellon resented Letitia's treatment of Randall.

Christian paused to reassess; Randall was the gentleman Letitia had betrayed him for, yet all he'd seen thus far of her attitude to the man seemed totally inconsistent with the love match their marriage was purported to have been. He made a mental note to learn more about Randall, especially about his and Letitia's marriage. But first . . . his apparently unquenchable protectiveness prodded him to ask, "Did anything occur during the time her ladyship and Mr. Randall were arguing in the study?"

"Indeed, sir, although not in the study." Mellon's eyes gleamed with vindictiveness. "Lord Justin Vaux, the mistress's brother, called to see the master. It was the master he wanted, not the mistress. He could hear the carry-on in the study, so he said he'd wait in the library. I led him there. He told me I didn't need to wait on him—it was latish by then. Said he'd show himself in once the mistress had left."

"So you retired?" His tone conveyed his surprise; Percival never retired while he was up and about unless he, himself, ordered him to.

Mellon looked stricken. "I wish I hadn't now, but his lordship's often here—makes himself at home, and the master had mentioned earlier that he was expecting him, so, well . . . it was clear he didn't want me about. So I went."

Even without glancing at Letitia, Christian had little doubt how to interpret Mellon's statement. Justin hadn't liked Randall, and had therefore called frequently, "making himself at home," supporting Letitia—very likely keeping an eye on her. That was revealing in itself. Although Justin and Letitia were close, they'd never lived in each other's pockets. And there was Hermione, too. Christian glanced at her, and wondered if Letitia's protective attitude had some specific cause beyond basic family instinct.

Clearly, Justin had made his dislike of Randall sufficiently obvious, hence Mellon's rabid dislike of him.

"So beyond that point you have no further knowledge of events." He caught Mellon's eye. "You can't say for certain that Lord Vaux left the library, went into the study and met with your master."

Mellon's lips pinched. "No, but I can say he didn't leave until more than an hour later. My room's above the front door, and I heard it open and shut. I got up and looked out—just to be sure—and saw Lord Vaux making his way down the steps and onto the pavement."

"Which way did he turn?"

"Left. Toward Piccadilly."

Christian cocked a brow at Letitia.

Arms again folded, she was glowering, quietly smoldering, but there was worry behind her eyes. When he waited, she reluctantly vouchsafed, "Justin's lodgings are in Jermyn Street."

Mellon had given the correct direction without hesitation; he most probably had seen Justin leave. Christian thought, then asked, "If anyone else had called on your master last night, after Lord Vaux left, or even before, would you have known?"

"Indeed, sir—my lord. If they'd rung the bell, I would have heard—it rings in my room as well as in the kitchen. Even if they'd knocked on the door, I couldn't help but hear, my room being where it is."

There seemed little point in suggesting he might have been deeply asleep. "Very well." Christian turned toward the bloodstain on the floor. "Let's move on to this morning. What happened once you came downstairs?"

"I was in my pantry seeing to the cutlery for the breakfast table, when Mrs. Crocket, the housekeeper, came to tell me that the tweeny who does the study of a morning couldn't open the door. I went straight away, thinking perhaps the master had gone to his study early. Sometimes he does lock the door. But when I knocked, there was no reply, not even when I called. Then one of the footmen looked through the keyhole—I was surprised he could, as the key should have been in it. He turned green and said the master was lying on the floor, and there was blood." Mellon paled.

"What happened then?"

"We tried to force the door, me and the two footmen, but it wouldn't budge. We were thinking of breaking a window and putting someone through when one of the maids told us the scullery boy could pick locks. We got him up here, and he managed to open the door. We rushed in . . ." Mellon's eyes were drawn to the bloodstained floor. ". . . and we found the master there, dead. Quite dead."

His voice quavered on the last words. Christian gave him a moment to compose himself.

He glanced at Letitia; her face was chalk white. "I realize this is distressing"—he addressed the comment more to her than Mellon, then returned his gaze to the butler—"but if you could describe how Randall was lying—on his back, or on his face?"

All color drained from Mellon's countenance. "On his back, my lord." His jaw worked. "There wasn't much of his face left to speak of."

Letitia made a small choked sound and turned away; hand at her throat, she stared out of the window. Hermione had paled but was less distressed.

Tamping down a disconcertingly strong urge to suspend the interview to spare Letitia, who would certainly not thank him, Christian forged on. "So it would seem Randall was facing the fire, and his attacker. I understand there were two glasses of brandy on the side table—had they been drunk?"

Mellon rallied at the change of subject. "Both had been sipped, but neither drained."

"Where, exactly, was the key?"

Mellon looked toward the door, and pointed. "There, on the floor—by that knot in the wood."

Hermione shifted. Christian glanced at her, and saw she was attending avidly. He glanced at Letitia; she was attending, too, but not with the same intensity. He looked again at Hermione. Her eyes were wide; she was definitely tense. Without looking at Mellon, he said, "Put your finger on the spot."

Mellon obeyed. "The best I can recall, it was here."

Hermione's eyes hadn't left Mellon, but as he straightened, she glanced at Christian expectantly.

Unsure what was going on, he looked at Mellon and asked the obvious question. "How do you imagine the key got there?"

"I can't rightly say, my lord."

"If you had to guess?"

"I think . . . that Lord Vaux locked the door behind him, then slipped the key back under the door."

Christian nodded. That seemed the most likely explanation, except . . . "Why would Lord Vaux do that? If he'd just murdered your master in gruesome fashion, why go to the bother of locking the door and slipping the key back inside?"

Mellon frowned, unable to answer.

"To give himself time to scarper."

The words drew all eyes to the door; they came from a whippet-thin individual who'd appeared in the hall. One glance at his ferrety features and Christian knew who he was.

Letitia had stiffened to a scarifying degree. In tones worthy of the haughtiest duchess, she said, "Dearne, permit me to introduce Mr. Barton. Of Bow Street."

She didn't need to say anything more; her tone effectively conveyed her contempt. Clearly Barton had already succeeded in thoroughly putting up her back.

Deliberately mild, Christian nodded to Barton. "Lady Randall has asked me to investigate the circumstances surrounding her husband's death. Might I ask why you imagine Lord Justin Vaux has, to use your phrase, 'scarpered'?"

Barton wasn't at all sure how to act toward him; Christian left him to make up his own mind, which resulted in Barton opting for caution. He answered civilly. "In light of the circumstances, I've been around to his lordship's lodgings. I was given to understand that her ladyship here"—Barton glanced at Letitia—"sent a message requesting his presence earlier, but had received no reply. Not surprising, as his lordship has disappeared."

Letitia looked startled, and shocked. So did Hermione.

"Disappeared?" Letitia stared at Barton; Christian could all but see the wheels in her mind churning. Then she sniffed and looked away. "I daresay he's gone to the country to visit with friends. It is August, after all. I suspect, Mr. Barton, that your 'disappearance' is nothing more than that."

Barton looked pugnacious. "Would you say his lordship normally leaves for country parties in a tearing rush late at night? With his man, who hadn't had any warning?" When Letitia said nothing, Barton went on, "Because that's what happened according to his landlord who lives downstairs."

After a moment Barton glanced down, drawing all attention to what he carried in one hand; it appeared to be a cloth garment, folded many times. "And then there's this."

He shook out the garment, revealing it to be a gentleman's coat. "Would this be one of your brother's, your ladyship? Do you recognize it?"

Letitia frowned. She walked closer, considering the coat's cut. "It looks like one of Justin's." Halting before the coat Barton obligingly displayed at arm's length, she raised her brows. "Is it from Shultz?" She reached for the left lapel.

Barton whisked the coat away. "You might want to be careful about touching it, your ladyship. There's blood on it, see—most likely your husband's."

Every drop of blood drained from Letitia's face.

Christian was at her side instantly, before he'd even thought. *"Barton."* The single word resonated with menace, yet was nothing to what he felt. His hands had fisted; he battled an urge to strike the runner. His tongue itched to tear strips off the man, but . . . they needed to learn what he'd discovered. "Did the landlord have any idea where his lordship was headed?"

He'd barked out the question. Barton stiffened; he wanted to refuse to answer, but didn't dare. "No."

"Did he know how they left—in a hired carriage, or did

Lord Vaux drive his curricle?" He glanced at Letitia as he asked; lips tight, she nodded. Justin did indeed keep a curricle in town.

Barton had noticed the interplay. Eyes dark with suspicion, he nevertheless grudgingly conceded, "His lordship drove off in his curricle."

"Do you have any further light to shed on this matter? Any information at all?"

"No, my lord. The body's been taken to the police surgeon. When he's done with his examination, the corpse will be released to her ladyship for burial." Barton used the word "corpse" deliberately, his gaze sliding to Letitia.

Christian battled an almost overpowering urge to throttle the man. "Very good." His harsh tones had Barton looking his way again; he caught the man's eye. "When that time comes, you—personally—will inform Mellon, and he will convey the information to me. Her ladyship is not to be disturbed with this matter again. Any query you may have, you may make through me." He held Barton's gaze. "I trust I make myself plain?"

His last words came out in a menacing purr, much like a lion anticipating his next meal. Letitia heard, not just the words but every nuance they conveyed, and could have kissed him.

Unfortunately, she couldn't, not now, not ever again, but he clearly still cared, somewhere in his heart, for her. She'd spent all her life among men like him; she knew how to read their signs.

Under Christian's hard gaze, Barton nodded. "As you wish, my lord."

Christian inclined his head. "Good." He paused, then added, "Rest assured that any pertinent information we find that sheds light on Randall's murder will be conveyed to you at the earliest opportunity."

Letitia turned her head and stared at him. He was being conciliatory—to the enemy! That was an olive branch if she'd ever seen one. She was about to draw breath and unleash some of her suppressed feelings—on which of them, Christian or Barton, she hadn't made up her mind—when Christian caught her eye.

Just a look—one pointed, intent glance—and, inwardly grumbling, she grudgingly shut her lips.

Folding her arms again, she fixed Barton with a chilly— icily furious—look.

He glanced her way, then returned his gaze to Christian and nodded. "I'll be on my way, then." He bobbed a general bow, then turned and left.

At a nod from Christian, Mellon followed, closing the door—the inches-thick oak door—behind him.

The instant it shut, Letitia let her temper loose. "How *dare* he!" She drew a huge breath. And raved on.

Christian glanced at Hermione. Although she remained silent, she clearly egged her sister on, agreeing with every dramatically and forcefully elucidated sentiment. Her enthusiastic "Hear, hear!" was clear in her eyes, in her whole being.

Resigned, he leaned back against the edge of the heavy desk and watched Letitia rant and pace, then rant some more. No one ranted like a Vaux—they had the activity down to a fine art. He was quietly amazed at how inventive she still was; colorful phrases and strikingly adverse comparisons—"addlepated, imbecilic moron with less wit than a dormouse"—tripped from her tongue with barely a pause for breath.

Better to let her get it out of her system. That was the Vaux's folly, their foible; all that natural energy had to be released.

Eventually finishing her dissection of Barton, his progenitors, and potential offspring, she swung around.

And fixed him with a fiery glare. "And as for you—how *could* you? You slapped him down well enough to begin with—and I thank you for that—but after one agreement, *one* halfway reasonable comment, you patted him on the head and let him go! Worse—you all but promised to share whatever we find!" Halting a pace away, she glared into his eyes; with him propped against the desk, hers were level with his. "What the devil were you thinking?"

"That he might learn something we need to know." Christian kept his voice mild; it reflected how he felt. He smiled, as always amused; he'd never been affected by Vaux histrionics, which was one point that always fascinated the Vaux. Almost without exception others got extremely nervous when they let their tempers loose; most tended to edge away, or escape if they could. Not him. He found their unbounded, unleashed energy refreshing. For all their apparent venom, they were never intentionally malicious; contrary to what many thought, they were neither dangerous nor insane.

Their temper tantrums were all fireworks; not in the least harmful if handled with care, and capable of being highly entertaining.

Especially as no Vaux had ever held his immunity against him. Certainly not Letitia.

His calm words had given her pause. She considered him through eyes in which the searing flame of her temper was slowly dying; he could almost feel the energy in the air around her fading.

"There's an old but wise saying," he offered. " 'Keep your friends close, and your enemies closer.' "

Something changed in her face; a coolness slid into her expression. "Well, as to that, you would surely know."

There was a quality in her tone he neither recognized nor could place. She held his gaze for an instant, then turned away. Her gaze passed over the bloodstain on the floor, then she started for the door. "If you've finished here?"

He straightened, glanced around. "Yes." He fell in in her wake, pausing to allow Hermione to proceed him through the doorway. "But I have more questions for you two."

Without comment Letitia led him across the front hall into the room diagonally opposite the study. She gestured as she swung to face him. "The front parlor. I tend to sit here more than in the drawing room."

To his left lay an archway leading deeper into the house; through it he saw ranks of bookshelves packed with books. He pointed. "The library?"

When she nodded, he headed that way. Letitia and Hermione followed.

The library was a good-sized room with floor-to-ceiling bookshelves covering much of the walls; halting in the middle of the room, he surveyed the books filling them. "Randall?"

"Yes. Not that he ever read them."

He glanced at Letitia. "He bought them, but didn't read them?"

She shrugged. "He didn't read. He could read, of course, but he never read a book, not that I saw."

Christian glanced again at the shelves. Many of the Vaux were bibliophiles. Most read voraciously; even Letitia would occasionally be found with her nose in a book. The idea of a total nonreader marrying into the family seemed . . . odd. And while it wasn't unheard of for a gentleman to set up a library just for show, there were a lot of books in that room.

As if sensing his thoughts, Letitia said, "Perhaps he saw them as an investment."

Walking past him, she went to a wing chair by the fireplace. A book had been left open on the small table beside it. She picked it up, then softly snorted. "Justin. This is what he was doing while he waited for me to leave Randall."

He'd followed her and looked over her shoulder. "Seneca—*Letters from a Stoic.*" His lips quirked. "Appropriate reading for a male Vaux."

She laid the book aside and turned to face him. "What else did you want to know?"

He gestured to the wing chair; she sank into it as he waved Hermione to its mate. Once they were both seated, he looked down at them. "If we want to shift suspicion from Justin, we need to reconstruct the crime and demonstrate that someone else had the opportunity to kill Randall."

Step by step he took them over what they knew, from the

time Letitia returned home through the chaos of the following morning. The exercise got them nowhere.

He grimaced. "Barton's right—the most obvious suspect is Justin."

"Perhaps," Letitia grimly conceded. "But he didn't do it."

"The key," Hermione said. "Don't forget that. You said it yourself." She fixed Christian with large eyes. "Why would Justin do such a thing? It makes no sense, not if he were the murderer. So he can't be the murderer."

Christian looked into her eyes, and wondered, not if but what she was hiding; that wasn't the first time she'd spoken in Justin's defense.

He glanced at Letitia; after spending a few hours in her and Hermione's company, he felt increasingly certain that the Vaux temperament was as he remembered it. They hadn't changed. Letitia's betrayal of him aside, loyalty, especially of the familial variety, was ingrained. Letitia had—he felt certain with no real thought for herself—walked across the gulf between them, braving whatever wrath he might seek to visit on her—whatever price he might ask—to gain his help in clearing Justin. Hermione demonstrably felt the same. The question in Christian's mind was whether she'd acted on that feeling, and if so, how.

He fixed Hermione with a direct look. "Do you know anything more about what happened last night?"

She blinked, slowly, then shook her head. "No. Only what I told you."

He didn't believe her. From the corner of his eye he noticed Letitia was also now regarding her sister with a slight frown. But she said nothing.

Both, he felt perfectly certain, would lie through their teeth if that's what was needed to protect Justin, even though the Vaux rarely lied . . . and family loyalty worked both ways.

It was very possible Justin was acting to protect . . .

He looked at Letitia, waited until she felt his gaze and raised her eyes to his. He studied those eyes, eyes he knew very well in all their green and gold splendor, eyes he'd in the past always been able to read. "Tell me you didn't kill Randall."

She blinked, but continued to return his steady regard. He saw her make the connection, her mind following the path his had trod. Her brows rose fractionally. "I didn't kill Randall." An instant passed, then she grimaced and added, "I often felt like killing him, but no, I didn't. I wouldn't. No more than Justin would."

And that, Christian reflected, was the right answer. In contrast to Hermione, he had no doubt whatever that Letitia was telling the truth.

He nodded. "Very well. That leaves us with one large and immediate question. Where is Justin?"

Chapter 2

After dining alone and reviewing and digesting the conversations and interactions of that afternoon, Christian—much to the disgust of his more vengeful side—felt compelled to call again at Randall's house.

Not that he had any interest in the house; it was its mistress who drew him.

He'd thought he'd understood where he and she now were vis-à-vis each other, yet there were undercurrents between them he couldn't explain. When he'd taken his leave of her that afternoon and she'd given him her hand, he'd grasped it—and felt her pulse leap, her breathing tighten.

Felt everything in him respond.

She reacted to him as she always had, if anything even more intensely—just as he was affected by her. He hadn't expected either to be so, had assumed she'd loved Randall with all her considerable heart and soul, and that her attraction to him and his to her would consequently have faded, if not died.

Not so.

As he strode briskly down South Audley Street, his more vengeful side—the side her betrayal and marriage to Randall had brought into being—sneered. Contemptuously reminded him how he'd felt when Barton had so distressed her with Justin's coat, how helpless he'd been to suppress the primitive response to protect and defend her—one that, at that intensity, only made sense if he loved her. If, in his heart of hearts, he still, despite all, saw her as his.

His to protect, even if she was no longer his to possess.

His position, he cynically admitted, was pathetic.

Inwardly frowning, he neared Randall's house, a block south of Grosvenor Square—and saw, to his considerable surprise, every window ablaze with light, much as if a ball were taking place. Mystified, he went up the steps and rapped sharply on the black crepe-draped door.

Mellon looked flustered when he opened it; leaving his cane with the man, Christian strolled into the drawing room—and discovered the reason why.

The large room was packed with women. Ladies. A swift survey informed him they were all Vaux—those of the main line together with innumerable connections.

The Vaux were one of the very oldest ton families. They were all but legendary, one of those families everyone knew of and kept track of, a recognized cornerstone of society. Christian noted a few males among the crowd, all more senior than he, but the company was predominantly female— and all were talking.

Luckily in whispers and the soft tones considered appropriate to a house in mourning; he could hear himself think. Because of the crowd, many of whom were standing, and being Vaux were of the tall, commanding type of female, he was only seen by those in the groups nearest him. And while those ladies stopped talking long enough to take due note of him, to bob curtsies or nod as appropriate to his rank, they quickly returned to their hushed conversations.

Randall might not have been a Vaux, but he'd married one of their leading lights. His death therefore was of considerable note to the wider family, something to be acknowledged by attendance at this gathering, not a wake for the departed but a show of support for the bereaved.

Locating Letitia on a chaise by the hearth, Christian made his way toward her. Cleaving a path through the crowd, most of whom knew him, wasn't easy; charm to the fore, he progressed by slow stages.

Which gave him time to study his target.

Seated between her paternal aunts—Lady Amarantha Ffyfe, Countess of Ffyfe, and Lady Constance Bickerdale, Viscountess Manningham—Letitia presided over the assembly with a calm, composed air.

Her expression clearly stated she knew this gathering had to be, and she was perfectly ready to host it and play her part . . .

Except she didn't look bereft.

She hadn't earlier, either, but he'd put that down to her concern for Justin, something that, in her, might be strong enough to override grief. Temporarily. But as he neared the chaise, he could see no evidence that she'd shed so much as a single tear for Randall.

In another female, he might suspect repressed grief, some emotional blockage that kept the woman in question in a state of emotional denial, barring all expression and the release of grieving. But the Vaux lived for emotion. The only way they knew to survive was firmly in the here and now, immersed in the immediate moment and unashamedly giving their emotions full rein.

Witness Letitia's storm of the afternoon. That's what happened with Vaux. They were, as one, single-minded when in the grip of their latest flight.

Letitia's current flight should have been grief, but there was no sign, not even a hint, of that emotion when she raised her eyes to his face, giving him her hand as he bowed before her.

Her clear-eyed composure unsettled him; to gain time to regroup, he turned to acknowledge her aunts.

Lady Constance arched a brow at him. "Letitia mentioned she'd appealed to you over finding Justin. Not that the Continent might not be the best place for the boy, all things considered, but it would be nice to know where he's gone."

"Nonsense!" Lady Amarantha waved that aside. "He should come back and face his trial. It's not as if anyone would convict him."

Christian blinked; he looked to Letitia for guidance.

She promptly stood. "If you'll excuse me, aunts, I must speak with Dearne."

"Of course, dear," Lady Constance said. "But later we must talk about the funeral."

Promising to return and give that subject its due, Letitia grasped his arm and steered him toward a corner of the room; while others stopped them to express their condolences, to which she replied with her prevailing calm, they reached their destination in good time. Astonishingly, not one of those who spoke with her seemed at all perturbed by her lack of outward grief.

Turning to stand beside her and look out over the room, he bit his tongue against the urge to ask, baldly, whether she'd loved Randall. The question plagued him, yet he wasn't sure he wanted to hear the answer.

He'd always assumed she'd been head-over-ears in love with the man; that was the only circumstance he could imagine that might have been strong enough to make her turn aside from the promises they'd exchanged. Her promise to him that she would wait until he returned from the wars, that she would be no other man's—that she loved him.

If she hadn't loved Randall, why had she married him?

Why had she broken her promises to him?

Confusion wasn't the half of what he felt.

In contrast, she clearly felt none. Surveying the company, she softly snorted. "They may be here because they're family, but the truth is Randall's murder is likely to be the juiciest scandal of the season. I can't imagine what might trump it, especially with the rumor of Justin being involved."

He frowned. "Has that got out?"

"Oh, yes." Contrary to her lack of grief, there was no doubt of her anger. "Quite a few mentioned it in their greetings—they'd heard about it, including that Justin has disappeared—*fled,* as they're putting it—long before they crossed this threshold."

Christian looked down the room—at Mellon, hovering just inside the doorway.

"Indeed." Letitia had followed his gaze. "I have absolutely no doubt Randall's senior lackey is who we have to thank for that. He's always hated Justin—hated, not just disliked."

"Why is that? Justin, after all, is his master's brother-in-law."

She lifted a shoulder. "I have no idea." She turned to face Christian. "We need to clear Justin of suspicion as soon as possible. The rumors will be rife by tomorrow."

He met her gaze. "I'll start searching in earnest tomorrow, but unless he's merely gone to visit friends, or is staying somewhere reasonably obvious and hasn't in fact deliberately gone to ground, then flushing him out isn't going to be easy."

She frowned. "I've racked my brains, but I have no clue where he's gone. He didn't mention leaving town."

After a pause, Christian asked, "Why is it that no one seems to expect you to be wailing and tearing your clothes?"

"I'm a Vaux—I wouldn't tear my clothes."

"Possibly not, but you should be wailing."

She met his eyes briefly. "Sorry, no wailing tonight. Nor any crying, either—it does terrible things to my complexion."

He looked at her, simply looked. While she felt the weight of compulsion in his gaze, she had no intention of explaining why she wasn't grieving for Randall. Especially not to him. Such an explanation would inexorably lead to further questions, ones she had even less interest in answering.

Their past was past. The promise of it dead and buried. Gone.

Stolen from her.

By Randall, and him.

Which was the reason she was making not the smallest

pretense of grief or sorrow. Her agreement with Randall had ended on his death; she was free, now, to behave as she felt. Her only surprise was that, as Christian had remarked, none of her extended family seemed at all shocked by her lack of feeling; she'd thought she had done better at pretending to love Randall over the years.

She surveyed the room. "I wonder how long they'll stay?"

About another hour was the answer. She wasn't entirely surprised that Christian, denied the explanations he wanted, remained by her side, his charm disguising his determination.

When she'd squeezed fingers and touched cheeks with the last of the ladies and thanked them for their concern, she turned to him, met his gaze and arched a brow. "Well?"

He glanced around the now empty room, large and peculiarly lifeless; although it was furnished in expensive style, as she'd informed him, it wasn't a room she favored. His gaze returned to her; he waved to the door. "Let's go to the library."

The library, she assumed, because it wasn't her domain. She acquiesced with a nod, gracefully turned and graciously led the way.

All too aware that he prowled in her wake. The image of a stalking lion popped into her head. With his fairish brown hair, combined with his loose-limbed grace and the power inherent in his large body, the analogy was peculiarly apt.

But when they reached the library, he seemed somewhat at a loss. She sat in one of the armchairs by the hearth and watched him prowl the room, idly inspecting titles as he worked his way closer.

When he finally arrived before her, he stood frowning down at her. "I checked at the obvious clubs—Justin's not staying at any of them. I'll make the same rounds tomorrow and see if I can find anyone who's sighted him."

Christian paused, wishing he could simply ask her outright about her marriage. The trouble with interrogating her was that she rarely if ever lied; instead, as she'd demonstrated earlier, if she didn't want to answer a question, she simply wouldn't. Even if he could bring himself to browbeat her by enacting some dramatic scene, being a Vaux, she'd only trump whatever efforts he made.

Catching her gaze, holding it, he stated, "It would help—greatly—if you simply told me everything you know that might affect this situation." *Including how you felt about Randall.* "I'm clearly missing vital pieces of the story."

And not only over the issue of Randall's death.

She merely raised her brows at him in that coolly superior way female leaders of the haut ton had perfected. "I have nothing to add to what I told you earlier."

He had no intention of being so easily dismissed. "What was the subject of your argument with Randall—the one last night?"

She hesitated, clearly debating if that was a piece of information she could offer as a sop. She decided it was. "It concerned Hermione. Randall had hatched a nonsensical scheme to marry her off to the Duke of Northumberland."

"Northumberland? He must be in his dotage."

"He is, but that was of no concern to Randall. He wanted the connection to a dukedom. Being connected to an earldom—" She broke off.

When she didn't continue, he dryly supplied, "Wasn't enough?"

A faint flush touched her pale cheeks—anger, not embarrassment. "Indeed."

"And the argument?"

Her gaze strayed to the empty hearth. "He'd been trying to convince me to support the notion over the last few weeks. Last night he pressed me to take Hermione on a visit to Northumberland's estate. I refused."

When she didn't elaborate, he prompted, "You argued with him for more than twenty minutes."

Gaze still on the fireplace, she shrugged. "He put his case in detail, but of course I would never agree to such a thing."

Her tone suggested that Randall was a fool to think she would . . . in the circumstances. *What circumstances?* Gritting his teeth, he quietly asked, "Why 'of course'?"

He'd hoped her abstraction would have her answering before she'd thought, giving him some insight into her increasingly curious marriage. Instead, she slowly turned her head and looked at him. Steadily. Then simply said, "I would never countenance Hermione being used in such a way."

Every answer he wrung from her only raised more questions—such as why Randall hadn't understood that. Christian held her gaze, and felt his own temper stir. She wanted him to clear Justin of suspicion, but would offer only limited information.

For whatever reason, she was determined to tell him nothing of her marriage.

And suddenly, unexpectedly, that was the most urgent point he wanted to know.

He took one slow step closer, then leaned down, clamping one hand on each of the chair's arms, caging her. Bringing his face much closer to hers, looming over her.

His nerves flickered; the scent of jasmine—the scent she'd always worn—teased his senses.

She didn't press back, retreat, didn't react in any fearful way to the blatant intimidation. Belatedly he remembered she'd always found his size—that he was significantly taller, heavier, and larger than she, and therefore capable of physically dominating her—exciting.

A lick of desire slid down his spine. He studied her eyes; at such close quarters in the dimly lit room they gleamed like beaten gold, shadowed and mysterious, giving nothing away. But her breathing had quickened. Her lips, when he glanced at them, had parted.

"If you recall"—his voice had lowered to a gravelly purr; slowly he brought his gaze back to her eyes—"I've yet to set a price for assisting you in finding Justin."

The air between them all but crackled. Her lids lowered,

but then she forced them up and locked her eyes on his. "Finding him, and clearing his name."

Her words were breathless. His lips quirked. "Indeed. But finding him comes first." He let his gaze drop to her lips. While he considered how to phrase his demand.

He wondered how her lips would taste now. . . .

Wondered what he should ask—what she might give. . . .

As if following his thoughts, she slowly stiffened, steel infusing her. He was jerked to full awareness when her lips firmed.

He glanced up at her eyes—and found them blazing.

"Just find Justin, and I'll pay whatever price you care to name."

The words rang with outright challenge. Raising her hands, she pushed against his shoulders—hard enough to make him straighten and step back.

She rose. Proud and haughty, she met his gaze, held it for a pregnant instant, then turned and swept toward the archway. "When you've found Justin, let me know."

Christian watched her disappear into the parlor and inwardly swore.

Transferring his gaze to the cold hearth, he ran his hand through his hair. His temper quickly cooled; his arousal was less forgiving. Reassessing his position didn't take long.

Turning, he stalked out of the house, picking up his cane and going quickly down the steps, then striding away along the street.

If finding Justin Vaux was what it would take to get him what he wanted, he'd find Justin Vaux.

Letitia knew the ton. It was the circle she'd been born into, in which she'd been raised, and in which she'd spent all her adult life. To her the ton wasn't a fixed entity, but a fluid, dynamic cosmos that wise ladies navigated and—if they were truly powerful—learned to manipulate.

She hadn't yet reached master status, but she was by no means a novice when it came to manipulating her peers.

Consequently, the next morning she dutifully donned her weeds, but rather than sit at home in the darkened front parlor, she called for her carriage and set out for the park. Hermione went with her, but after the previous evening's event, their aunt Agnes, who lived with them and assisted Letitia in chaperoning Hermione, elected to remain abed.

"I thought," Hermione said, her gaze on the coachman's back, "that most widows remained indoors for at least the first few weeks."

"Usually," Letitia conceded. "But we are Vaux. Not even the most censorious dowager will expect us to sequester ourselves, not with a murder in the family." She paused, then added, "Indeed, they'd most likely be highly disappointed if we did. And we're hardly cavorting—merely taking the air." Heaven knew, after last night she needed it.

Although the day was fine, a warm breeze gently teasing curls, flirting with ribbons, and rather irritatingly playing with her veil, as it was August, there were far fewer carriages drawn up by the verge in the park than was customary during the Season.

Those of the ton with country estates—which was to say most of the nobility—were presently on them, enjoying the summer and more bucolic pleasures. That still left a core of the aristocracy in residence, along with minor branches and connections, those whose sole residence was in the capital and who hadn't been invited to someone else's country house party this week.

While sorely in need of fresh air to blow the cobwebs—and the sensual miasma invoked by Christian Allardyce—from her brain, Letitia had another purpose—to assess the reaction of the ton to the news of Randall's murder.

One couldn't successfully manipulate society's thinking without knowing the current situation.

She directed the coachman to draw in to the verge in a

large gap between two landaus. The separation between her carriage and the others was sufficient to establish that she wasn't courting gossip, wasn't openly inviting discussion of Randall's sensational death.

"I can see Lady Cowper climbing down from her carriage," Hermione whispered. "She's heading this way."

"Good." Letitia glanced at the lawns nearby. "You'll have to give up your seat—the ladies won't want to mention murder with your delicate ears about. I suggest you stroll, but don't go far."

Somewhat to her surprise, Hermione nodded. "All right." Gathering her parasol, she opened the carriage door. The footman hurried to assist her to the ground.

Hermione loved listening to her elders gossip. Letitia, eyes narrow, studied her sister, suspicious, wondering . . . but then Emily Cowper reached the carriage and she had to give her attention to her ladyship, and the numerous others who followed in her wake. Emily, who had known her since birth, claimed precedence as an old family friend and joined her in the carriage. Most others merely stopped by the carriage's side, to offer their condolences and hear whatever she felt able to tell them of the recent shocking events.

As she'd predicted, given that she and Hermione were appropriately garbed in black bombazine and she evinced no desire to encourage those stopping by to linger, their presence elicited no censure, especially not with Emily Cowper, patroness of Almack's, sitting so solicitously beside her.

Letitia knew her ton.

As she'd expected, there were many who, along with their condolences, were only too happy to recount what they'd heard. To her dismay, the universal theme was that Justin, in a fit of the famous Vaux temper, had brutally slain his brother-in-law. Whether his temper had been aroused on his own account, or on hers, or on Hermione's, was the chief point of conjecture.

No one—not one person—questioned Justin's guilt.

Letitia was grateful for her veil; she'd never been especially good at hiding her feelings, and she certainly wouldn't have been able to conceal her mounting dismay as lady after lady simply *assumed* Justin was Randall's murderer.

The veil also allowed her, when from the corner of her eye she caught sight of a group amassing a little way from the carriage, to cut her eyes in that direction.

What she saw horrified her. What was Hermione doing?

Her sister, animated and exclaiming, stood at the center of a circle of fascinated ladies, young and old, all hanging on every word she uttered, increasingly hotly.

She was defending Justin. Letitia didn't need to hear Hermione's words to know that was so.

Swallowing a curse, she immediately developed a headache. Excusing herself to Lady Cowper and the other three ladies with whom she'd been speaking, she dispatched the footman to fetch Hermione with a message that she was needed immediately at the carriage.

Her sister broke off in mid-tirade, and ignoring those around her, came hurrying over. She gripped the carriage's side. "What's happened?"

Supremely aware of curious eyes, and even more curious ears, Letitia gestured weakly. "I have the most *dreadful* headache—we need to return to the house."

Hermione frowned, surprised by the headache, something she knew Letitia rarely suffered from. "All right." The footman opened the door and she climbed into the carriage.

Letitia gave the order to return to South Audley Street in a suitably faint tone.

Both footman and coachman were Randall's people. While she could have spoken quietly enough to leave the coachman unaware, the footman, perched directly behind the seat on which they sat, was another matter. She resigned herself to holding her tongue—and her temper—until they reached the house.

Nevertheless, as they turned out of the park and into Park Lane, she couldn't resist asking, "What were you talking so animatedly about?"

Hermione's face took on a mulish cast. "Justin. I was telling them all that he couldn't possibly have murdered Randall."

As Letitia had feared. Behind her veil, she pressed her lips tight and said no more.

She reined her ire in while they traveled through light traffic back to the house, then waited some more as they descended from the carriage and climbed the steps. When they entered the front hall, with Mellon hovering, with entirely assumed calm she dispensed with her veil, leaving it with her gloves and reticule on the hall table, then, her movements invested with increasing tension, she swept into the front parlor. "Hermione, I'd like to speak with you. Now."

Her sister blinked, then followed. Looking back at Mellon, Letitia instructed, "Please shut the door."

Reluctantly, Mellon did. After eight years he knew the signs of a storm brewing, but with the door shut, he wouldn't be able to hear clearly, not unless she screamed.

Not certain that she wouldn't, once the door was shut she swung on her heel and stalked into the library.

Mystified, starting to frown, Hermione followed more slowly in her wake.

Letitia's irate stride carried her to the fireplace. Dragging in a huge breath, she swung around and pinned her sister with a furious gaze as she paused in the archway. "What in heaven's name did you think you were *doing*?"

Hermione's mulish look returned. "I was defending Justin. Someone needs to, and I didn't hear you saying much at all when those ladies came up to the carriage."

Letitia struggled to find calm enough to form a coherent reply. She hauled in another breath, held it for an instant, then flung up her hands. "I know you've only limited experience of the ton, but you have to pay attention! You cannot—absolutely *must not*—defend Justin. Not with words. All that does—all it will have done—is confirm in everyone's mind that he is in fact guilty."

Hermione frowned. "Why? I was telling them specifically that he *isn't*."

"And why is *that*?" Letitia looked pointedly at her sister and answered the question, "Because you think he did indeed kill Randall."

She started pacing before the hearth; when Hermione's frown deepened to a scowl, she went on, "That's how all those around you in the park will interpret your words. To the ton, a verbal denial is second best to an admission. A *heated* denial—and I saw how strongly you were speaking—is tantamount to outright confirmation."

The belligerence in Hermione's face slowly faded. "Oh." After a moment, in a small voice, she asked, "Have I made things much worse?"

Still pacing, still trying to work off her temper, Letitia waved her hands. "More difficult, perhaps, but I don't believe our position is irretrievable. I'll just have to work harder to steer perceptions in the right direction."

Hermione watched her for a minute, then asked, "How will you do that? Steer perceptions?"

"By seeding doubt. For instance, when those ladies mentioned Justin's guilt, I was slightly startled, then puzzled that they'd come to such a conclusion. I didn't try to argue them around, but instead left them with the suspicion that perhaps what they'd heard wasn't what really happened." She waved again, pacing further. "To manipulate the ton, you have to use guile and subtlety, not direct words."

Hermione's lips formed an *O* of comprehension.

Letitia's pacing—now fueled more by burgeoning concern that contrary to what she'd told Hermione, her sister's misguided efforts might just have sunk their cause—led her deeper into the shadowed library—far enough that she noticed a pair of highly polished Hessian boots.

The boots encased a pair of long legs. Halting, she whisked her gaze upward to Christian's eyes; he was sitting in an armchair in the shadows, watching her. "What are you doing here?"

Her greeting was in no way encouraging, but he smiled nevertheless. The smile of a man who knew her well—well enough to know her temper was largely spent.

"I came to ask for information with which to pursue your errant brother, and"—his gaze switched to Hermione—"to again ask your sister what she knows."

She swung to face Hermione in time to see her sister fight to banish consciousness from her expression. "Whatever you know, please tell us."

When Hermione met her gaze, anxiety and even a touch of fear in her eyes, she urged, "We're trying to help Justin—we can't do that effectively without, as Dearne put it, reconstructing the crime. If you know something, anything relevant, we need to know."

Hermione hesitated, then pressed her lips tight and shook her head.

Letitia sighed. "You're not helping, dearheart. You must tell us—"

"I *can't!*" Hermione's response was almost a wail. Letitia got the impression she wanted to stamp her foot, but then her eyes filled with tears. "I . . . I don't know *anything.*"

Spinning about, Hermione ran back through the archway.

An instant later they heard the parlor door shut.

Letitia closed her eyes and sighed again, this time feeling the accumulated tension and energy flowing away, leaving her drained.

Eyes closed, she stood there, before the hearth in Randall's forgotten library, and tried to relocate her mental feet.

She sensed Christian draw near. She hadn't heard him move, but her nerves ruffled as only he had ever made them do.

"She obviously knows something." His voice, low and deep, came from beside her.

"Obviously." She didn't open her eyes.

"Why do you think she isn't telling us—not even you?"

His quiet tone, his patient voice, led her mind where she didn't want it to go. But she refused to back away from the truth. Her belief in her brother's innocence was absolute; nothing could shake it. Opening her eyes, she moistened her lips, half turned to face him. "She won't tell us because what she knows makes Justin appear guilty."

Christian's gray eyes held hers. "Yes." A moment passed, then he asked, "Can you accept that he might be?"

She forced herself to think, to consider it—rationally rather than emotionally—but emotion in this instance was too strong. "No." She shook her head. "He didn't kill Randall. Justin might be popularly known as a rake and a gamester, as a profligate hellion, but he's no murderer."

Calmly she met Christian's steady gray gaze. "You know that as well as I."

After a moment he nodded. "Unfortunately, the ton doesn't share our opinion." He moved back a little, giving her space to breathe. "What did Hermione do?"

She told him.

"How much damage did she cause?"

She glanced at the archway, but Hermione hadn't returned. "Considerable, unfortunately. Some of the most avid gossips, finding that I wasn't about to feed the scandal, had passed from me to her. She largely undid what I'd done, and then went further."

She frowned, imagining the outcome and how she might deal with it.

"What are you planning?"

She glanced up, met his eyes. "I'll have to appear rather more than I would like, but it has to be done." Raising a hand, she brushed back a loosened lock from her temple, noted that his eyes followed her hand. She turned away. "As I told Hermione, I need to seed doubt—and now I need to do it in far more minds. If the ton grow convinced beyond shaking that Justin is guilty, proving him innocent won't be enough to clear his name. Even if he's officially exonerated he'll never recover his standing. I can't let that happen. One day he'll be the Earl of Nunchance and head of the House of Vaux."

When Christian didn't reply, she glanced at him. Hands on his hips, he was staring at the floor, a frown marring his handsome face. She grasped the moment to study it, felt as always a visceral tug—searched for distraction and recalled that he'd come to ask for information. "What did you want to ask me?"

He glanced up. She saw him think back—clearly whatever had caused that frown had been something else.

"I need to know the names of Justin's friends and associates. However many names you know."

She grimaced. "That's not all that many." She thought, then recited, "Ludwell and Arkdale. Geoffrey Amberly. Rittledale. And Banningham. Those are all I know for certain, at least over the last years."

Christian nodded; he lowered his arms. "I'll ask around and see what I can learn." He stepped closer. "We need to locate Justin and get him to tell us what went on. Tell Hermione that's what I intend to do."

Letitia's eyes widened, but she held her ground. Inclined her head. "I will. But she's stubborn."

He held her green-gold gaze. "Aren't you all?"

Once again they were close; once again excruciating awareness arced and all but crackled between them. The past seemed tangible, a web of feeling threatening to snare them anew. Yet . . . seeing the deep worry clouding her eyes, he couldn't resist lifting one hand and gently touching the back of one finger to her pale cheek.

Her eyes flared. Ruthlessly suppressing his answering response, he lowered his hand and stepped back. "I'll let you know what I learn."

With a brisk salute, he turned—then turned back. "One thing. Barton's outside, keeping watch. If Justin sends word, or by some chance you find you can get a message to him, warn him not to go to his lodgings, or to come to this house." He hesitated, then said, "Tell him to come to mine."

She studied his eyes, then nodded "All right."

With a vague wave, he turned and left her—standing before her husband's empty hearth.

Christian swung down the steps into the street and set off for Grosvenor Square.

All those who caught a glimpse of his face gave him a wide berth.

One part of him—the vengeful part—couldn't believe what he was doing. That, once again, he was falling under the spell of Letitia Vaux, the Jezebel who'd ripped his heart from his chest and then later thrown it away.

Wanting to knock Barton's teeth down his throat was one thing; given how the runner had behaved, he would probably have felt as strongly had it been any gently bred lady. Or so he'd tried to tell himself.

But today . . . it was one thing to discover that he still lusted after her as intensely as he ever had, but to allow himself to feel *tender* toward her—what sort of self-flagellating moron was he?

Even more to the point, how had his plans of revenge, admittedly vague and unformed, degenerated to such a degree? To where he now wanted to comfort her, to soothe her and ease her way?

A scowl darkening his features, he strode along and couldn't think of an answer. The truth was, when he'd seen her today, bowed down not only with worry for her brother but having to battle the ton's perceptions, and then shouldering the additional burden Hermione had unwittingly created, all because she understood that for them, in their circle, family came first . . . he'd understood, to his soul he'd been touched, and he'd felt . . .

Something he hadn't felt in years.

Reaching the pavement before his front door, he halted and stared at the highly polished panels.

The truth was . . . even though he knew that she hadn't truly loved him, that contrary to what he'd believed, all that they'd shared in the past had been nothing more than a passing fancy to her, it didn't seem to matter.

He'd loved her then.

And he still did.

Dragging in a breath, he slowly let it out, then marched up the steps and let himself into his house.

Chapter 3

Christian spent the rest of that day trawling through the likely haunts Justin Vaux might have retreated to, innocently or otherwise. That Justin's man had gone with him suggested a stay somewhere; when nothing came of inquiring at the obvious places—White's, Boodle's, Crockfords, and the smattering of other clubs a nobleman of Justin's age and ilk might frequent—Christian turned to more serious scouting.

Later that evening, using the Bastion Club as a base, along with the support Gasthorpe provided by means of his small army of messengers and footmen, Christian sent out inquiries along the main highways out of London, especially those leading to the ports in the south and southeast, searching for some sighting of Justin's curricle.

Since returning to London, he'd glimpsed Justin numerous times in the clubs, but hadn't spoken to him. Letitia's brother hadn't made any effort to speak with him either, but courtesy of those vignettes gained across crowded rooms, Christian knew Justin had grown into his family's legacy; few seeing him, even in a greatcoat, would forget him, and with his striking good looks, his height, and that hair, most could be counted on to remember if asked.

Unfortunately, as he discovered the next morning when he returned to breakfast at the club, no one recalled sighting Justin over the last days along any of the stretches of highway he'd targeted.

He was finishing his breakfast and mulling over his options when Tristan, Lord Trentham, another club member, strolled into the dining room. His eyes lit at the sight of the maps Christian had spread over the table. "Gasthorpe mentioned you were involved in something. Anything I can help with?"

Christian grinned and waved to a chair. "I didn't expect anyone else would be in town yet."

Sitting, Tristan sighed. "Lenore apparently needs new gowns, and of course she needs to check on her uncle and brother." He hooked a thumb in the direction of the house next door. "She's over there at the moment, but then she's heading to Bond Street." He brightened. "So I'm at loose ends, and therefore yours to command."

Smiling understandingly—all of them missed the action of their former lives—Christian gave him a brief outline of the issues surrounding Randall's murder, omitting all mention of his previous association with Letitia.

Tristan saw through his ploy. "And you've been drawn into this because . . . ?"

Christian held his gaze steadily. "I know the family of old. Our estates are in the same region."

Tristan studied his face, then smiled. "I see."

But to Christian's relief, he said nothing more.

Transferring his attention to the maps, Tristan asked, "Where have you searched so far?"

Christian told him.

After some discussion, pooling their contacts they organized a network of more detailed inquiries, effectively drawing a tight circle around London. After dispatching Gasthorpe's messengers, Christian surveyed the map and their lists with grim satisfaction. "That, at least, should tell us whether he's left town, or has gone to ground somewhere within our circle."

Tristan met his gaze. "You think he's hiding?"

Christian nodded. "Yes, I do. What I don't know is why."

* * *

That evening, Letitia attended a select soiree at the home of Lady Lachlan, one of her multitude of connections. A family gathering, more or less. Garbed all in black with a filmy veil shading her features, she relentlessly projected the stance she wished to establish—that while she would pay all due observance to the ton's sensibilities regarding mourning dress, that while she would not dance, nor indulge in any other form of entertainment, she had absolutely no intention of hiding herself away.

Aside from all else, hiding herself away wouldn't help Justin.

Events such as this provided her only real opportunity to gauge what the gentlemen of the ton thought. Unfortunately, as she quickly discovered, they, one and all, had followed the ladies' lead.

"Dreadful business," Sir Henry Winthrop, a distant cousin, opined. "Can't think what got into Justin's head."

"*Justin's* head?" Letitia looked perplexed. "I'm afraid I don't follow."

Sir Henry blinked, then smiled avuncularly and patted her wrist. "I don't suppose you do, m'dear. Not the sort of thing a gentlewoman should think about, heh?"

Before she could disabuse him of that ludicrous notion, he was hailed by someone from across the room; excusing himself, he left her side.

The younger gentlemen were even worse.

"That temper, you know. Always thought it would get the better of him one day." That from a Lachlan acquaintance.

The reply, from Mr. Kenneally, an Irishman known for his dissolute ways, "I heard he can be quite ferocious when roused. No holding him," left Letitia literally speechless.

When Christian unexpectedly appeared by her side, she fell on him as the only safe outlet for her increasing ire.

"They're making Justin sound like a madman!" Facing Christian, she fought to keep her voice down. "The way they're talking, it's as if the infamous Vaux temper is an affliction. A prelude to insanity!"

Christian eyed her cynically. "The family, you included, have been perfectly content to be known as the vile-tempered Vaux for generations. You can't expect people to suddenly forget."

She sent him a glittering glance. "You know we're not that bad."

"Yes. But then I know the Vaux rather well." The subtle emphasis he placed on the latter words might have had her blushing, but through the veil he couldn't tell. "It was your great-grandfather who started it, wasn't it?"

"Yes, and he truly was a bona fide terror. From the stories my grandfather related, he must have had the most vicious tongue known to man. Not that my grandfather was all that much better, but by all accounts he was an improvement. My father, as you know, could never be described as a comfortable person, but no matter how verbally violent we might be, we're not—never have been—*physically* dangerous."

"Except when you throw things."

"We never throw things at people, and our aim is good. You can't ask for more." She dragged in a breath. "But none of that—the truth—seems to matter!"

Clutching his sleeve, she swung around and pointed at a youthful gentleman. "Do you know what Finley Courtauld said?"

Through her grip on his arm, Christian sensed just how strung up she was. She proceed to relate numerous comments either made to her or that she'd overheard, all confirming the ton's solidifying belief that Justin Vaux had, in a fit of the famous—or infamous—Vaux temper, beaten his brother-in-law to death.

Her own temper was not just showing but spiraling—to a dangerous degree.

He closed his hand over hers on his sleeve, squeezed until she stopped her escalating rant and looked at him. When she did, he said in a perfectly even voice, "You're feeling unwell. Come—I'll take you home."

Through the filmy veil she narrowed her eyes at him; her lips had firmed into a thin line.

He returned her gaze steadily; they both knew that if she remained in Lady Lachlan's drawing room and continued in her present vein, she would risk reaching the stage where her temper slipped its leash and took over.

And they both knew how histrionically violent, how dramatic and sensational, the outcome was all but guaranteed to be.

She humphed, and looked across the room, locating their hostess. "Only because I can't afford to create a scene at this moment, on this topic."

"Indeed," he replied dryly. "The *ton* really doesn't need a demonstration of just how violent—verbally or otherwise— a Vaux can be."

She humphed again, but consented to be led across the floor, to make her farewells, rather brittlely, to Lady Lachlan, then to walk with him into the front hall, where they waited while her carriage was fetched.

Although Letitia preserved a rigid silence, he knew that her temper, once aroused, wasn't that easy to deflect. To douse. The Vaux temper didn't respond to logic, reason, or control, not once a certain point was reached, a point she'd already passed. There were a few distractions that would work, but although one—the most effective—occurred to him, given their public location, it wasn't a viable option.

When he handed her into the carriage and then sat beside her, he could sense the storm building within her, increasingly potent for being suppressed.

She waited until they'd started rolling to release it. "I can't imagine why everyone—simply *everyone*—is being so willfully obtuse! Can't they see . . ."

She ranted and raved, calling into question the mental acuity of a sizable portion of the ton, ruthlessly stripping bare their foibles, exposing all, the shallowness and jealousy, to a relentlessly clinical verbal dissection.

Much of what she said was correct. She was a highly intelligent observer of her world, and her memory for minor details of people's lives was remarkable in its depth and clarity. He sat back and listened, knowing she needed nothing more than the occasional monosyllable from him.

The journey to South Audley Street wasn't long enough for her to run down. As the carriage slowed, then halted before her—Randall's—door, she cut off her tirade, hauled in a huge breath and held it. Let him hand her down and escort her up the steps and into the house without a word.

He followed her into the front parlor.

She halted, half turned and cast a rapier glance back, not at him but at Mellon. Randall's butler plainly recognized the signs of an impending explosion; he'd paled and remained hovering in the hall, making no attempt to come closer.

"You may retire." She spoke quietly, slowly, each word bitten off. "I require nothing more from you tonight."

Under her gaze—one promising all manner of dramatic retribution should he remain an instant longer—Mellon paled even more, bowed and scurried away, his alacrity testifying to prior experience of such unvoiced threats.

The instant he disappeared, Letitia made a hissing sound; swinging around, she stalked back to the door, slammed it shut, then turned to Christian. "Did you *see*? Outside? That ghastly weasel of a runner is across the road, still keeping watch."

Raising a hand, she ripped off her veil, along with the comb anchoring it. She flung it on a chair. "I'd like to strangle Mellon"—she curled her hands as if fastening them about the butler's neck—"for visiting this whole nightmare upon us. Then again, he has the intellect of a flea. Presumably he can't help being a dolt. Regardless, I don't know where the authorities' brains are—how they can countenance . . ."

She paced, ranted and raved. Hands were flung freely,

skirts were kicked out of her way, fingers were wagged and stabbed for emphasis.

Christian stood in the center of the parlor and watched the show. As always, he was the rock, unaffected by the storm, while she was the lashing waves, the fury and tempest. She circled him, all fire and brimstone, lightning and raw emotion. He waited, knowing she'd talk herself to a standstill, or at least to a point where her mind reasserted control and she refocused on the here and now.

He had time to study their surroundings. This was her room—the difference between it and the rest of the house, at least all the other reception rooms, was pronounced. This was Vaux territory, her domain, richly and sumptuously furnished, a feast for the senses. Two sofas faced each other across the fireplace; matching sofa tables across the back of each held large crystal vases filled with flowers. Other tables and two armchairs were arranged about the room. The candelabra and most ornaments were of gleaming silver. Silks and satins were the primary fabrics, the colors jeweled-toned blues and greens touched with gold—vivid and dramatic hues to create the perfect setting for a vivid and dramatic lady. The effect was of unabashed sensual luxury.

Yet her presence was restricted to this room. He wondered why.

Eventually she halted and frowned at the fabulous green and gold rug. Then she turned her head and looked at him. Her eyes still sparked; her temper had yet to die. "And then there's you." Her lips curved, as cynical as he often was. "Playing your own game." She swung closer, halting directly before him. She looked into his face, studied his eyes. "What have you learned?"

He arched one brow. Let a moment tick past before answering. "We finally found someone who saw Justin in his curricle in the early hours of the morning after Randall was killed. An ostler at an inn on the outskirts of the city—on the Dover Road."

"Dover?" Looking down, she frowned. "There's nothing at Dover."

Other than the packet to Calais. Christian saw no value in stating the obvious.

She shook her head. "He won't be going to Dover."

Which, despite appearances to the contrary, was his— and Tristan's—experienced conclusions. "We think he's deliberately laying a trail to make it appear he fled the scene, and then the country."

She looked up at him, still frowning. "He's deliberately making himself look guilty?"

"That's the way it . . . feels." Instinct more than fact had informed his and Tristan's opinions.

Her frown deepened. "But . . . *why?*" Swinging away, she flung out her hands. "Why do such a *senseless* thing?"

He had one very good idea, but it wasn't wise to suggest it, given her still fraught state. His supposition was all but guaranteed to send her into another bout of histrionics, albeit aimed at her brother, not him.

She suddenly swung around and strode back to him. "We have to find Justin. We have to locate him wherever he is, and bring him back and exonerate him in the eyes of the authorities and the world." Halting before him, even closer this time, eyes locked on his, she jabbed a finger into his chest. "You have to *do something!*"

He caught her finger.

She frowned, tugged, but he didn't let go. Lifting her gaze to his eyes, she narrowed hers in a glittering, dangerous glare.

Which had entirely the opposite effect on him than she intended.

Through his hold on her hand, he could feel the tension thrumming through her. Her temper was another form of passion; her earlier outburst had opened the floodgates, leaving her passionate, sensual self very close to her surface.

It had been twelve long years since they'd been this close.

He looked into her eyes, and saw desire and heat well even as her lips firmed.

"I think," he said, refusing to let her hand go even when she tugged again, "that it's time to discuss a down payment."

He was playing with fire and he knew it.

Knew her fire all too well.

Had never forgotten it.

"Just for getting a sighting?"

He smiled intently. "Consider it an incentive to learn more."

Her eyes couldn't get any narrower; they gleamed like molten gold. With her hand trapped in his, no more than an inch separated them, separated the black bombazine covering her breasts from his chest.

"What, then?"

Her voice had lowered, her tone provocative, challenging, demanding. A tone that, despite all, certainly despite her intention, racked his arousal one notch higher.

She held his gaze. "What do you want?"

The answer was obvious. "A kiss."

"A kiss?"

Her expression was, to him, transparent; she'd guessed his direction regarding payment correctly. She wasn't surprised by his choice; instead, she was . . .

Angry all over again. He saw the flash of temper in her eyes in the instant before she wrenched her hand from his slackened grasp, snapped, "Very well," reached up with both hands, framed his face, moved into him—and kissed him.

With all the passion her temper had stirred.

With all the heat, all the fire pent up inside her.

It was a relief to let it go. Letitia let every reservation, every barrier she had, all the walls she'd erected over the long years to bank her passion, fall. Simply fall to the ground.

Let all the yearning in her passionate soul free.

He wanted a kiss? Very well. She would give him one,

one he wouldn't soon forget, and gain as much as she gave—
for one long moment revel as the woman she used to be.

His.

She wasn't the least bit surprised when he reacted, when
he wrapped his arms about her and hauled her against his
chest. It had always been like that—her passion effortlessly
igniting his.

His lips firmed, then he tilted his head, the kiss changed
and he was in command, so he could part her lips and invade
her mouth and lay claim.

And send her senses soaring.

Heat poured through her, welled and swelled and spread.
She could feel it in him, that same helpless reaction, in the
hot kisses he pressed on her, the scorching heat between
them as he stole her breath, then gave it back.

Need and desire infused her, and him, there, potent and real
in the hardness of his lips, in the grip of his hands on her back.

She would have laughed if she could have, thrown back
her head in sheer joy. In the indescribable delight of feeling
alive again, of feeling lust, desire, and physical need again.

Of being his again, for however short a time.

She grasped the moment voraciously, tunneled her fingers
into his hair and gripped his skull, clung, hung on as they
swirled in the spiraling vortex that had risen up and seized
them. Frankly reveled in the knowledge that she could still
lure him, could provoke the languid lion to action, and more,
could still arouse him.

That last was beyond question. The hard ridge pressed
against her belly was testament enough to his state. As were
his increasingly hungry, nay ravenous, kisses.

She urged him on. Reached up and wound her arms about
his neck, pressing against him in flagrant invitation.

Need flared deep inside. Hotter than she remembered,
molten and greedy.

And suddenly the kiss wasn't enough.

Dragging her hands from his hair, she pressed her palms
to his shoulders, ran them *slowly* down his chest, savoring

the heavy muscles that seemed harder, heavier, than she recalled.

She knew what it felt like to touch his skin, to feel it against hers. The memories surged, brilliant moments that had tided her over all the long years since. They erupted into her reeling consciousness, and compelled.

Then his hands were on her, closing about her breasts and kneading, sculpting her body, blatantly possessive, and she had to respond.

To his heat and his need and his desire.

To the passion he pressed on her through the kiss, through the commanding, demanding caresses that set her skin afire, that flayed her nerves with sensual pleasure, and an explicit promise of more to come.

She had to have that more.

Had to make him want as she did, make him desire as she did. To strip away the studied calm with which he faced the rest of the world and touch the real man—the warrior, the ruthless demanding conqueror—beneath.

The knowledge that she could had always thrilled—a thrill she'd never thought to feel again. But he was there, arms like steel trapping her, his lips on hers, his tongue plundering her mouth, his large hard hands sliding down to cup her bottom and shift her provocatively against him again . . . and nothing else mattered.

She pressed his coat wide, fell on the buttons closing his shirt, returned his kiss with a fervor to match his. To taunt, to incite, to demand.

And he gave her what she wanted, dropped every last shield and joined her on that primitive sensual plane on which they'd always danced.

She wasn't even aware when they sank to the floor, to the silk rug that lay between the sofas.

Christian drew her down beside him. Thought had long flown. Instinct ruled.

In asking for a kiss, he hadn't expected this—an explosion of need, his as well as hers, a raging fire in his blood he was unable to deny, to control, to even guide. A conflagration from which there was no drawing back.

She was the heat he'd been searching for, the warmth, the life. She was raw passion and need, a bright, slender, scorching flame he'd never been able to forget.

Yet he'd forgotten the danger of playing with fire.

She'd set him alight, and now he burned.

No other woman had ever been able to cinder his control, not in any circumstances and certainly never with just a kiss.

His only consolation was that on the plane of need they'd breached, she had no more control than he.

She wanted him with the same urgent scorching passion as he wanted her. In that, nothing had changed.

As he slid free the last button closing her bodice and yanked the fabric aside, slid his hand beneath and with a flick of his fingers dispensed with her chemise, and finally, finally, after twelve long years, set his hand to her firm flesh, she arched into him, then sighed.

So did he. For one finite moment he savored the silken skin beneath his palm, then she wriggled, urgent and demanding, and he bent his head and set his lips to her flesh— to taste and possess and drive her wild.

How long he managed to string out the heated moments, he couldn't tell, but he doubted it was long; they were both too hungry—their passions too long denied—too desperate for all that they both knew could be to linger.

As he pushed up her black skirts and exposed her long legs, ivory pale and so familiar just a glimpse of them sent yet more heat racing to his groin, he didn't even wonder whether she would stop him.

She'd found the buttons at his waistband, then she found him—and his world rocked. He paused, eyes closed, felt every touch of her too knowing fingers, their hungry, greedy stroking, felt her simple possession like a brand, not just on his skin but in his brain; head back, he groaned.

Heard the delighted chuckle she gave.

That acted like a spur, pricking sharp and deep, as she'd known it would. In this arena, they'd always wrestled for supremacy, and while he usually won, she held enough power in her Vaux soul, enough passion, to challenge him.

To provoke him as no other woman ever had. Ever could.

Even as he thrust one knee between hers, forced her legs apart and touched her, even as his fingers delved in her wet heat, stroked, then penetrated, then thrust more deeply— even as she gasped and clutched his upper arms, a supplicant surrendering to her master, breathlessly, wordlessly, begging him for more—he knew it was all illusion. That he was as much her slave as ever she was his.

He yielded to the urgent tug of her hands, yielded to his own raging desire, and moved over her, spreading her thighs and settling between.

The jolt to his memory of being there once again, his flanks clasped by her long, firm thighs, his hips cradled by hers, the blunt head of his erection bathed by the scalding heat of her welcome, might have been powerful enough to jerk him back to sanity, but she raised her hands and framed his face—and drew his lips down for a searing kiss.

Cindering any hope of rational thought.

Trapping him once again in their mutual conflagration. She shifted beneath him, and the flames roared.

He reached down, found her knee and lifted it to his hip, opening her beneath him.

Then he thrust in.

Thrust home.

Her body arched under his. She moaned, the sound trapped in their kiss; her body clutched his, tightly, then beneath him she melted.

A small climax, he realized, but he'd be damned if he let her escape with just that.

He needn't have worried. The instant he started to move within her, each stroke slow, long and deliberate, she was with him again.

Although a touch surprised by the small explosion—just because he'd entered her, for heaven's sake—Letitia had no intention of settling for just that. Now she had him exactly where her body craved him, she was determined to wring every last iota of pleasure from the event.

From the chance that had somehow materialized to give her senses, for so long starved, succor.

So she reveled in the sensations of him, so rigid and heavy, so incontestably male, moving within her. She met him and matched him, wound her leg about his hips and drew him still deeper. Gloried at his moan, at his surrender as he took every last inch she offered and filled her.

Opening her senses, she drank in, soaked up, every little pleasure—the weight of him pressing her to the floor, his hips pinning hers as he drove repetitively deep within her, his chest heavy against her aching breasts—a delicious ache she'd all but forgotten—his lips still locked over hers, his mouth still feasting on hers, his tongue mimicking his possession of her in a flagrantly erotic way.

With joyous greed she grasped every chance to let her rejected, shriveled, almost moribund passionate soul milk all it could from the encounter, all it could of what he and circumstance had conspired to deny her for twelve long years.

All his thirst for revenge and her dramatic temper had today, between them, unwittingly unleashed.

So she strove for no control; she simply wanted.

She made no effort to guide or direct; she simply urged him on. Urged him to ride her as hard as he would, as deeply as he wished, amazed to discover that he seemed as desperate, as driven, as she.

To revisit all they'd had. To touch the heat, the incredible flaming peak, again.

To at the end, all flushed skin and damp flesh, hands grasping, locking, fingers clenched, lungs so tight they burned, lips fused, mouths melded, blind and desperate searching for release, let desire wield its whip and drive them the last little way, to crest the peak together.

To together soar over the edge and into the void.

To fracture and fall, in passion's embrace to let pleasure claim them.

To shatter them, and fill them.

With a golden glory she hadn't felt for so long it made her weep.

Spent, he slumped upon her. She could feel his heart still racing, pounding in his chest, feel the tempo echo where they joined.

She drew a slow, shallow breath, then raised a hand, wiped the tear that had slid from beneath her lashes, paused. Then, hesitantly, driven by an urge she had no wish to name, she raised her hand to his hair and, tentatively, caressed. When he settled under the caress, her heart contracted. She continued, gently ruffling his hair, just as she used to.

A quiet, tender minute ticked past. His heartbeat gradually slowed; his breathing eased.

She wasn't sure if what she felt was her parched heart shattering, or if the sensation in her chest was of that same parched heart, refreshed by the last moments, slowly swelling, returning to life.

The latter was unwise, and would most likely prove self-destructive, at the very least exquisitely hurtful. He hadn't loved her, not as she loved him, and never had, no matter what she'd thought. It would be foolish beyond permission to imagine that had changed, especially given how he now thought of her.

Regardless, she could control her heart no more than she'd been able to control the passion of the last minutes.

Any more than she'd been able to control it all those years ago.

Finally, he stirred, withdrew and moved off her—only to slump heavily on his back alongside. Luckily, the silk rug was large.

Reaching down with one hand, she flicked her skirts down over her knees, not out of any sense of modesty—with him she had none—but because, with passion fading, the air felt cool.

They lay side by side staring up at the ceiling.

When he gave no sign of breaking the silence, she decided that, as his hostess, it fell to her to do so.

"That wasn't supposed to happen." Her voice was low, sultry—even more raspy than it usually was.

Christian felt more than heard the words, as if they were some damnable caress, stroking down his chest and lower. Inside, not outside; not stroking his skin but his very nerves.

Nerves she'd—they'd—just sated to an extent he hadn't recalled as possible.

He felt her sidelong glance, knew she was waiting for him to make some response, but . . . he simply couldn't find the words. Could barely find his brain, let alone assemble sufficient wit to have a coherent conversation.

Especially not with the scent of jasmine everywhere around him.

The physical vortex they'd created had been wild enough—mind-bending, senses-scrambling, shattering enough. But the emotional whirlpool it had left behind was . . . at least for now, more than he could cope with.

He felt battered, raked raw.

Her hand in his hair, gently stroking as she always had before, had shaken him to the depths of his soul.

Regardless, he knew he had to regroup, at least enough to take his leave.

She'd been studying his profile. She definitely seemed more well-grounded than he. From the corner of his eye he saw her lips quirk—recognized the fleeting smile as one of smug, feminine satisfaction.

Before he could summon the will to react, it faded. Her expression grew closed, shuttered.

He turned to look at her as she looked away.

And pushed herself to a sitting position.

She started to rebutton her bodice. "No one has ever

claimed a Vaux failed to honor an obligation." She glanced at him, briefly met his eyes. "I don't imagine any Allardyce would either."

Bodice closed, she swung her legs beneath her and got to her feet. She shook out her skirts, then met his eyes again.

Her lips had thinned. "Consider what just occurred as a significant payment against our account." She straightened, and looked haughtily down at him. "Now you have to prove yourself worthy of your hire."

The look in her eyes told him very clearly that she'd correctly divined, and was totally unimpressed by, his ill-formed intention of using her payment to exact some convoluted revenge.

One fine brow slowly arched; he was fairly certain she could, even now, read the few thoughts his brain had managed to assemble. He'd forgotten just how well she knew him.

"I'll find Justin." His voice came out as a resigned growl.

That infernal brow of hers arched higher. "Good." With a crisp nod, she half turned toward the door. "You can see yourself out."

When he made no further comment—in his present state unnecessary speech was beyond him—she merely raised both brows, swung on her heel and swept out of the room.

Leaving him lying in disarray on her fabulous silk rug.

He waited until he heard the door click behind her, then he groaned and sat up. Upright wasn't much of an improvement; he still felt . . . stunned, blindsided, reeling.

He knew what he'd intended—just a kiss, a taunting, teasing one that would have left her wanting and reminded her of what she'd turned her back on.

He knew what had happened—she'd seized his intention and turned it back on him, and with typical Vaux disregard for safety had unleashed a maelstrom that had plunged them both back into the past.

Back into each other, and not just physically.

He knew what had occurred, even now could recall each stunning instant with startling clarity—feel her taking him in, even feel her hands on his overheated skin, burning him, branding him.

What he didn't know was why.

And even less did he know what it meant.

She—they—between them had taken a step back through time, as if the intervening years hadn't mattered. As if all that had happened in those years didn't truly exist, not on the same plane.

As if all that had occurred in those years hadn't affected what lay between them.

He didn't understand how that could be so. She'd walked away from her promise to wait for him and happily married another man. When he'd returned briefly to assume his title after his father's death, he'd heard that her marriage to Randall was widely regarded as a love match—there being no other explanation for a lady of Letitia's birth and family circumstances marrying so far beneath her.

Yet tonight, on the exquisite green and gold silk rug in her parlor, they'd plunged into the past—and it—every moment, every touch, every gasp—had been exactly as it had been before.

If anything, even more intense than before.

Even to that moment afterward when she'd gently tumbled his hair.

Everything had been the same—yet given what had happened between then and now, how could that be?

Mentally shaking his head, he got to his feet and righted his clothes.

Then he headed for the door, dousing the candles as he went. The front hall was in darkness. He opened the front door, set the latch to lock behind him, and stepped out into the balmy night.

Walking home through the darkness helped clear his head.

By the time he reached his front door, he'd clarified at least two points.

While he didn't understand what had happened, he intended to find out.

And although he'd intended the price for his services to be nothing more than, at the most, a fleeting liaison, he'd changed his mind.

Now, he wanted a great deal more.

Chapter 4

Exactly what he now wanted of Letitia Randall née Vaux was a point Christian hadn't yet decided. The following morning, he put that matter—defining his prize—aside, and concentrated instead on winning it.

He and Tristan met at the club. Over breakfast, they reviewed all they'd been able to glean over the past days concerning Justin Vaux.

"He's twenty-six—no longer a wet-behind-the-ears whelp." Pushing his empty plate away, Tristan sat back. "From all I could gather, he's viewed by his friends as a curiously sober sort. 'A reliable man,' to quote one."

"Aside from his temper, presumably," Christian dryly replied.

Tristan inclined his head. "Oddly, however, while everyone acknowledged it—his temper's existence—it didn't seem to feature in, to influence or color in any real way, their experience of him."

Christian snorted. "The Vaux are largely frauds." When Tristan looked his query, he elaborated, "They do have tempers—histrionic and dramatic ones. Ones that rely on the tongue for expression." He considered, then said, "One should perhaps remember that while the Vaux have never been warriors, they've always been valued by the most powerful in the land—for their tongues. They've been diplomats, envoys, all manner of messengers and ambassadors. Most of the males in the senior line have served in that capacity at one time or another."

"Not the sort of delicate missions normally entrusted to those who can't control their tempers."

"Precisely. They can control themselves when they wish, at least to a manageable degree. However, the truth is they love—to the point of addiction—the drama and sheer energy they can let loose, and so if there is no pressure to rein their tempers in, they don't. Won't. Instead, they indulge themselves, to the general terror of all those around to hear." His lips curved. "Mind you, I have it on excellent authority that the current generation are but a pale imitation of the ancestor who gained the family their nickname."

Tristan snorted. "Probably just as well, although that hasn't in this case stopped the ton from attributing a murderous impulse to the infamous Vaux temper." He met Christian's eyes. "Which brings me to our next point. Quite aside from any temper-induced fury, nonwarrior that he is, could Justin Vaux have killed his brother-in-law, especially in such a brutal manner?"

Christian held Tristan's gaze for some moments before saying, "I can imagine him killing with a pistol—a single shot. Or with a sword thrust. What I find difficult to imagine is him committing the unnecessary violence. By all accounts there was very little left of Randall's face."

Tristan grimaced.

"And," Christian went on, "while admittedly I haven't met Justin since he was fourteen, even then he was a stickler in some respects, quite rigid in his adherence to our codes. Again, a Vaux trait. I can imagine him killing Randall—quickly and cleanly, even strangling him—but what I cannot imagine is him doing so and then fleeing. If Justin had killed Randall, brutally or not, he would have been the one to raise the alarm. Quite aside from it being unusual for a Vaux to decline to appear in a scene of high drama, they're incredibly proud, something that goes bone-deep, alongside their stubbornness."

Tristan pressed his lips together, then stated, "Everything you've said—all we've found and all we feel—about Justin Vaux suggests, strongly, that he's acting to protect someone."

Christian nodded. "I agree."

"So the question is: Who?" Tristan shifted. "Let me play devil's advocate. Could Lady Letitia have killed Randall, and Justin then acted to protect her by deflecting attention to himself?"

Christian had already considered it. "I can readily believe Justin acting in that way—it would fit his character as I know it to a T." He met Tristan's gaze. "But equally I know, absolutely, that Letitia did not kill Randall. While I admit she had, on the surface, a motive of sorts in opposing Randall's plans for her sister, she could have—and would have—dealt with that easily enough by other means. In that disagreement, the power lay with her and she knew it. Beyond that, she has no motive. And beyond that again, I seriously doubt she has it in her to intentionally kill anyone, and if she'd unintentionally harmed Randall, lethally or otherwise, not being the sort to readily lose her wits, she would have summoned assistance immediately."

Tristan held his gaze steadily. "As devil's advocate, I would have to point out that she might not have done the actual killing."

It took Christian a moment to realize what Tristan was implying.

As understanding dawned, Tristan went on, "If, as it appears, the marriage had deteriorated, it's not inconceivable that Letitia has a lover. Perhaps she schemed with her lover and he killed Randall. Or perhaps the lover acted on his own initiative and killed Randall without her knowledge. As for motive, who can tell what goes on between man and wife— what passions and jealousies might come into play?" Tristan broke off, then continued, "I was going to suggest that perhaps Randall's death came about in self-defense, but that won't wash given the injuries."

"Indeed." Christian hesitated. "I don't believe that Letitia has a lover, certainly not a recent one." He didn't want to believe that she might, even now, have a lover in the wings. He forced himself to evenly say, "But I can't swear to it." He straightened from his slouch. "I'll make discreet inquiries."

They revisited the items on their investigative list. "So we have three fronts," Christian summarized. "Justin Vaux— both his whereabouts and any hint of a motive, on neither of which we have any firm information. Secondly, we need to confirm if Letitia has a lover, and therefore some motive beyond what we know, and if said lover might be involved."

"And lastly," Tristan said, "Randall himself. We need to know much more about him, especially if neither Justin Vaux nor his sister are the murderers."

Christian grimaced. "Indeed. Once we eliminate them . . . at present the field is empty."

"Which is going to make it doubly hard to argue the Vaux's combined innocence."

Christian nodded and stood. "I'll look into Randall and his circumstances, and inquire about any lover Letitia may have. But first I've an appointment with Pringle—I asked him to take a look at Randall's body."

"An excellent idea. Meanwhile I"—Tristan rose, too— "will scout through the clubs for more pertinent information on Justin Vaux—whether anyone knows of any reason he might have headed to Dover, or if, as we suspect, he was merely blazing a trail for us to waste time following."

Christian met Pringle in an anteroom off the police morgue.

While the dapper little surgeon washed his hands, he happily recited a list of Randall's injuries. "Those to the face are the most severe, of course—extremely heavy blows with the poker. And yes, before you ask, it was Randall's poker that was the sole weapon. No hint of any other blunt instrument coming into play."

Picking up a waiting towel, Pringle turned to look at

Christian. "What was most interesting, however, was that he wasn't killed by the blows to the face and the sides of his head." Pringle grinned at Christian's look of surprise. "Indeed. The gentleman was killed with one lucky blow to the *back* of his head." Raising a hand, now clean, Pringle indicated the base of his skull.

Christian frowned. "Why a 'lucky' blow?"

"Because it was delivered with far less force than the blows to the face. In many men, it wouldn't have killed them. Randall had a thin skull, as it happened, so it did for him. Regardless, the killing stroke—administered first—was weak and definitely struck from behind. All the rest—the blows to the face and sides of the head—came later."

Disappointment settled in Christian's gut. "So in your opinion, a woman could have delivered the blow that killed Randall?"

Unaware of the importance of the question—that the chance to *eliminate* a female as the murderer was what had prompted Christian to ask him to examine Randall, and then pull strings, using his rank to arrange it—Pringle grinned. "Indubitably. Any reasonably tall woman could have done it—I say tall so the angle of strike fits."

Letitia was definitely tall.

Christian fell silent, digesting the news.

But Pringle hadn't finished. "What, however, in my humble opinion, a woman *couldn't* have done was deliver the blows that came later."

Christian refixed his attention on the surgeon. "You're sure?"

Pringle pursed his lips, weighing the question, then nodded. "Perhaps a strong woman from the circus might have, but any normal woman simply would not have been able to impart such force, even with him laid out on his back and her standing over him. Whoever struck those after-death blows was a male—a grown man. I'd stake my reputation on it."

Christian inwardly grimaced at the scenario taking shape in his mind. "How long after death?"

Again Pringle pursed his lips. This time he took longer before he answered. "My best estimate—and I stress it's only an estimate, this is an inexact science after all—would be at least fifteen minutes after death. Possibly as many as thirty, but not much longer. The injuries caused by the heavy blows were bloody—there was definitely some blood, but in none of the injuries, nor in the relevant reports, can I find sufficient blood to suggest the man's heart was still pumping. It wasn't. He was already dead, and from what else I saw on the corpse, for at least a little time."

"So it looks like he was first struck down when he was facing . . . the desk?"

Pringle considered, then nodded. "Again I'm going by the reports, but there wasn't any indication he'd been moved other than being turned over, which of course he was. And yes, with the knowledge that he was first struck from behind, not from the front as was assumed, he was indeed facing the desk, not the hearth."

Randall had been facing away from the person who had shared a drink with him. The person who'd sat in the other armchair.

Christian tucked the information away and refocused on Pringle. "Do you have any insight into why anyone would deliver those blows to the head and face of an already dead man?"

Pringle nodded. "Indeed I do. A guess, of course, but I believe it bears examining." Laying aside the towel, he reached for his coat. "Those later blows were extremely deliberate, struck with concerted, focused force. Any notion they were the product of some frenzied attack is purest fancy. No. Those blows were administered, I believe, to achieve precisely what had been achieved before you called me in. The police doctor didn't look closely enough—he assumed that the blows to the face and sides of the head killed Randall, and that, as I said, would exclude any woman as a suspect.

"I believe," Pringle caught Christian's eyes, "that the postmortem blows were administered with the sole objective of hiding—disguising, if you will—that a female could, in fact, have been the murderer."

Christian nodded; the scenario in his head had solidified.

"Just as well you called me in when you did," Pringle went on, shrugging into his coat. "If I hadn't got here this morning, it would have been too late. They're releasing the body to the undertakers as we speak—he'll be buried this afternoon."

Christian already knew about the funeral; he nodded again. "Thank you." He waited until Pringle settled his coat, then shook his hand and left him to make his report to the police.

Christian paused on the steps outside the dismal gray building. The raucous sounds of the bustling city surrounded him but made little impact on his senses. His mind was focused on what he was increasingly sure had happened in South Audley Street four nights previously. Justin Vaux had administered those dreadful blows to his already dead brother-in-law's face, and then fled, leaving a trail any child could follow, all to draw attention from, to protect, the person Justin believed had killed Randall.

Letitia.

Christian walked back to his house in Grosvenor Square, using the journey to turn Pringle's findings and his deductions over in his mind; with every step, every minute thus spent, he only grew more convinced that his conclusion was correct. Justin had acted to protect Letitia.

Why, as ever, was what he didn't know.

Regardless of Pringle's assertion that a tallish woman could have killed Randall, Christian knew, with the same absolute, unshakable conviction he'd felt from the first, that Letitia hadn't delivered that killing blow.

Who had—for if his scenario was correct it couldn't have been Justin—was the other major question he'd yet to address.

Reaching the steps leading to his front door, he started up, then paused. An instant ticked by, then he turned and looked across the square at the house directly opposite.

He considered the sight for a further minute before, straightening, squaring his shoulders, he went down the steps, crossed the street, and followed the path through the park filling the square, eventually reaching his senior paternal aunt's door.

He knocked, and was admitted—with some surprise—by her ladyship's butler, Meadows, who informed him their ladyships—Lady Cordelia Foster, Countess of Canterbury, and her sister, Lady Ermina Fowler, Viscountess Fowler—had just sat down to luncheon in the smaller dining parlor.

Girding his loins, he allowed Meadows to show him in.

"Christian, dear boy!" Seated at the end of the smaller table—still long enough to seat twelve—Cordelia waved him to her. A still handsome woman now in her late fifties, she was surprisingly energetic and remained a force to be reckoned with among the ton—even with the improbably blond curls that framed her face.

He obliged, crossing to her chair and placing a dutiful kiss on the cheek she offered, then circled her to perform the same greeting with the sweeter tempered Ermina, a milder version of Cordelia but no less observant.

"Come and sit!" Cordelia waved imperiously to the chair on her left. Meadows was already setting a place there. "As you're here and we're lunching, you can lunch, too."

Although he hadn't intended to, he was happy enough to fall in with her wishes; Cordelia's chefs were invariably excellent, although they never lasted long.

He sat, then eyed the dishes the footmen Meadows waved in placed before them. "You're new chef is Austrian."

"Clever boy! Yes, indeed, Frederick is my new find. Quite a novel craze, Austrian dishes. They say Wellington and the others brought back the taste after the Congress of Vienna. The congress was a complete failure, of course, but the food, apparently, was excellent." Cordelia glanced at Meadows as the last dish was set in place. "Leave us, please, Meadows. I'll ring if we need you."

"Very good, ma'am." Meadows bowed low. "My lord." With a second deferential bow to Christian, Meadows retreated.

The instant the door closed behind him, Cordelia fixed Christian with an interrogative eye, the same gray hue as his own. "Well, my boy—what do you need to know?"

The direct attack had him blinking.

Ermina smiled gently—and closed in for the kill. "Well, dear, you never do appear without a summons, not unless you need something from us, which is usually information."

Her earnest soft gray gaze was quite enough to make him inwardly squirm.

Ermina's smile deepened as she shook out her napkin. "I daresay it's about Letitia and this dreadful business of Randall's murder."

Christian glanced from her to Cordelia. From the eager gleam in Cordelia's eye, she was only too ready to answer whatever questions he had; clearly, delicacy and tact would be wasted. "Indeed." Delicacy and tact aside, he wanted to reveal as little as possible; his aunts rated among the most well-connected gossips in the ton. "As you say, Randall has been murdered, and so the question of whether Letitia has a lover, and whether together or separately, for the obvious reason, they killed him, naturally arises."

Both his aunts stared at him. Their expressions initially suggested shocked surprise; that was quickly replaced by censure.

Cordelia snorted. "For *men* the question might 'naturally arise,' but I assure you no such nonsensical thought has surfaced in any female brain within the ton." With that statement, uttered in a tone even he would think carefully about questioning, Cordelia returned her attention to her plate.

From across the table, Ermina shook her head at him. "No, dear—you're quite wrong in even suggesting such a thing. Even putting such an outrageous suggestion into words."

It hadn't seemed outrageous to him—Letitia was a highly passionate woman—but there was clear rebuke beneath Ermina's words.

"Letitia is a Vaux, after all," Ermina informed him with not a little dignity. "I would have thought you would know what that means. She has taken no lover—absolutely not—not in all the years since she wed that man. We never did approve of him, of course—there was something not quite right there, as I've always said."

Chewing, Cordelia nodded. She swallowed, then said, "Not that he—Randall—was ever anything other than polite. He always behaved just as he ought, but . . ." She waggled the beringed fingers of one hand. "There was just *something* that didn't feel quite right about him." She mulled for a moment, then rallied. "But enough about him—he's dead and gone. As for Letitia, as Ermina said, she's a *Vaux,* for heaven's sake—they're sound, fury, and high drama on the surface, but absolutely unshakable rock beneath. A vow for them is sacred. Nothing would induce them to break one, and Lord knows you must have noticed how stubborn they are."

He'd known that, all that, but . . . Letitia had broken her vow to him. Why not her vows to Randall? He felt a pang of unaccustomed jealousy . . . for a dead man.

Shaking off the feeling, burying it, he returned to the point at hand. "So, no lover?"

Cordelia snorted. "Absolutely not."

Late that afternoon, his mind grappling with a number of irreconcilable "facts," Christian stood in the graveyard of the church in South Audley Street and watched George Martin Randall's earthly remains laid to rest a mere two blocks from his house and close to the center of the ton's world.

Given that, the lack of mourners was remarkable.

The short service in the church had been brief. Very brief. No one had come forward to read the eulogy. Letitia, it transpired, hadn't known any of Randall's friends, and as none had called or written to convey their condolences, the minister made the best job of it he could, but his knowledge of Randall was cursory.

Letitia, Hermione, Letitia's aunt Agnes, and Randall's servants had made up the congregation in the church; other than Christian, no one else had attended. As was customary, all the females and the younger males had returned to the house at the close of the service, leaving Christian, Mellon, and two older footmen to observe the interment.

The only other observer was Barton, the Bow Street runner. Christian spied him watching proceedings from the shadow of a monument, no doubt imagining he was inconspicuous. Barton scanned the cemetery, as did Christian rather less obviously, but no one else appeared at any time—not even after the sods had been cast and the mourners drifted from the grave.

Christian found it difficult to comprehend the startling absence of any friends. Given that Randall had been murdered, the ton's ladies—those who would otherwise have been present to support Letitia in her grief—had not been expected, but where were Randall's male acquaintances, let alone friends?

Regardless of the nature of his demise—indeed, even more so because of it—they should have turned out, one and all.

Yet not one gentleman had appeared. As a comment on a life lived within the ton, that was extraordinary.

Admittedly the ton were only just returning to the capital for the autumn session of Parliament, and perhaps some who might have known Randall had yet to hear of his death, yet this absolute dearth of acquaintances seemed bizarre.

As he left the graveyard, Christian heavily underscored his earlier mental note—he had to find out more, a lot more, about George Martin Randall.

Chapter 5

Later that evening, deliberately later than a gentleman would normally call on a lady, Christian rapped on the door of the house in South Audley Street.

Mellon opened the door and promptly looked scandalized.

Christian ignored him and walked in. "Please inform your mistress that Lord Dearne requests a few minutes of her time."

Mellon blinked, then recalled himself and bowed. "Ah . . . I believe her ladyship has already retired, my lord."

All the better to rattle her. "I doubt she'll be abed yet." Christian looked down his nose at the obsequious Mellon, then raised one brow. "My message?"

Flustered, Mellon turned to the drawing room. "If you'll wait in—"

Christian strolled toward the front parlor. "I'll wait in here."

Mellon dithered, then surrendered and flapped away toward the stairs.

Smiling intently, Christian walked into Letitia's domain and looked around. On the end of one sofa table, a candelabra still burned, bathing the silk rug in golden light and shadows.

The sight brought the phantom scent of jasmine back to his senses. Tightened his belly and his groin.

He drew in a breath and looked around the room, and

felt her there, around him. While he waited—he knew she wouldn't hurry—he studied her things, searching for some insight into how she'd changed in the twelve years they'd been apart, but there was nothing he saw that seemed in any way different. More intense, more powerful, more well-defined, perhaps, but in all respects she was still the same Letitia Vaux he'd fallen completely and irrevocably in love with more than thirteen years before.

She'd grown, matured, but she hadn't changed.

Presumably that meant that the same rules applied—that the ways he'd used to deal with her in the past would still work.

He had to learn more about Randall, and most especially about Letitia's marriage to the man. Whatever else Justin Vaux was, he was sharply intelligent; he had to have had some compelling reason to believe Letitia had killed Randall. Christian needed to learn what that reason was in order to do what Justin had obviously felt needed to be done—protect Letitia from suspicion.

That was his logical, rational reason for what he was about to do.

His emotional reason had nothing to do with Randall's murder, but everything to do with his marriage.

"He's *what*?" In her bedchamber, seated before her dressing table mirror, still in her black gown but with her long hair tumbling about her shoulders and back, Letitia turned to stare at Mellon.

"He said he'd wait in the front parlor." Mellon all but sniffed. "Quite at home he seemed."

Letitia felt her temper stir. "I daresay." Turning back to the dressing table, she set down her brush. She held her own gaze in the mirror for an instant, then said, "Tell him I'll see him in the library. Show him in there, and shut the doors to the front parlor."

In the mirror she watched as Mellon, his lips pinched in disapproval, bowed and withdrew.

Her lips quirked; ironic that in this she agreed with Mellon. If he could have told her how to avoid Christian Allardyce, now Marquess of Dearne—a nobleman accustomed to getting what he wanted and ensuring he always did—she would happily fall in with any plan.

But she knew how futile running from a large and powerful predator was; he would only pursue her all the more intently. And from past experience she knew that if pushed, he could, and would, act with a supreme disregard for convention every bit the equal of her own.

They were who they were; society's rules only applied if and when they chose.

As the door closed behind Mellon, her dresser, Esme, engaged in laying out her nightclothes on the bed, straightened. "Do you want me to go down with you, my lady? It is late, and you being so recently widowed and all."

Letitia glanced at her and smiled fondly. Esme, whom she'd brought with her on her marriage, tall, lanky, and rather severe, but an excellent dresser, was the only servant in the household she trusted. "Thank you, but no."

Whatever Christian had in mind, she had a strong notion she would need privacy to deal with him. "Lord Dearne probably has more questions."

She could imagine he would have. When they'd parted the previous night, her temper had been on edge, hard and bright, sharpened by disappointment that he'd actually followed through on his plan to use her vow to give anything in return for Justin's safety to try to hurt her. To in some small measure pay her back for what he thought she'd done. To make her want him again, and then perhaps deny her.

Regardless of what his plan had been, she'd refashioned it in a way that had resulted in an interlude she could accept. What had been between them was still there; she hadn't been entirely surprised that that was so.

As for the power of it . . . that had been both a surprise and a delight.

She'd slept better last night than she had for twelve years. Not since the night she'd seen him off to the wars.

And the sight of him afterward, the way he'd just lain there—as if sensually flabbergasted—had gone a long way toward salving any slight she might have felt. All in all, last night had gone far more her way than his.

Which almost certainly explained why he was waiting downstairs in the library.

Not the front parlor; she was far to fly to the nuances of place to let him use the lingering echoes of last night to distract her.

He'd stood by her side at the funeral that afternoon, but in public, on such a somber occasion, they'd exchanged only the barest greetings. He'd been nothing but unfailingly supportive; she'd leant on his arm, and been grateful he'd been there.

By now, however, he'd be champing at the bit, wanting to know everything. Ready to demand she tell him all that she was well aware he didn't know—all she still had no intention of telling him.

Years ago he'd made his decision—and by that made his bed and hers, and made them separate. Now he'd come back from the life he'd chosen, but if he thought, with Randall conveniently dead, she'd blithely open her heart to him again, he would learn he was mistaken.

Pride was one of the few comforts left to her, pride that regardless of her wishes, she'd done the right thing.

She wasn't about to let him take her pride from her. Wasn't about to explain to him what his long ago decision had wrought. Wasn't about to—ever—let him know what that decision had cost her.

How many heartbroken days and nights.

How many lonely years.

The sudden swell of emotion snapped her back to the here and now, to her reflection in the mirror.

She studied her eyes, then deciding she'd made him wait long enough, she considered her hair, debating whether to wind it up into a quick knot. She was otherwise fully dressed, gowned, hooked and laced.

Her hair down, a silky, shining, shifting veil, would distract him more than it would her. He'd seen it down before, usually rippling over her nakedness.

She smiled approvingly and rose.

She glanced at Esme. "Don't wait up for me. Dealing with his lordship might take some time."

Unhurriedly, she left the room and headed for the stairs. A vivid memory of when they'd first met swam across her mind. As she started down, she recalled, and felt her lips curve.

She'd been barely sixteen. He'd been twenty-two. They'd met at a local fair; they'd seen each other over the bric-a-brac stall. Their eyes had met—and that had been that.

He'd been atrociously handsome, even then. The sight of him in his guardsman's uniform had literally made lesser women swoon. While she'd never done anything so maudlin, seeing him standing tall and proud, the wind ruffling his light brown hair, she'd certainly understood her weaker sisters' affliction.

For her, however, looking hadn't been enough.

It hadn't been enough for him either.

In rapid succession they'd become acquaintances, then friends, then sweethearts. He wasn't always in the country; he was often called away. But every time he returned, their connection only seemed stronger, more definite, something that linked them each to the other and grew with every passing day, regardless of whether they were together or not.

Needless to say, they'd spent every moment they could together.

But they hadn't become lovers until nearly a year later, when he'd come home and then come north to tell her that his upcoming assignment would see him on the Continent for some considerable time. That he was going into danger had been implicit; she hadn't needed to be told.

It had been she who'd grasped the moment, who had

pulled him down into the hay in the old barn and insisted he educate her in the ways of passion.

Not that he'd fought all that hard, but she'd been well aware that she couldn't leave it to him to initiate any intimate link. Men like he had certain lines they wouldn't cross, and seducing her—even though he'd intended eventually to marry her—had been one of those lines. While she was usually a stickler for honor, in that instance she hadn't seen the point.

Even now, after all the lonely years of nursing a broken heart, she still couldn't find it in her to regret those passionate moments, those long interludes over one glorious summer when she'd given him not just her heart—that had already been his—but her body and her soul.

The memories still burned bright; for long moments they held her.

Then she blinked, and realized she'd halted outside the library door.

Drawing in a deep breath—girding her loins—she reached for the doorknob.

Only to have the door swing open.

Christian stood there, frowning down at her. "I presume you're intending to join me at some point?"

She struggled to keep her lips straight. He would have heard her footsteps approach, then stop outside the door.

Thankfully, he didn't know what had held her immobile.

With the faintest lift of her brows—she could do arrogant every bit as well as he—she glided past him into the room. And saw the book open on the table beside one of the armchairs by the hearth—instantly appreciated the scene he'd set, that he'd expected her to walk into—he calmly reading while waiting for her.

Memories of them in flagrante delicto had ruined his preparation.

The Fates, she decided, were on her side tonight.

Halting before the fire, she turned to face him. "You have more questions, I assume?" Chin high, she locked her eyes on his.

Saw the exasperation that swam through the gray orbs.

Christian didn't bother to hide his frustration. He needed answers—answers he was well aware she wouldn't want to give.

And she was stubborn, and intractable, and ungovernable, and generally uncontrollable. He'd tried to set the scene so she'd be at least a little off-balance. Instead she'd already evened the scales. "I had a surgeon I know examine Randall's body. What he found showed that, contrary to all assumptions, Randall was killed by a single, relatively weak blow to the back of the head."

"The back?" She saw the implications in a blink. "So . . . the person who was in the other armchair, sharing a drink with him."

"That's my interpretation. Others might have a different view."

She frowned. "What different view?"

"That you killed Randall, and that later Justin delivered the blows to Randall's face in order to conceal your involvement."

She paled. "I didn't kill Randall."

He nodded. "I know. But Justin thought you did. At the very least he believed you might have." He trapped her eyes. "Let's assume Justin came upon Randall already dead. Dead of a relatively weak blow to the back of the skull from the poker conveniently nearby, a blow a tallish woman—you, for example—could easily have struck. We know Justin had heard you and Randall arguing—violently as usual. When he came upon Randall dead, he instantly jumped to the conclusion that you'd killed him—and set about covering up what he thought was your deed."

She was frowning more definitely now, following his argument, not, he noticed, protesting his reasoning.

The hope grew that, in her need to find her brother, she would answer the myriad questions crowding his brain.

He moved closer, so he was standing before her, a little to the side so he wasn't directly confronting her; he'd try persuasion first. "Why did Justin believe you had killed Randall?"

She glanced at him, puzzled, met his eyes—but her puzzlement wasn't over Justin's reason, but that he'd done what he had. She saw him searching, and refocused—recalled his question, and put up her shields. She looked away. "I have no idea."

He looked down. The rug beneath their feet wasn't anywhere near the quality of the one in her parlor. "Letitia." He tried to keep his tone even, patient. "It's patently obvious that the rift between you and Randall went far deeper than his views on Hermione's future."

"And that, my lord, is none of your business."

Her tart accents had him looking up—directly into hard hazel eyes.

"If Justin was so misguided as to believe I might have—in a fit of Vaux temper, no less—killed Randall—and yes, I accept that it appears he did just that—then presumably he had some reason. When you find him, you might try asking him—not that I imagine he'll share details of my private life, not with you."

He felt his lips thin, felt control and success slipping from him. "Letitia—"

"Don't you 'Letitia' me." Her eyes narrowed to shards. She faced him directly. "You have no right to demand to know details of my marriage. You gave away that right years ago."

No, he hadn't. She'd *taken* that right away from him. He felt his face set, clamped down on his temper. "That's not how I recall it."

She opened her eyes wide. "It isn't? How do you recall it, then?"

The flagrant challenge hit him like a gauntlet in the face. "Like this." He caught her arms, yanked her to him and crushed her lips with his.

She resisted—tried to hold firm, passive, against him—for all of two heartbeats.

Then the fire that, apparently, never stopped smoldering between them leapt to life. Hungry and greedy, eager for more, heightened and strengthened by the previous night's encounter.

Wanting more.

To his immense relief, she did. She made no secret of her desires, let them rise to meet his freely, slid deeper into his arms, pressed against him, and invited.

Satisfaction. Satiation. Consummation.

He knew that was where they were headed, that it was already impossible to change their course—that there was no real reason, at least none in his overheated brain, they should. She was a widow, and he was free. There was nothing to prevent them from indulging the passions that flared so hotly, so powerfully, between them.

But tonight he had another goal he hoped to achieve along the way. Passion was, in his experience, the only force strong enough to override her stubbornness. The only lever he could use to get her to tell him something that, for whatever incomprehensible reason backed by her feminine will, she refused to divulge.

So he gave her what she wanted, but held part of himself back. Enough to remain in control. Such as control was when they were together like this, wrestling in the flames.

That's what it felt like, all greedy hands, heat and fire. Igniting at a touch, built by each passionate caress until it spread like wildfire beneath their skins. And they burned.

He waited until they both were—then waited some more.

Waited while he sat her on the edge of the big library desk, bared her breasts, then tasted his fill.

Until she was gasping; until, head back, she was clutching his head to her, reveling in his skill, in the increasingly hot caresses he pressed on her. He hadn't been celibate for the last five years—not since he'd discovered she'd married. He'd learned a few things she didn't know in that time, things he was very ready to share with her.

Things that would put her in the state most conducive to him getting some answers.

She was sitting on her gown, effectively encasing her legs and hips in stiff bombazine. He touched her through the fabric, caressed until she moaned, then with a scorching kiss—one that nearly cindered his plans—she made her wishes known.

In response he eased her off the desk, propped her against it, then drew her skirts up as he went to his knees before her. She blinked down at him, her eyes heavy with desire and clouded with lust, arched a brow when he caught her gaze. He inwardly smiled, knowing she'd relish the sight of him on his knees before her. She'd relish the sight even more when he was done.

He lifted her heavy skirts up and back, exposing her long, long legs; running his hands up the long curves from her calves to her hips, he pushed the skirts high, then tucked the fabric behind her so it was trapped by her hips against the desk's edge—out of his way.

So that the only veil between him and the curls at the apex of her thighs was her filmy silk chemise. He ran his hands up beneath it, and she shuddered.

He looked up and saw she'd closed her eyes; a line of concentration furrowed her brow. He let his hands explore her jasmine-scented skin, the swells and hollows he'd first claimed so long ago; he hadn't taken the time—had had no time—to reacquaint himself with them last night.

Tonight he took his time, until she grew restless. Until her hand tightened in his hair and she settled against the desk, parting her thighs. He glanced up at her, caught a glittering glimpse of gold and green from beneath her lashes. He smiled, and accepted her invitation, watching her face as, with the backs of his fingers, he lightly stroked the crisp curls at the apex of her thighs, then turned his hand and slid his fingers into the haven between, and caressed. She closed her eyes. He found her entrance and circled, time and time again, until her breasts were heaving, until her fingers tightened painfully in his hair. He slid one long finger into her, penetrated her to his full reach, then stroked slowly out. The tension holding her didn't ease, but her grip on his hair did. He pressed in and stroked again, and eased closer.

Letitia shuddered. Pleasure spilled down her veins in a never-ending stream, one he continuously fed. The sight of him supplicant at her feet went some way to deadening her irritation with him—this, once again, wasn't supposed to have happened.

But it had, and she wasn't about to argue. Wasn't about to deny herself the pleasure he and only he could give her.

Especially as he was so intent, and so assiduous, in doing so.

He knew how to pander to her senses; he clearly hadn't forgotten. He knew just when to wait, when to take, when to demand. When to command.

Her hand in his hair helped keep her upright as the telltale tension, all fire and bright, glittering sensation, built and rose inexorably within her—fed, expertly orchestrated, by his caresses, explicit and increasingly intimate.

Then he grasped her thigh and parted her legs farther. She felt him shift. A shiver of expectation slid down her spine as she waited for him to rise, to lift her and impale her.

Fill her.

Instead she felt the rough rasp of his beard on her inner thigh, simultaneously felt his hair brush her belly, through her hand on his head realized he'd pressed his face closer.

Then she felt his tongue and realized why.

"Christian!"

She fought to lift her lids, managed to crack them open a sliver, enough to look down and see. . . .

On a moan, she closed her eyes again. Let her head fall back, felt her fingers clench in his hair.

As he did diabolical things to her with his tongue. With his mouth and his teeth and that wicked tongue made love to her there.

Her senses stretched, expanding to take in the novel sensations, her body, her nerves, greedily rejoicing.

He knew what he was doing—knew how to wind the sensual rack he'd placed her on tighter and tighter until she thought she would shatter, only to ease off, let the tension slacken, draw her back from that glorious edge just enough to keep her from falling over.

And then he'd push her forward again. Stoke her fires, build the sweet tension until she was just about to—

His mouth left her. His breath washed over her swollen flesh as he breathed, "Did Randall ever treat you to this?"

She frowned. "Of course not." Then she realized and amended, "He wasn't . . ." In the end, she gestured. She couldn't think well enough to lie.

His wicked tongue rasped slowly over where she was most tender and she gasped. "Accomplished?"

"Much of a lover. For God's sake—"

"Is that what you held against him?"

"No." She struggled to open her eyes, to drag air into her parched lungs so she could tell him what she thought of his methods of interrogation, but no doubt sensing her intent, he went to work with his mouth again, and she couldn't find the strength.

Couldn't fight her way free of the drugging sexuality, the sheer eroticism of his actions, especially once he brought his hands and clever fingers into play as well.

Then he drew back to suckle, oh so gently, on the delicate bud just beneath her curls, at the same time testing, teasing, the entrance to her sheath with two large blunt fingertips.

"But you did dislike Randall." He made the statement quickly, while changing the angle of his attack.

She decided no answer was required.

Another minute of excruciatingly exquisite pleasure passed, then he lifted his head. "Why was that?"

He had her balanced on the cusp of the storm, on the bright sharp edge of the peak of oblivion. She had to tip over, had to have that one last touch—

She opened her eyes and looked down into his, breasts heaving as she dragged enough air in to say, "I didn't dislike Randall. I *hated* him. With an absolute passion."

A passion as strong as her love for Christian, but that she kept to herself.

She glared as well as she could. "Satisfied?"

His lips curved—intently. "For now."

Between her thighs, he shifted his hand, thrust his fingers deep—and she shattered.

Finally, finally, *finally*.

Letting her head fall back, she gloried in the waves of intense pleasure that rolled through her, sharp, bright, primitively right. She didn't question that last, simply acknowledged it.

He rose to his feet, caught her as her knees buckled, supported her when she slumped against him, and with his hand still buried between her thighs, spun the pleasure out and out, until it faded.

She sighed and settled against him—waited for him to release his erection and take what he wished of her, take his pleasure in her, slake his desire for her.

Instead he held her trapped between his hard, aroused body and the edge of the never used library desk; bending his head, he whispered against her hair, "Why did you hate Randall?"

She let her lips curve but kept them shut. That was one question she wasn't going to answer. Would not answer, no matter what he did.

No matter what state he reduced her to.

When she said nothing, he cajoled, "Leti-tia," drawing her name out as he used to do.

Rather than learn what he might try next—and as she still needed a moment more to regain control of her limbs—she informed him—teased him with, "Justin was right. I would happily have killed Randall if I'd been the sort of person who killed people. And while I wouldn't do anything so scandalous as to dance on his grave—although the temptation did occur to me this evening—I certainly won't be shedding so much as one tear on his tombstone." She paused. "Which reminds me—I better order one."

Raising her hands to Christian's upper chest, she pushed, leaning back as she did so she could see his eyes. "Shall we get on with this?"

The look he gave her was that of a man pushed too far, but she knew how to fix that. How to circumvent any inclination to argue or question her further.

Bracing one hand on the planes of his chest, she lowered the other, flicked the buttons at his waist free, slid her hand into his trousers and curled her fingers about his hard length.

His jaw clenched. She could see him debating how long he would let her play before he again took charge. She smiled, leaned into him, moving him back a fraction, then sank down.

To her knees, just as he had.

Locking both hands around his heavy member, she admired her prize—then opened her lips and applied them to the blunt head of the thick shaft, lightly licked, then slowly slid her lips down, taking him in as she'd heard the act described, hoping she was doing it correctly.

From the sound that strangled halfway up his throat, given the way his hand clutched in her hair and held her rather than pushed her away, she wasn't far wrong.

She'd heard about this years ago, had had more than a decade to fantasize about having him at her mercy. Now at last she had him where she wanted him, she wasn't about to let him go without learning a great deal more.

Without confirming firsthand what drove him to desperation.

She set herself to that task with her customary enthusiasm.

Christian couldn't breathe. Both his hands had lowered to tangle in her hair. The desk beside him gave him some support; without it he might have collapsed in shock, in complete and totally unexpected sensual overload.

Her mouth on him there . . . he'd never even imagined it. Not all ladies were aware of the act, nor keen to devote themselves to a man's pleasure in that way.

Letitia clearly saw advantages—he should have known she would, but he hadn't thought . . . couldn't think. . . .

Her tongue curled around him and he heard himself groan.

Her small hands found his sac, weighed, toyed, then caressed—and he knew, despite the carnal delight, that he couldn't—wouldn't—last much longer.

He fought to give her as long as he could, to take the delicious torture, but then she became more intent, and he had to slip a finger between her luscious lips and prise them from him.

Pull her up against him, grasp her hips and hoist her up.

She needed no directions; she wound her long legs about his hips, angled her hips and sank down as he thrust up. He buried his aching erection in her heated sheath, felt her stretch and take him in, then cling. Clutch. Caress.

They'd come together in this fashion on long ago nights, in illicit interludes in darkened parlors and gardens. In gazebos and conservatories.

Memories rolled through him, but they couldn't dim, couldn't touch, the glory of the moment. She arched, head high; hands on his shoulders she rose up on him, then her eyes locked on his and she slid down, down, taking him all as she lowered her head and brought her lips slowly down on his, wound her arms around his neck—and surrendered.

Let him have her as he would.

Let him lift her, then slowly impale her again, let him battle desire and need to drag the moments out, to savor her body in all its feminine glory freely yielded.

In that instant she made him hers again, totally captured his soul again, for as her green-gold eyes, heavy-lidded with passion, met his, there were no barriers, no shields, no screen to veil the reality that shone in their depths.

He held her steady and rocked into her; her lids fell and he thrust again, deeper, filling her completely.

Thrust again and felt the mouth of her womb.

Felt it and her sheath contract, felt the ripples of her release caress his entire length, held his breath, tried to rein in his galloping heart to cling to the moment for just an instant more, but she pulled him over, took him with her.

They shattered together, tumbling headlong into the abyss of satiation.

Warmth surrounded him as it never had with any other woman. Her warmth, her fire, her passion.

All he'd craved for the last twelve years, and she was in his arms once more.

He slumped back against the desk, holding her in his arms, unable to move, too sated to care.

Letitia eventually stirred. She could, she knew, grow seriously addicted to the feeling of golden pleasure, the inevitable sensation of aftermath she always experienced with him, flowing like sweet honey through her veins.

Such an addiction would not be wise.

But she didn't see any harm in gorging on what he freely offered.

Of course, he'd thought he would get answers to his questions by reducing her to mindless, quivering need. So she'd given him answers, much good would they do him.

She should be furious, but the revelation that she could, if she wished, sweep *him* away—sweep aside his control and reduce *him* to mindless, quivering need—went a long way toward dousing her temper.

Indeed, as she wriggled and he obliged and, moving very carefully, disengaged and set her on her feet, she couldn't help feeling a trifle smug.

Unfortunately, her limbs were still too exhausted—

wrung out and boneless—to support her; she wobbled, but he grabbed her, gathered her in and settled her against him. Feeling strangely like purring, she nestled against him and let contentment claim her.

Let her mind assess where they now were, and what she should say, how she should go on.

Eventually, summoning every ounce of censure she could lay her tongue to, she coolly informed him, "Your inquisitorial methods did not impress. Don't try to question me like that again. And just to make sure we're quite clear on the matter, there will be no more payments of any sort until you find Justin."

She paused, thought, then frowned. "Incidentally, in light of the down payments and incentives you've already received, have you learned anything yet?"

Christian inwardly sighed. With one hand he absent-mindedly readjusted his clothing while he told her about Tristan and their inquiries. "Tristan called around this afternoon." He glanced at her face as he said, "Did you know your brother is no longer—indeed, may never have been— the profligate rake he's purported to be?"

She frowned in quite genuine puzzlement. "No." She met his eyes. "What have you—or your friend—heard?"

"It appears that, sometime since coming on the town, or thereabouts, Justin has . . . turned over an unexpected leaf. He's in reality highly circumspect in his associations, and conservative to a fault, especially with money."

Because he was watching, Christian saw the comprehension flare in her eyes—at the mention of money. But the Vaux were wealthy, always had been. They were major landowners, in similar circumstances to himself. "It appears," he continued, "that with Justin there's no gambling, that he's not the least interested in frittering away his patrimony as the bulk of his peers are. Admittedly none of his friends couch it in miserly terms, but rather that he simply isn't interested in losing large wads of cash, and they can't recall that he ever was. He also seems to have developed a monk-ish attitude to women, not complete abstinence but . . ."

Still studying her face, he summed up Tristan's and his own findings. "Justin seems to have taken a very mature line from a relatively early age. As if something happened that shocked him to his senses much earlier than is the norm."

She reacted to his guess that there'd been something—some event she knew of—that had affected her brother as he'd described; he saw speculation light her eyes.

Equally saw her expression close as she shuttered herself against him.

Shutting him out, despite what they'd just shared.

Despite the fact he was searching for Justin.

He caught her gaze, asked anyway. "Do you have any idea what happened to make Justin . . . so different from what one might expect?"

She looked at him and baldly stated, "No." She was lying, and knew he knew she was.

Before he could say anything more, she drew back out of his arms, shook her skirts into place, then, buttoning up her bodice, calmly walked away from him.

Toward the door.

She spoke as she walked, facing away from him. "I'm sure you know your way out by now. Do lock the door be-hind you."

His lips thinned. "Letitia." He waited until she paused, but she didn't look back. "Whatever you and Hermione do, don't forget about Barton."

"He's still out there?"

"Yes. I spotted him when I came in."

"He's obsessed."

"Very possibly. Catching Justin would help his career."

She hesitated, then inclined her head, still without look-ing back. "I'll bear that in mind—and warn Hermione." She proceeded to the door. Opening it, she went through; turning, she looked back at him as she reached for the doorknob. Met his eyes across the room. "Good night." Her lips curved slightly. "Sleep well."

He narrowed his eyes on the door as, quietly, she shut it.

Dealing with the Vaux had never been a simple matter.

Throughout the next day, Christian devoted himself to finding Justin Vaux, and tried his damnedest to keep his thoughts from Justin's infuriating sister. Infuriating, and enthralling.

The following morning he set off for South Audley Street early. Reaching Randall's door, he strode past it, then crossed the street to where he'd spied the top of Barton's head; the man had ducked into the area beside a house's steps to avoid his gaze as he'd scanned the street.

Halting on the street above the crouching runner, who'd taken refuge on the steps leading to the house's basement, he mildly inquired, "If I might ask, what do you think you're doing?"

A moment ticked past, then Barton heaved a put-upon sigh and stood. He had to look up to meet Christian's eyes. "I'm keeping a close watch on the deceased's house. On the scene of the crime."

Christian studied the unprepossessing man. "And by doing so you hope to achieve . . . what?"

Barton tried his best to look superior. "It's a well-known fact among us runners that, more often than not, the murderer returns to the scene of the crime."

"You believe that?"

"Indeed, m'lord. You'd be surprised how many villains we catch simply by being patient and keeping a solid watch." Barton eyed him a touch suspiciously. "'Specially in the night hours. People tend to think no one will recognize them in the dark."

Christian held the man's gaze and let his brows slowly rise. "Is that so? Well in that case, as to Randall's house, you can expect to see me coming and going rather a lot—in the nighttime as well as during the day."

"Be that as it may, m'lord, we haven't figured you for this crime."

"No, but one might imagine my presence in the house might deter the villain."

Barton frowned. "No saying what villains will do, but the way I see it, chances are Lord Justin Vaux will try to speak with his sisters. I plan to be here when he comes calling."

Recognizing that nothing was likely to dissuade the runner from continuing his watch, Christian wished him luck and left.

Returning to Randall's house, he knocked on the door. When Mellon opened it, he walked in. "Are the ladies down yet?"

Mellon took his cane with reluctance but was forced to admit, "Yes, my lord. But they're just sitting down to breakfast."

"Excellent. I'll join them. You may announce me."

Mellon clearly wished he had some other alternative, but accepted the inevitable and did so.

Letitia greeted him with a sparkling gaze—one of anger, although not directed at him. She waved him to the chair beside her, barely waiting for him to exchange greetings with her aunt Agnes and Hermione, the other two at the table, before informing him, "I went belowstairs this morning looking for my dresser, and discovered that runner in the kitchen, talking to Mellon as if they were old friends, and scrounging breakfast while he was at it!"

Which explained why Mellon had quit the room the instant he'd finished announcing Christian, all but sliding past him in the doorway.

Engaged in scrounging breakfast himself, Christian asked, "As I found Barton in the street just now, I take it he beat a hasty retreat?"

Letitia glowered. "He did once I'd finished with him."

Christian helped himself to the ham Agnes passed him.

"He apparently swears by the old saw that the murderer always, eventually, returns to the scene of the crime."

Addressing herself to a mound of kedgeree, Letitia sniffed. "So I gathered."

They all ate for some moments in silence. Then the footman returned with a fresh pot of coffee. Letitia dismissed him once he'd set the pot down. "Please close the door after you, Martin."

The instant the door clicked shut, she looked at Christian. "Have you found Justin?"

She'd kept her voice low.

Christian shook his head. Sitting back, he set down his knife. "We've searched in all the likely places and found no sign. Last night it occurred to me that I might have been going about our search the wrong way."

She frowned. "How so?"

By not taking sufficient account of Vaux intelligence. Something he'd been guilty of in other respects. He picked up the coffee cup Agnes had filled for him; she and Hermione were as eager as Letitia to hear his report. "As I said, we've been hunting for your brother everywhere one might expect to find him, to no avail." He took a sip of coffee, then caught Letitia's eye. "I thought perhaps it was time to ask where the very *last* place you'd think to find him would be."

Hermione, also frowning, said, "You mean the place he'd be least likely to go?"

Christian nodded.

Letitia's face cleared. She exchanged a glance with Hermione, then shrugged. "Nunchance. That's the one place you can be certain he *won't* be."

Christian saw the light. "Yes, of course. I understand he's had a falling out with your father."

Letitia's lashes screened her eyes. "You might say that."

From her tone, he surmised it would be fruitless to ask why.

Puzzling over his words, she fixed him with a frown.

"But I can't see how that gets you any further. Justin definitely *won't* be at Nunchance." She hesitated, then—perhaps because he hadn't asked—consented to explain. "My father has grown rather worse with the years."

Recognizing the wisdom of telling him enough so he would understand that Justin really wouldn't be at Nunchance Priory, their family estate, Letitia hunted for the right words. "Some years ago something occurred that set Justin at loggerheads with Papa. Unfortunately, my marriage to Randall only added to the tension. Rather than fading over time, as I'd hoped, that tension escalated to a major rift, to the point where now they can't be in the same room without coming to verbal blows. No, even worse than that—flaming rows the like of which even our family hasn't seen for generations."

She held Christian's eyes. "You know what they're like. They're quite capable of tearing strips off each other, lacerating and painful, and they're equally stubborn, so there's no hope of reconciliation because neither will back down."

Reaching for her teacup, she shrugged. "Over the last years, Justin has only visited Nunchance at Christmas, and then only for a fleeting visit on the day, to see me and Hermione and the rest of the family. I honestly don't think he and Papa have exchanged a civil word in all that time."

Sipping her tea, she considered the possibility that Justin might have sought refuge at Nunchance—perhaps staying out of their father's sight—but she couldn't see him being that cautious. More specifically she couldn't see him reining in his pride to that extent, enough to hide like a felon in his family home. She shook her head and set down her cup. "Wherever Justin's gone, he won't be at Nunchance."

Turning her head, she arched a brow at Christian. "So what are you planning?"

He met her gaze briefly, then looked across the table—at Hermione. Her sister remained oblivious, busy slathering marmalade on her toast.

"I have various avenues to pursue—I'll let you know if I hear anything promising." His gray gaze returned to her face. "Incidentally, everything we've uncovered about your brother's life since we last spoke has confirmed his . . . somewhat novel direction. Far from being a wastrel and a hellion, he's a son to make any father proud."

Letitia merely nodded, wondering where he was heading with that comment—where he was trying to lead her.

He held her gaze, unhurriedly searching her eyes. "You don't seem all that surprised that Justin should be the antithesis of his reputation."

Ah. *That* was where he was heading. She smiled. "As a loving older sister, I can only rejoice at his exemplary sense."

"Indeed. But you also know why Justin is as he really is." He arched a brow at her. "I don't suppose you'd care to enlighten me?"

She held his gaze, then shook her head. "Knowing that won't help you find Justin."

"I see." Christian smiled easily and inclined his head. "In that case, ladies, if you'll excuse me, I'll return to the hunt."

He rose, bowed to Agnes, nodded to Hermione, then looked at Letitia.

Frowning, she asked, "What are you going to do?"

He looked down at her, let his smile grow edged. Softly replied, "You knowing that won't help me find Justin."

Her mouth dropped open, then she shut it with a snap and glared at him.

Unperturbed, he saluted her, then turned and walked out of the room.

Entirely confident that she would work out where he was going soon enough—and that she would follow.

He set out an hour later, driving out of Grosvenor Square in his curricle with his pair of prime chestnuts between the shafts. The long drive north was very familiar, yet the necessary tacking to get out of London's crowded streets, then threading through the traffic clogging the Great North Road—the mail coaches, the wagons and drays—

commanded his attention, so that despite the length of the journey, he had little time to think.

His ultimate destination was Nunchance Priory, but he wanted to time his arrival there, so he'd decided to stop at his home, Dearne Abbey, for the night.

He pulled up in the graveled forecourt as twilight was taking hold. His staff were ecstatic to see him.

"I'll have your room ready in a jiffy, my lord." Mrs. Kestrel, his housekeeper, all but rubbed her hands in glee. "And Cook set a roast on the spit the instant we heard you were back."

Christian acknowledged her enthusiasm with an easy smile, then turned to his steward, hovering hopefully at the mouth of the corridor leading to the estate office, and gave himself up to business.

Later, he dined in solitary state—there was no one else, not even a distant impecunious cousin, in residence—then he elected to climb the stairs to the long gallery to reacquaint himself with the extensive, uninterrupted views across the fens to the Wash.

The view at the best of times was a lonely one. Mile upon mile of low, flat fields with the sea a distant silver-gray glimmer on the horizon. What houses there were were cottages, built low and largely swallowed by the never-ending fields.

The abbey was built at the very edge of the fenland, on a slight rise, with its back to the limestone cliff that marked the boundary of the low lying land. The house dominated its surroundings, a large Palladian mansion of perfect proportions built on the old abbey ruins by his grandfather.

Christian stood at one long window and looked out across the fields, into the deepening twilight. He owned much of what he could see, highly fertile land that guaranteed his and his family's financial future.

Yet the huge house around him lay empty. For the first time since returning from the Continent and properly taking up the mantle his father had bequeathed him, he felt the weight of it. Sensed in his new life, as in this house, a lack, a hollowness wrapped in elegant calm, peaceful, serene, but empty.

Barren.

Folding his arms, he leaned against the window frame and looked out as the light faded and night slowly crept across the land.

This house—his house—was waiting. Ready, in perfect condition, fully staffed with people eager to serve. Yet he'd made no move to claim a bride, to bring her there, and start a family that would—once again—fill the corridors with laughter and gaiety.

The house was made for that, for an active, bustling family. Something his aunts, Cordelia and Ermina, would certainly remember with fondness, and look forward to seeing again.

That was what lay behind their disapproval, increasingly severe, of his continuing unwed state. They'd offered to help, of course, but when he'd refused, politely but categorically, they'd been wise enough to desist; stubbornness wasn't solely a Vaux trait.

Not surprisingly, that thought brought Letitia to mind. Into his mind, filling it.

For long moments she was with him again; she was the only woman he'd ever envisaged there—standing beside him, her arm linked with his, looking out over his fields.

She was the only woman he'd ever imagined making a life with—making a family with.

The only woman he'd ever wanted in his bed—there or at Allardyce House.

He'd known the truth years ago, and it still remained true. She was the one his heart and soul desired.

Unbidden, the dreams he'd had of them long ago rolled back into his mind, dreams he'd spent years embellishing, building them, clinging to them through all the long years he'd spent deeply embedded in an alien culture, an enemy land. They'd been his inner refuge, his strength.

The emotions wound into those dreams roiled through

him, unexpectedly intense. Reawakened and given new life by his recent hours with her, the her who'd stood at the center of those lost dreams.

For they'd been false . . . as had she.

His reaction to that fact was as violent as it had ever been. He still didn't understand how, or why, she'd done as she had.

All that mattered was that she'd married Randall.

And killed his dreams.

Lowering his arms, he went to push away from the window frame, but stopped.

Looked out across the quiet night and wondered how much he still wanted those dreams.

She was now a widow; she still responded to him as she always had.

He no longer knew what she felt for him—something, certainly, even if it wasn't what he'd thought. She hadn't been in love with him as he'd been with her.

But did that matter?

The truth was . . .

For long minutes more he stood looking out unseeing, wrestling with the question of how much he was willing to give—to bend, to forgive, to accept—to recapture a semblance of those long-ago dreams.

Chapter 6

He bowled through the Nunchance Priory gates at mid-afternoon the next day. The long, winding drive was, he noted, in excellent repair, the trees shading it old but well-trimmed. The lawns and gardens that surrounded the house were neat, but not rigidly so, comfortable and colorful with rambling roses tumbling over walls, their perfumed blooms nodding in the warm breeze.

Beyond the changes expected of the years, all was as he remembered it.

He pulled up in the circular forecourt before the huge, rambling, late Tudor mansion. It had indeed been a priory, one linked to the abbey at Dearne; whereas the abbey hadn't withstood the ravages of time and the various assaults visited upon it, the priory had escaped the old wars relatively unscathed, and succeeding generations of Vaux had preserved and added to its red-brick magnificence.

Leaving his curricle and horses in the care of a suitably reverent groom, Christian looked up at the long facade, at the many leaded windows that winked and blinked at him. The Allardyces and the Vaux were neighbors of sorts; while they didn't share any boundaries, they were the two most senior families in the area and throughout the generations had been close acquaintances, if not always as close as friends.

That had been one reason both families had looked upon his and Letitia's long-ago romance with benign approval, if not outright encouragement. No Vaux and Allardyce had married before, but once the idea bloomed, everyone had concurred that it was high time the families established a closer bond.

Then he'd gone to war, and Letitia had married Randall, and all thought of closer ties in this generation had faded. But the underlying acquaintance had not.

Climbing the shallow front steps, Christian tugged the bellpull.

When the butler, a thoroughly imposing specimen, opened the door, Christian smiled easily. "Good afternoon, Hightsbury. Is your master at home?"

Hightsbury recognized him and unbent enough to return his smile. "Indeed, my lord. Do come in. And may I say what a pleasure it is to see you here again. If you'll wait in the drawing room, I'll inquire as to the master's pleasure."

Christian consented to cool his heels in the elegant, formal drawing room; naturally, being a Vaux domain, it was also a cornucopia of rich and colorful visual and textural delights.

He barely had time to absorb their combined impact before Hightsbury returned.

"If you'll come this way, my lord. His lordship is in the library."

Following Hightsbury down the long, wood-paneled corridors, remembering what little Letitia had said about Justin's falling out with their father, he considered how to approach the coming interview.

Hightsbury opened a tall door, went in, and announced, "Lord Dearne, my lord."

"Heh?" A white-haired figure hunched over a large desk swung around to peer at the door.

Christian was momentarily taken aback; the earl appeared swathed in a dressing gown—then he realized it was a long, soft, dun-colored coat of the sort serious scholars wore to protect their clothes from ink stains.

He smiled and went forward.

The earl peered at him from under bushy white brows.

His hair stood up in tufts, as if he'd tugged at it; Christian saw the odd ink stain in the tumbled locks. All in all, the earl's reputation as an irascible, unpredictable eccentric appeared well-founded.

But there was nothing at all vague in the sharp hazel eyes that met his.

The earl inclined his head; his expression was relaxed but his eyes were watchful. "Christian, my boy—good to see you again."

Christian half bowed. "Sir."

Lord Vaux studied him, increasingly intent. They exchanged a few words about Christian's aunts, then the earl waved him to a chair to one side of the desk. "And to what do I owe the pleasure of this visit, heh?"

Christian sat, his gaze skating over the papers scattered across the long desk. Most appeared to be rough notes, others looked more like treatises, extensively annotated and overwritten. He returned his gaze to Lord Vaux's face. "I'm unsure how much you've heard from London, sir, but I believe Letitia informed you of her husband's murder."

Lord Vaux nodded, his gaze increasingly sharp. "She did. And I've since heard that some have cast my son as the murderer."

Christian inclined his head. "Unfortunately, that 'some' encompasses the better part of the ton, and, I believe, the authorities."

"*Nonsense!*" Lord Vaux scowled. "My son may be many things, but a murderer he is *not*."

"Indeed. However, it appears Justin has deliberately cast himself as the most likely candidate." Christian smoothly went on, "I understand you and he have had a falling out."

When he waited, pointedly polite, for some response, the earl's eyes sparked and his lips thinned. Eventually he barked, "We don't speak. That's common knowledge. The why concerns no one but ourselves. What's that got to do with Randall's death?"

Christian inclined his head placatingly, hiding his surprise at the strong undercurrent of bitterness in Lord Vaux's voice. "I have no idea. However, I believe you should know . . ." Sticking strictly to what he knew for fact, he outlined what he'd discovered and why he'd concluded that Justin had acted as he had to divert suspicion from Letitia.

As he spoke, Lord Vaux's bitterness receded, but his scowl grew darker. He did not, Christian noted, find Justin's supposition of Letitia's guilt of sufficient note to comment. Indeed, his lordship followed and accepted his son's logic without protest.

Christian ended his recital with a summation of their lack of success in locating Justin. Somewhat to his surprise, Lord Vaux's expression turned thoughtful; he cast a quick, surreptitious glance at a bookcase across the room. From the corner of his eye, Christian saw a gap—a space where a tome was missing from the regimented row.

There were books aplenty lying on various tables and chairs around the room, but he would have taken an oath that Lord Vaux knew where every single volume in his extensive library was—except for the missing book.

Remembering the book left open on the table in Randall's library, Christian longed to ask if the missing work was Seneca's *Letters from a Stoic*, but he was as yet unsure—all personal feuds aside—just where Lord Vaux stood when it came to protecting his son.

Indeed, once he'd reached the end of his report, Lord Vaux regarded him with a wary, faintly suspicious air. "If I might ask, just how did you come to be drawn into this, Dearne?"

Not his name, but his title. Christian held his lordship's hard gaze. "Letitia, realizing—correctly, as it transpired—that Justin was going to be the prime suspect, appealed to me for help in proving his innocence."

"She did?" That information had Lord Vaux regarding him in an entirely different light; hope, along with blatant interest and curiosity, now colored his tone.

Although he'd never formally spoken, never asked for Letitia's hand, his interest in her had been common knowledge twelve years before. "Indeed." Studiously bland, Christian continued, "She and I have been working together, both to locate Justin and, as I believe will become increasingly necessary, to discover who killed Randall." He considered his now relaxed host. "Apropos of the former, I thought it might be useful to visit here and ask if you have any idea where Justin might be."

The earl's eyes started to shift toward the gap on the shelves, but he suppressed the impulse. He fixed his gaze on Christian. "No." His gaze remained steady and direct. "I have absolutely no notion where my son might be."

He was telling the literal truth, but, as Christian now did, he suspected his son and heir was somewhere close by. At the very least he'd dropped in on his way to wherever he'd gone.

Christian felt certain Justin hadn't gone far. "I fear that you might shortly hear some rather distressing reports from the capital."

"Faugh!" Reverting to his usual Vaux temperament, the earl pulled a face and made a dismissive gesture, conveying his absolute contempt for such reports. "I've friends in the capital—I know what's being said. Absolute *poppycock*! The very notion . . ."

Christian inwardly smiled, and settled back to enjoy his lordship's more colorful side.

When Lord Vaux realized he wasn't in the least perturbed by his blunt and in some cases rather strong language, the earl relaxed even more and continued his rant, encouraged by having an appreciative audience.

Christian listened and learned; his lordship had much the same style of temper as Letitia and, if his memory proved correct, Justin—sharp, incisive, informed by a ruthless ability to see beneath most people's surfaces. It seemed increasingly obvious that the earl cherished his scholarly life and had used his supposedly infamous temper to protect his privacy. And still did. Ruthlessly and relentlessly, with a full measure of Vaux stubbornness.

He eventually ran down, appearing oddly energized from having vented so much spleen on the distant ton. He eyed Christian approvingly. "A great pity you and Letitia didn't tie the knot all those years ago. But . . . well, water under the bridge, I suppose." He looked down, and with one liver-spotted hand, shuffled his papers.

When Christian made no comment, the earl glanced at the windows, beyond which the shadows had started to lengthen. He looked at Christian. "I would take it kindly if you would consent to dine with me—and remain for the night, of course. I don't get many visitors." He snorted. "Well, the plain truth of it is I neither encourage nor abide many visitors, but you'd be doing me a favor if you would stay—Hightsbury and the rest of them worry so when I go for long periods without speaking with anyone. Must be . . . well, weeks since anyone called."

Christian muted his grin to an easy smile of acceptance. "I'd be delighted to join you. Better than driving back to Dearne in the dark."

"Indeed. Precisely. Obviously you should stay." That set-tled, the earl pointed to a bellpull on the wall. "Ring that, would you? Hightsbury will show you to a room. Tell him we'll dine at seven."

With that, the earl turned back to his papers. Letting his grin widen, Christian rose and crossed to the bellpull, hav-ing achieved exactly what he'd intended when he'd arrived.

He waited until he was walking down a corridor from the gallery in the majestic Hightsbury's wake to ask, "Hights-bury, have you or any of the other staff seen Lord Justin recently?"

The tension that instantly infused the butler's already rigid spine was answer enough.

Halting beside a door, Hightsbury set it wide, revealing a comfortable bedchamber. He fixed his gaze on a point above Christian's head—no mean feat—and replied, "No, my lord. We haven't seen Lord Justin for some time."

"I see." Christian nodded amiably and walked into the room.

"I'll have your bag brought up immediately, my lord."

Walking to the wide window, Christian looked down, then glanced back and smiled. "Thank you, Hightsbury. I believe I'll go for a walk around the grounds until it's time to dress."

That news did not make Hightsbury happy; the struggle he waged to find some acceptable way to dissuade Christian—a marquess—from a perfectly acceptable pastime showed in his face. Eventually accepting that there was nothing he could do, he bowed low. "As you wish, my lord."

Christian watched as Hightsbury departed, pulling the door closed behind him. Brows rising, he turned back to the window and looked out on the extensive gardens and, beyond that, the even more extensive park that he now recalled surrounded the priory. "You're here somewhere, Justin—the question is where."

He started his search in the stables, using the excuse of checking on his valuable pair to confirm that Justin hadn't left his precious horses—apparently his sole tonnish vice— or his curricle in the care of his father's stableman.

Christian wasn't surprised to discover that he hadn't; that would have been foolish, and Justin was no fool.

Nevertheless, judging from the head stableman's dark looks, Justin and his horses were not far away.

Leaving the stables, Christian walked toward the house, studying it from the rear. It was not a true Elizabethan manor, lacking the classic E shape. Instead it had many and varied wings and additions, making it difficult to be sure, once inside, just where in the structure one was.

Lots of unexpected rooms tucked here and there in which to hide.

And that wasn't taking into account priest holes and the like.

Resigned, Christian strolled slowly around the house,

taking note of every window. Most on the first floor—all the bedchambers and apartments—had their curtains drawn to preserve the furnishings inside from the sun. He located only two sets of uncurtained windows on that level—those of the bedchamber he'd been given, and a set at one end of a short wing, no doubt the earl's apartments.

On the second floor, some windows were curtained, others not. He would have to check the rooms on that floor. Many of the uncurtained rooms might be empty, stripped of furnishings, yet others . . .

He changed direction and headed for the house. The attic rooms, above the second floor, were universally uncurtained, but they would be servants' quarters, nurseries and the like; aside from all else, he didn't like his chances of finding his way through the maze that was certain to exist up there.

Going in through the open front door, he climbed the main staircase to the second floor and, taking due note of landmarks so he wouldn't get lost, started to work his way through the rooms.

It didn't take long to realize the staff were keeping a eye on him. A procession of maids with empty chamber pots, footmen with extra tapers, and in one case an empty coal shuttle, all passing him on the way to nowhere in particular, was a fairly clear sign. At first he considered it encouraging, but as the minutes passed, he realized that they were more curious than concerned.

The conclusion was obvious: Justin wasn't inside the house, or at least not on the second floor.

Quitting that field, he started down a secondary stair. Glancing out of the landing window, he saw a conglomeration of buildings tucked away behind a stand of mature trees. The buildings—barns and similar structures, most likely the home farm—weren't visible from the house except from certain vantage points.

Continuing down the stairs, he strode outside. As a landowner himself, he could always ask intelligent questions about crops and yields.

But it soon became apparent from the amused gleam in the farmer's eyes that Justin wasn't cowering in any barn, or anywhere else amid the farm buildings. As for the farmhouse itself, Christian couldn't stand upright inside without constantly dodging beams, and if anything, Justin was a touch taller.

Accepting defeat for the moment, Christian headed back to the main house. Despite his lack of success, he remained convinced—increasingly so—that Justin was somewhere on the priory lands.

Twilight was spreading its subtle fingers across the landscape when he reached the house and entered through the garden hall. The instant he turned into the corridor that joined the front hall, he heard Letitia's voice.

"How long has he been here?"

Out of habit, he'd been walking silently. He halted and listened.

"He arrived this afternoon, my lady," Hightsbury replied.

"Not last night?"

Christian raised his brows and started walking once more. She was asking after him, not her missing brother.

He turned a corner; the front hall lay directly ahead.

He was still cloaked in shadows, some twenty feet from her, when, as if alerted by some sixth sense, Letitia turned and looked at him.

"There you are."

"As you see."

As he emerged from the shadows, she searched his face. He raised his brows faintly, resigned.

Correctly divining that he'd yet to find Justin, she grimaced, and turned back to Hightsbury. "I assume Mrs. Caldwell has my room ready."

"Of course, my lady. I'll tell her you're here."

"Please do. And tell her I'd like a bath. Esme is with me—no need for a maid. But please send up the water as soon as you can."

Hightsbury bowed. "Indeed, my lady."

Letitia turned and took Christian's arm. "Come walk me to my room."

He settled her hand on his sleeve and, without argument, fell in with her wishes.

As they climbed the stairs, he murmured, voice low, "What took you so long? I thought you'd be here before me."

"I assume you stopped at the abbey, so I would have been, except that I couldn't leave yesterday—I'd promised to attend Martha Caldecott's dinner, and if I'd cried off at that late stage, she would have been left with thirteen, and in this season finding another to fill the gap would have been difficult, and—" She paused to draw breath. "—when we find Justin and prove he's innocent, Martha's one of the ladies I'll need on my side to spread the word."

"Ah. I see. In that case, might I suggest we join forces and devote ourselves to the task?"

They'd reached the long gallery, well out of Hightsbury's hearing. She halted; drawing her hand from his sleeve, she faced him. "Hightsbury said you'd gone wandering about the house. Where have you searched?"

"Inside and out, but only as far up as the second floor."

"No sign?"

"None. In fact, I'm fairly certain from the way the staff have been behaving that I haven't even got close."

She frowned.

He studied her face, then asked, "Could you ask them, appeal to them? Would they tell you?"

Grimacing, she shook her head. "Their loyalty, first and last, is to my father, and after that to Justin. If he's told them not to tell me, they won't. Nothing I can say or do will sway them—they'll adhere to Justin's orders come what may."

"But you know this house well, all the nooks and crannies, all the hidden and half-hidden rooms. You probably know this place better than Justin—you've spent more of your life here than he."

She tilted her head. "That's true. So what do you suggest?"

He looked up. "The attics. I haven't even seen the attic stairs yet."

"You won't. They're hidden." She thought, then said, "It's too late to go up there now—it's almost time to dress for dinner."

Christian studied her face, her focused expression. "And your bath will grow cold."

She narrowed her eyes at him. "Indeed. Regardless, our best time to search the attics is after dinner, while the servants are gathered in the hall belowstairs, having theirs. Papa is all but guaranteed to retreat to the library the instant the covers are drawn. We can pretend to have tea in the drawing room, pretend to be fatigued after our journeys, and retire as soon as we can."

He saw nothing in her plan with which to quibble. "Very well." He met her eyes. "I'll see you in the drawing room."

Letitia nodded and left. Christian stood in the gallery and watched her walk away down a corridor; absently he noted which door she chose. Without real thought, he stored the information in his memory, then turned and headed for his room.

The one part of the evening Letitia hadn't foreseen was her father's contribution. She wasn't the least surprised that her eccentric sire evinced not the smallest degree of grief over Randall's demise. What stunned her was that instead he appeared to have stepped back twelve or so years—or rather, seemed intent on behaving as if those intervening twelve years hadn't existed.

Not for any of them.

Especially not for her and Christian.

The instant her father stumped into the drawing room and set eyes on the pair of them standing before the empty hearth, his eyes lit. He chuckled as he came to her and offered his cheek. And proceeded to comment on what a handsome couple they made.

By the time she'd shaken off her shock—he was usually guaranteed to grumble and grouse and grump through any meal—he and Christian were engaged in a discussion of her finer points.

As if she'd been a horse.

She immediately took charge of the conversation.

And her father immediately tried to wrest the reins back.

Christian, of course, understood perfectly. Amused, he walked between them, her hand on his sleeve, to the dining room.

There was no telling what, if given free rein, her outrageous sire might say. The only way Letitia could think of to distract him was to focus the conversation firmly on his bête noir, namely Justin.

"I tell you it's simply unbelievable what the ton are saying. I even heard someone remark . . ." She prattled on, deliberately choosing comments that would most effectively ignite her sire's ire.

Christian, of course, did nothing to help; he sat back as course followed course, his eyes on her, occasionally switching to her father when he grew colorfully irate, but his gaze always returned to her, with a glint of amusement lighting the slaty gray, a subtle smile curving his lips, and his ears flapping.

He'd expected her to follow him, had expected to sit at a table with her and her unpredictable father; it seemed clear he'd hoped to discover, uncover, rather more than just her brother.

If she could have, she would have boxed his ears, verbally at least, but she had to keep her wits focused on her father.

"I honestly can't believe that Justin had the gall to think I'd murdered Randall. Do I look like a murderess? Do I have an evil glint in my eye? It can't be the color of my hair. But regardless, I can't help see what's happened as anything other than ironic—the ton believing it was he for precisely the same reason he believed it was me. . . ." She glanced swiftly at Christian, saw he'd noted the point. Mentally cursed.

"Humph!" Her sire sat back, waving aside a vegetable tureen. "Regardless, can't say I blame anyone for believing it of either of you, all things considered."

To her horror, Christian looked up from helping himself to another serving of roast beef. "What 'things'?"

"Well . . ."

Letitia tried desperately to catch her father's eye, but he was looking at Christian, opposite her.

Then her father waved generally. "Randall, of course." To Letitia's relief, her father's peripatetic attention swerved back to her. "I still can't believe you married the bounder."

She glared at him. She'd married the bounder to save him and the family, as he damned well knew. For one finite moment her temper threatened to snap its leash for good and all, but then she glanced at Christian—waiting, hovering, wanting to know—and she forced it down, drew a huge breath, held it for an instant, then calmly—awfully—stated, "I do not believe we should continue this conversation. Randall is dead, after all."

Her father, from whom she'd been very careful to hide the depths of her hatred for Randall—and equally, thankfully, the heights of her love for Christian—grumped, but subsided.

Christian narrowed his eyes at her, then gave his attention to his beef. She looked around, saw the platter was empty, and dispatched a footman to the kitchen for more. Anything to keep the twin banes of her life occupied.

At last the meal ended and, as she'd predicted, her father excused himself and returned to his library.

Christian dutifully refused her offer to retreat and leave him to enjoy a solitary brandy; he prowled at her heels as she led the way back to the drawing room. Claiming to be exhausted after the journey from London, she requested the tea trolley be brought in immediately. She and Christian made a show of pouring and sipping, then left the trolley in the drawing room and headed for the stairs.

It was only as she was climbing them with Christian beside her that she solved the riddle of the strange look on Hightsbury's face as they'd passed him in the front hall and she'd airily informed him they were retiring immediately.

Hightsbury, and no doubt the rest of the staff, assumed she and Christian were "retiring" to the same bed.

Conscious of a wayward stirring of her interest, she shot a sidelong glance at Christian. She wouldn't be surprised if he was thinking—or assuming—much the same as the staff, but she'd drawn a line and intended to stick to it.

No more payments until after he'd found Justin. Aside from all else, she couldn't afford more—not yet. Not while there was Justin's safety between them, complicating things.

She hadn't yet decided how they should go on, didn't even know what more—a brief affair, a longer liaison—he might want of her. Such matters were potentially too fraught to be dealt with now, not with Randall's murder and all its possible ramifications hanging over them all.

Christian noted her silence—not so much unusual for her as unusual in its absorption. He wished he knew what she was wrestling with; even more, he wished he knew what the circumstances of her marriage to Randall—the earl's "things"—were.

He'd hoped having her and her father together might lead to some revelation, however small, but all he'd gained was that tantalizing reference; all else was ongoing frustration.

Letitia's marriage to Randall was the central pivotal issue behind all that had occurred. It was the reason for Justin's actions. It was the reason Letitia and her father weren't entirely in accord.

He wouldn't be surprised if it was also the critical issue underlying Justin's rift with his father. As far as he could make out, the timing fitted.

Not much else did. Letitia's self-confessed hatred of Randall—in no way assumed—didn't explain why she'd married the man. Likewise, the earl's assertion that he couldn't understand why she had made no sense. Admittedly that last had set Letitia off, so was probably an exaggeration, but there had to be some kernel of truth or she wouldn't have been so irate.

They reached the gallery. Letitia halted and faced him.

He met her eyes, let his gaze travel slowly down until it rested on her skirts. "There's sure to be heaps of cobwebs up there. Do you want to change your gown?"

"All bombazine gowns are the same, in my opinion." Her brisk tone testified to her impatience. Having checked the gallery for lurking footmen, she turned and beckoned. "Come on. I'll show you the attic stairs."

The most interesting aspect about the attics at Nunchance Priory were the stairs leading to them. That, at least, was Christian's opinion when, an hour later, they descended said stairs and, dusty and not a little dirty, returned to the gallery.

"Nothing." Letitia looked both disgusted and vindicated. "I had hoped I was wrong and he'd holed up in the old nurseries, but clearly no one has been there for years."

"Judging by the dust, decades." He brushed a clinging cobweb from his sleeve.

"Yes, well, you wanted to look. So we've looked. Everywhere. Justin—as I warned you—isn't here."

He told her of the missing book in her father's library.

She frowned. "That does sound as if he were here. But he must have been just passing through." She glanced up at his face through the shadows. "Do you think he might have fled to Scotland?"

"He's a Vaux—anything's possible."

She humphed, looked down—looked anxious.

He inwardly sighed. "I honestly think he's somewhere close. I just don't know where." When she looked up again, he asked, "What about nearby buildings, further out from the house?"

When nothing registered in her face, he suggested, "What about the farms? Would he claim refuge with your workers, those he grew up with?"

She frowned, didn't immediately reply, but then shook her head. "I'm sure there are some who would happily hide him, but he won't go there."

He tilted his head. "You sound very sure."

"I am." She met his gaze. "He won't go to them because he'll know that by now he might be a wanted felon. He won't put other people—people who trust him—at risk by asking them for help."

He grimaced. That rang only too true. The Vaux were honorable and chivalrous to a fault.

Except for Letitia breaking her vow to him.

He looked at her through the gloom. "Why did you marry Randall?"

Even in the poor light, he saw her shields—shields she'd largely dropped over the last days—snap back into place. Shutting her off from him.

"That, as I've told you, is none of your business."

It felt as if a wall had sprung up between them, the separation was that absolute. Given their history, given she was otherwise open and straightforward, that wall was unsettling, disturbing.

She held his gaze, direct and determined, then inclined her head and turned away. "Good night. I'll see you at breakfast."

He watched her walk away through the shifting shadows, and debated whether, despite her chilly dismissal, despite—or even because of—that wall, he should follow. Her "not until you've found Justin" still rang in his brain; regardless, he doubted she'd deny him. Refuse him. When it came to what flared between them, she was as caught, as addicted, as he.

And it wasn't as if she was promiscuous. No lovers, not a one, yet she'd accepted him back as her lover with neither resistance nor hesitation. She still felt something for him; he was still special to her.

Yet . . .

After his visit to the abbey, he was no longer certain just what he wanted of her. More, yes, but how much more?

While he didn't know the answer, he'd be wise to tread carefully with her. The Vaux had tempers; they also had long memories.

Sinking his hands in his pockets, he turned to look out of one of the long gallery windows, waiting for the impulse to follow her—still pricking like a spur—to fade.

Frustration dragged at him, taunted him, on levels too numerous to count.

Minutes ticked by. He was about to turn and head for his room when he saw a light—a pinprick, no more—bobbing through the trees.

He leaned closer to the glass, watched for long enough to confirm that the light was moving steadily away from the house.

Purposefully away from the house.

He told himself it would be a maid out on a tryst.

"But if it isn't?"

He glanced to left and right, noting landmarks in the gardens to fix the direction, then left the window and ran silently downstairs.

The gardens of Nunchance Priory were extensive and, as Christian discovered that night, if not precisely overgrown, then distinctly mature. The trees were old, large and full-canopied; they cast inky black shadows that swallowed what little light the quarter moon shed. Pounding through the formal gardens, he'd plunged into the ornamental shrubberies beyond. Thick bushes abounded; paths meandered, garden beds unexpectedly forcing them this way, then that.

He considered himself lucky when he finally glimpsed the bobbing light still moving away some distance ahead of him. Keeping it in sight wasn't easy; in the dark, over unpredictable terrain, he couldn't keep his eyes glued to it without risking a fall.

Mentally cursing—the constantly changing landscape no doubt looked lovely on a warm summer's day—he forged on. Luckily, whoever was carrying the light wasn't moving fast.

Once he reached the park proper, long stretches of sward shaded by well-spaced large trees, his way became easier. He managed to close the distance between himself and the light bearer. Eventually he made out that the light came from a lantern, partially screened, its bearer a small, dapper individual he hadn't previously seen.

Justin's man, perhaps. He was carrying a large tray, the lantern dangling from one hand.

They were well away from the house when the light suddenly disappeared. On a silent oath, Christian rushed forward—and only just stopped himself from falling over the edge of a bank.

The area beyond looked like a large scoop had been taken out of the side of a rise; within it, a wooden hunting lodge, small, discreet, lay bathed in the faint light of the moon.

Smoke drifted from its chimney.

He watched as the lantern bearer approached the door, halted before it, juggled the tray, knocked once, then entered.

Slowly, intently, Christian smiled, then turned and circled the bank, dropping onto the downward slope. He found the path that led through the rough grass to the lodge's door. Silently, he circled the small building, checking for other exits. Other than shuttered windows, he saw none.

Satisfied, he stepped up to the narrow covered porch, rapped once on the door, then opened it and entered.

He stepped into the lodge's main room—sitting room, dining room, kitchen combined. Justin Vaux sat at the main table, his hand poised above his fork, about to eat the dinner his man had just delivered.

Closing the door, Christian walked in. He nodded at Justin's plate. "The roast beef's excellent."

Justin, who'd been staring, increasingly nonplussed, frowned. "What are you doing here?"

Pulling out a chair on the opposite side of the table, Christian dropped into it. "Looking for you."

Justin picked up his fork. "Oscar just told me you've been searching the house. What I don't understand is why."

"Because Letitia asked me to find you."

For a long moment, fork frozen in midair, Justin held his gaze. "She did?"

Christian made a "Here I am" gesture.

Justin looked rather pleased. He picked up his knife, waved at the plate. "I assume you've eaten, so you won't mind if I do."

"Not at all." Christian settled back.

"Wine?"

"Thank you." He hid an appreciative grin as Justin signaled to his man, who'd been eyeing Christian much in the way a duck might eye a wolf. No matter what one thought of the Vaux, they had style.

Once they were both supplied with goblets of a fine claret—doubtless culled from his father's extensive cellar—Christian sipped, and said, "Your father wasn't aware you were here, but unless I miss my guess, he now suspects."

Justin shrugged. He didn't look up.

Christian let him eat for a few minutes, then inquired, "Tell me, was the book you borrowed from his library the Seneca?"

Justin looked up, frowned. "Yes. How did you know?"

"You were reading the same book in Randall's library that night. I noticed you were not quite halfway through. When I—and your father—saw a book missing from his shelves, I assumed it was that."

Justin raised his brows. "So you braved the lion in his den, did you?"

Christian smiled, but declined to be diverted. "What happened that night at Randall's house?"

Justin continued eating. Christian waited, unperturbed.

Eventually, Justin replied, "I went in to see Randall. He'd asked me to call—we'd had a disagreement about . . . investments. We spoke for a short time—argued—then I lost my temper, picked up the poker and struck him."

Although naturally pale like his sister, Justin had paled further; Christian noted the haunted look in his eyes. He was twenty-six, and had almost certainly never seen a dead man before. That he'd felt forced to commit what he almost certainly viewed as a despicable act on a corpse would stay with him all of his life. In trying to protect Letitia, he'd already paid a price.

Justin lifted a shoulder and returned his attention to his plate. "I'm sure you know the rest."

Christian sipped his wine, then said, "I know you didn't kill Randall."

Justin's head came up; he frowned. "You couldn't know that." After a telltale second, he added, "Because I killed him."

Christian swung to face him directly across the table. "No, you didn't." He held Justin's gaze; from the corner of his eye he could see Justin's man—Oscar—looking both more interested and more hopeful by the minute. "Randall was already dead when you found him. He was lying facedown, his head toward the desk. He'd been felled—and killed—by a single relatively weak blow to the head, delivered with the poker which was lying nearby."

Justin simply stared at him, his expression tightly checked.

"I don't know why you did what you did, but I can guess. Tell me if I'm wrong. When you arrived at the house, you heard Letitia arguing violently with Randall. You retreated to the library, picked up the Seneca, started to read, and lost track of time. When you realized, the house was quiet. You went to Randall's study, found him dead, and assumed Letitia had killed him. You then set about making sure the authorities would never suspect a woman had killed Randall by obliterating his face."

Christian paused. "It worked, by the way, at least at first. But when a more experienced surgeon examined the body, he noticed that the major blows were struck after death." Both Justin and Oscar were hanging on his every word. "Of course, the authorities still have you in their sights. No doubt they'll argue you delivered both sets of blows, but we, of course, know differently. However, to return to your actions, you even sacrificed one of Shultz's creations by smearing Randall's blood on the sleeves, then leaving it in your lodgings for the runners to find."

He smiled, not humorously. "Runners might not be able to discern the importance of smears versus splatters, but I'm not so blind. You then left your lodgings—in a noisy rush so your landlord would notice—and headed out of town on the road to Dover, made sure you were seen at a hostelry on the outskirts of the city, then you turned around, cut straight back through town and came here. You didn't stop at any inn, but nursed your own horses through the journey, so there was no one to say that you'd come this way."

Christian smiled again, this time in reluctant appreciation. "You actually did quite well in making yourself look guilty. Certainly the authorities are convinced. Unfortunately for you, there were two things wrong with your plan, both to do with your sister."

Justin looked wary. "Letitia?"

Christian nodded. "She refused to believe you were guilty. And she didn't kill Randall either."

Justin blinked. His gaze grew distant, the frown on his face indicating that he was going back through the events of that fateful evening.

Christian gave him a moment, then said, "Justin, I need you to tell me exactly what happened that night. Letitia won't rest until you're exonerated, and, if it comes to that, neither will I."

Justin flicked him a look that was part irritation, part assessment. After a moment he said, "If I tell all I know, Letitia will look guilty. If it wasn't me, then she's the most likely." He frowned more definitely. "I still don't understand how—"

When he broke off, Christian supplied, "How it couldn't be she? How it could be anyone else?"

Justin met his eyes, then pulled a face and nodded.

"I have to admit, I don't at this point either, but then I'm missing some of the most pertinent facts." Christian sat back. "Some of which you have. If you tell me all, I might be able to work it out."

Justin studied him—his face, his eyes—for a long moment, then said, his eyes steady on Christian's, "I'll tell you all if you promise one thing. You have to swear on your honor that you'll keep Letitia out of this—that you'll keep her safe. I couldn't bear it if she had to sacrifice anything more for the family, and especially not for me." Justin held his gaze. "Will you give me your word?"

Christian returned his unwavering regard. "You may take that as read."

A large part of the tension that had held Justin faded. He searched Christian's face one last time, then nodded. He forked up the last morsel on his plate, chewed, swallowed, then set down his knife and fork and pushed the plate aside; Oscar stepped in and whisked it away.

"In that case . . ." Justin reached for his goblet. "It happened much as you said. What more do you need to know?"

"You said Randall had asked you to call. Why, and at what time was he expecting you?"

Justin paused, then, eyes on Christian's face, replied, "He sent a message that morning. Said he wanted to talk to me about some investment and asked me to call after two."

Christian frowned. "He was advising you about investments?"

Justin shook his head. "He was trying to lure me into debt. He'd tried to encourage me to gamble. When that didn't work, it was collecting. Investments was his most recent tilt."

"Why?"

Justin tipped his head in the direction of the house. "He wanted Nunchance." When Christian looked his befuddlement, Justin continued, "Randall was very wealthy, but he didn't have a country estate. He wanted one, but once he'd seen Nunchance, nothing else compared. So he was looking at ways to become the next owner. I know he'd made inquiries into breaking the entail. It's difficult, but it's not impossible—not if you're connected to the family, have unlimited funds, and the present incumbent is in Newgate."

"He was trying to bankrupt you?" Christian was having a hard time comprehending.

"Yes. Just as . . . well, never mind that. But that was what he wanted to chat to me about. I, of course, didn't appreciate the summons, but I was curious to learn what he would say this time, so I called that evening. I knew he'd be in because I'd met Letitia earlier and she told me he'd cried off from going to some dinner with her."

"But when you called, Letitia was with Randall."

Justin nodded. "She'd come home, and was already in full flight. I knew what it was about." His gaze flicked to Christian's face.

Christian nodded, rather grim. "Hermione."

"Another case of Randall trying to use our family to his own social-climbing ends. Regardless, on that topic, I knew I could leave him to Letitia—she wasn't going to budge. I could hear how serious she was."

"So you went to the library." Christian leaned forward. "Do you know what time that was?"

"I left White's at ten, so it was after that. . . ." Justin's frown cleared. "The clock in the library struck ten-thirty as I was settling with the Seneca."

"Good. So at half past ten Letitia was screeching at Randall, and you were in the library. What time was it when you left?"

"It was the silence that finally registered. I was surprised it was so quiet and I looked at the clock." Justin met Christian's eyes. "It was after eleven-thirty—eleven-forty, give or take a minute. I remember because I was amazed at how deaf I'd been—I'd sat through both the hour and the half-hour chimes and hadn't noticed."

Intent, Christian nodded. "What happened next?"

"I set aside the Seneca and went to see if Randall was still downstairs. The house was totally silent, all the other rooms dark. The door to his study was shut, but I could see light beneath the door—a lamp was still burning. I thought he was still working—he often worked late. I opened the door expecting to see him sitting behind his desk. Instead . . ."

After a moment, frowning, Justin went on, "At first I thought he'd swooned and fallen. I went in, touched him, then saw the dent in the back of his head. If the lamp hadn't been on that end of the desk, I wouldn't have seen it—there wasn't much to see. I checked for a pulse and then looked into his eyes—he was dead. Then I saw the poker lying on the other side of him."

Justin fixed his eyes on Christian's face. "Given the whole . . ." Searching for words, he gestured. ". . . *situation* between Letitia and Randall, and how that had echoes in this business about Hermione, I honestly thought he'd pushed her one step too far. That she'd seen red, picked up the poker when he turned away from her, and struck him. And killed him."

"You didn't think to go up and ask her—see her, find out, what state she was in?"

Justin grimaced. "I honestly didn't know if she *knew* she'd killed him—as I said, the blow wasn't that easy to see. She might just have struck him, not realized she'd struck so hard, then just flung down the poker and stormed out. Not the most likely thing, not with anyone else, but with her and Randall . . . well, it wasn't inconceivable."

"And you weren't really thinking all that clearly."

"Well, no. All I could think about was that she'd killed

him, and all because of her marriage to him—all to protect the family, and that even then, she was protecting Hermione. . . ." Justin's jaw hardened. "I just thought it was time someone in the family protected *her.*"

Christian had question upon question crowding his mind—about Letitia, her marriage, the "situation"—but he forced himself to concentrate first on clarifying what had happened that night. "Let's say it was eleven forty-five when you entered the study and found Randall dead. Mellon saw you leave the house, and he admitted he'd already been in bed for a time."

Justin nodded. "I told him to take himself off, that I'd see myself in."

"So he said. But Letitia must have left Randall shortly after that. You know your sister—she might rant, but the longest she'll go for is ten minutes, then she runs out of steam, runs out of temper—and usually storms out and away from whoever she's screeching at. In this case Randall. And that's exactly what she says she did—so she must have left Randall at, say, ten thirty-five. Ten-forty at the latest."

Frowning, Justin nodded for him to continue.

"So you find Randall at eleven forty-five, and wield the poker—but according to my knowledgeable surgeon, while Randall was definitely dead before you struck him, he'd only been dead for fifteen to thirty minutes at most. Not the hour that would have been the case if Letitia had killed him."

Justin looked incredulous. "Someone else was there?"

Christian nodded. "It appears someone else saw Randall between she and you."

"I didn't hear anyone else arrive." Justin grimaced. "Not that I necessarily would have."

"Mellon swore no one did." Christian reviewed what he now knew. "We'll have to follow that up later, once we're back in London." He refixed his gaze on Justin's face. "Let's leave the mechanics of Randall's death aside and concentrate on motives. What is it about Randall's marriage to Letitia that explains all this?"

Justin blinked, then stared, expressionless, at him. Then he blinked again. "You don't know?"

"Obviously not."

Justin let his puzzlement show. "But why hasn't she told you?"

A rhetorical question, but he gritted his teeth and replied, "You'll have to ask her. But for now, why don't you tell me."

Justin's perplexity turned to a frown. After a long moment he said, "It's not my place." His frown deepened, then he shook his head. "I can't understand *why* she hasn't told you. *Before*, I can understand—you never went near her, and so never gave her the chance . . . not that if she'd wanted to she couldn't have created a moment. But now she's asked you for help, and you've been seeing her for what? Six, seven days? And she *still* hasn't told you?"

Christian looked at him. "Just tell me."

There was that in his voice that brooked no further argument.

Justin met his eyes, raised his brows fleetingly, then capitulated. "I knew you and Letitia planned to marry, that she'd sworn to wait for you to return from the wars."

He wasn't surprised; Justin and Letitia had always been close.

"All was well until eight years ago. All just rolling along as it usually did, then suddenly—no warning whatever—m'father informed us, Letitia and me, that we—the Vaux, the family—were bankrupt."

Christian blinked.

Justin saw and grimly nodded. "Indeed. Somehow, he'd run through the entire fortune, and it wasn't a small amount."

"How?"

"Investments." Justin's lips curled, and Christian knew what had turned him so conservative. "Somehow or other—it was never clear—the whole lot had gone. Worse, we were in debt, and sinking fast. There was no way back, no way out. Except . . . at just that time, Randall, who Letitia had met but only in passing, made an offer for her hand. The pater refused, of course—when Randall pressed, Papa intimated that the family weren't flush with funds. Not long after, Randall came back—with a complete and accurate summation of the family's finances, and a plan to resurrect them."

"Let me guess—the plan included Letitia marrying him." He heard himself ask the question, but part of his mind had already disengaged. Was already absorbed with another, quite different question.

"Not included—the plan was *contingent* upon their marriage. And not just that. There were conditions. Some of them I don't know—once she'd decided she had to do it, Letitia took it upon herself to finalize those with Randall. I do know that part of the agreement was that there would be no hint whatever that Letitia had married to secure the money—that he'd bought her, as it were. He insisted, and she ultimately agreed, that to the ton and the world, the marriage had to appear to be a love match."

"Was there any chance Randall was in any way connected with the bad investments your father made?" Again the words fell from his lips perfectly sanely; inside his skull, a chant of *Why, why, why?* was starting to pound.

Justin met his eyes. "There was no hint of it." Then he added, "Not then."

That recaptured his attention; he narrowed his eyes. "But now?"

"When Randall started proposing investments to me, I got suspicious. Knowing why he was doing it, there was just too much of an echo with the past. I started asking around. I haven't found anything definite, but . . . the feeling's still there. That if all those years ago we'd looked more carefully, we would have found a connection."

"Is that what's behind your rift with your father?" Some small part of his mind persisted in filling in the gaps. The rest was consumed with more pressing issues.

Justin sighed, closed his eyes. "Yes. I couldn't—still can't—forgive him for losing all that money. For putting all our futures at risk, for being the reason Letitia sacrificed herself—her happiness, the future she should have had—to secure ours." He opened his eyes. "That's what I can't stand—it still rankles. Every time I see him."

Christian nodded absently.

A moment ticked past. He was about to push back from the table—to pursue the urgent need building inside him—when Justin, who'd been broodingly studying him, said, "You know, I take it back. I *can* understand why Letitia hasn't told you. You should have known how it was. She loved you. The only thing that might have swayed her was duty to the family—you had to have known that."

The observation gave him pause. He hadn't known that because . . .

Regardless, a lack of faith on his part didn't excuse the oversight—the slight—implicit in Justin's story. He dragged in a huge breath. "I . . . see."

He could hardly speak—couldn't think. The emotions churning inside him were so powerful he wasn't even sure he could stand. He pushed up from the table. "If you'll excuse me . . . I'll see you in the morning."

Puzzled, curious, but after one glance at his face not about to detain him, Justin nodded.

As he reached the door, Justin called, "You may as well bring Letitia with you tomorrow. She'll be happier once she sees me."

He raised a hand in acknowledgment but made no reply. He had no idea what state Letitia would be in come morning.

He might just have strangled her by then.

Leaving the lodge, he strode swiftly, increasingly quickly, back to the house.

Chapter 7

Letitia heard Christian's footsteps an instant before he flung open the door to her room. Catching the door's edge with one hand, his gaze pinned her where she sat swiveled around in surprise on the stool before her dressing table, then he stepped into the room—and slammed the door behind him.

He stalked toward her, glowering furiously. More angry than she'd ever seen him, angrier than she'd thought he could be. His face was pale, his nostrils pinched. As he drew near, his eyes reminded her of thunderheads, roiling and dangerous.

"Why the hell didn't you tell me why *you married Randall?"*

The words were uttered with such vehement force, a lesser woman would have quailed.

Unimpressed, she swung her legs around so she was facing him, and arched her brows. "And what good would that have done? Now, so long after the fact?" She realized the implication, and calmly continued, "From which question I take it you found Justin. Where is he?"

Halting before her, he glared down at her. "In the lodge in the park."

She frowned. "Damn! I'd completely forgotten it existed. I thought it was derelict—Justin's the only one of us who's ever had any interest in it. Of course, over recent years he's spent much more time here than I have. I've hardly—"

"Don't change the subject."

She looked up into his face. "I thought Justin was the subject. Or is that the object? Of our search, that is. Now we've found him—"

He grabbed her by the shoulders and hauled her up so they were face-to-face. "Why, why, *why?* Damn it, *why* didn't you send for me? *Why in all Hades did you marry that bounder instead?*" His roar all but echoed through the room. "Why didn't you give me a *chance* to fight for you— for us?"

She looked into the turbulent tumult of his gaze, saw his hurt fury, the accusation, sensed his rage through his grip on her arms.

Felt all the old rancor she'd suppressed for years rise up and swamp her.

She lifted her chin, perfectly evenly replied, "Why didn't I tell you?" She widened her eyes at him. "But I did. At least, I tried. I wrote to you—sent for you. *Begged you for help.* My letters were returned unopened. They didn't know of you at the Guards."

Her last words sent a chill through Christian, effectively dousing his ire. He searched her eyes. Realizing how hard he was gripping her arms, he eased his hold. Simultaneously he ransacked his memories, confirming that all those years ago . . . he never had told her what he'd actually been doing on the Continent. Never told her that while he was a major in the Guards, he hadn't been serving with any of the regiments.

"Justin even went to Horse Guards and asked." Her voice remained studiously uninflected. "They admitted you'd once been a serving officer, but they said you were off their books and they didn't know where you were."

He looked into her eyes, melded gold and green, and sensed her banked fury. His mind was reeling, his mouth dry; he moistened his lips. "I—"

"So there I was." She spoke over him, clinging to that same, terribly even tone, as if she weren't speaking of an event that had critically, cataclysmically, affected her.

"If I agreed to marry Randall and pretended it was a love match, I could save my family from certain ruin. If I didn't agree . . ."

She met his gaze, her own hard and unforgiving. "You tell me—what choice did I have? My lover, my sweetheart, my closest friend, who I *thought* loved me, had deserted me. Vanished from the face of the earth. Deliberately. We contacted your people—even they didn't know how to reach you."

Only his father's solicitor had known whom to contact, and she hadn't known about him. Because he hadn't told her. He'd blithely assumed he'd be able to write to her, but once he was in deep cover in central France, it simply hadn't been possible.

Her lips curved in a bitter, brittle smile. "So please don't suggest that I betrayed you. I know that's what you've thought all these years. Well you can wallow in self-pity as long as you choose, but don't—please don't—ever expect me to indulge you. I didn't betray you." Head rising, smile fading, she sucked in a tight breath. "If anyone was betrayed, it was *me*."

He swallowed, released her, lowered his hands. Eased back a step. His gaze locked with hers, his mind was a swirling jumble of unfinished—unfinishable—thoughts. All he'd known as fact, the framework underpinning his smoldering anger, had been ripped away, his perceptions turned literally upside down. He didn't know how to defend himself—didn't see how he could.

He took another step back.

Fury lit her eyes and she came after him. She jabbed a finger into his chest. "I had a *right* to your support and consideration, even then. You gave me *neither*." Her voice grew in volume and dramatic force. "You hadn't even seen fit to speak to my father, so I couldn't appeal to him, or to yours, for help. Couldn't suggest that there might be another way out rather than by me marrying Randall."

He flung his hands out to his sides. "You *know* why I didn't speak—we discussed it. I might have been killed, and you were so young—you would have been tied to me, mourning me." He held her gaze. "Christ, I would have given a king's ransom for you—you know that."

"Indeed? Much good did that do me." Eyes glittering, she advanced and he gave ground. "Where *were* you, Christian? Where were you when I needed you?"

Raising one hand, she halted. "No, wait—don't tell me. I believe I know." Her eyes blazed. " 'Keep your friends close, but your enemies closer.' Isn't that the motto you swear by? Isn't that what you *chose* to do, all those years ago?"

He stopped backing away. "It wasn't like that."

She narrowed her eyes. "Oh, yes it was. You chose to go and play not just soldiers but spies, to get even closer to the enemy. You left behind your friends—you left *me* behind—for that. For the *thrill*."

She held his gaze. "You needn't think to deny it. I know you rather well, if you recall. We aren't so very different—you just hide all your passion behind an imperturbable mask while I let mine show. You *lusted* after excitement—that's what drew us together in the first place—so when a certain gentleman crooked his finger and offered you the chance, you grabbed it—and went. For twelve years."

"I wasn't doing nothing all those years."

"Oh, I'm quite sure you weren't." She started to pace; he was forcefully reminded of a cat lashing its tail. "I'm quite sure you were indulging your craving for excitement to the hilt. But you didn't want me to know about that. You didn't trust me enough to tell me about your new if temporary life. Instead, you left me here, alone, unclaimed, unspoken for, to weather whatever storms fate sent my way. As it happened, fate sent Randall."

He dragged in a huge breath, ran a hand through his hair. His chest felt as if it had been put through a mangle. He looked into her expressive face, saw all she'd held back, all she'd felt for so long—finally saw what had built the wall he'd sensed between them—and didn't know how to breach it, how to reach her.

Only knew he had to.

Her lashes lowered, screening her eyes. She, too, drew in a breath, and held it. He sensed her drawing back, reining her temper in, realized that—the Vaux love of drama notwithstanding—she wasn't going to, didn't want to, lose it. Not now, not with him.

That seemed strange. Here, surely, was a grand stage—a grand passion tailormade for her to indulge in to the very top of her bent. A matter in which she was totally in the right, and he totally in the wrong.

But rather than rail at him, she turned away. Which only made him feel even more desperate. Head rising, she walked back to her dressing table. "One thing." Her voice was cool, clear; she didn't glance back at him. "I will not be blamed for doing what had to be done—not by you, not by anyone."

Reaching her dressing stool, she stepped around it and sat. With dreadful calm, she reached up to unpin her hair. "Close the door behind you."

He looked at her, for long minutes studied her, then he walked slowly forward until he stood directly behind her. He searched the face in the mirror—a face he knew better than his own, one that had inhabited his dreams for so many years he'd lost count.

A face that now was shuttered against him.

He hadn't realized she could do that. He was certain, would have sworn that before—before he'd left her twelve years ago—she'd never be able to hide any of her vibrant emotions from him.

But the years between—the years with Randall—had taught her how to veil her inner self, to hide her feelings—to shield her heart.

The heart that once had been his, unreservedly.

"I'm sorry."

The words fell from him, direct from his heart.

Her eyes sparked anew. She looked up, in the mirror met his gaze. *"Sorry?"* Temper, disgust, and disbelief mingled in her tone; her eyes were burning disks of fury. "Sorry for all the years I lay beside that man? Sorry for all the nights I had to put up with his rutting?" Her voice changed. "Do you want to hear that he was a dreadful clod of a lover? Because he was. You at twenty-three knew far more than he ever learned."

There was nothing he could say, nothing he could do to defend himself against the accusation in her eyes. He held her gaze, forced himself to, and hoped she could see how much he hurt, how much her words had cut him, how much he now bled, for her.

She seemed to. She drew another careful breath, again drew back from her dangerous edge. She refocused on her reflection; her face stony again, she reached up and pulled another pin from her hair. For a moment he wasn't sure she was going to say anything more. He was floundering, trying to find some verbal way forward, when she drew in an unsteady breath and in a voice devoid of emotion stated, "You left me. You made my bed for me, and I was the one who had to lie in it—with Randall."

He didn't want to ask, but he had to know. They'd always—in the past—been open with each other. "Can you forgive me?"

Again she didn't immediately answer, but continued pulling pins from her hair. Then he sensed rather than heard her sigh. "If you want the truth, I honestly don't know."

He heard, knew that *was* the truth—and it terrified him. Sent a sheet of ice-cold fear cascading through him.

To have her within his grasp and lose her again . . . he knew, in that instant, that he couldn't bear that. Couldn't live with that.

That he had to, somehow, find a way to recapture lost dreams—his, and hers.

She pulled out the last pin and her hair tumbled down, falling across her shoulders in a dark mahogany wave. The sight held him; he watched as she picked up a brush and applied it to the silky locks.

A minute ticked by, then he turned away. He knew, beyond doubt or question, that if he left her now, backed away from her revelations, he would never win her back. Stopping by a chair, he shrugged out of his coat, set it over the chair's back, then unbuttoned his waistcoat, then set his fingers to his cravat.

Wielding her brush, she glanced at him, frowned, opened her mouth . . . after a moment she shut it again. She studied him for a moment more, then rose and, brush in hand, walked to the window. Slowly brushing, she stood looking out at the night.

He unraveled his cravat, dispensed with it and his waistcoat, then sat on the chair to pull off his boots. Setting them aside, he rose, yanked his shirt from his waistband, loosened the collar. He glanced at her, then, unlacing his cuffs, crossed silently to her.

Halting behind her, close, he waited while she finished brushing out one long tress, then slid the brush from her fingers and placed it on the chest of drawers beside the window.

She said nothing, did nothing.

He reached for her, wrapped her in his arms and simply held her. Waited, his cheek against her sleek head, until at last she relaxed, until she leaned back against him. He tightened his hold, swore on his heart, on his soul, that he would never again let her go.

Bending his head, he pressed a kiss to her temple. Murmured, "I have one last question. When you came asking for my help, why didn't you say anything? Why didn't you mention what's been standing like a six-foot-thick wall between us?"

He wasn't sure she'd give him an answer; he couldn't demand one. Her hands resting over his at her waist, she continued to look out into the night.

Then she lifted one shoulder. "Pride, I suppose. That was all that was left to me."

He tried to keep them back, but the words came out anyway. "Was it really so easy to hate me?" He used the term in the full knowledge that she never did anything by half.

Her chin rose. "It's become a habit."

"Break it." Not demand, not command. A suggestion.

"Why?"

The response he'd expected. He turned her to him, into his arms. Looked into her eyes. "Because of this."

He bent his head and kissed her—and knew he would have only this one chance. One night to give her reasons to try again. One night to make her believe in him again.

One night to find some hope that she would trust him again. Sometime.

That sometime she would be, again, as she had been long ago.

His.

Unquestionably. Incontrovertibly. Irrevocably.

He knew well enough not to try to overwhelm her, but kissed her gently, waited for her response before coaxing her into more. She kissed him back, tentatively at first, as if she hadn't yet made up her mind to allow him into her bed—even though they both knew she had.

Although he hadn't seen them, he tasted tears on her lips. On her tongue when he parted her lips and surged inside. He gathered her closer and deepened the kiss, let her feel all she did to him, and all he did to her.

Let her sense how much she meant to him.

No screens. No veils. No reservations.

The time for those was past.

She was, as always, liquid fire in his arms, but this time the fire was contained. The flames licked, tantalizing, tempting, but the fire was banked, controlled. She didn't burn and sear him, didn't try to set him afire as she usually did, didn't fight for supremacy—for the reins—but held back, hung back, and left it to him to stoke their blaze.

So he let their passions rise, but slowly, tiny step by step, so there was no raging inferno to sweep them both away. So that they stepped hand in hand into desire, then let desire unfurl into full-blown passion.

Let passion escalate degree by degree . . . until it blossomed into need.

Letitia let him persuade her. For once let him lead her down the familiar path rather than rush ahead, so that for once he had to coax, rather than restrain.

She let him kiss her until her senses were reeling, let him fill her mouth and make her yearn.

Let him seduce her.

Not because she'd forgiven him.

Not because she'd made any decision about him, but because she felt she was owed this.

That for all the long years—the lonely, deadening years—that for all her long ago heartbreak, she deserved recompense—a recognition of the sacrifice she'd had forced on her, by circumstance and him, all those years ago.

So she gave him her mouth and let him claim her, surrendered her body and let him caress her—let him trace her curves, with his too-knowing fingers circle, tweak, press, knead, until she grew breathless, restless and needy.

Let him make love to her.

Let him strip away her gown, her petticoats; with a sigh, she felt her chemise drift away. Felt the coolness of the night air on her skin—a long-ago pleasure she'd all but forgotten—the sensation heightened, gently at first, later excruciatingly, by the heated touch of his hands, followed by the hot brand of his mouth on her throat, traveling slowly on to her breasts, then later still laying a fiery path over her stomach to ultimately taste the soft flesh between her thighs.

Gasping, senses reeling, her skin flushed and damp, she let him, on his knees, hold her before him, his hard hands gripping her bottom, supporting her while, his soft hair tangling with her curls, he worshipped her with his lips, his mouth, his tongue, let him use his expertise to ensnare her completely, then let him drive her up, up and over the shining peak.

Glory broke like the sun over her; heat and pleasure fragmented, washing through her veins as molten delight.

Her legs buckled. She gasped; helpless, she gripped his shoulders. Shuddered as, her senses returning, she grew acutely aware of passion's lash as at her core he supped, licked. Savored.

She didn't have strength left to stop him, to do more than gasp as he spun the pleasure out. Eyes closed, she let her head loll back, and with a soft moan let delight sweep through her.

Let the intimacy of his possession sink into her.

At last he drew back; he looked up at her, then in one fluid movement stood and swung her up into his arms.

He carried her to her bed, flung back the covers, then laid her on the cool sheets.

She was restless, but didn't want to show it. Didn't want him to know how much she physically craved him. Forcing herself to lie still, through the dimness she watched as he stripped off his shirt and trousers. Naked, he stood by the bed, bathed in faint moonlight; silver gilded the heavy planes of his shoulders, etched the hard lines of his face. He studied her as she studied him, then he stepped closer and climbed onto the mattress.

It gave under his weight. Fully aroused, he came to her, let himself down on her and covered her. Reached down, caught her thighs and spread them wide. Settled his hips between, the blunt head of his erection at her entrance, then, his shadowed gaze locked on her face, with one long, controlled, unrelenting thrust, he joined them.

She smothered a gasp, couldn't stop her body from arching in delicious reaction. His size still felt new to her, something she might once have known but had yet to grow accustomed to again. Yet to reach the stage where his penetration didn't impinge overwhelmingly on her senses.

Lips lightly—irrepressibly—curving, she let her lids fall, let her body respond as he withdrew and thrust again, deeper still, then he settled into a slow, steady rhythm—a long, slow ride into paradise.

Opening her other senses, she let herself enjoy all she'd missed—his large, hard body, the wide acres of his chest, the heavy muscles banding it, the faint but excruciating abrasion of the crinkly hair that adorned his chest as it rasped her tightly furled nipples. Beneath him, pinned to the soft bed by his much greater weight, she quietly gloried in the indescribable delight of gripping his tight buttocks and feeling him driving into her, feeling the long, heavy weight of his erection thrusting and retreating deep inside her.

Regardless of all else, he knew how to please her—exactly how to pleasure her. How to delight and satisfy her.

She took all he gave her, gathered it in as her due.

Christian felt every nuance, was awake and aware to every racing beat of her heart, every flutter of her lashes, every soft sound that spilled from her lips, every moan he wrung from her. Every tensing of her fingers on his skin.

He'd never made love to any woman as he did to her that night. Never been so conscious of, so focused on, the intertwining of emotion with the physical act. Never had the act meant more, never had he needed it to mean so much, to carry so much emotional weight—the full measure of what he could no longer hide. Dared no longer hide, no longer had any reason to hide—all that he felt for her.

She'd never been passive in her life, yet that night she watched and waited, took, accepted, but held herself back. Not physically but emotionally.

It wasn't a cold coupling; between them such a thing simply couldn't be. Yet there was an emptiness within it that, he realized, her love used to fill. Used to fill and overflow.

He hadn't noticed its absence during their recent interludes; the firestorm of her passions, and his, had concealed the lack. But he sensed it now. And felt the loss keenly.

He looked down at her as she lay beneath him, glorious as ever in her passion; her mahogany mane flung across the pil-

STEPHANIE LAURENS

138

lows, the faintest of curves to her lips, she rode with him, her hips undulating with each deep thrust, her breasts caressing his chest as he drove harder and harder into her luscious body. Her thighs gripped his flanks, her fingers tensing, sinking into his flexing buttocks, urging him on; within, her sheath, scalding and slick, gripped him and held him, released, then received him.

She was with him, yet not, reserved in some indefinable way that she never had been before, some elemental part of her withheld. He saw it, sensed it as the peak reared before them and they hovered, senses suspended, then they tumbled, fell, plummeted through the void, and in that searing, gasping, mindless moment when their senses imploded and ecstasy roared through and they clung . . . when they drifted back to earth, they were still two separate people.

Where before there'd always been a sense of shared joy, of complete fusion in the moment, of a loss of self that was somehow glorious, now there was only physical satiation.

Complete, deep and mind-numbing, yet not—for him nowhere near—as satisfying.

He couldn't believe she didn't feel the same, that she didn't feel and mourn that loss.

That she didn't wish it were otherwise.

He collapsed upon her, too racked to move. His head on her breasts, her shallow breathing in his ear, his heart still thundering in his chest, with the night air laying cooling tendrils over their slick bodies, he fought for breath—and waited.

Prayed.

At last—*finally*—she raised a hand and gently slid her fingers through his hair.

He closed his eyes, swallowed as incalculable relief swept through him. Simply lay there and took comfort in what he knew to be an instinctive, habitual caress.

In his mind's eye he followed every slide, every flick of her fingers, every little touch that made up that caress.

Wallowed in what drove it.

All was, thank heaven, not lost. Her love—the one thing he now most wanted in life—still lived.

To win it back . . . all he had to do was convince her to trust him with it again.

Convince her that loving him again would be safe.

Prove to her that he would never again hurt her, never let anyone or anything hurt her.

He remained where he was, hungrily, greedily, savoring the sensations of her sated body cradling his. Clinging to the moment, the quiet glow, he wondered how one went about mending a broken heart.

Chapter 8

Letitia wasn't easily shocked, but when she woke the next morning to the inescapable sensations of a large, warm—not to say hot—male body spooned around hers, she very nearly leapt from the bed.

She did sit up. Struggling out from under a heavy arm, she stared, mouth acock, then looked across the room to the windows they'd left uncurtained—at the sunshine streaming in.

"Christian!" She jabbed his shoulder. When he didn't respond, she jabbed his upper arm, leaning closer to hiss at him, "You have to wake up and go to your room!"

Over all the times they'd made love, she'd never spent the night in his arms. Never woken to find him beside her.

Exasperated—and not a little panicky—she jabbed again, and he moved—but only to wrap one huge hand about her fingers.

And draw her inexorably back down. . . .

"No!" She tried to pull back, but had no purchase. "We can't!"

He rolled over. Looking sinfully sleep-tousled, he cocked a lazy brow at her. "Why not?"

He continued to drag her closer, until, frustrated, she let herself tumble across his chest. All but nose-to-nose, she glared at him. "Because my maid will be here with my washing water and I absolutely refuse to be discovered in flagrante delicto with you in this bed."

He smiled, slow, sensual, teasing. "Don't worry." He reached for her nape. "I locked the door."

She narrowed her eyes at him, swiftly replayed his stormy entrance the previous night. "You did not. You slammed it."

Large and warm, his palm caressed her sensitive skin. "I got up during the night and locked it."

She blinked. "You did?" She frowned, trying to imagine why he'd thought to do so. Why he'd planned . . .

He gripped and drew her head down. "Stop thinking. Come and enjoy something you never have."

She found herself lowering her lips to his. She halted just before their lips met. "What?"

He lifted his hips and she felt . . . his morning erection.

Her eyes widened. "Oh."

"Indeed." He drew her down the last inch, into the kiss.

She let him, wondering, tantalized. Seduced.

She'd heard about men's proclivities in the morning, but as she'd never shared a bed all night with him—and had actively discouraged Randall from spending one more minute with her than he absolutely needed to—she'd never had a chance to experience . . . the different, strangely compelling sensations of making love when they were already warm and relaxed beneath the covers.

When there were no clothes to remove, no barriers separating their warm skins, so that from the very first touch they stepped onto a higher level of intimacy, yet one that, presumably because the outcome of their tangling naked limbs was all but preordained, held much less urgency, much less driving need—much more simple, tactile pleasure.

Sensual pleasure of a depth and breadth she hadn't previously known. She let him show her, let him settle her astride him, lift her and ease her down so she took the rigid length of him deep, let him lie back and fondle her breasts as she—clinging to the lazy languor of the moment—rode him slowly.

The end, when it came, was lazy, too. Warm pleasure, bright as the morning sun, welled and spilled down her veins, the glory heightened when he locked his hands about her hips and thrust upward, again, and again, then on a long groan joined her.

One hand tangled in his hair, she lay in his arms, and let the warmth and the peace of the morning hold sway—for just a little while.

But outside the door, locked or not, reality waited.

She stirred, pushed against the weight of his arms across her back. He held her for an instant, pressed a kiss to her temple, then helped her up. Without further argument he rose, found his clothes and donned them, then, passing her on the way to the door, he caught her to him for one last, sweet kiss, then with a salute, left her.

Eyes narrowed, she stared at the closed door for a full minute, then shook her head and crossed to the bellpull to ring for Esme.

Twenty minutes later, in yet another black gown, this one of fine silk crepe, she descended the stairs and headed for the breakfast parlor. She swept in, inclining her head gracefully to Hightsbury in acknowledgment of his bow—and only then remembered that her father invariably breakfasted in his library.

Leaving her to entertain his guest.

Blotting his lips with a napkin, Christian rose and, with an easy smile, drew out a chair for her—the one next to his.

She hesitated. His eyes challenged her. Chin tilting, she swept forward and sat. After resetting her chair, Christian resumed his seat beside her.

Hightsbury had anticipated her needs; tea and toast magically appeared before her. She smiled at the butler, then, bending to the pressure of a large knee against hers, said, "Thank you, Hightsbury. We'll ring if we need you."

Evincing no surprise at being dismissed, Hightsbury bowed and left them.

She turned her gaze on the far less predictable male alongside. "What?"

Christian raised his brows at her bald query. "I thought,

all things considered, that you might wish to know my intentions."

Lifting her teacup, she opened her eyes wide at him over the brim. "You have intentions?"

"Indeed. And as you feature prominently, I thought I should mention them."

She searched his eyes, unsure whether to encourage him or not.

He didn't wait for her to make up her mind. He looked down at his hand, resting by his plate, at the gold signet ring on his little finger. "I was wrong—wrong not to tell you about my peculiar commission, wrong to leave you without any means to reach me."

Her gaze locked on his face. He had her full and complete attention.

Forcing himself to sit still and not squirm, he went on, "Twelve years ago, when I was younger, and, yes, caught up in the romance of being a spy, I made that mistake. I adhered absolutely to the 'tell no one more than they need to know' rule. If I had the time again, I'd act differently, but I can't rewrite history."

Glancing up, he met her gaze. "You said fate had thrown Randall in your path—now it appears fate has stepped in and removed him from your life. Which leaves the way open for me."

Her eyes flashed.

He held up a staying hand. "Before you erupt, know this—I freely admit to the mistake I made twelve years ago, but I'll be damned if I pay for it for the rest of my life." He caught her gaze. "And I'll be damned if I let you pay for it any more than you already have."

Her eyes slowly narrowed to slits. Her lips thinned. After a long moment she inquired, in her sweetest voice, "Don't you think that's rather presumptuous? Just a touch over-arrogant, even for you?"

He held her gaze and bluntly replied, "No." After a second, he went on, "My service to our country cost us both, but you far more than me. But the war is over, my service is past, and now Randall's dead, there's no reason for either of us to keep paying in any way whatever." He hesitated, then went on, grasping the thistle of complete exposure, "The future we envisioned twelve years ago—it's still there, waiting for us if we wish to pursue it. I intend to." He paused, then, his eyes still locked with hers, said, "No more secrets between us—I wanted you to know."

Once again he couldn't read her eyes. Couldn't see her thoughts in her expression.

A full minute ticked by, then she looked away, sipped, and set down her cup. "Times change."

"True, but people like us don't. What used to be between us is still there—not exactly the same perhaps, it's evolved as we have, but the strength, the depth, the power of it is, if anything, even greater."

She drew in a slow breath. "Perhaps, but . . . I no longer know if that—the future we envisaged twelve years ago—is what I, now, want."

He'd expected that, had known she wasn't likely to throw her arms around his neck and encourage him to speak with her father then and there. And if the implied rejection still stung, he told himself it was far less than he deserved for, as she'd correctly termed it, deserting her.

Regardless, he wasn't about to accept any dismissal, certainly not yet. Reaching for his coffee cup, he evenly replied, "I'm prepared to wait for however long it takes for you to make up your mind."

He sipped, aware of the sharp, frowning glance she leveled at him.

Sometime last night he'd made a decision, one that had kept him in her bed. That morning, he'd sought to draw her back to him; instead he'd discovered how elusive she could be, how much her own person.

Discovered how independent and strong-willed she'd grown.

Discovered that she was no longer someone he could

dominate and lead, but instead—given she was his goddess and, courtesy of their past, he was cast as a contrite supplicant—he might very well have to follow.

Regardless, he'd never been more certain of his path.

She continued to regard him suspiciously as she crunched her way through a piece of toast.

He clung to silence. He'd said all he had to—told her his intentions and that he would wait, that he wasn't going away. The ball was in her court; the next move was hers.

Pushing away her empty plate, she patted her lips and goddesslike decreed, "I believe I should speak with my brother."

Letitia hadn't requested any escort on her walk to the old lodge, yet given Christian's statement—of his intentions, no less—she wasn't surprised that he was ambling beside her, easily keeping pace as she marched along.

Despite his forthrightness over said intentions, she had no real belief that she understood his motives. Being well acquainted with his baser traits, she knew it was possible that he was acting out of protectiveness and using their connection to keep her close, to help manage her as matters unfolded.

In men like him, protectiveness toward women like her was ingrained, and while in the past it had grown out of his possessiveness, she could no longer be sure that was still the case.

Could no longer be certain he truly wanted her.

Could not be certain his "intentions" weren't simply a reflection of what he thought he ought to do, ought to feel. How he thought he should now behave with respect to her, the lover he'd effectively jilted.

She wasn't at all pleased with Justin for telling him her secret; whether if left to herself she would ever have told him, she honestly didn't know. That point was now moot because Justin *had* told him—but she didn't, she'd realized, know what else her idiot brother had seen fit to reveal.

Reaching the lodge, she swept through the door with con-siderable force. Christian followed rather more slowly.

Her gaze fell on her brother, seated at the table, about to tuck into a heaped plate of ham and eggs.

She pinned him with a narrow-eyed glare. "How *dare* you?"

Justin eyed her measuringly. "How dare I what?"

"How *dare* you share details of my private life—includ-ing the reasons behind my marriage to Randall, which you swore never to reveal—to *him*." She flung out a hand toward Christian, now blocking the doorway.

Justin shrugged. "Randall's dead. Christian isn't." With his knife, he pointed as if directing her attention. "He's here."

"I *know* he's here, but that gives you no right—I gave you no leave—to divulge my personal secrets!"

Justin frowned, his temper rising to match hers. "Well, someone had to. You hadn't bothered to tell him. Not even after Randall's death!"

"I would have told him *sometime*, but that's not the point!"

"So what is the point?"

"The point is—"

Christian walked forward and pulled out a chair. He didn't wait for permission from Letitia—certainly didn't wait for her to sit—before settling at his ease. Leaning back, patient, he waited.

Letitia paced along one side of the table, raging at her brother across the expanse. Glowering, Justin tracked her movements, his cutlery unused in his hands.

Arms and hands flying, Letitia ranted; scowling blackly, Justin gave as good as he got. For his part, Christian said not one word, far too wise in Vaux ways to attempt to intercede; far better for both to air their tempers, to let the pent-up emotions free. While Letitia might be berating Justin over his "disloyal revelations," that was only her principal com-plaint; if it hadn't been that, she would have been upbraiding him over his attempt to deflect suspicion from her by encouraging it to fix on himself. Justin, meanwhile, although dogged in his defense of Christian's right to know the long-ago truth, was equally irritated by her refusal to accept his grand sacrifice.

Eventually, Christian knew, they'd run down. Letitia, he estimated, had at most a few minutes more left in her. Justin might have greater stamina—not that he would wager on it—but he wasn't truly angry, more irritated with her for calling him to account for a fault that, in his eyes, was hers.

Christian focused on her face, faintly flushed, eyes sparkling. Despite her protestations, he did wonder if she would ever have told him of her own accord. Knowing her pride, knowing how deeply she'd despised Randall, he doubted it.

As he'd predicted, she eventually sighed, and rubbed the center of her forehead. "This is getting us nowhere."

Justin opened his mouth, caught Christian's warning glance and grudgingly shut it. Tightening his grip on his knife and fork, he looked down at his plate. Only to discover that his man, Oscar, clearly a veteran of Vaux affairs, had slipped a cover over the dish.

Without a word, Oscar reached past Justin and whipped the cover off.

Justin grunted his thanks and cut into an egg. "There's no point carrying on. What's done is done—now we have to deal with it."

Having run out of steam, Letitia plopped down on the chair Christian pushed out for her. "I still can't believe you thought I'd killed Randall."

"If you'd been able to hear yourself that night, you wouldn't have any great difficulty." Justin shoveled in some ham, studied her while he chewed. He swallowed and said, "At least Hermione's safe from any further matrimonial machinations."

Letitia nodded.

After their outburst, both needed a moment to recoup. Inwardly smiling, Christian took charge. "Now that we can all think, might I suggest it's time to focus on the problem before us?"

Letitia and Justin turned their heads and regarded him with identical expressions suggesting neither was sure which problem he was alluding to.

He enlightened them. "If Letitia didn't kill Randall—which we know to be fact—and Justin didn't kill Randall—which we also know to be the case—then who *did* kill Randall?"

They both stared at him, then frowns slowly darkened their handsome faces.

"We now know Randall was killed between the time Letitia left him, and the time Justin went to the study to speak with him." For Letitia's benefit, Christian sketched the information from Justin and Pringle that had enabled him to establish that point.

Her frown deepened. "Mellon must know something."

"Possibly. But equally, Randall might have been expecting someone and let them into the house himself. Mellon could well have been en route to his room at the time, and so not have heard the door." Christian looked at Justin. "What do you know of Randall? I never met the man—describe what type of man he was as best you can."

Justin thought as he finished off the last of his ham; pushing away his empty plate, he grimaced. "He was something of an enigma. You imagined he would fit the normal mold—he certainly seemed to outwardly—but the closer you got and the more you learned of him, he . . . just didn't match expectations."

"There were no friends at his funeral," Christian said. "No male acquaintances of any degree."

Justin's brows rose; his gaze grew distant. "Now you mention it, I can't recall ever meeting him with anyone he introduced as a friend. He knew others, of course, and was known by others, but it was all the usual passing acquaintances one has in the clubs. In his case . . . I can't think of anyone I'd name as his friend."

Refocusing on Christian, Justin went on, "That's what I mean about him not meeting expectations. What gentleman of the ton has no friends?"

Christian inclined his head. "Regardless, it had to be a friend—at the very least an acquaintance he trusted—who murdered him, given the position of the body and the two glasses on the table near the hearth."

Justin nodded. "So we need to look for Randall's friends. Whoever and wherever they might be."

"We need to return to London. That was Randall's base— that's where we'll learn more." Considering Justin, Christian frowned. "You, most unfortunately, are our best source of information on Randall. You might not know anything specific—like who his friends were—but you almost certainly have information tucked away in your head, the sort that if we learn a name, you might be able to tell us more."

Justin shrugged. "So I'll return to London with you."

"You can't!" Letitia told him. "Thanks to your earlier efforts, you've succeeded exceedingly well in casting yourself as the murderer."

"Indeed." Christian met Justin's eyes. "And there's a runner haunting Mayfair who's determined to hunt you down."

"So I'll go to ground."

Christian nodded. "The question is: Where?"

"Not at your lodgings—Barton, the runner, has already been there. And you mustn't come near Randall's house," Letitia said. "The little weasel is keeping a watch in the belief the murderer—meaning you—will return to the scene of the crime."

Justin's brows quirked. "I suppose that cuts out my clubs, too."

"And unfortunately Barton knows I'm helping, so Allardyce House won't be safe, either, especially not with my aunts and sisters dropping by whenever the fancy takes them." Christian met Justin's eyes. "If either of my aunts see you, it'll be all over the ton inside an hour."

"Yes, well, that consideration eliminates our aunts,

too." Letitia frowned. "There must be somewhere safe you can go—somewhere we can easily reach you to pick your brains."

They all fell silent, thinking.

Eventually Christian stirred. "As a stop-gap we can use my private club, the Bastion Club. It's in Montrose Place," he added for Justin's benefit. "Ultimately that will come under Barton's eye, too, but for a few days it'll be safe enough. Meanwhile . . . there's an ex-colleague who might agree to give you refuge. If he's still in London and if he's so inclined."

Christian thought for a moment, then nodded. "I'll need to return to London and ask him. If he agrees, I'll send word. Until then, I suggest you remain here." He glanced at Letitia. "As you doubtless counted on, everyone knows that Nunchance is the last place on earth you'll be."

Letitia pulled a face. Justin grinned.

Christian rose. "I'll head back to town immediately."

Letitia bounced up from her chair. "I'll come with you. I need to get back to Hermione." She swooped on Justin and bussed him on the cheek. "Thank you, brother mine, for trying to protect me, however misguided your efforts."

Justin snorted, caught her hand and squeezed it. But he was looking at Christian as he said, "Just take care that in exonerating me, you don't color yourself as the murderer instead."

Christian's lips curved in a wry smile. "As it happens, courtesy of your earlier sterling efforts to throw everyone off the scent, the only way we'll succeed in exonerating you now is by identifying and producing whoever did, in fact, kill Randall."

They left Nunchance within the hour, bowling south in Christian's curricle, his powerful chestnuts between the shafts. A parasol shading her face, Letitia sat back and watched the scenery flash by. Esme would follow in the carriage with her luggage, but for herself . . . she was determined to stick by Christian's side.

She knew him. If she let him, he'd plant her in a drawing room—or in her front parlor—and leave her there while he went out hunting Randall's killer. It might be perverse of her, yet despite the contempt if not outright hatred she'd borne her husband, she felt a real need to see his murderer brought to justice—not solely on Justin's account, but on hers, too. That murder had been committed within her household deeply offended her at some fundamental level.

Murder was not something that could be tolerated in a tonnish house; she was sure that was one of those maxims ladies such as she were brought up to revere.

Regardless, she meant to play an active role in the hunt.

They halted on the road for lunch, but didn't dally. Once they were bowling along again, this time behind a pair of flighty blacks, she said, "You were speaking the literal truth, weren't you—about us having to identify and catch whoever killed Randall in order to exonerate Justin?"

Christian held the horses in as a mail coach rumbled by, then let the reins flow again. "Unfortunately, your brother overlooked a number of factors in scripting his little drama. Clearing him of suspicion from the authorities will be straightforward enough—that we can do with evidence alone."

"But clearing him of suspicion from the ton—clearing his *name* so he'll be accepted in society again and be able to marry well—for that . . ."

"Indeed." With a flick of his wrist, Christian sent the restive pair racing past a lumbering carriage. "To achieve that, we'll need to produce not just factual proof, but the murderer himself. Nothing else will do."

Letitia humphed. "If I know the gossips—and I do— we'll even need to prove that the murderer, whoever he is, doesn't know Justin. Or me. Or even Hermione."

"As none of you know any of Randall's friends, that, at least, shouldn't be too hard."

Letitia mulled over the issue of Randall's friends—the odd circumstance that, after eight years of marriage, she had absolutely no idea who they were. She'd had no interest in her late husband's life—no interest in him; their social paths had remained by her decree disconnected.

Not that Randall had minded.

As if following her train of thought, Christian asked, "Did Randall accompany you to the usual functions?"

"Yes, but only the major ones, or those where he knew certain other guests would be—those with whom he wanted to rub shoulders." She thought back. "He wasn't all that socially inclined, not in tonnish terms, but he did like to be seen, to claim his place, as it were, every now and then."

Another mile swept by, then he asked, "I assumed that he married you for your social connections. Wasn't that the case?"

She grimaced. "I assumed the same, but the answer was yes and no. I was more like . . . oh, a trophy. At least that's how I felt. Not so much a person as an object, something to be acquired and put on a shelf to be admired, but otherwise . . ."

That, she realized, was a reasonably accurate summation of her marriage. There never had been any pretense, at least not between them, that Randall had married her for love, not even for desire.

Unprompted, she murmured, "Our marriage was more like a civil truce. I didn't like him, I didn't respect him, but we'd made an agreement and I stuck to it. And for all that I detested him, so did he."

She wasn't surprised when Christian asked no more, but she knew he had more questions—ones he couldn't, had no right to, put to her. Such as how often Randall had shared her bed. The answer was far less than she'd expected, but Christian didn't need to know that. Didn't need to know that courtesy of her earlier association with him, she'd had the confidence and the ammunition to drive Randall away— and keep him away. He'd never asked her who her lover had been, so he'd never known to whom he was being compared.

All he had known was that he didn't measure up—not in any way.

With a younger brother and more male cousins than she could count, she'd known where the major chink in men's armor was. Reducing Randall to a near impotent state, at least with respect to her, hadn't been too difficult.

She'd gained control of that aspect of her marriage, and had otherwise largely lived a life apart from her husband. Unfortunately that meant . . .

As they rolled into London, she sighed. "I do hope you have some idea of where to search for Randall's friends, for I freely admit I have none."

Christian glanced at her. "No man is an island. Donne was correct. Randall will have had some connections somewhere."

He looked up at the sky. They'd made good time, yet late afternoon was edging into evening. "It's too late to call on that colleague I mentioned. I'll take you back to the house."

Letitia wrapped her shawl more tightly about her as the shadows of the buildings engulfed them. "Hermione and Agnes will be waiting to hear."

They weren't the only ones. After halting briefly in Grosvenor Square to pick up one of his grooms, Christian drove on to South Audley Street. Tossing the reins to his groom with instructions to walk the horses around to the mews behind Grosvenor Square, he alighted and handed Letitia down. As the curricle moved off, he glimpsed a familiar head ducking behind the area railings opposite. Inwardly shaking his head, he turned and climbed the steps to where Mellon, struggling to hide his disapproval, and failing, stood holding the door.

Shrugging off his heavy greatcoat, he left it with the butler, then walked into the front parlor. Letitia wasn't, as he'd expected, seated on one of the sofas regaling Hermione and Agnes with their news. Instead, she stood poised by one of the front windows, peering—glaring—past the lace curtains. "That horrible little man is still there! Did you see?"

Lips quirking, he halted by the sofa opposite the one Agnes and Hermione occupied. "However reluctantly, one has to give him credit for unswerving devotion to his cause." He nodded to Agnes and Hermione.

Letitia humphed, and turned back into the room. Joining him before the sofa, she sat, allowing him to sit, too.

"So Justin's perfectly all right—you spoke with him?" Eyes bright, almost painfully eager, Hermione leaned forward.

Letitia nodded. "The idiot thought he was protecting *me*." She described where Justin had been hiding and what they'd learned from him.

At the end of her recital, she glanced at Christian. "You may as well stay for dinner—if you haven't any other pressing engagement?"

When he inclined his head in acceptance, she rose and headed for the bellpull. "We need to put our heads together and decide what to do next."

He waited while she summoned Mellon and gave the order for an extra place at dinner. He'd have to question Mellon again, but now was not the time. He shifted his gaze to Hermione. She was biting her lower lip, clearly chewing on her thoughts. In the circumstances, she was currently at the top of his interrogation list.

When Mellon retreated and Letitia returned to the sofa, Hermione looked up at her. "So you don't think Justin killed Randall—and you're looking for the real murderer?"

Flopping back down beside Christian, Letitia nodded. "To clear Justin's name completely and beyond question, as we must—the future head of the House of Vaux cannot carry the stigma of being suspected of murder in even the least degree—then we have to produce the real murderer, and have him convicted of the crime."

Mellon returned to announce that dinner was served. They all rose and repaired to the dining room. As he took his seat alongside Letitia's at the end of the table, Christian noted that no expense had been spared—not with the highly polished table, a stunning example of the craftman's art, nor with the silver and crystal, both on the table and on the sideboard against the wall. Expensive artwork, curtains, rugs, and satin-striped upholstery completed the room, along with an elegant crystal chandelier.

Flicking out his napkin, he glanced at Letitia. "Did you entertain much?"

She looked up, then, as he had, looked around the room. "A little, but not as much as I might have." Realizing the significance of his question, she added, "And they were always my friends and acquaintances—the only names Randall ever suggested were politicians or ton figures he wished to meet and talk with, not people he already knew."

Seated opposite Christian, Agnes shook her head. "He never did bring people home." Agnes looked at Letitia. "Not even when you and Hermione were out." She glanced at Christian. "When Letitia takes Hermione with her, I usually remain at home. And people like Randall always overlook the old ladies of the world."

At their peril. From the light in Agnes's eyes, Christian surmised she'd kept a closer watch on Randall—and very likely Letitia and Hermione as well—than any of them knew.

Agnes looked down as the soup course was placed before her. "Sadly, rack my brains though I have, I can't offer any suggestions as to Randall's friends."

"Nor can I." Hermione picked up her soup spoon.

Conversation lagged as they worked their way through the fish course, the entrée, then moved on to dessert. Throughout, Hermione frowned abstractedly at her plate.

Christian waited until the footmen withdrew, then under the table nudged Letitia's knee. She looked at him. When he directed her gaze to Mellon, standing correct and upright behind Randall's empty chair, she blotted her lips with her napkin, then waved an imperious hand. "You may go, Mellon. We won't need anything more."

Mellon would have preferred to stay and satisfy his curiosity—he'd heard their earlier comments about his late master's friends—but he had to bow and withdraw.

When the door closed behind him, Letitia turned to Christian—to discover him regarding Hermione with that steady, gray, impossible-to-escape gaze of his.

Hermione, wrapped in her own thoughts, remained oblivious.

"In order to expose Randall's real murderer—as we must—we need to learn exactly what went on here on the night he was killed." His gaze still on Hermione, Christian laid his napkin on the table.

Recalling that her sister knew something about that night that she'd yet to share, Letitia, too, fixed her gaze on Hermione.

Who finally looked up.

Finding both Letitia and Christian focused on her, Hermione glanced at Agnes, only to see her aunt also waiting patiently to hear what she would say.

Hermione grimaced. She brought her gaze back to Christian's face. After a moment of studying him, she said, "Before I tell you what I know about that night, swear to me that you'll make sure Justin's safe."

Letitia opened her mouth to utter a blanket assurance; Christian stopped her by closing one hand about her wrist.

Holding Hermione's gaze, he said, "I swear on my honor as an Allardyce, and as Dearne, that I will do everything in my power to see your brother cleared of Randall's murder." He arched a brow at Hermione. "Good enough?"

She nodded. "Thank you."

"So what did you see?" Letitia frowned. "And how did you come to see anything at all?"

Christian squeezed her wrist again, then released her. To Hermione, he said, "Start with your evening, before you went to bed."

Hermione looked down at her fingers, smoothing the hem

of her napkin. "Agnes and I had a quiet evening. I was already in bed when Letitia came home." Her gaze flicked up to Christian's face. "My bedroom is above the study." She returned her gaze to the napkin. "I can't hear people *converse* in there, no words, but I can hear loud noises. I heard Letitia railing at Randall—I knew it was something about me, but I didn't know what." She glanced at Letitia. "You kept saying it was nothing, but it was obviously something—enough of a something to have you screeching."

Letitia made a dismissing gesture. "The issue died with Randall. It's . . ."

Hermione arched a brow. "Dead and buried?" She nodded. "I did wonder whether that was, at least in part, behind what I later saw—or thought I saw."

When she didn't immediately go on, Letitia opened her mouth—Christian grasped her wrist and silenced her again. She shot him a weak glare but desisted. Grudgingly.

"So I heard Letitia ranting." Hermione picked up her tale. "Then I heard her slam the study door and storm up the stairs and into her room. I thought, after that, that I'd be able to fall asleep." She paused. "I was just dozing off when I heard Randall and another man talking—I couldn't hear the words, I never can, but I could hear the rumble of their voices. I tried to sleep, but couldn't, then I heard a thud. A heavy thud.

"I listened, but the voices had stopped. I told myself it was the door shutting, or something like that . . . only I knew it wasn't. I know the sounds in that room, and I'd never heard a thud like that—sort of soft but heavy."

Christian asked, "Did you notice the time?"

She shook her head. "My candle was out. I kept trying to fall asleep—I don't know for how long. I kept imagining what that thud might be. I actually thought it might be a dead body. In the end, I knew I wasn't going to sleep until I knew, so I got up to go and see. I thought that the worst that might happen was that Randall might be at his desk—he often worked late. If he saw me, I was going to say I couldn't sleep and was heading to the library for a book. But I had to dress—I wasn't going to get caught by anyone in my dressing gown."

"Did you hear anything while you were dressing?" Christian asked.

"Or going downstairs?" Letitia put in, trying to hurry things along.

Hermione frowned. "No—not until I was on the landing. I didn't use the main stair, but the one in my wing. It comes down in the corridor past the study. When I reached the landing, I heard the study door open. I hadn't taken a candle—I could see well enough—so I crouched down on the landing and looked through the banisters."

She glanced at Letitia, then at Christian. "I saw Justin come out of the study. I didn't see his face—he turned and looked back into the room, then he walked on to the front door." She paused, caught by her memories. "I would have called to him, but he seemed . . . strange. Stunned, I suppose, now I know what he'd done. Even then, I suspected something bad had happened, so I didn't say anything, just watched him open the front door and walk out, then he pulled the door closed behind him."

Straightening in her chair, Hermione paled, but met Christian's eyes gamely. "I waited a little, everything was quiet, then I crept down the stairs and looked into the study. I didn't go in—I could see enough from the doorway. I . . . I thought Justin had killed Randall. It was so *horrible* . . . but I'd never liked Randall—never liked that Letitia had had to marry him no matter how much she pretended it was a love match. And, well, he was dead now—that was obvious. But I didn't want Justin to be caught, so I thought . . . the only thing I could think of doing was to lock the door and slip the key back inside. I hoped it would look like the key had fallen out of the lock later—perhaps while they were beating on the door. I knew no one could possibly think Randall had taken his own life, but I thought having the door look like it was locked from inside would at least confuse things."

Christian grimaced. "In that you succeeded, but Mellon knew Justin had called to see Randall and later left."

"But I didn't know that," Hermione said. "Justin might have just arrived and Randall had let him in—I couldn't tell. Anyway, the key was in the lock, Randall usually kept it there, he sometimes did lock the door—so I locked the door, slid the key back inside, and went back upstairs."

She wrinkled her nose. "I didn't get any sleep, though."

Christian could imagine. He considered, matching Hermione's story with Justin's, then he looked at Letitia, frowning in concern at Hermione, then at Agnes, who was patting Hermione's hand.

For her part, Hermione seemed relieved. It was she who asked, "So what will you do now?"

Both Letitia and Agnes joined her in fixing inquiring gazes on him.

Deciding no harm could come of sharing his deductions, he glanced at the door, confirmed it was shut, then in a voice that wouldn't carry, said, "I believe what happened was that after Letitia left Randall—while Justin was reading in the library after having dismissed Mellon—someone else called on Randall, someone he was expecting, given Mellon didn't hear the doorbell. His visitor was someone he knew, someone he trusted. That person sat in the chair by his study fire and they shared a glass of brandy."

"So the person was almost certainly a man," Letitia pointed out. "Very few women drink brandy."

He inclined his head. "So this man and Randall chatted amiably—Hermione heard no shouting. Then Randall rose, headed for his desk, presumably to fetch something—and the man picked up the poker and hit him on the head. Randall fell, dead. His murderer dropped the poker, then—presumably via the front door—left the house."

All three of his listeners were nodding.

"So," he concluded, "our next step is to learn who the friend Randall entertained that night might be. And to confirm, if we can, how he got into the house, and how he left it."

All three women's expressions grew determined.

"And whoever he is," Hermione said, "*he's* Randall's murderer."

Letitia was pleased Christian had shared his thoughts so freely—without her having to drag them from him—but what she now wanted to know was how he proposed to learn who Randall's mysterious friend-cum-murderer was. However, not wanting to encourage Hermione to think she could play any role in their hunt, she waited with what patience she could muster until Hermione and Agnes retired.

The instant the door shut behind them, she swung to face Christian, once more seated beside her on the sofa in her parlor. "How—"

He pulled her into his arms. Into a kiss. Not a scorching one. One she might, if she'd put her mind to it, have resisted.

But she didn't resist. Instead found herself melting into his embrace. Mentally cursed, but by then it was too late.

He kissed her until her wits had long flown, until she was breathless, and achy, and thinking of things she'd had no intention of thinking about—sins she'd had no intention of committing—until he'd kissed her.

When he lifted his head and looked into her eyes, his heavy-lidded with the passion and desire that always—always—lay between them, she could barely marshal one coherent thought. And that one . . .

She fought against the drugging tide, tried to reorient—knew she had questions she wanted to ask, but couldn't lay her mind to any of them. Blinking, she tried to reassemble her wits.

Before she succeeded he was on his feet, and she was on hers, and he was towing her to the door.

She couldn't even manage a frown. "Where are we going?" Even to her ears she sounded more interested than scandalized.

He glanced back as he opened the door. "Upstairs. To your room."

When she stared at him, faintly stunned, he raised his brows. "You didn't think I was leaving, did you?"

She honestly didn't know what she'd thought.

And before she could decide what she *should* think—of his presumption, of his high-handed, arrogant assumption that she would, after just one kiss, be sufficiently besotted to fall in with his plans . . . she had.

"This room?" He pointed to her door.

She started to nod, stopped herself, but he'd already opened the door and was towing her inside.

And then the door was shut and she was in his arms, and nothing else mattered.

She was distantly aware that that shouldn't be so, but as her clothes fell like autumn leaves to the floor and his clever hands and even cleverer mouth found her bare skin, she couldn't remember why.

Couldn't summon a single reason against indulging with him.

Couldn't see why she shouldn't let her starved soul free, let it rejoice in the pure sensuality he brought to her. That he offered with both hands, with his mouth, with his body.

That he fed her with each kiss—scorching and possessive now—that reached her through each touch, each explicit caress, each frankly possessive stroking of her valleys and planes.

In the heat and the fire that followed, in the familiar passions that she and he ignited, that raged as they always had between them, cindering reservations and all ability to think in a conflagration of need. Overwhelming and sustaining. Demanding and succoring. Needing and caring.

The give and take between them had never been complicated. Always direct, always unmasked. Every time they came together, she could only glory that that hadn't changed—not in the least.

She knew why she lay back and welcomed him into her body. She wasn't so sure she understood why he was there. But after the eight lonely years she'd spent in that bed, she was in no mood to deny herself the absolute irrefutable proof that her sensual side still lived.

That the passionate self who delighted in physical pleasure that she'd buried when she'd married Randall hadn't died.

Had been resurrected in all her feminine glory.

By him—her long-ago lover.

Sunk deep in the slick heat of her luscious body, her long legs about his hips, her long, svelte form undulating in uninhibited concert beneath him, Christian could only close his eyes and give thanks that—in this at least—she wasn't about to deny him. Wasn't about to shut herself off from him.

He hadn't been sure. Hadn't known whether she would suddenly pull back—whether she would let him remain this close while she made up her mind.

To his mind, this was his only hold on her—the only certain way, the only certain times, he would have to reassure her. To make her believe in him again, that he would always be there, there to love her every night and every day.

She raced up the peak, and dragged him with her. No matter how firmly he tried to hold back, she knew how to command him, how to shred his control. How to take his hand and *leap*—over the edge, into the void, into the pulsing heart of their passion.

They burned together, shattered together, gasping, clutching, holding tight as they flew . . . then clinging as they slowly spiraled down to earth again.

Into each other's arms again.

If last night had seen him take a new direction, tonight had given him hope. As he disengaged and, with a smothered groan, rolled onto his back and gathered her to him, felt her curl against him, he couldn't imagine what he would do if she tried to remain apart from him. If she decided against him and tried to cut their ties.

A week or so ago when she'd come to him for help, he hadn't known that what ruled him now still lived within him. Now he did. Now he felt it, knew it—would, could, no longer deny it. Had no wish to deny it. A week of being with her again had brought him, if not precisely full circle, then to a similar place, a similar state of emotional acceptance to that he'd reached twelve years ago, yet now he was older, wiser, more appreciative of his needs, and hers.

She had to see—he prayed she would see—that if twelve years ago they'd been an ideal couple, now they were even more so, not less. That the years had given them both more depth, greater strength.

Deeper passions.

"What do you plan to do next?"

Her words breached the fog of pleasured aftermath. Clearly the years had also given her a greater ability for recuperation. "I . . ." He replayed her demand, heard the conciseness in her tone, realized she expected to be told—and she was testing to see if he would share. "I need to question all the staff, Mellon and the footmen I spoke with earlier included. Someone must have let Randall's mysterious friend in, or if not, have some experience of him from some other time."

He hesitated, then, adhering to the new script he'd written wherein he held nothing back from her, said, "But first, I should call on that colleague of mine." He glanced at her face, through the dimness met her eyes. "I don't know if he's in town, or has resigned his commission and gone to the country, but if he's here and agrees, he's one of the few I would trust to hide Justin, and he has the resources to help our investigation in other ways, too—if he's free and so inclined."

She studied his eyes. "Who is this colleague?"

He drew a deep breath, let it out with, "His name's Dalziel.

I'll go to his office tomorrow morning—he's usually at his desk reasonably early."

"I'll come, too." Her eyes were mysterious, but her tone carried a warning.

He nodded, and gathered her closer. Settling his cheek on her hair, he meekly said, "We can go after breakfast."

Chapter 9

It was just after ten the next morning when Christian ushered Letitia into the anteroom of an office buried in the labyrinthine depths of Whitehall. Sweeping in, head high, she noted the nondescript clerk who glanced up, then came to his feet in a rush.

"Ma'am—I think you must be 1—" The clerk broke off as Christian followed her through the door. "Ah . . . Major Allardyce. I'll . . . ah." The clerk's eyes went again to Letitia, then returned to Christian. "Shall I see if he's in?"

Letitia found the clerk's performance revealing, but she had an ace up her sleeve. "Kindly inform your master—I believe he calls himself Dalziel—that Lady Letitia Randall née Vaux is here to see him, together with Lord Dearne."

The clerk all but goggled at her. She was aware of the sharp glance Christian shot her, but when the clerk sent him an imploring look, he endorsed her request with a nod.

"Ah . . . ." Still the clerk hesitated. "If you'd like to take a seat. . . ?" He gestured to three bare wooden chairs lined up along the wall opposite a plain wooden door.

She turned her head, examined the chairs. "I don't believe that will prove necessary." She looked back at the clerk, saw him still dithering and, exasperated, made a shooing motion with one hand. "Go."

The clerk went.

Fascinated, Christian eyed Letitia, but her face gave nothing away. Could she really know. . . ? He'd assumed he would have to introduce her, explain his connection to Dalziel . . . he recalled she'd known he'd been off spying. He hadn't told her, but she'd mentioned a certain gentleman who'd crooked his finger . . . somehow she'd found out about Dalziel. He turned to look at his ex-commander's door.

Just as it was yanked open.

Dalziel filled the doorway. He stared across the ante-room, not at Christian—at Letitia. Not a flicker of emotion disturbed his austere features, yet Christian could clearly hear his mental cursing.

Letitia regarded him with haughty calm. "There you are. I assume you have time to see us?"

Dalziel's gaze flicked to Christian, then returned to Letitia's face. "Of course. Pray come in."

He stood back, holding the door. Letitia swept past him and entered the inner sanctum. Christian followed more slowly. When he drew level with Dalziel, his ex-commander met his eyes.

Dalziel's eyes were a deep dark brown; reading them was never easy. In this case, however, Christian could see his exasperation—and his resignation—quite clearly.

Closing the door behind his clerk, who scurried out—a mouse escaping the presence of two lions and a lioness—Dalziel waved them to the chairs before his desk. As he sank into the chair behind it, he regarded them stonily. "This had better be serious."

Letitia raised her brows, haughtily superior. "It is. Naturally. As you've no doubt heard, my husband was brutally murdered and my brother is suspected of the crime."

Dalziel regarded her expressionlessly for a moment, then quietly corrected, "Stands accused of murder."

Letitia frowned, not understanding the distinction.

Dalziel glanced at Christian. "I heard yesterday afternoon." To Letitia, he said, "The authorities have sworn out a warrant for the arrest of Lord Justin Vaux. The charge is that he killed his brother-in-law, your husband, George Randall."

Letitia looked exasperated. "*Drat* them! Couldn't they wait?"

Glancing from one to the other, Dalziel raised his brows. "From which I take it you're here to tell me Justin didn't do it, and there's some mystery over who did."

Letitia nodded. "Yes. Precisely. Helpful of you to grasp the facts so quickly."

There was a hint—just a hint—of sarcasm in her tone; Christian knew her well enough to know she'd intended it.

Dalziel had heard it; he hesitated, but—to Christian's immense surprise— declined to respond.

Or declined to prod a thus far rational Vaux?

The notion that his ex-commander was well acquainted with the Vaux was confirmed by Dalziel himself. His gaze on Letitia, he said, "You may spare me the protestations regarding Justin's innocence. I may not know him well, but I know enough of him to accept that it's highly unlikely he committed the crime as I heard it described."

He shifted his dark gaze to Christian. "Tell me what you know."

Christian complied, chapter and verse. Dalziel was particularly interested in Pringle's report.

"That," he said, "isn't common knowledge. Indeed, it weakens the authorities' case considerably—they can't have Justin bludgeoning Randall to death in a fit of manic temper on the one hand, only to say that he actually killed Randall first with a gentle, lucky tap on the head."

"Exactly." Letitia went on, "Given that, along with everything else, it seems patently obvious that Randall was killed by some mysterious friend who saw him that night between me and Justin."

Dalziel regarded her, then glanced at Christian. "So who was this mysterious friend?"

"That," Christian said, "is what we don't know." He related what little they'd learned from Justin, and his own observations thus far. "So finding who Randall called friend isn't as simple as one might suppose."

Dalziel was frowning. "That's . . . very strange."

"And if you add the suspicion that Randall was attempting to lure Justin into debt, it becomes even stranger." Letitia regarded Dalziel severely. "But the principal point here is that in order to clear Justin's name within the ton, we need to not just prove he didn't do the deed, but, as matters now stand—and I assume the swearing of that warrant will only make things even worse—we need to produce Randall's real killer."

Still frowning, Dalziel looked at Christian. "We need to learn who else had reason to want Randall dead."

Christian caught his gaze. "We?"

Dalziel's lips twisted wryly. "The royal 'we'—you, me, and anyone else we can call in. Who else is in town?"

"Trentham. I doubt anyone else will have come up yet."

Dalziel nodded. "Enough to go on with."

"We have another problem—Justin is our sole albeit poor source of reliable information on Randall. He's been closest to him—indeed watching him—for the last several years."

"Eight years," Letitia supplied. "Since I married Randall."

Christian inclined his head. "So we need Justin here, not at Nunchance—"

"But you have nowhere to hide him." Dalziel held Christian's gaze for an instant, then looked at Letitia, at her hopeful, expectant expression. He sighed. "Very well—I'll undertake to house the whelp in secret."

Letitia flashed him a brilliant smile. "Excellent."

Dalziel looked back at Christian. "Tell him to come to your club—I'll whisk him away from there. He'll need to leave Nunchance in the evening so he'll reach London in the small hours." He glanced again at Letitia. "His description will have been circulated to the watch, and very likely to all the posting inns. He'll need to be careful."

Letitia nodded. "I'll write and tell him."

"As for the rest"—Dalziel transferred his attention to Christian—"I suggest we meet at the Bastion Club." He glanced at a clock on a nearby cabinet. "Shall we say three o'clock? I'll see what I can learn from the authorities, if they have any more information that might give us a clue as to who the real murderer might be."

He rose. Letitia and Christian came to their feet.

"Until three, then." Letitia gave Dalziel her hand.

He took it, bowed, then released her.

As she turned and swept to the door, Christian caught Dalziel's eye. "No further sign of our old friend?"

He was referring to a traitor buried deep within the ton; their group of ex-spies had run across his tracks several times over the last year, but despite their—and Dalziel's—best efforts, he'd managed to evade them, twice by committing murder.

Dalziel shook his head. "Not a whisper." He looked around the room. "I need to be here for a few weeks more." His lips twisted as he turned back to Christian. "This latest start of the Vaux should help fill in the time."

Christian saluted. "I'll let Trentham know about the meeting. He'll be there."

Dalziel nodded. "I'll see you then."

He resat at his desk; Christian headed for the door.

Following Letitia into the anteroom, Christian shut the door behind him. He was, he realized, on the cusp of solving a mystery that had plagued the Bastion Club members for years. Dalziel wasn't Dalziel's real name. His identity had always tantalized them; although they'd discovered any number of people who knew it, they'd never been able to persuade any to divulge it. Now, although Dalziel—Royce Whoever-he-was—had avoided any mention of his address, presumably where he intended to hide Justin, obviously Justin would shortly learn it, and thus learn his identity.

Even more obviously, Letitia already knew it.

He smiled benignly at the clerk, and rather more delightedly at her. "Come." He waved her to the outer door. "Let's find a hackney to take us back to Mayfair."

* * *

"No, I will *not* tell you his real name." Letitia shook her head and stubbornly set her lips.

Exasperated, Christian slumped back against the hackney's seat. "Why, for heaven's sake? It's patently obvious you know it—that you know him, Royce Whoever-he-is. That quite a few ladies of the ton know who he is. Why can't we know?"

"It's not a matter of keeping his name a secret. That's not the point."

He cast her a saber-edged glance. "What is the point?"

She heaved a huge sigh. "The point is that mentioning his name, whether to his face or otherwise, anywhere in the ton and, I suspect, even beyond, is forbidden. Absolutely not done."

He stared at her. "Why?"

"Because it was so decreed years ago—even before my come-out. It was one of those things my aunts instructed me in before I came to town. I don't know exactly how long the edict has been in place, but there you have it—anyone caught breaking the rule can be assured of instant ejection from the ton."

He frowned. "Is this one of the Almack's patronesses' rules?"

"No, although they certainly support it. It was a rule—an edict—laid down by all the most powerful ladies of the ton, and, as I heard it, many of the gentlemen agreed. It's been in force for . . . well, it must be something like fifteen years."

He couldn't fathom it. After a few minutes of slow rocking through the traffic, he asked—begged rather plaintively, "Can't you just whisper it to me?"

"No!" She frowned at him severely. "No one speaks his name—that's the rule. Aside from anything else, he would know."

She wasn't going to change her mind.

He heaved a huge sigh. He'd got so *close*.

The carriage slowed. They'd reached South Audley Street.

Letitia glanced at him. "I can't see why you're so exercised—you'll learn the truth soon enough."

Before he could question her further, the carriage halted and she leaned forward and opened the door. "I'll meet you in Montrose Place at three. Until then . . ." A footman had come down the steps to assist her; she gave him her hand and alighted. On the pavement, she looked back at Christian. "I'm going to circulate and do my best to play down the rumors of Justin's guilt."

He hesitated, then nodded and saluted in farewell. Dalziel's news about the warrant had shaken her; she no doubt wished to ascertain how widely known that development was.

With a nod she swung away—then halted, stared along the street. All but hissed. "That damned runner! Did I mention I found him in the library this morning? I've given orders he's not to be admitted without my express permission, or unless he has a warrant, or both. If he wants to keep watch on the scene of the crime, he can damn well do it from outside."

With another fulminating glare, she swung away, forged up the steps and swept through the door Mellon was holding open.

Christian watched the door close, then smiled. "St. James," he called to the jarvey on the box. It was time to do a little social scouting of his own.

They met as arranged, delighting Gasthorpe and his staff, who were feeling rather redundant with so little to do.

Tea and ginger biscuits appeared in the library where Christian, Letitia, and Tristan gathered; the "no females beyond the front parlor" rule was long dead. While Letitia poured, Christian outlined for Tristan what they'd learned from Justin and Hermione, how the events on the night of the murder now appeared, and briefly detailed their meeting with Dalziel.

He'd barely finished when a familiar heavy knock

sounded on the front door. A moment later Gasthorpe entered to announce, "Mr. Dalziel."

A misnomer if ever there was one; they may not know his name, yet of one thing they were certain—Dalziel was one of them.

He walked in, his eyes briefly meeting theirs. He exchanged nods with Letitia, accepted a cup and saucer from her, then she handed the rest of the cups around and they sat and got down to business.

Dalziel spoke first. "I contacted the Bow Street magistrate in charge of the case. He and his minions are convinced Justin did the deed. A warrant for his arrest has indeed been sworn, and a runner, Barton, has been assigned to hunt him down."

Letitia grimaced but didn't comment—to the relief of all three men.

Christian quickly, succinctly, listed the facts they knew, establishing the likelihood that Randall was killed by someone he knew, most likely a friend, who'd visited the study between Letitia leaving it and Justin entering.

"It sounds as if he expected his killer." Tristan glanced at Letitia. "Just to cover the obvious, have you checked his diary?"

Letitia shook her head. "He didn't keep one."

Christian frowned. "Not at all? No address book even?"

"Nothing. I don't know how he managed, but he kept all that sort of thing in his head."

Dalziel raised his brows. "Not so hard if you don't have many friends."

"He must have had some," Christian said. "We need to learn who."

"We need to make a list." Tristan rose and, taking his cup, went to sit at the library desk. He pulled out a sheet of paper, checked the pen, then dipped it in the ink pot. "Friends." He wrote. "Need to identify." He looked down at his handiwork. "I'll ask around the clubs. Given I'm in no way connected with the Vaux, I might learn more than you." He looked at Christian.

"I'll see what I can learn via other avenues," Dalziel put in.

Tristan and Christian exchanged a glance, but forebore to ask what other avenues their ex-commander had in mind.

"With any luck," Letitia said, "once he's had time to think of it, Justin might, by the time he reaches here, have remembered something more."

"That covers the direct approach," Dalziel said. "For the indirect, what do we know of Randall himself—his background, family?" He looked at Letitia.

She met his gaze. A long moment passed, then she pulled a face. "You're not going to believe it—in hindsight it seems quite amazing—but I know of no family. None. As for his background . . ." She raised a helpless hand. "I know our man of business looked into his financial state before our marriage, but other than that . . . he was educated, well-presented, was established in our circles, was wealthy and personable enough." She paused, sipped. "I suppose we saw no reason to look further."

"So . . ." Dalziel's voice had grown softer—more intent. "No family known, no school, no university, no connections known." He raised his brows, met Christian's gaze. "Our man becomes more and more of a mystery."

Tristan had been frowning. "Place of birth?"

Letitia shook her head. "Not even that." She paused, then added, "I can't even tell you which county he hailed from— he never said, never even dropped a clue that I recall."

Dalziel looked at Tristan, who obediently dipped the pen and started writing. "So we've lots more to learn about Randall's personal background." He switched his gaze to Letitia. "What about his financial background? He was wealthy, so where did his money come from? Was he involved in any schemes—investments, developments? You mentioned your family's man of business had checked earlier."

She nodded. "I'm sure he'll have some of those answers, at least as things were eight years ago."

Christian caught Dalziel's eye. "If we want to investigate Randall's finances we should use Montague."

Dalziel nodded.

"Heathcote Montague," Letitia stated, "and his father before him, have always handled the Vaux family affairs—it was he who looked into Randall's financial state."

"Perfect." Dalziel set down his empty cup. "We can rely on Montague to ferret out whatever there is to find in Randall's financial dealings."

Tristan was busily scribbling. Christian said, "I'll go and see Montague."

"I'll come, too." Letitia reached for a ginger biscuit. "He'll want my permission before he speaks of Vaux family business."

The men all nodded.

"Which brings us to the connected subject of Randall's will." Dalziel cocked a brow at Letitia.

She looked taken aback, then frowned, as did Christian. "Yet more oddity—the funeral was days ago and yet we haven't heard a word of any will. What *is* going on?"

The three men exchanged glances.

Christian leaned forward, setting down his cup. "Do you know who Randall's solicitor was?"

To his relief, Letitia nodded. "Griswade, Griswade, Meecham and Tappit. They're in Lincoln's Inn Fields."

"So," Tristan said, writing, "they're on our list to be visited, too."

Letitia brushed crumbs from her fingers, her expression unimpressed. "I'll inquire about Randall's will."

Christian made a mental note to go with her.

"Right." Sitting back, Dalziel steepled his fingers. "We've avenues to pursue—facts to assemble. What about motive?"

When Letitia raised her brows, Christian elaborated, "Money, power, or passion—Randall will have been killed for one or the other."

"Or any combination thereof," Dalziel added.

"Power seems unlikely," Tristan suggested. "A prime element of power, at least in our world, is influence. If he had no friends . . ."

"He liked to meet and be seen with powerful people," Letitia said, "but I never sensed he had any interest in exploiting such acquaintances. In using them for anything." She frowned. "He just didn't seem interested in developing such connections."

Dalziel caught Christian's eye and shook his head. "The more we learn of George Randall, the less he seems to conform to any recognizable type. For someone who, as I understand it, presented as unremarkable, he seems to have led a highly eccentric existence."

Christian nodded. "So if power wasn't involved, then leaving aside the obvious—money—is there any hint this might be a crime of passion?"

Dalziel snorted. "Other than the Vaux being intricately involved?"

Christian's lips quirked; he inclined his head "Other than that."

Letitia narrowed her eyes at them both, but her heart wasn't in her glare. After a moment she said, "I honestly can't see Randall being involved in any situation that might have given rise to a grand passion in another—not enough for that other, or even someone associated with them, to kill him."

Dalziel arched a brow. "Are you sure you're not biased?"

She shot him another look, but shook her head. "No. I don't think so. It's not that . . ." She frowned at the biscuit plate—now empty—then sighed. "Randall wasn't . . . well, like us. While I routinely gave thanks for that, he simply didn't have the same drive."

They all knew precisely which drive she was referring to, and given her beauty, her unquestionable desirability—her temper notwithstanding—that, too, rated as odd.

Dalziel rubbed his temple. He glanced at Christian. "You

see what I mean—this man, the bits we keep learning of him don't mesh into any recognizable whole."

Letitia was still frowning. "Justin might know with more certainty, but I'm *almost* completely certain Randall never had a mistress—at least not while we were wed. That simply wasn't where his interests lay."

"If there's any long-term connection, it's likely to be mentioned in his will," Tristan said, still busily making notes.

"But if his interests didn't lie in that direction"—Dalziel fixed Letitia with an interrogatory look—"what was his principal focus in life?"

She answered readily. "Business. He was always involved in this or that—even that night, he cried off from a dinner because he wanted to attend to some business."

Dalziel sat up. "Did he have any business associates?"

Letitia dashed his hopes. "When I say 'business,' I mean letters, papers, documents. He was forever in his study poring over some report or proposal. He often worked late into the night, dealing with such things." She paused, then added, "I think he acted as his own man of business. I never heard of anyone calling who might be such a person."

"I'll check with the butler," Christian said. "He should know."

Dalziel nodded. "So as far as we can see at present, motive appears to be the most usual, and most obvious—money. In some way or form."

He glanced around, but no one disagreed.

"So we need to learn who stands to profit from Randall's death."

"Even better," Christian said, "who profits from Randall's death *now*."

"True." Dalziel nodded. "If money's the motive, there's likely some reason he was killed at that time."

"At that meeting between associates." Tristan looked up from scanning his list. "So when will we meet again?"

They discussed who would do what, when, and decided to reconvene in two days' time.

Letitia rose, pulling on her gloves. "Justin should be in London by then, so we'll be able to see if anything we learn means something more to him."

"Meanwhile"—Dalziel straightened his long legs and got to his feet—"while we all have our avenues to pursue, the most pertinent aspect is—"

"Who stood to benefit from Randall's sudden death." Letitia nodded regally to Dalziel and Tristan. "Gentlemen— I'll see you in two days."

She turned to the door and Christian, who struggled to hide a grin; if Dalziel had thought he would be in charge, he was fast learning otherwise. She arched a brow at him. "I thought to go and see Montague tomorrow morning."

He nodded. "I'll call for you at ten."

Airily she replied, "I'll see you then. My aunts and their families are dining in South Audley Street tonight—I must oversee the preparations."

With a graceful inclination of her head that included them all, she swept to the door.

Christian inwardly debated, but in the end let her go. Given the upheaval of the last days, a little time apart might be wise.

They met again the next morning, and journeyed into the city, to Heathcote Montague's office within a stone's throw of the Bank of England.

Christian had sent a note the previous afternoon. Montague was waiting, ready to greet them—to express his condolences to Letitia and bow to Christian.

He ushered them into his office, waited until they'd settled in the chairs before his massive desk, then he sat in the chair behind it and opened the file box that waited on his blotter. "Dreadful business, but I understand there's some question about your late husband's finances."

"Indeed." Letitia set her reticule in her lap and waved at Christian beside her. "You may speak freely before Lord Dearne."

"Excellent. Well, I looked up the research I did on Mr. Randall at the time of your marriage, my lady. Eight years ago, I admit I was still in my father's shadow somewhat, but all the relevant issues"—he studied a document he extracted from the box—"appear to have been covered. Since then, of course, I haven't had reason to inquire into Mr. Randall's finances—he wasn't a client of mine." He glanced at them. "What is it you wanted to know?"

Letitia glanced at Christian, a clear invitation to lead the questioning.

"I understand," he said, looking at Montague, "that Randall was very wealthy at the time of his marriage. From where did that wealth derive?"

Montague briefly glanced at the contents of his box. "Ah, yes, here it is—a very sound fortune consisting primarily of conservative financial instruments of one sort or another, holdings in the funds, and some very solid investments."

Christian nodded. "But where did Randall's money initially come from? The seed capital, as it were? By your account, at the time of his marriage he had large sums of money sitting in various deposits—but where did he get that money in the first place?"

Montague blinked. For the first time in all the years Christian had known him, he appeared at a loss—momentarily. Then he frowned and delved back into his box. "That's a very good question. . . ." He eventually unearthed a sheet of paper. Straightening his glasses, he read it. His frown deepened. "I understood—well, assumed in the face of nothing speaking to the contrary—that it came from his family?" He directed a questioning look at Christian.

Who shook his head. "For various reasons—including that we know of no family—that doesn't seem likely. Ton or gentry, a family with that level of wealth would have been more widely known. Do you have any information on his family and background?"

Montague now looked troubled. He went back into the box and came up with another document. "Randall attended

Hexham Grammar School. I didn't do the search for his birth certificate myself, but I have it recorded that he hailed from Hexham." Lowering the sheet, he looked at Christian. "Given he went to the grammar school—I believe it has an excellent reputation—I assume that means the family has, or had, a certain social and financial standing."

"Normally that's true, but there are exceptions." Christian glanced at Letitia, who was as puzzled as Montague. "Randall may have attended the school on a scholarship. Many larger grammar schools have such things."

He looked at Montague. "Clearly we need to dig much deeper into Randall's background, but at least you've given us a place to start—Hexham Grammar School. We'll follow that up, but we have an even more urgent need to learn of his current financial state. We need to know of any recent activities, where his money was at the time of his death, where his income derived from, if he was involved in any scheme, any development, whether he'd gone into business in any way whatever, whether he'd made any unusual transactions in recent days—in short, every possible detail of his recent life that had anything to do with money."

Montague looked at them, then beamed. "You've come to the right place."

"Well," Christian said as the hackney they'd hailed rumbled out of the city, "that certainly confirms Dalziel's observation—the more we learn of your late husband, the more a man of mystery he becomes."

Letitia frowned. "I'm not at all thrilled to discover how very little I knew of him. It seems rather bizarre in hindsight, but . . . well, I suppose we all took him at face value."

"I'm surprised your father—if not your aunts—didn't demand to know all about his family."

Letitia grimaced. "They probably did, but that would have been after we were married, and Papa would just have scowled, growled and told them to go away. He asked Montague to check Randall's finances—that, after all, was the point of the marriage—but as for family . . . as I said, Randall was perfectly presentable, and in the prevailing circumstances, not to say panic, his ancestors were a great deal less relevant."

After a moment of trying to imagine it, Christian asked, "What about the wedding? He must have had family or friends there—a groomsman at least."

But Letitia shook her head. "We were married very privately, here in town. Justin was his groomsman." She grimaced. "That was mostly my doing. It was a travesty of a marriage—it seemed appropriate it commence with a travesty of a wedding. Randall wasn't concerned. The story we put about was that it was an out-and-out love match and we were so urgent to tie the knot we wouldn't wait for a big wedding to be organized."

"That must have gone down well with your aunts."

"Not to mention all our many connections. But by the time they learned of it, all was done and finished. They grumbled a bit, but . . ." She shrugged.

Christian studied her expression, serene now, but he could imagine what she must have felt—a lady of her nature, and a Vaux besides—to make do with such, as she'd termed it, a travesty of a wedding. It would have been the antithesis of her dreams.

He made a mental note—a vow—for later. If he got the chance. If she gave him the chance.

The hackney swayed as it turned into Trafalgar Square, reminding him of their unexpected destination. He frowned. "I don't understand why you're so keen to share this with Dalziel immediately."

She was peering out of the window. "Because he might well have contacts in Hexham who can make inquiries at the grammar school."

He frowned. "Do you know that he does?"

"No. I suspect that he might." She turned her head and met his gaze. "Let's just go and tell him and see."

Dalziel's clerk looked up as they entered. He didn't wait

to be asked but immediately rose and went to tap on Dalziel's door. He was back in seconds to bow them into his master's presence.

Immersed in paperwork, Dalziel signed a sheet, then rose. Once Letitia sat, he subsided again and fixed her with a patently false mild look. "Yes?"

Without embellishment, she related what they'd learned from Montague. "So, you see, the place we need to start asking questions about Randall's family is in Hexham." She fixed Dalziel with a pointed look. "I thought you might know how to make inquiries there without Christian having to travel all that way."

His expression unreadable, Dalziel held her gaze for a pregnant moment, then straightened. "Consider it done. The grammar school will have records. I'll get whatever there is in them sent down."

Letitia beamed. "Excellent."

Dalziel looked less pleased. "Is there anything else?"

His servile tone suggested he fully expected to be asked to supply cream buns for their next meeting. Seeing Letitia's eyes start to narrow, Christian stepped in—before she could take his ex-commander up on his unvoiced offer. "I've sent word to Justin—he'll come down to London tonight, to the club."

Dalziel looked at him and nodded. "I'll whisk him away tomorrow night. It might be useful to have him at our meeting tomorrow afternoon."

Letitia rose, gathering her reticule. "Have you learned anything else about Randall?"

"Not yet." Dalziel met Christian's eyes as they both got to their feet. "What's rather more surprising is the answers I'm *not* getting." He didn't elaborate, but nodded to them both. "I'll see you tomorrow at four."

Christian followed Letitia from the office. As they emerged into the corridor outside the anteroom, he murmured, "Hexham, hmm? Yet another man of mystery."

Letitia smiled, but refused to say more.

*   *   *

She was not smiling later that afternoon when they arrived at the offices of Griswade, Griswade, Meecham and Tappit in Lincoln's Inn Fields to be informed that, yes, while the solicitors had been notified of the unexpected demise of Mr. Randall, the partner who dealt with his estate—Mr. Meecham—was presently away attending another client in Scotland and wouldn't be back until late that night.

Letitia subjected the head clerk, a wizened individual, to her most haughty stare. "Can't someone—Griswade, Griswade, or Tappit, for instance—read the will in Meecham's absence?"

The clerk cast a nervous glance at the closed doors around his station. "They could, ma'am—but they've declined."

"Declined?"

Before matters grew too fraught, Christian stepped from behind Letitia to stand alongside her at the railing behind which the clerk was perched at his raised desk. "Waiting for Meecham's return seems an unnecessary delay, given the will is unlikely to be complex. Randall was buried nearly a week ago."

Again the clerk glanced around, then he leaned nearer and lowered his voice. "It was the runner that did it. All ready to come and read the will after the funeral, Mr. Tappit was, as was right and proper, until that red-breast turned up on the doorstep and demanded to see it."

Letitia stiffened.

"Did he see it?" Christian quickly asked. He grasped Letitia's elbow.

The clerk sniffed. "Of course not. Mr. Tappit and Mr. Griswade both told him no—and when he pushed and pestered, telling them it was a case of foul murder and all, well, they decided it would be better—more appropriate—to wait until Mr. Meecham got back and let him handle it, he being the one who knew the client and his affairs."

Christian squeezed Letitia's elbow in warning; it sounded as if Meecham was the one they needed to see anyway. "Very well." He fixed the clerk with a hard gaze. "Please convey to your masters that once Meecham returns, the reading of Mr. Randall's will cannot be further delayed. Its contents are, unsurprisingly, of pressing interest to Lady Randall, and her friends."

He imbued the last words with quiet significance.

Beside him, Letitia, her spine ramrod straight, looked down her aristocratic nose at the clerk. "Please tell Mr. Meecham that I will expect to see him tomorrow morning. I, and Lord Dearne, will be expecting him."

The clerk all but curtsied in his fluster. "Indeed, my lady. Of course, my lady. I'll be sure to tell him."

Christian caught the clerk's eye as he stepped back from the rail and uttered just one word. "Do."

Letitia swung around and he released her; he fell into step protectively behind her as, head high, she made her exit.

Chapter 10

Later that evening Christian sat in Letitia's parlor, sipping brandy while she sipped tea. On the sofa opposite, Hermione sat idly dreaming, while beside her Agnes industriously knotted a fringe.

It was a quiet moment, one to savor at the end of a long day.

He glanced at Letitia beside him. Relaxed, she'd slipped off her slippers and drawn her feet up beneath her skirts. Agnes had primmed her lips at the informality, but hadn't said anything. For himself, he was pleased that Letitia had patently reverted to her long-ago unconsciousness of him.

After considering those long, curled legs for several moments, he let his gaze travel slowly upward, to her face. As she sipped, he realized her mind was not as relaxed as her limbs; her gaze hard and sharp, her eyes were fixed unseeing on the rug. It wasn't their previous interlude on said rug she was mentally reviewing; the evolving situation over Randall—the continuing revelations that underscored how little she'd known him—was seriously bothering her.

Understandably, yet there wasn't anything she could do about it, which was what, he suspected, lay behind her suppressed ire.

Having to swallow the delay over the reading of Randall's will, even if only for a day, and the further irritations of Mellon having—without her knowledge or consent—taken it upon himself to inform Randall's solicitors, and Barton's never-ending presence outside the house, had contributed to the pressure building within her.

That, in part, was why, instead of parting from her after their return from the city and going on to his clubs, he'd stayed by her side. She'd been stunned when he'd suggested accompanying her on her afternoon drive in the park.

As he'd expected, his presence beside her had effectively hauled the dowagers' and sharp-eyed matrons' minds from all interest in her brother. He hadn't had to do anything, simply sit beside her and smile at those who nodded, and thoughts of marriage had replaced thoughts of murder in all the relevant female minds.

Except hers, of course.

Nevertheless, she was too experienced not to see what he'd done. To his surprise, the moment she'd realized, she'd grown a touch flustered; he'd glimpsed consternation in her eyes, an unexpected crack in her usually polished composure.

She'd seen him looking, noticing, had dragged in a breath, and the moment had passed. She'd continued dealing with her peers with her customary air—and had largely ignored him.

Yet even though she doubtless suspected he had other, ulterior motives—such as introducing the concept of he and she as a possible match to the pertinent part of the ton— she'd still been grateful for what he'd achieved. To her mind, any topic of gossip was better than the murder, even if that gossip was about her.

She'd been grateful enough to invite him to dine, albeit grudgingly.

He'd accepted, not solely because one night apart had, at least for him, proved separation enough, but also because he knew that it was at times like these that she—her temper— most needed distraction. That she most needed someone about who could distract her.

Agnes, shrewd as could be and a Vaux herself, seemed as aware as he of the brewing storm. She studied Letitia's face, then said, "At least that solicitor will be here tomorrow, and we'll have the matter of the will settled and done with. One thing out of the way."

Letitia roused herself. "Indeed. Assuming he actually arrives."

"He will." Christian caught her eye as she glanced at him. "We might learn of friends or associates through Randall's bequests. We should definitely gain a better understanding of his current finances, enough to know if there's any hint of a motive there."

"And you'll learn who inherits this house." Agnes started to pack up her fringe. "Which is a not unimportant detail, especially when you have the likes of Mellon to deal with."

Letitia raised her brows. "There is that."

"What will you do," Hermione asked, "when the murderer's found and the dust settles? Will we keep living here?"

Letitia tilted her head. "I don't know."

Christian kept his lips firmly shut.

"I'll have to think about it." Draining her cup, she reached out and set it back on the tray. She looked at Agnes as her aunt stood. "Are you going up?"

"Yes—it's time." Agnes looked at Hermione as Christian got to his feet. "Come along, miss. Make your good-nights and you can help me up the stairs."

Hermione smiled sleepily; she'd already smothered a yawn or two. Uncurling her legs, she stood. "Good night, L'titia. 'Night, Christian." Then she focused on Christian. "Or should I call you Dearne?"

He smiled. "Christian will do." Hermione might be bidding fair to becoming an unconscionable minx, but she'd always been on his side.

Given the way Agnes was eyeing him—not openly censorious but prepared to be so—he'd need all the support he could get.

He half expected Agnes to ask when he was leaving; as he had no intention of doing so, that would have proved awkward, but just as he was bracing for some such pointed query, she humphed and nodded a good-night. "I'll no doubt see you in the morning, Dearne—at the reading of the will."

If he had his way, she'd see him at the breakfast table, but that might be pushing the boundaries too far. He bowed and murmured his good-nights.

Once Agnes and Hermione had left and the door was closed once more, he sat again, relaxed once more beside Letitia.

She was staring into space again, brooding. He studied her face, considered what he could see in it, heard again the subtle warning in Agnes's tone. Despite her eccentric, old lady ways, Letitia's aunt was neither blind nor slow. She knew what he wanted, and didn't disapprove—just as long as he did right by Letitia.

This time.

Agnes, he realized, scanning his recent memories of her—of when he'd seen her, always with Letitia there with them—felt strongly protective toward her niece. Which seemed odd. He wouldn't have thought Letitia needed protecting. . . .

The knowledge came to him in a wave, simply washed over and through him—and he saw what he should have from the first. Something that explained her odd attack of nerves in the park that afternoon. Something that meant he would have to tread carefully—*very* carefully—if he wanted to reclaim her.

Agnes was right. Letitia was vulnerable—horribly, critically, emotionally vulnerable. Over him. *Because* of him.

He'd hurt her badly once, unintentionally perhaps, but that hadn't made the hurt any less.

Now he was back, he could hurt her again—that was what lay behind Agnes's warning.

He wasn't above taking an eccentric old lady's warning to heart.

Especially as it suggested Letitia still felt for him all she ever had.

He glanced at her, and this time understood the responsibility he hadn't recognized all those years ago. When he'd gone off to war, gone off to play spies, and had left her to fend on her own.

Guilt tightened his chest, but guilt wouldn't help either of them.

He was waiting, watching her, when eventually she turned her head and looked at him. Searched his face, then arched her brows.

Her message was clear: While she wouldn't summon Mellon and have him shown out, neither would she make the first move.

Before, long ago, she almost always had.

But now, if he wanted her, he had to ask. He had to make his desire plain, lay it out, no veils, no screens, before her.

And pray she would welcome it.

Raising a brow in reply, he reached for her hand.

Got to his feet and drew her to hers, waited while she slid her feet into her slippers. If he kissed her on the sofa, they might never leave it. And Mellon would still be about.

When she straightened, he brought her hand to his lips. His eyes locked on hers, he kissed her fingertips, then turned her hand and pressed his lips to her palm. Let them linger just long enough for her to feel their heat, then he lifted his head. With his hold on her hand, he tugged gently, drew her a step closer, then, still holding her captive with his eyes, bent his head and pressed his lips to her wrist.

To her leaping pulse.

Letitia tried to keep her mental distance, knew she should, but she was already enthralled. By the warmth in his gray eyes, by the banked fire behind them. By the touch of his lips on her sensitive skin, commanding yet not demanding, luring rather than seducing.

Before, she'd always been so eager—so damnably impatient that he'd never had to work. Never had to tempt her.

His lips moved over her skin, hot with promise but gently, until an equally gentle flush rose under it, and beckoned him further.

Lifting his head just a little, he drew her closer still, let her hand fall to his shoulder as his arm slid around her and he drew her, still gently, in. Against him, but she wasn't trapped. Wasn't crushed. He bent his head again—stopped just before their lips met. Waited a heartbeat so she could sense his hunger—and hers—then he closed the gap and fed her.

Soft kisses. Like gentle rain on parched ground they made her bloom—coaxed her senses to slowly unfurl. Teased her nerves with the promise of paradise until she parted her lips on a sigh.

He didn't enter, instead drew back. Whispered across her lips. "I want you, and you want me. For tonight, let that be enough."

She blinked up at him, wondering, knowing he wanted much more. "But will that be enough?"

The words drifted from her lips to his.

He kissed her again, a tantalizing touch.

And didn't answer.

Instead, he murmured, his voice deep and low, "Invite me to your bed. Let me come to you there. Let me lie with you there . . . and let what will be, be."

That, she could agree to without reservation. What would be would be regardless.

Her eyes on his, she drew back. Caught his hand as she did, then stepped back, turned and led him from the room.

Led him up the stairs to her bedchamber, waited while he shut the door, then led him to the end of her bed.

Turning to him, she waited. In the flickering light of the candle Esme had left on her dressing table, she met his eyes. Felt rather than saw the desire in the gray—for once took the time to savor it.

His thumb moved over her fingers, stroking, then he released her hand, stepped closer. Raising both hands, he framed her face, tipped it up to his. Looked down for one long moment, searching her eyes, then he bent his head and kissed her.

Longingly.

Hungrily, yet his hunger was reined. Greedily, letting her taste his wanting, yet holding back, not taking.

She wouldn't have stopped him if he had, yet this time she was content to follow. To let him show her what he wished.

To let him deepen the kiss degree by degree, until a tide of response, of a longing to match his, rose up and swamped her. Swept away both restraint and thought. Left only sensation and feeling to cling to.

She clung, and her soul rejoiced.

Christian held to the slow pace, to the slow steady beat of his drum, held her to that so he had a chance to show her the other side of passion's coin.

So he could weave what he felt for her into each caress, invest each slow kiss with his need of her. Let her taste his desire on his lips, on his tongue, let her feel it in the slow, steady claiming.

She grew restless, reached for him. Releasing her face, he caught her hands, stepped into her as he eased her arms behind her. Anchoring both her wrists in one hand, he trapped them at the back of her waist, holding her within that arm.

With his free hand he trapped her jaw, angled her face so he could continue the kiss—draw it out until she was breathless. Then he shifted his lips to her temple, cruised over her ear and down to press a hot caress in the sensitive hollow beneath.

She murmured, and tried to shift into him. He held her back, kept at least an inch between their bodies. "Not yet," he murmured, and ducked his head, tipping her jaw so he could trace the long, arching line of her throat with his lips. She shuddered beneath the caress, and grew less rigid. More pliant. Willing to cede him the moment, to see what he wished to give her.

He pressed his lips to the pulse point at the base of her throat, felt more of her impatience fall away. Breathing in, he drew the scent of jasmine into his lungs, held it there, close to his heart.

Lifting his head, he found her lips again, kissed her again.

Still slow, still hungry. Lowered his hand to her breast, let the warm mound fill his palm.

She reacted instantly—immediately wanted him to release her hands so she could sink them in his hair and set the pace. He knew, but still he held her, kept her hands trapped while he kneaded, while his fingers searched and, through the black silk crepe, found and circled her nipple.

Her kiss grew hungrier, more demanding, yet still he held her back. Forced her to feel his unhurried assessment of her bounty. He traced, stroked, ran his thumb over the furled peaks, until her breasts were swollen and firm, straining beneath the confining silk.

Only then did he consent to move on. It was the work of a minute to slip the black buttons closing her bodice free, releasing the pressure. Holding her to their kiss, he found the lacings at her back and swiftly undid them.

She sighed when he released her hands and slid her gown from her shoulders, down her arms, let it slide slowly down her slender body until it slithered over her hips and down her legs to puddle on the floor.

Leaving her clad only in her fine silk chemise and even finer silk stockings. And they were black, too—dark veils too insubstantial to fully screen her white skin. The filmy chemise shifting over her curves distracted him.

Letitia saw, and felt a spark of amazement lance through her desire. He'd seen her naked often enough; to see him transfixed now was a curious delight. She shifted, stretched, watched his eyes track her breasts, her hips, trace her waist through the screening chemise.

Setting one hand to his shoulder, she slipped off her slippers, stepped out of her discarded gown and into him.

To her surprise, he caught her, his hands locking about her waist. Holding her as she was, the tight peaks of her breasts just brushing his coat.

An excruciatingly tantalizing caress; she needed to get closer, to ease the ache in her heavy breasts, but he held her trapped.

He looked into her face, searched her eyes, her expression, in the dim light. She had no idea what he saw, but then he bent his head, still moving far too slowly for her liking. But at least his lips closed on hers, and this time his tongue surged deep into her mouth. Not in any fury of desire, not as it usually was between them, all fire and unleashed passion, but with a slow intent, a measured, unhurried, almost languid claiming that somehow, to her reeling senses, was strangely erotic.

With her lips and tongue, she tried to urge him on, to make him go faster, to ignite the flames that between them usually roared and drove him.

To return to the familiar.

But he wouldn't, not this time. He held to his slow beat, and refused to let her push him. Even though the heat between them was palpable, he kept it at simmering, steadily burgeoning, escalating, but totally under his control.

A shiver went through her as she realized what was so different—so sensually exciting it was setting her nerves flickering, skittering, with expectation.

Control. His.

Whenever they'd come together in the past, neither had exercised any real measure of control—for herself, she'd never sought it, and she'd always, in the past, been able to cinder his.

Not this time. As the kiss went on, spun out, and left her slowly whirling along the outer edges of a vortex of pleasured delight, she felt all resistance fade.

He wished her to know this, and so she would. The conqueror within him, a being she'd always known existed beneath his debonair charm, wasn't going to give her any choice.

A primitive shudder of anticipation ran down her spine.

He sensed it; he paused in his slow, devastatingly thorough claiming of her mouth, then the kiss changed. Deepened. As one hand drifted from her waist.

She felt the brush of his fingers as they slid beneath the

hem of her chemise. With his fingertips he traced—slowly—upward from her hip along her side to the underside of her breast.

Moving slowly, smoothly, he palmed it. At last skin-to-skin, he closed his hand about her flesh and the flames leapt.

Just so far. They flared and fell as he touched her—everywhere. As he claimed every inch of her skin—unhurriedly, explicitly, as if he had all night and intended to use it.

His desire, his absolute intent to make her his, to claim her, brand her, reached her through his touch. Through every caress of his hard hands, through every sweep of his palms as he sculpted her body. Through every slow, languid, thorough exploration.

It almost felt as if he were learning her anew, as if those long-ago times had been in some other life and they were both different people now.

As if he were claiming her for the first time.

That thought filled Christian's mind; that was indeed his intention. Always, before, he'd let her have her head, let her burn and take him with her—let them plunge unrestrained into passion's fire and be consumed. Never before had he extended himself, never before had he fought to give her this. Never before had he held the flames back so she might see what, to him, beneath the flames and the fire, being intimate with her was all about.

He'd always hidden the emotion that, from the first, had driven him with her.

Tonight he held the flames back, and laid his heart and soul bare before her.

He was who he was, and that was something she understood.

But not something he'd before let her see. Never completely. Never clearly. Hardly at all.

Tonight was different. Tonight he intended to love her—and let her see.

She kept trying to push him, to let the flames free, but if

he truly wished, he could hold her back. Could keep her with him, gasping, breathless, as he caressed every inch of the lush body he would possess.

Her breasts were a delight he savored at length, purely with his hands, knowing she ached for more. "Later." He breathed the word across her swollen lips then took them again in a long, deep kiss, one sufficiently demanding to keep her absorbed—that together with his caresses left her no mental space to gather her resolve and press him. To summon the will to reach for him and touch him as she usually did.

The long sweeping planes of her back, the graceful indentation of her waist, the flare of her hips—he learned them all anew, as if he were some pasha and she his latest acquisition, his newest slave.

He set his thumb to her navel, and pressed in and out in a rhythm she knew very well. Her hands were on his shoulders; they shifted to his throat, fingers curling over his nape as she clung. He sensed the heat rising within her, drew his thumb from her navel and skated his hand down.

With the backs of his fingers he brushed the crisp curls at the apex of her thighs. Felt her shudder, felt her fingers tense.

He drew back from the kiss, eased back and looked at her—at her body, skin flushed and heated, all but quivering with need, screened by the filmy black veil of her chemise.

The sight had rocked him; it still aroused him. Her skin was so white, pearlescent in the dimness. He'd never had a widow in her weeds before. Nevertheless . . .

One hand on her waist, anchoring her, with his other he grasped the chemise, gathered a handful and drew it up. She obediently lifted her arms and wriggled. He pulled it up, free of her hair, then let it fall.

Immediately she reached for her garters.

He stopped her, caught her hands again in his, moved her arms back and once again locked them in the small of her back. He drew her full against him. She looked up, eyes wide—struggling to hide the effect of his clothing rasping her sensitized skin.

"Leave your stockings on."

His voice was a bass rumble, coming from deep in his chest.

Letitia made out the words—had just enough brain left to decode them. Her skin felt alive, her nerves aroused by his caresses and now shocked into heightened awareness by the realization he was fully clothed while she was . . . naked but for her black garters and black silk stockings.

It wasn't modesty that had her reeling.

How had he done this? How had he—

His mouth came down on hers, and she stopped thinking.

Could only feel as his hands locked on her hips and he half turned her and steered her back the few steps until her legs hit the end of her bed.

It was a high four-poster bed; the footboard behind her calves and knees ended lower than the top of the mattress.

His hands gripped and he lifted her, but he didn't throw her back on the bed as she expected; he sat her on the edge of the mattress.

He let go of her and stepped back.

Dazed, adrift—not knowing this script—she blinked up at him. Put her hands behind her on the silk coverlet and braced her arms to lean back so she could. Saw his lips curve in a smile that was all arrogant conquering male.

"Spread your legs." His eyes trapped hers. "Wide."

A shiver ran down her spine. Slowly, she complied.

Then watched his gaze lower from her eyes to her lips, to her breasts, swollen, peaked, fine skin flushed from his earlier ministrations. Watched his gray eyes grow darker, stormier, as they skated down over her ribs, over her waist and belly, to fix on the soft flesh she'd willingly revealed to him.

She felt that flesh throb, dampen. As his eyes devoured.

"Good." The word was a guttural growl. He stepped closer, between her spread knees. The bed was high so it was easy for him to lean down and kiss her, draw her once more into the drugging, enthralling exchange. Then he set his hands to her body again.

Reduced her to gasping, trembling need before he consented to touch her between her thighs, to stroke her, part her folds—at long last slide a long finger deep into her sheath and give her the first part of what she wanted.

He eventually eased a second finger in alongside the first, to her immense relief. But then, his hand still working steadily between her thighs, he drew back. And looked at her.

She opened her eyes and looked at him. Watched him watching her. Saw herself through his eyes, naked but for her stockings, her legs spread, his hand between, pleasuring her. He was still fully clothed; he wasn't touching her anywhere else.

What she saw in his face had her shuddering. Biting her lip against a moan, she closed her eyes—and felt the slow scorching burn of passion controlled. More intense, more powerful, more potent. With every slow, possessive thrust of his fingers he pressed that on her.

She felt it swell, felt it fill her. Her gasps turned to pants; her inner flames coalesced and brightened.

He sensed it and drew back. Eased his fingers back so they were only just penetrating her, playing at her entrance in the slickness he'd drawn forth.

Her whirling senses slowed; a protest was on her lips when she felt him lean close. Planting a large hand on the bed beside her, he leaned down—and set his mouth to her breasts.

On a half gasp, half moan, she let her head loll back.

She wanted to hold him to her, but her arms were too weak to support herself on just one.

So she had to sit there, propped on her arms, and let him do what he wished to her. Let him taste her, savor her. He licked, laved, suckled. Her breasts, her shoulders, then her navel. The outer curve of her hip, the junction where thigh and hip met, the long upper sweep of her thigh.

While he lazily and unhurriedly claimed her with his mouth, his fingers continued to stroke between her thighs.

Until she thought she'd go mad.

At last he knelt between her knees. By then she was so heated, so tense, so desperate, she made not the slightest demur when he drew his fingers from her, slid his hands beneath her bottom and gripped, held her and shifted her, then replaced his fingers with his mouth, with his tongue.

Tasted her there, and as he had elsewhere, licked, laved, and suckled.

Slowly. Thoroughly. Unhurriedly.

She thought she might die.

He'd made love to her this way before, but not like this. Not with such intent control, such slow purpose.

The same purpose she suspected he'd had throughout—to possess her utterly. Completely.

Helpless, more alive than she'd ever been, more aware of the intimacy of the act than she'd thought possible, she had to lie back and let him do as he wished—let him love her as he would.

Let him overwhelm her senses and reduce her to mindless need, to a craving that reached to her bones.

Until she needed to feel him inside her with such desperation it hurt.

Until she was thrashing, sobbing, pleading.

Then he held her down and took her with his tongue.

Possessed her utterly. As he wished.

She heard herself scream, luckily breathlessly. A massive wave of heat rose, then broke over her and dragged her down. Into a whirlpool of fire, of flames that leapt and roared. The fragile furnace within her couldn't contain the conflagration. It shattered, shards of heat flying down every nerve, eventually slowing and sinking into her flesh, to melt and warm.

As reality, still heated and flushed, returned, she felt battered and racked by the intensity of the release—the explosion he'd wrought.

That he wasn't—wouldn't be—finished with her, she knew. Even through the miasma of spent passion she could feel the familiar emptiness within. An emptiness she'd never felt except with him—an emptiness only he could fill.

She opened her eyes, through the shadows saw him walking toward her.

He'd shed his clothes, doused the guttering candle.

He was totally naked. Fully aroused.

He was hers.

She knew it—for the first time since they'd come together again, possibly the first time ever, she felt that in her bones.

She was too wrung out to move. She lay there and watched him come to her.

He reached the end of the bed, loomed over her, then he sank both fists into the coverlet on either side of her and leaned nearer to look into her face. He searched her eyes, then stated, "Don't say a word. Don't try to do anything."

She simply blinked, and obediently held her tongue.

He eyed her suspiciously, but then drew back. Pressing his hands beneath her, he lifted her. Kneeling on the bed, he moved up it, then laid her back down with her head on the plump pillows.

He followed her down, and covered her.

Found her lips and covered them with his.

As his hands found her body and stroked.

She arched into him, inviting his touch—begging for it. He languidly traced, caressed, effortlessly possessed, and she sighed. She'd expected flames and their usual explosive passion, but this was loving of a different sort—strung out, nerves tense and aching—waiting for the next touch, the next kiss, the next act of communion.

Which always came. He was a dark, possessive male who loved her in the dark, who made her ache, then fed her, who commanded her senses, filled her mind, and took slow, unhurried possession.

Not just of her body. Not just of her mind.

He was familiar, yet not. He was different, and so was she. They were no longer the young lovers who'd found each other—their other halves, their soul mates—so easily. Too easily, perhaps.

Now they were older, wiser, now they both knew the value of what they'd had. Of what they'd lost.

Of what, she knew, he wanted to reclaim.

Find again, take again, hold again.

As she writhed beneath him, helpless and yearning, soothed by his hands, by his lips, by the slow build of heat that wrapped them about, that cocooned them in her bed, she honestly didn't know if they would ever be that way again.

Only knew she would be with him in trying again.

In attempting to find their way forward again.

A different way, perhaps.

Like this.

Even though this was the bed she'd shared with Randall, he'd never been her lover. The man in her arms had been— still was—her one and only.

Her one and only love. If there was a way forward for them, she'd be a fool to turn away.

The moments rolled together as they tangled on her bed; she was no longer interested in rushing ahead. This enveloping, caressing warmth was new, precious; it held passion and desire, but also something deeper. Something finer.

She'd always been passionate, but this was passion on a different plane, a deeper desire, a stronger yearning.

Her hands spread on his back, she held him to her, shifted beneath him as she kissed him back—only to be overwhelmed by the kiss he returned, only to fall back and let him surge in and fill her mouth. Let him take it, mimicking the way he would take her body soon . . .

They'd held off as long as they could; she suddenly knew it—sensed he did, too. With his thighs, he spread hers wider, settled between; she felt the blunt head of his erection at her entrance.

She expected him to simply thrust in and fill her. Instead, he broke from the kiss.

His breathing as ragged as hers, he reached around, caught her hands, one in each of his, and dragged them up, anchoring them in the pillows above her head, locking them there in one hand.

Their gazes met. Across the few inches of heated shadows between them, their eyes locked, held.

With his free hand he reached down, gripped her hip, tilted her hips beneath him.

And entered her.

Slowly. His eyes on hers, holding her, his weight pinning her beneath him, he pressed into her body relentless inch by inch . . . so slowly she felt every second of his possession. Every tiny nuance as he penetrated her, stretching her sheath, filling her.

Completing her.

He didn't stop until he'd filled her to the hilt.

His eyes still on hers, he drew back—slowly, totally controlled—held back for an instant, then surged slowly in again.

The friction was intense.

The sensations filled her mind.

She closed her eyes, arched beneath him.

He continued to fill her, to command her body and her, to swamp her senses with pleasure and delight until her fingertips burned.

Until her body was afire beneath his—and his burned, too.

Not with their usual flashfire, but with something more powerful. More intense, more all-consuming.

It surged from deep within them—finally wrenched all control from him.

In those last moments they were together again, helpless again, at the mercy of what, together, they'd evoked.

Something stronger, more wondrous, more earth-shatteringly glorious.

It racked them, wrecked them, broke them with its glory. Flung them into that never-ending void.

Drained them.

They floated back to earth in each other's arms. She had no idea how long it had been since she'd led him to her room, to her bed. Since she'd given herself into his arms.

Only knew, beyond thought, beyond doubt, that she belonged there.

As satiation dragged her down, her only thought was a wish that their future might be.

Her only reservation was a fear—that she wouldn't, despite all, find the courage to trust him with her heart again.

Christian stirred sometime in the long watches of the night. Dawn was not yet here, but he knew he had to leave. Agnes notwithstanding, he couldn't push the woman in whose arms he lay, whose body lay curled around his.

He felt her closeness to his bones, simply lay and savored it for long moments. Her hair was a tumbled mass flung over his chest, the weight of the soft silky veil a subtle benediction.

She'd always been flagrantly, blatantly, possessive—in the past. Since he'd returned . . . although from the first of their recent encounters she'd been as fiery as his memories had painted her, not until tonight had she relaxed and accepted him to the point of once again sleeping wrapped around him.

Claiming him as hers even in sleep.

His lips relaxed. He was, if not totally satisfied—he wouldn't be that until she was his wife—content enough with what he'd achieved.

Out of protective habit, his gaze focused on their surroundings, scanned the room—and his content faded, replaced by a powerful wish that they were somewhere else.

In some other bed.

Preferably in his bed at Allardyce House.

Anywhere but in the bed Randall had bought for her.

Had bought for the bride he'd bought.

Chapter 11

Mr. Meecham arrived in South Audley Street at eleven o'clock the next morning. Letitia had elected to receive him in the drawing room, reasoning, Christian suspected, that the greater formality would provide a better stage for the occasion.

When Meecham was shown in, she was seated on the chaise, gowned in her most severe bombazine, flanked by Agnes, equally austere in a dark slate gray gown.

From his position behind the chaise at Letitia's shoulder, Christian watched as, having been announced by Mellon, Meecham, a short, rotund individual dressed somberly in his best black, bowed low, then came forward with a tripping gait.

Features arranged in a patronizingly compassionate expression, Meecham halted a yard away, bowed again, and declaimed, "If you would permit me, my lady, to convey our most sincere condolences on the passing of your late husband." Without waiting for any acknowledgment, Meecham continued, "Mr. Randall—"

"Was murdered."

The blunt statement—and the tone in which Letitia uttered it—threw Meecham entirely off his stride.

He all but goggled at her. "Ah . . . yes. So I was given to understand."

"Indeed. That being so, I'm sure you can understand that we wish to hear the details of my late husband's will without delay." Imperiously she waved Meecham to a straight-backed chair positioned for the purpose a few yards before the chaise, a small table beside it. "If you would sit, perhaps we might proceed."

Her tone was so cold, Christian was surprised Meecham didn't shiver. With one last glance at her, then at Christian, who met it blandly, he crossed to the chair and sat down. Pulling his briefcase into his lap, he opened it and drew out a thin sheaf. He regarded it, then with appropriate gravity laid it on the small table. "The last will and testament of Mr. George Martin Randall."

He glanced at Letitia. "As you are the sole principal beneficiary, my lady, we may proceed without further ado."

The words had barely left Meecham's lips when a heavy knock fell on the door.

Letitia shifted her gaze to the door. *Not* Mellon was her first thought; no butler knocked like that. Before she could decide whether to bid whoever it was to enter, the door opened—and Barton walked in.

Halting, he nodded to her, then to Christian. "If you'll pardon the intrusion, my lady, I humbly request to be present when the will of the late Mr. Randall is read. It's imperative we—the authorities—know what's what with the inheritance."

Letitia narrowed her eyes on the runner. "Humbly request" her left foot. She was about to remind him he was forbidden the house when Christian's hand closed on her shoulder.

She turned her head and looked up at him. He leaned down, head bent to whisper, "He'll be able to get the details when the will is lodged with the courts—probably later today. Letting him stay and listen now isn't going to change anything, but it might mean he mellows and becomes less intrusive, less of a bother to you."

A powerful consideration. She raised her brows fleetingly, then, smoothing her expression into one of haughty indifference, she turned back to Barton. "You may stay." She pointed to a straight-backed chair against the wall. "Provided you sit there and keep silent."

Barton frowned, but accepted with good enough grace.

Once he'd sat rather gingerly on the chair, Letitia looked again at Meecham. "You may proceed."

Meecham had recognized Barton, presumably from his partners' description; his expression suggested he'd anticipated an ugly scene and was relieved to have been spared. He'd fished a pair of pince-nez from his waistcoat pocket; perching them on his nose, he held up the will, and read.

Once he got past the verbose preamble, matters became more interesting. Letitia saw Barton pull a notebook from his pocket, open it, lick his pencil, and start scribbling. Glancing back, she saw Christian, too, had pulled a small black book from his pocket; he and Barton took notes as Meecham detailed Randall's estate, all of which had been left to her.

Meecham paused after that section, casting his eye back over the list he'd just read. Randall's property had been described not in value but in kind—the house in South Audley Street, his investments in the funds, in various other bonds, and a third share in the Orient Trading Company, which had as its address another legal firm on Chancery Lane. "A very tidy fortune," Meecham opined.

Letitia glanced up and back at Christian. He quietly said, "Montague will be able to tell us more."

Meecham cleared his throat, drawing all attention back to him. He fixed his gaze on Letitia. "That's what will come to you, my lady, plus any and all residuals after the following bequests."

Letitia had to force herself not to lean forward. Barton, she noted, didn't seem interested in the bequests; frowningly studying what he'd written, he'd stopped taking notes.

"The first bequest," Meecham intoned, "is to a Mr. Trowbridge, of Cheyne Walk in Chelsea—'the Glockstein clock that resides in the study, in recognition of our long friendship.' The second bequest, also in recognition of long friendship, is of the Stuart crystal pen and inkwell set, also from the study, to a Mr. Swithin, of Curzon Street, London." Meecham paused, then went on, "Those are the only two bequests beyond the household. The other bequests . . ."

While Meecham worked his way through the usual long list of small bequests to household staff—Mellon, the two footmen, Randall's long-serving cook among them—Letitia turned and looked inquiringly at Christian.

He nodded, spoke quietly. "At last we've some names—some people we can ask."

"Perhaps they're away, and so missed his funeral."

"We'll see." With his head, Christian directed her attention back to Meecham, who was summing up.

"So the bulk of the estate passes to Mr. Randall's relict—Lady Letitia Randall—outright, no covenants and no restrictions bar the customary one." Meecham looked at Letitia and colored faintly. "That is to say, if you were to bear Mr. Randall a child after his death, then the estate is held in trust—"

"You need not concern yourself with that eventuality."

Letitia's tone—colder and more final than any grave—gave Meecham pause, but then he gathered his courage and with an attempt at delicacy suggested, "Your pardon, my lady, but it *is* possible—"

"No, Mr. Meecham. No child of Randall's is possible, at least not by me. My late husband and I have not been . . . close for some years."

Meecham's color deepened to an unbecoming purple. "Yes, well." He fell to shuffling his papers. "If that's the case, then the estate passes to you unreservedly."

"Very well." After a moment Letitia asked, "Is there anything more?"

Meecham assured her there was not; he went on to outline his role in registering the will with the courts.

Christian let the words roll past him; his mind had snagged on Letitia's "some years." He didn't doubt she was speaking the literal truth, even possibly understating it;

"some years" explained a number of things—her short fuse when he pulled her into his arms, for one.

For a woman of her passions, "some years" must have seemed a lifetime. Just as it had for him over the years he'd been celibate, expecting to return to her.

He wasn't sure if it was the notion of tit for tat—that she'd been as deprived as he—or the more fundamental realization that Randall and she hadn't been intimate for years that so buoyed him.

Regardless, when Meecham rose, bowed, and took his leave, he was feeling distinctly mellow.

Barton rose as Meecham turned for the door. "Just one thing I wanted to check with you, Mr. Meecham."

Meecham halted. "Yes?"

"This estate of Mr. Randall's—it's quite a fortune if I understood correctly?"

"I don't know the precise value—you'd need to consult a financial expert for that—but I would venture to say that taken together the properties and funds I listed would amount to quite a considerable sum."

"And," Barton pressed, "all that considerable sum passes to Lady Randall here?"

"Yes, that's right. Hers to do with as she pleases."

Barton thanked Meecham and let him go. He made a note in his book, then, closing it, turned to Letitia, still seated in state on the chaise. "A considerable sum makes a very good motive for murder, I've always found."

Letitia didn't shift a muscle; her voice dripped icicles as she said, "You can't seriously be suggesting I murdered Randall."

"No—but I would suggest you're very fond of your brother, and if he'd needed money, then killing Randall would, through you, serve him just as well."

A long silence ensued. Christian considered stepping around the chaise to get between Barton and Letitia, but then she spoke, her voice dreadful in its calmness, "I believe you know your way to the door."

Barton hesitated; Christian prayed he had enough nous not to further prod her. Then Barton bowed stiffly and turned away.

Just as he reached the door, Letitia spoke again, and there could be no doubt whatever of her feelings. "Incidentally, Barton, should you enter this house again without a warrant, rest assured I'll have the watch summoned and see you thrown out on your ear."

Barton had paused in the doorway. A moment ticked past, then he continued on without looking back.

Christian rounded the chaise. He reached for Letitia's hand; as the door clicked shut, he drew her to her feet. "At last we have two specific names to pursue—although I don't know either. Do you know Trowbridge or Swithin?"

She had to think to answer—had to put aside her rising temper to do so; it took her a moment of blinking up at him before she succeeded, and frowned. "No, I don't—at least not in the sense of having any real acquaintance. I know nothing of Swithin—I've never heard of him—but I've heard of Trowbridge."

"It's lunchtime. Let's go into the dining room and put together what we know, so this afternoon, when we meet the others at the club, we'll have a concise report."

Frown easing, she nodded, her mind having switched, as he'd intended, to a topic that held more interest than railing over Barton. "Yes. All right." She glanced at Agnes. "Aunt, are you ready to eat?"

Agnes nodded. "An excellent idea." Her gaze was on Christian. He stepped around Letitia and helped Agnes up.

Nodding her thanks, Agnes shook out her gray skirts, then headed for the door. "You're very good, Dearne."

Christian hid his smile and offered Letitia his arm. Already engrossed in assembling all she knew of Trowbridge, she absentmindedly placed her hand on his sleeve and let him steer her to the door.

*   *   *

In mid-afternoon Christian escorted Letitia down the steps of Randall's house and into a hackney. Ordering the jarvey to drive them to the park, he climbed in, shut the door, and sat beside her.

He watched, but as the hackney drove off, Barton made no move to quit his position opposite the house. As the hackney turned the corner, Christian saw him settling back against the area railings, arms folded, his gaze locked on Randall's door.

"He's staying there?" Letitia asked.

"It looks like it. Nevertheless, we won't take any chances." He glanced at her. "A short walk will do us good."

They left the hackney at the corner of Hyde Park, then crossed the street and ambled a short way down Grosvenor Place. They'd passed Grosvenor Crescent when Christian halted, scanning the street behind them. "No sign. He didn't follow us."

"Good." Letitia set off at a brisker pace. "It's this way, isn't it?"

They reached the club shortly before three o'clock. Admitted by Gasthorpe, who confirmed he was housing a visitor, they went up to the library, Letitia all but taking the stairs two at a time.

There, they found Justin, at his ease, sharing a tale with Tristan. Both rose as Letitia swept in.

Her gaze raked her brother. She nodded. "Good. You managed to get yourself here without breaking your neck."

Justin grinned. "Good afternoon, sister dear." He leaned down to buss her cheek.

Christian offered his hand. "How was the drive down?"

"Utterly uneventful," Justin replied, with all a Vaux's contempt for such a happenstance. "It's bad enough in daylight—at night it's dead boring."

Sinking into a chair, Letitia rolled her eyes.

The men had barely reclaimed their seats when a knock sounded on the front door. A minute later Dalziel entered.

His gaze swept the room, locating, and remaining on, Justin's face.

Justin's eyes went wide—he clearly recognized Dalziel—Royce Whoever-he-was—even though there had to be a good ten years between them. Justin slowly got to his feet. "Ah . . . you must be Dalziel." He held out a hand.

With a nod of approval, Dalziel grasped it. "You'll be staying with me, out of sight. I'll come for you later tonight—no need to take any chances whatever, given the authorities' current bent."

"I should thank you—"

Dalziel silenced him with an upraised hand. "Time enough for that later. For now"—he surveyed their small company—"what have we learned?"

"Randall's will was read this morning," Letitia stated. "Dearne has the details."

Extracting his notebook, Christian ran through both Randall's estate and the bequests. The latter, unsurprisingly, became the focus of discussion.

Tristan in particular pounced on the names. "Trowbridge and Swithin—those are the only two gentlemen I turned up who anyone even suggested might know Randall as more than a nodding acquaintance." He glanced at Christian. "I covered virtually every male haunt of tonnish gentlemen—at least those where we go to meet with friends. Many knew Randall by sight, yet none admitted to friendship, nor did I find anyone who could name any of his friends. Trowbridge and Swithin were mentioned solely as gentlemen my sources had seen Randall talking to on more than one occasion. That was the sum of it—interesting that they weren't known as his friends, yet he names them as longtime friends in his will."

"Indeed." Christian frowned. "Especially as it seems he has met them in recent times, and all live more or less in London, Swithin within a few blocks."

"Was the will recent?" Dalziel asked.

"Two years old," Christian replied. "Recent enough." He looked at Justin. "Any ideas?"

Justin grimaced. "I've seen Randall speak with Trowbridge, and Swithin, too—I only know their names because he mentioned them in passing. On different occasions, each stopped him to have a word when he was with me—although they stepped aside, I got the impression it was simply that—a word or two. Nothing of deep import. But . . ." He grimaced again, and looked at Letitia. "If one goes by how people stand—how close, how relaxed they are—then it did seem as if he knew them well."

"It sounds as if Swithin and Trowbridge go on our list of potential friends-cum-murderers." Dalziel raised a brow at Justin. "Can you think of anyone else—anyone Randall classed as friend, whether by word or deed?"

"I've spent the last days racking my brains, but other than Trowbridge and Swithin, who I did recall, there's no one else I can name, or even point to. Looking back, it's really quite bizarre, but Randall simply didn't appear to have the usual circle of male acquaintances all other gentlemen do."

Frowning, as they all were, Tristan asked, "How did he spend his evenings? Surely he must have had some social circle of sorts?"

It was Letitia who answered. "He spent a lot of his evenings in his study. Often to all hours. Business, he said, although I never knew what." She grimaced. "I had no interest in knowing, so never asked." She paused, then added, "And I'm not sure even if I had asked, that he would have told me. He was rather secretive about his financial affairs."

"That's true." Justin looked at Tristan. "He probably spent half his evenings out—sometimes with Letitia at dinners, and sometimes trawling the clubs, but at least in the latter case, on the times I went with him or saw him out and about, it always seemed that he was there to see and be seen, not to do anything specific like meet someone or play cards or dice. He'd walk through the rooms, stopping and chatting with whoever was there. If you watched him long enough, you'd see him just keep walking until he'd passed everyone, and then just walk out again. Most never noticed, but I did because I watched—it always struck me as deuced strange."

A moment passed, then Dalziel said, "So we have Swithin and Trowbridge as possibilities, and no one else. What do we know of them?"

Letitia shook her head. "I never encountered them with Randall—I never heard him mention them, nor heard that they'd called at the house. Swithin I've never met at all—I know nothing about him. Trowbridge I have met socially— we've been introduced." She glanced around. "He's something of an authority on paintings and sculpture, and as the latter is currently very popular with the ladies of the ton, Trowbridge is in demand. When I met him it was at a private exhibition of figurines—he was one of the critics the hostess had invited. But that's all I know of him, although courtesy of Randall's will, we now know he lives in Chelsea."

"That's more or less all that I managed to learn about Trowbridge," Tristan put in. "As his and Swithin's were the only names I turned up, I asked around very quietly. Trowbridge seems well established within the ton. All I heard about Swithin, however, was that he was known as a canny and very private investor."

"Clearly we need to learn more about Trowbridge and Swithin." Having stolen his thunder, Letitia turned to Dalziel. "I presume you haven't heard anything from Hexham yet?"

Dalziel shook his head. "I've sent word to contacts I have there—they'll visit the grammar school and see what they can find, but it'll be a day or two yet before they send anything back. However, I also made inquiries through other, closer sources, hoping to turn up something on Randall. Unfortunately, all I turned up were negatives—he's never been in any of the services, never attached to any government department or embassy, never had a position in any ministry, royal house, or parliamentary enterprise. Nor was he ever connected with the church—as deacon, sexton, or any such capacity."

Letitia wrinkled her nose. "So my late husband remains an enigma."

No one argued.

Christian broke the silence. "Have any of you heard of the Orient Trading Company?" When they all shook their heads, he went on, "Randall owned a third of the company—we should find out who the other owners are. It's possible that company affairs provided someone with a motive for murder." He looked down at his notebook. "Letitia and I have to visit Montague anyway, to ask what he's learned regarding the original source of Randall's wealth, and now also to give him the details of Randall's estate so he can give us an estimate of its worth. As part of that, he'll need to assess the Orient Trading Company—I'll ask him to ferret out the other owners, and whether the company is profitable, too."

"Do." Dalziel looked around. "It seems we all have clues to pursue. I'll continue to see what I can uncover regarding Randall's background. I'll also see what I can learn about the company."

Tristan nodded. "The Orient Trading Company sounds like an import-export business—I'll see what I can learn of them around the docks and through the shipping companies. Alongside that, I'll keep pursuing Swithin—we know far too little about him."

"Indeed." Letitia glanced at Christian. "I'm sure I can arrange to come up with Trowbridge socially—that might be the best way to approach him about his connection with Randall. I could mention the bequest."

Christian nodded. "Good idea. I'll go with you. We'll concentrate on Trowbridge. Otherwise, for the company and Randall's finances, it's Montague we most need to alert— we'll do that as soon as we can."

They all rose, pleased to have something to sink their teeth into. All except Justin, who clearly felt left out.

"You'll just have to grin and bear it," Letitia informed

him, "for I'll never forgive you if you give that weasel Barton the satisfaction of taking you up." She hugged him. "Stay . . . where you're told to stay, and don't be a nuisance."

Justin rolled his eyes but settled back into a chair to read a book readily enough. Dalziel had already departed, having ordered Justin to be ready to leave the club at two the next morning.

Letitia followed Christian down the stairs. "Dalziel at least is taking the threat of the authorities seriously."

Christian snorted. "He should know—he's one of the authorities' ultimate threats."

Gasthorpe, as ever efficient, had a hackney waiting. Letitia climbed in; Christian told the jarvey to take them to South Audley Street, then joined her.

To find her frowning at him. "What about going to see Montague?"

He shook his head. "It's nearly five o'clock. We'd never make it in time—he'll have left his office before we reach it."

"But—" She stared at him. After a moment she asked, "Don't you know where he lives?"

Her impatience had resurfaced. "No." Then he added, "And even if I did, I wouldn't use the knowledge. There's nothing he could accomplish tonight."

Slumping back against the seat, she grumped, "He could *think*."

Leaning back, he smiled, caught her hand and held it. "We'll go and see him first thing in the morning. Until then, you'll simply have to possess your soul in patience."

Patience was not a Vaux trait. Letitia wasn't sure she had a patient bone in her body. However . . . she did have other matters to attend to—even if she hadn't yet divined just how she was supposed to eradicate the assumption that appeared to have lodged with quite ridiculous firmness in the majority of the grande dames' minds.

That evening she stood in the middle of the Marchioness of Huntly's drawing room, and wondered where—and how—to start. While she'd assumed Christian's appearance beside her in her carriage in the park the previous afternoon would engender a certain amount of speculation, she hadn't anticipated just how rabid and deep-rooted that speculation would be.

Her initial intention—to simply ignore all comments—had been rendered ineligible when her hostess, one of the most influential females in the ton, had commented, in her calm, collected, commanding voice, on how pleased she was to see Letitia and Christian together again.

Huh! They were together in the sense he'd escorted her there—but together in the wider, long-term sense, in the sense of having a future together . . . as to that, she still didn't know.

And the last thing she wanted was to get hemmed into a corner by the ton's expectations. To have her decision effectively taken out of her hands—she was perfectly aware that could happen if the ton's assumptions were allowed to grow unchecked. Admittedly, as a Vaux she could ultimately do whatever she pleased and the ton be damned—something the ton, perversely, would accept as perfectly normal for a Vaux—but she currently had enough scandal in her life; she didn't need to court more.

And she would infinitely prefer that the grande dames stopped watching her and Christian like beady-eyed eagles.

Or was that gossipy vultures?

Regardless, the conclusion was obvious—she needed to pour ice-cold water all over the ideas blossoming beneath the various coiffures bobbing about the room.

Around her, the guests at the extremely select soiree filled the elegant room with a multitude of murmuring voices. With Randall so recently dead, soirees of this nature were the only "entertainments" she felt it was permissable for her to attend. Of course, ever since Randall's sensational demise, the flow of invitations had dramatically increased, ladies she barely knew inviting her to afternoon teas and the like.

Much good would it do them. She'd chosen to attend the marchioness's event because she'd known all the most influential ladies—those whose thoughts she most needed to monitor—would be present. Beyond managing the opinions society held of her, Justin, and her family in general, she had little interest in social affairs, not with Justin in hiding and Randall's killer as yet unmasked.

And Randall proving even more peculiarly secretive in death than he had in life.

She'd left Christian with a bevy of gentlemen discussing political affairs; neither he nor she needed support in this arena.

Surveying the company, she wondered which grande dame she ought to approach first.

A sharp rap on her arm—not from a hand but the head of a cane—answered her question. Summoning a delighted smile—perfectly genuine; she knew who her accoster was, and no lady was more relevant to her task—she turned and met a pair of obsidian eyes. "Lady Osbaldestone! How lovely."

She didn't curtsy—Lady Osbaldestone's title was inferior to her own; instead she grasped her ladyship's beringed fingers, squeezed gently as she leaned in to touch cheeks.

"Well, miss." Lady Osbaldestone transfixed her with an incisive gaze. "So you're a miss again, after a fashion, and not a moment too soon in my opinion. You wasted enough years with that man—I can't say I view his demise as any great loss. And I see Dearne's come to his senses, which is exactly as it should be."

"Dearne's been a great support in tracking down Randall's murderer." Letitia knew she had to adhere firmly to that line; her ladyship had one of the shrewdest brains in the ton. "I fear I wouldn't have known where to start."

Lady Osbaldestone's black eyes regarded her unblinkingly. A second ticked past, then her ladyship said, "To be blunt, my dear, I'd heard that the authorities had your brother firmly at the top of their list."

Letitia waved dismissively. "You know what the authorities are like—they have to have *some* name on their list, so they put Justin's on it. As his is the *only* name they have, ergo he's at the top, but that will change once they have the correct suspect."

"And Dearne is helping you locate this suspect?"

"Indeed. He was kind enough to agree to assist. With his background, he's the perfect gentleman for the job."

Her ladyship's lips quirked. "Indubitably." A subtle smile curved her lips. "I doubt, my dear, that you'll find many who will argue that point."

Letitia blinked, replayed her words—and inwardly cursed. She hadn't been referring to Christian's past with her. She quickly said, "His experience in . . . er, covert operations, as I believe they're termed, has proved very valuable—"

She broke off; from the amusement glowing in Lady Osbaldestone's black eyes, she wasn't advancing her cause. Where were the right words? Ones that weren't ambiguous?

"I quite understand, dear." Lady Osbaldestone patted her hand in a way that suggested she truly did. "And here comes Helena—you must tell her precisely what you told me. She won't have been so entertained in years."

Letitia had to fight to keep her eyes from narrowing as they both turned to greet the shorter, slighter—but no less powerful—Duchess of St. Ives, or Dowager Duchess as she preferred to be styled in a very public attempt to spur her only son, now the duke, into marrying.

"My dear Letitia!" The duchess enveloped her in an exuberant, scented embrace, touching first one cheek, then the other, to hers. "Such a happening! I would offer my condolences, but then again, while I did not know your late husband well, one cannot imagine that his absence is devastating."

The duchess was French. Outrageous was her middle name. She could give—and over the years had at times given—the Vaux a run for their money.

"Letitia was just telling me that Dearne's been helping her find Randall's murderer." Lady Osbaldestone leaned on her cane.

"Excellent!" The duchess opened her lovely pale green eyes wide. "So useful to have a gentleman about who has more than one string to his bow, *nein*?" She beamed at Letitia.

Who inwardly sighed. If she decided to break with Christian, she would simply have to weather the scandal.

Nevertheless, while she chatted with Lady Osbaldestone and the duchess, then after parting from them, with various others, she continued to adhere to her story that he was merely helping with the investigation into Randall's death. Nothing more.

Much good did it do her. Her aunts Amarantha and Constance were a case in point; they cornered her, literally, and demanded to be told all.

"Such a wonderful thing—well, I know one is not supposed to say that over a death," Constance quickly amended, "but really it's very hard to mourn Randall. I've tried to think of him, but it seems we hardly knew him."

It seemed no one had, Letitia thought.

"And anyway," Amarantha declared, "he's dead—and you and Dearne aren't." She fixed her intent hazel gaze on Letitia. "So what's afoot? Randall murdered, Justin vanished, and Dearne hovering protectively—you can't tell me that's not going to be the story of the season."

Letitia set her jaw. "I don't wish to feature as the story of the season."

"Pshaw!" Amarantha waved aside the comment. "You're a Vaux—you can't simply suspend your heritage. The haut ton expect us to entertain them—and I have to say that currently you and Justin are doing a fine job of it."

"Indeed—I haven't had so much attention in years," Constance stated. "I vow I'm mobbed wherever I go, with ladies—and gentlemen—wishing to know 'the Truth.'" Constance edged closer; Letitia all but had her back to the wall. "So what should we say?"

Letitia told them precisely what she wished them to say.
Much to their disappointment.

Constance picked at her spangled shawl. "I can't imagine
why you think people are going to swallow such a tale—that
the only thing between you and Dearne is this investigation."

"And anyway," Amarantha informed her, "the investigation's not what they want to hear about. Randall being murdered and Justin having to disappear until the real murderer
is caught and the authorities get themselves straightened out
is all very well, but it's the *romance* everyone really wants
to know of."

"Indeed?" Letitia arched one brow. In her haughtiest manner—not all that effective against her aunts—she
stated, "If and when—and I do stress that *if*—there is anything to report on the romance front, rest assured I will let
you know." She inclined her head to them both. "And now if
you'll excuse me, I must find the withdrawing room."

Grudgingly, they stepped aside and let her go; she retreated to lick her wounds—or more specifically, to soothe
her aggravation.

On the opposite side of the room, Christian found himself in his aunt Cordelia's sights. Ermina had fluttered about
him earlier but hadn't settled; Cordelia, in contrast, looked
determined on an interrogation.

She trapped his gaze, her own unflinching. "Is Justin
Vaux guilty or not?"

That one was easy. "Not."

"Indeed?" One brow arching, Cordelia turned and pointedly looked across the room.

Following her gaze, he had no difficulty locating Letitia
as she glided through the guests; her height, combined with
the fabulous richness of her dark red hair, made her easy to
spot.

"If that's the case, then I suggest you move smartly to establish that point. More, to prove his innocence. Otherwise
. . . suffice it to say you might well find yourself facing a
hurdle you won't wish to front."

He let his lips curve although there was no real amuse-ment in the gesture. "Thank you, Aunt." On a murmur he added, "What would I do without your sage counsel?"

Cordelia snorted. "Indeed. While I'm sure you've seen the point yourself, in your usual arrogant fashion you won't let it bother you. But if you're anything like your father, you'll have forgotten that it's not just you involved—*you* might be perfectly willing to stare down the ton, but will she let you?"

Christian blinked.

"Exactly. Think about that—and then, if you're serious about claiming her, you'd better get cracking on proving to all the world that Justin Vaux is utterly blameless in the mat-ter of his brother-in-law's murder."

Having said her piece, with a regal nod, Cordelia swanned off.

Leaving Christian with the uncomfortable realization that she was right. He knew the ton would be shocked beyond measure if he—Dearne—married the sister of a convicted murderer. But as Justin wasn't guilty . . . and, moreover, as Letitia was so keen to clear Justin's name—to ensure he was known to be innocent rather than simply not proven to be guilty—there had seemed no problem, no hurdle in his path.

The problem, the hurdle, would however eventuate if they weren't successful, and Randall's killer slipped through their fingers.

If that happened, then even if Justin was no longer sus-pected of the murder, he would still, in the ton's eyes, be assumed to be guilty.

And his sister . . .

"Damn!" He muttered the word beneath his breath. Much as it pained him to admit it, Cordelia was entirely cor-rect. While he wouldn't let society dictate whom he married, the plain fact was, in such circumstances, Letitia wouldn't marry him.

She would refuse to fill the position of his marchioness.

She would not—he knew beyond question that she would not—allow him to bring disgrace to his family in that way—through her.

He looked for her, searched the crowd, but couldn't see her. She must have stepped out; he wasn't worried—she'd be back. He'd used his town carriage to bring them there; the butler knew him and her, and would send word if she tried to leave on her own, which she knew.

So she'd be back soon—and then they would leave.

He would take her back to South Audley Street. Although he'd much rather take her to Grosvenor Square, he doubted he could win that argument yet. One night soon he would, but not tonight.

Tonight he would stay with her in Randall's house, no matter how much that irked him. Regardless, he would be spending every night henceforth with her, the better to wear down any resistance she might have to accepting her future as his wife.

He was perfectly prepared for any battles on that front, perfectly confident of winning them, but as his aunt had reminded him, there were other aspects to this engagement.

Cordelia was right—he needed to prove Justin innocent.

He needed to find Randall's killer—soon.

Chapter 12

Christian accompanied Letitia to Montague's office the next morning.

Montague was delighted to see them. He eagerly copied Christian's notes on Randall's current estate. When he came to the third share of the Orient Trading Company, he paused, brows rising. "Now that's interesting. I didn't find any mention of that when I looked into his finances before the marriage—but that was eight years ago." He made a notation on his pad. "We'll certainly find out everything we can about the company."

Letitia frowned. "It doesn't ring a bell? It's not an investment company?"

Montague shook his head. "I've never heard of it. Most likely it's a private company. But we have their representative's address, so the details shouldn't be hard to extract."

"Have you uncovered anything about Randall's original source of funds?" Christian asked.

"No, unfortunately." Montague's expression darkened. "I have to say that's proving most . . . intriguing. I haven't yet been able to track down any source prior to him setting up his London accounts when he moved to the city twelve years ago. But it has to be there—I will persevere."

Reflecting that Montague's choice of the words intriguing and persevere was apt—when it came to finances, he was a stickler for detail and a terrier for facts—Christian nodded and rose. "We'll leave you to it."

"To that"—Montague shuffled his notes—"and to toting up Randall's present considerable wealth—which will necessarily involve a complete analysis of the Orient Trading Company's worth." Looking up, he smiled, then rose as Letitia did. He bowed to them both. "You may leave all that to me."

They did. Returning to South Audley Street, they alighted before Randall's steps. Barton stupidly let Letitia get a glimpse of him. Even across the width of the street, her contemptuous dagger-eyed glance scorched.

Christian drew her up the steps and through the door.

Ire lit her eyes. "That man!" Reaching up, she unpinned her veil. "Don't you know anyone at Bow Street?"

Taking her arm, Christian steered her toward the dining parlor; Mellon had informed them that Hermione and Agnes were already at the luncheon table. "I probably could get Barton removed, but they'd only put someone else on the case." He met Letitia's eyes. "Much as he irritates you, he might well be a case of better the devil you know."

She humphed, and let him lead her to the dining table and seat her at its end.

Hermione and Agnes were eager to hear of developments. While the footmen and Mellon were in the room, they had to be circumspect in what they said, but when the fruit was set before them, Letitia dismissed the staff and had Mellon close the door.

Lowering her voice, she told Hermione and her aunt that Justin was in town and safe with friends.

"Well *that's* a relief." Agnes reached for a fig.

"Yes, *but*," Hermione said, "he can't be free again until we catch the murderer."

"Indeed." Letitia was concentrating on the fig she was peeling, yet Christian registered her tone, sensed the same thread of something more deadening in Hermione, too.

The Vaux tended not to deal well with "nothing happening."

He cast about for something to distract them. Remembered . . . "We haven't yet pursued the question of how the man Hermione heard talking with Randall that night—presumably the murderer—got into and out of the house."

A minor issue, but it would serve.

Busy neatly consuming her fig, Letitia slanted a glance his way. "You were going to question Mellon again."

"So I was. No time like the present." Swinging his legs from beneath the table, Christian rose and crossed to the bellpull.

When Mellon answered the summons, Christian, seated again, arched a brow at Letitia.

She waved to him to proceed. To Mellon, she said, "Please answer his lordship's questions."

Christian studied Mellon, standing between Letitia and Agnes on the other side of the table, for several seconds, before saying, "Mellon, think back to the night your master was murdered. Who, throughout all that evening, did you admit to this house?"

Mellon frowned, but answered readily enough. "Other than Lady Randall when she returned from her dinner, and the master when he came home at six o'clock, the only person I opened the door to was Lord Vaux, my lord."

Christian watched Mellon closely. "You admitted no other person, at no other time during that evening and night, whether through the front door or any other door. Is that correct?"

Mellon fixed his gaze above Christian's head. "Yes, my lord."

Christian leaned forward. "Tell me, Mellon, in your opinion is it possible that someone entered the house, or left the house, through the front door without your knowledge?"

Mellon opened his mouth, but then shut it. Christian was pleased to see he took time to think before answering. Nevertheless . . . "I can't say absolutely not, my lord—there were a few minutes between when I left Lord Vaux in the library and reached my room—but that was the only time anyone could have come in or out through the front door, or else I would have known, given as my room is directly above it."

Christian nodded. "And if they'd come in then, when did they leave, and if they left then, then when did they arrive—quite." He paused, then asked, "Is there any other door, or French door—any other way into the house other than through the servants' hall?"

"No, my lord. None at all."

Christian remembered. "There's a lane down the side. No entry from there?"

"Not to the front of the house, my lord. There's a gate at the side of the backyard, and as you will have seen, there's only a very narrow area behind the front railings. The drawing room and front parlor windows look onto that, but they aren't doors, and they're locked anyway."

Christian waved the windows aside. "There's clearly no other way anyone else could have got into the house." He caught Hermione's eye as she opened her mouth—breathed easier when she shut it. Looking at Mellon, he smiled. "Thank you, Mellon. You may go."

Mellon bowed, then cast a glance at Letitia. She waved a dismissal and he went.

Hermione managed to contain herself until the door shut. She even managed to keep her voice down. "But there *was* someone else there—I heard them." She glanced at Letitia. "I'm not making it up."

"We know you're not." Letitia looked at Christian. "What now?"

Carefully, he took Hermione step by step through her story again. She was unshakable in her certainty that she'd heard Randall speaking with some other man. "And it definitely *wasn't* Justin. I wouldn't mistake his voice—it's deep, like yours."

Christian raised his brows. "And the other man's wasn't?"

Hermione shook her head. "His was . . . lighter. Not light, but a medium man's voice. Nothing one would notice either way."

She remembered things far too clearly, in too much detail, for Christian to doubt her.

He sat back. "Very well. So what we're faced with is this. On that night some man, a friend of Randall's, gained entry into the house, how we don't know, spoke with Randall, and then hit him with the poker, killing him. How did that man get into and out of the house?"

They all sat back and thought.

"Not the house," Letitia eventually said. She caught Christian's eye. "Just the study—we don't know that he went anywhere else in the house. We have no reason to suppose he did."

Christian nodded. "Good point. So how did he get into the study?"

Letitia sat forward, leaning her elbows on the table. "If this was Nunchance, I'd say he'd got in through the secret passage. But this is a London town house—no secret ways."

Christian stared at her, at her face, for a long moment, then looked up—at the cornices—ornate—and the heavy rough plaster of the ceiling. Recalled similar plasterwork in the library and front parlor, and the wood half paneling that ran through most of the house. . . . "But this *is* an old house." Swinging around, he stood and stalked to the window to get a better sense of the thickness of the walls. Thick. Head rising, he pictured the front façade—of this house, and the one that abutted it, and the one beyond that.

He turned back to the table, caught Letitia's gaze. "This *isn't* a new London town house. It's a very old house that's been divided into three. It *is* of the vintage where secret passages and entrances were de rigueur."

Something else struck him. "Why did Randall buy this house—this particular house? Did he ever mention it?"

She thought, shook her head.

"He was a secretive man—if we've learned anything about him, it's that. He liked to hide things." He was already moving toward the door.

Behind him, chairs scraped. His hand on the doorknob, he turned back to see all three ladies on their feet.

Letitia's eyes were wide. "You think there's a secret passage leading to the study?"

He smiled intently. "I wouldn't be the least surprised."

They trooped into the study and started their search. Agnes, unable to easily bend or stretch, excused herself and retired, leaving the three of them tapping panels and poking at the ornately carved mantelpiece and the thick, lushly carved picture rail.

Letitia was working her way along one wall, pressing every knob in the intricately figured rail that ran along the top of the half paneling, when a knock fell on the front door. They all stopped searching, waited, listening to the low murmur of voices in the hall.

A second later the door opened to reveal Mellon. He announced, "A Mr. Dalziel has called, my lady. I've shown him into the drawing room."

Letitia straightened. "Please show him in here, Mellon."

Mellon looked disapproving, but retreated, restricting himself to a glance at the spot where his master's body had lain.

Two heartbeats later, Dalziel walked in. He turned and rather pointedly shut the door in Mellon's face.

Holding up one finger to enjoin their silence, Dalziel waited for half a minute, his hand on the doorknob, then he opened the door again.

They couldn't see past his shoulders, but heard him utter two words. "Leave. Now."

His tone suggested that whoever was there—presumably Mellon—risked fatal injury if he didn't immediately comply.

He must have left—at speed—because Dalziel smoothly shut the door and turned back into the room.

It wasn't good news making Dalziel so edgy; leaving the wall, Letitia moved to the center of the room, stopped and waited for him to join her.

Which he did, halting directly before her.

She was conscious of Christian drawing nearer, stopping

by her shoulder. She searched Dalziel's uninformative face. "What is it? Justin?"

Dalziel answered with a sharp shake of his head. "He's safely hidden where no one will think, or dare, to look for him." He held her gaze. "I've heard from Hexham." His voice low, he went on, "There's only one family called Randall in the area, or was—a farmer who had a decent spread outside the town. He and his wife are both dead, but he was warm enough to spare his only son from the farm when the boy was awarded a governors' scholarship to Hexham Grammar School. There, the lad did well enough, apparently, but the school lost track of him after he left."

Letitia held his dark gaze; she knew what he was telling her, but she couldn't—simply could not—take it in. After a blank moment, she said, "You're saying . . ." Then she shook her head, briskly dismissing the impossible. "That couldn't have been Randall. I couldn't have been married to a farmer's son."

Dalziel's lips compressed, then he murmured, "George Martin Randall. According to the school and parish records he would have turned thirty-four in April this year."

She stared, jaw slackening. "Good *God*!" Her voice was weak; she literally felt the blood drain from her face.

"Sit down." Christian grasped her arm and eased her back and down into the chair he'd set behind her.

Once she was seated, still stunned and shocked, he glanced at Dalziel. "That explains a few things."

"Indeed." Dalziel nodded curtly. "It also poses a host of new questions."

"But . . . how could. . . ?" Letitia gestured at nothing in particular, but they knew what she meant.

"Precisely." Dalziel glanced around the study—at the polished wood, the heavy desk, the books and curios on the shelves, the elegant chairs. "The 'how coulds' are endless. How could a farmer's son have achieved all this? More, although he was only thirty-four, he'd been wealthy enough, for long enough, to have simply become accepted by the ton."

"Wealthy enough to rescue the Vaux from gargantuan debts," Letitia said. "And so marry me—and through me become connected with and have the entrée to the highest levels of society."

Dalziel blinked.

Christian realized he hadn't known about the debts that had led to Letitia marrying Randall. Letitia, Justin, and their father had kept that secret well.

It was on the tip of Dalziel's tongue to ask—to confirm and inquire about the forced marriage—but then he glanced at Christian, his look plainly saying, *Later?*

Christian nodded.

Somewhat to his relief, a frown replaced Letitia's stunned expression.

"But why?" She looked up at Dalziel, then swiveled to look at him. "Why, why, *why*? It makes no sense."

After a moment, Dalziel said, "Yes it does. Just think— a farmer's son rises to live as one with the highest in the land." When they looked at him, he continued, "That has to be a dream, a fantasy many farmers, laborers, and the like indulge in. Randall didn't just fantasize, he made it happen. Found ways to make it happen."

"I don't understand."

They all turned to Hermione. She was leaning against the desk, arms folded, a frown identical to the one on Letitia's face darkening hers.

"Why would he want to become one of us? Why not just be a very rich farmer?"

Dalziel answered. "Status. It's something we take for granted, that we rarely if ever think of. We're born to it—we assume its mantle as our norm. But although *we're* barely aware of it, others are. They envy us what we barely notice—all the privileges we enjoy by right of birth." He paused, then went on, "While there are many who—out of our hearing—rail against our privilege, the truly clever . . . they try to join us."

Letitia hauled in a huge breath, let it out with, "In which endeavor Randall succeeded excellently well."

She was a part of his success.

She looked up, met Christian's, then Dalziel's, eyes. "That fits. Very well. It explains a lot of his attitudes that I never understood."

Dalziel nodded. "Very likely, but the most pertinent point for our investigation is that having succeeded so excellently well, Randall kept his success a secret. A very, indeed amazingly, closely kept secret. Who knew of his background? So far, we've found no one. No one even suspected. One might have thought that, having succeeded, he might crow—at least to close friends. But he didn't have any—something that now makes sense. Yet nothing we've uncovered suggests even secret gloating. He might have inwardly preened, but he didn't celebrate his success."

"He wasn't finished." Letitia met Dalziel's dark eyes, then looked at Christian. "He was set on taking Nunchance from Justin. And he wanted children." Her lips curved cynically. "Unfortunately for him, he forgot to specify that as part of our agreement. I believe he thought it simply followed as a natural outcome of my duties in the marriage bed, and strangely—perhaps because he was in fact a farmer's son— he never realized that I might have some way of preventing that."

The depth of her aversion for Randall showed in her eyes, then she turned back to Dalziel.

Who had started to pace. "Even so, his secrecy might well have been the reason behind his murder. His continuing plans, which made maintaining that secrecy even more important, only add weight to the thesis."

Letitia frowned. "I can understand him murdering someone else to preserve his secret, but how could such a secret have killed him?"

Dalziel halted. "I don't know, but such secrets are always

dangerous." He frowned, then glanced at the paneling, as if only then registering what they'd been doing when he'd entered. "What were you searching for?"

They told him.

He hesitated, clearly weighing what else he had on his plate against the challenge of finding a secret door. It took him all of five seconds to decide. "I've got some time—I'll help."

Which made four of them, which, as Letitia remarked, was just as well. The study was a cornucopia of carved wood. They divided the room into quarters and settled to their search.

Starting in one corner, she poked and prodded, mindlessly working her way along the paneling's upper rail; inside, her mind was awash with a litany of exclamations, all escalating versions of "a farmer's son?" It was, simply, unbelievable—unacceptable. For a lady of her rank and birth . . . it was more than shocking.

More than scandalous.

If it ever became known she'd stooped so low as to marry a farmer's son . . .

Halting, raising her head, she sucked air into suddenly parched lungs.

Farther along the wall, Christian glanced up, caught her gaze.

She looked into his eyes, into the unwavering, unshakable gray, and felt her reeling world slow, steady.

Her catastrophic secret would only be a disaster if it became known.

He arched a brow at her, plainly asking if she was all right.

Drawing in another breath, she nodded, and returned to her examination of the rail.

Later. She would deal with the potential for catastrophe later. At the moment, it was all she could do to get her mind to accept Dalziel's truth.

Ten minutes later she found a catch hidden in the moldings around one of the windows. Energized, she told the others. They came to look, then, while they all scanned the room, she depressed the catch.

A bookcase in the center of the opposite wall popped free of the stonework.

"My God!" Hermione breathed. "There really is a secret door."

Christian and Dalziel had already crossed to the bookcase. They didn't need to expend any huge effort to move it back—it swung open easily, and noiselessly, on well-oiled hinges.

Standing in the opening revealed, Christian, in a voice tinged with awe, said, "It's not a secret door—it's a secret *room*."

Letitia and Hermione joined the two men, then followed them down the three steps that descended into what truly was an amazing find.

"Trust Randall to have a secret room"—Letitia slowly pivoted, taking in the space—"to store all his secrets in."

That certainly appeared to be the room's purpose. In contrast to the study, which was neat and tidy, with no papers on the desk and a pristine white blotter clearly for show rather than use, this room was full of papers—stacked on both sides of the massive but well-worn desk and bulging from pigeonholes behind it—and a blotter that was crossed, recrossed, and rather tattered.

All of the available wall space was covered with shelves housing ledgers, stacks of files, document boxes, and tomes that appeared to be accounts, their spines marked in Randall's schoolboyish hand with dates and initials. The shelves stretched all the way to the high ceiling; a wooden ladder stood in one corner.

There was an old, serviceable lamp upon the desk—a large one of the sort clerks favored, that shed a wide pool of light when lit. The glass lamp-well was half full of oil, and the wick was charred, needing to be trimmed. There was hardly any dust anywhere. The room appeared to be in frequent use.

The desk, with its well-padded revolving chair behind it, sat halfway into the room, its back to the shelves covering the wall the room shared with the main body of the house. Letitia glanced back; the wall with the hidden door in its center was likewise covered in shelves, outside the space of the door itself. The wall opposite, abutting some deeper part of the house, was also covered in shelves.

The fourth wall—the one facing the desk—was the one of most immediate interest to them all. Both sides housed more ledgers, but between were two narrow windows flanking a wooden door.

They'd all been standing silently, pirouetting as they took it all in. Their gazes came to rest on the closed door. Christian walked forward, grasped the knob and turned; the latch clicked.

"Well, well." Opening the door wide, Christian walked through.

The rest of them followed, emerging into a small walled yard. Less than three yards wide, it ended at the lane wall. To the left, in line with the study-side wall of the secret room, a plain stone wall ran across, joining the lane wall. That wall was high—so high none of them could see over it, and no one in the area along the house's front could see into the yard where they stood.

Opposite, another stone wall ran from the house to the lane wall; again, it was sufficiently high so no one below, in the yard beside the kitchen, could see in, and they couldn't look over and down.

But they could hear voices floating up and over the wall; a few seconds of listening told them two maids were hanging out some washing.

The length of the yard from the front to the back matched the length of the secret room. Turning as one, they looked back at the house, at the way the roof line concealed the existence of the little room. Shaking her head in amazement, Letitia nudged Hermione back toward the door.

Christian made to follow, but Dalziel hung back, then turned and walked in the opposite direction, to the wooden door set in the lane wall. From where Letitia paused by the door into the room, she could see the heavy lock on the lane door. But when Dalziel grasped the handle and turned it, the door swung open—as easily and noiselessly as the door to the study.

Leaning out, Dalziel looked up and down the lane. Letitia knew what he would see—a cobbled lane too narrow for carriages, with a procession of wooden garden doors opening onto it. Unless one counted and watched the roofs at the same time, the unexpected door wouldn't appear out of place.

Drawing back, Dalziel closed the door. Turning, he waved them ahead of him back into the room. Once the room's outer door was shut and there was no chance of the maids below hearing them, he looked at Letitia and Christian. "I believe we've solved the mystery of how Randall's murderer came and went."

They were all silent for a moment, imagining it.

"I doubt Randall would have left those doors unlocked." Letitia wrapped her arms around herself. "He was always careful of windows being left open."

"The doors—all of them—would have been locked, but his murderer was a friend, one he was expecting." Christian reviewed the events of that night in his mind. "Randall wasn't expecting Justin that evening—no reason he wouldn't have made an appointment for a friend to call." He looked around. "Not just any friend, but one he did business with."

Dalziel nodded. "He unlocked the doors, and left them unlocked because he assumed his friend would shortly be leaving by the same route."

"Which he did," Christian said. "After he'd killed Randall."

Nodding again, Dalziel turned to consider the shelves.

Hermione had already wandered over to them. Tilting her

head, she peered at some stacked papers. "No wonder he spent so many hours, so many nights, locked in his study."

Dalziel glanced up the steps. "It might be best if we lock the study door."

"I'll do it." Hermione headed back into the study.

Letitia exchanged a look with Christian, then they joined Dalziel in staring at the shelves.

She shook her head. "I can't see any obvious place to start."

Christian sighed, walked to a shelf, and pulled down a ledger.

Within ten minutes they'd confirmed they were looking at the records of the Orient Trading Company. Encouraged, they spent the next twenty minutes wading through files, documents, and accounts.

Dalziel looked up, glanced at the ledger Christian held. "I have income, you have expenses, but all the entries are in some sort of code."

Frowning, Christian nodded. He and Dalziel had a more than passing familiarity with codes. "I don't think it's a keyed code." Glancing at Letitia and Hermione, he explained, "A code where there's a defined key—so once you have the key, you can read the code."

He looked again at the entries in the ledger. "This looks more like initials of things."

Dalziel grunted. "If so, then there'll be a pattern some-where, if we look long enough." He looked up at the tower-ing shelves of papers.

They all mentally groaned.

A clock chimed in the study. Letitia blinked, then reluc-tantly shut the ledger she'd been perusing. She looked at Christian. "If we want to catch Trowbridge this afternoon, we'll have to go."

Dalziel cocked an inquiring brow. Letitia explained, "I received an invitation to an afternoon exhibition of garden sculptures at Lady Hemming's house in Chelsea. Trow-bridge is one of the critics her ladyship has invited to grace the event and proffer opinions on the works. I'd thought to approach him there, in a social setting, rather than call formally."

"An excellent idea." Dalziel looked at Christian. "I'll continue here, but we should send for Trentham. He knows more about importing and shipping than I do—he might see something in these"—with a wave he indicated the walls of records—"I'll miss."

Christian nodded, closing the ledger he'd been examining. "I'll send a message—and I'll also see if Jack Hendon's in town. If we need to know about importing and shipping, no reason not to go to the source."

"Indeed." Dalziel looked at the shelves again. "I've a feeling we're going to need all the help we can get."

They arranged for Hermione to wait in the study, from where she could look out and keep watch on the street. When Tristan arrived, she would allow him into the study, then show him the secret door.

"One last thing." Dalziel set down the files he'd been perusing. "Let's find out how to open the door from this side . . . assuming it does open from this side."

Leaving Hermione in the study, they shut the secret door, then hunted. It was the work of a few minutes to locate the catch; the door did indeed open from both sides.

Letitia was about to leave the secret room when she recalled that both outer doors were unlocked. She mentioned it, along with, "So anyone who's ever seen Randall open the secret door from this side—his murderer, for example—has free access to the rest of the house."

Both she and Hermione wrapped their arms around themselves and shivered.

Dalziel exchanged a look with Christian.

Who looked at Letitia.

Just as she remembered. "I know where the keys are."

Spinning around, she climbed the steps into the study. Going to the desk, she opened the middle drawer and pulled out a small ring with two keys. Returning to the secret room, she headed for the outer door. "Barton found these when he searched the desk. Neither he nor I had any idea where they fitted—he tried them in all the locks in the house."

One key operated the lock on the door to the small yard. Unlocking it again, she opened the door and silently crossed to the laneway door. The second key locked it.

Relieved, she returned to the secret room, locked the outer door, then tossed the keys to Dalziel, now sitting in the chair behind the desk. "Leave them with Hermione if you leave before we get back."

He sent her a look—he didn't take orders at all well—but then saluted her and gave his attention to another ledger.

She turned to Christian. "Now we can go." She headed for the steps to the study. "Come on, or Trowbridge will have left before we get there."

After exchanging a resigned look with Dalziel, Christian turned, nodded to Hermione, and followed Letitia back into the house.

Throughout the journey to Chelsea, Letitia was uncharacteristically quiet, her silence punctuated by an occasional muttered, "I still can't believe it."

Christian understood her difficulty, and her consternation. If it ever became common knowledge that she, Lady Letitia Vaux, an earl's daughter, had married a farmer's son, she, and the Vaux in general, would never live it down. Despite Randall having deceived the entire ton, she, even more than her family, would bear the opprobrium. As dangerous secrets went, that certainly qualified.

She, of course, realized that; as the carriage rattled into Chelsea she fixed him with a tense look. "Who else might know of Randall's background? What about the alumni of Hexham Grammar School?" A hint of hysteria colored the words.

"I doubt they'd know," he answered evenly. "The school wouldn't advertise the social standing of their governors' scholars—the other boys would have imagined them impoverished gentry." He paused, then added, "If any had known, you would have heard of it long since."

She nodded tersely. "True. So!" She drew in a tight breath. "Who else needs to know the details?"

He'd anticipated that question, too. "The others who are helping us—Trentham, and Jack Hendon, if he's here. Without knowing that, they won't understand what we're dealing with. But you needn't worry about their discretion. They won't say a word—I guarantee it."

She searched his eyes. "You know each other's secrets, I suppose."

He nodded.

She softly humphed, and looked out of the window. "I'll have to tell Agnes—she'll need to know. But I'm not going to tell Amarantha or Constance. They'd have the vapors, and that would be just the start of it."

"There's no need to tell anyone who's not helping us unravel this mystery."

After a moment she said, "I'll have to tell Justin."

Given Justin's feelings over Randall and her marriage, her reluctance was understandable, but . . . "Yes, he has to know."

When she said nothing more, he added, "And at some point, you'll have to tell your father."

A moment went by, then, still looking out of the window, she murmured, "He already feels so guilty over me having to marry Randall . . . we'll see."

He left it at that, not least because they'd reached Lady Hemming's; the carriage slowed, joining the line of vehicles drawing up before her ladyship's front steps to disgorge their fair burdens. A survey of those alighting confirmed that this was another highly select event. To his relief, Christian noted a smattering of gentlemen among the female throng.

Lady Hemming greeted them effusively, thrilled to have Letitia grace her event. Randall's death was still a point of interest for the ton's avid gossips, and having Christian appear as Letitia's escort only heightened expectations.

Yet as they strolled into the crowd—a sea of color constantly shifting about the sculptures set up on her ladyship's lawn—Letitia's cool grace proved sufficient to keep the curious, if not at bay, then at least within bounds. They nodded and exchanged greetings, eyed Christian with open curiosity, but did not try to detain them or engage them in discussion of the "distressing events surrounding her husband's death."

Christian overheard the phrase more than once during their perambulation, whispered behind hands, eyes following Letitia and himself. Like her, he ignored both the whispers and the eyes.

"That's Trowbridge." Letitia halted by a bronze of a scantily clad nymph. She pretended to study the statue, but with a tip of her head indicated a gentleman standing before the next sculpture along. He was surrounded by a bevy of ladies, both young and old, who hung on his every word as he passed judgment on the piece.

Letitia continued to study the nymph, allowing Christian the opportunity to feign boredom and idly survey the group before the next statue.

Trowbridge was on the tall side of average, his hair an artful tangle of mousy brown locks, one of which fell artistically across his forehead. His features, while pleasant enough, were undistinguished, lacking the sharp angles and planes common among the aristocracy, but it was his dress that caused Christian to mentally raise his brows.

Trowbridge had elected to wear a coat of bold green, ivory, and black checks. His waistcoat was a perfectly matched spring green, the buttons on both coat and waistcoat large gold disks; his trousers were black. Instead of a cravat, he wore a floppy ivory silk scarf knotted about his throat.

Together with his gestures as he discoursed on the sculpture to the assembled ladies, the vision he presented made Christian wonder. . . .

"I seriously doubt he has the slightest interest in any lady—other than the statue, of course."

The dry comment from Letitia had Christian glancing at

her. Then he looked back at the group around Trowbridge. The ladies, one and all, appeared to be flirting outrageously with the man, while Trowbridge responded to the top of his bent. He frowned. "Do those ladies know that?"

"Of course." Slipping her hand onto his arm again, Letitia murmured, "That's why they flirt with him so openly—no matter how he responds, his preference for men makes him perfectly safe."

Christian's brows rose higher. "I see."

They circled, holding to their own company but keeping Trowbridge in view. Eventually some of the ladies drifted away, then, having expounded at length on the points of a statue of a satyr, Trowbridge stepped back, allowing those left a moment to reflect.

Letitia and Christian exchanged a glance, and moved in.

"Good afternoon, Mr. Trowbridge." Letitia gave him her hand. "I'm Lady Letitia Randall. We met at Lady Hutchinson's event."

Trowbridge smiled delightedly and with an extravagant flourish bowed over her hand. "Enchanted, my lady."

"Allow me to present Lord Dearne."

Christian exchanged a circumspect nod with Trowbridge.

"I wished to speak with you"—Letitia glanced at the ladies still studying the satyr—"to ask your advice on the relative merits of the pastoral style of works"—a wave indicated the pieces studding the lawn—"versus the humanistic style, from the viewpoint of long-term investment."

Trowbridge blinked.

Turning away from the satyr—and the other ladies—Letitia started to stroll slowly down the lawn toward the river wall that marked its far end.

Trowbridge necessarily kept pace. "I . . . er, don't really advise from an investment point of view. My interests are more on the artistic side—the skill of the artist in capturing his subject, his technique, the quality of execution. Sadly, investment value is more driven by what becomes popular, rather than by artistic merit."

Contrary to Christian's expectations, Trowbridge didn't halt, ready to part from them and return to his bevy of admirers. Instead he continued to stroll beside Letitia, his gaze on her face. Waiting.

She glanced swiftly back, confirming they were out of earshot of all other guests. "I see. Regardless, Mr. Trowbridge, I have something I wished to discuss with you."

"Yes?" Trowbridge's tone was frankly expectant.

Christian had fallen back, strolling a pace behind Letitia's shoulder, leaving Trowbridge's interrogation to her—at least to begin with. He drew closer as she drew breath and said, "I daresay you've heard about the murder of my late husband, and that the authorities suspect my brother of the crime."

Trowbridge's face blanked.

Glancing up, Letitia saw, waited. When he said nothing, simply stared at her, she went on. "I believe you knew my husband rather well—you and he were close friends, were you not?"

Trowbridge halted. "Ah . . . no. Not close. Not anymore. Not for many years."

Halting, too, Letitia raised her brows. "Indeed? Then it will come as a surprise to you that he left you a bequest in his will."

"He did?" Trowbridge was either an excellent actor or was truly surprised. "But I thought . . . that is to say, we'd agreed—" He broke off altogether. After a moment of staring into space as if seeking clarification, he refocused on Letitia. "I really don't know what to say, Lady Randall. Randall and I hadn't been more than passing acquaintances socially for . . . well, the last decade." He frowned. "What did he leave me?"

"You'll no doubt hear from his solicitor in due course. It was an antique clock—he said you'd admired it."

Trowbridge's face lit. "The Glockstein?" When Letitia nodded, he rattled on, "Indeed, it's a very fine piece. He came across it years ago and was wise enough to pick it up.

I was always envious. He even said it was knowing my taste that spurred him to buy it. Such ornate work on both the face and the hands. I've always—"

"Trowbridge."

Christian's deeper voice jerked Trowbridge back to blinking attention; he caught the man's gaze. "How did you know Randall?"

Trowbridge's eyes widened. "How?"

Christian felt his face harden. "Through what avenue did you first meet him? It's a simple enough question."

"Yes . . . but why do you want to know?"

"Because for obvious reasons we're hunting for Randall's killer, and a necessary part of our investigation is considering all who knew him well. He mentioned you in his will as a longtime friend, and if, as you intimated, you were green with envy over his acquisition of the Glockstein clock, then—"

"No, no!" Trowbridge waved his hands. "Good Lord. It wasn't like that. Our acquaintance . . . well, friendship as it was, was nothing like that." He looked sincerely horrified. "If you really must know, we met at school."

Letitia opened her mouth. Christian silenced her with a look. "Which school?"

"Hexham Grammar School."

Christian looked into Trowbridge's large, slightly protuberant blue eyes. "Did you know Randall was a farmer's son?"

"Yes, of course. We . . . ah, he wished it kept secret. Especially when he went up in the world." Trowbridge glanced at Letitia, as if conscious of what such a secret would mean to her.

Christian grasped the moment to ask, "And what about you, Trowbridge? Have you come up in the world, too? Are you, too, hiding something?"

Abruptly Trowbridge looked him in the eye. "Patently, I'm hiding nothing at all." He held out his arms, hands spread, inviting them to view him as he was. "From which you may infer that deception isn't my strong suit." He glanced at Letitia. "It was Randall's." He looked again at Christian. "If I had half his talent, I would, without doubt, be more circumspect. As it is . . ."

Again he gestured, turning the movement into an extravagant bow. "If you'll excuse me?"

With a nod, he turned away, and walked swiftly, rather stiffly, back up the lawn.

Shoulder-to-shoulder, Christian and Letitia watched him go.

"I'll lay odds," Christian murmured, "that he's from a lower class family, too. That he was another governors' scholar. His natural . . . flair, for want of a better word, is his disguise—in our circles quite an effective one."

Letitia snorted. "If we're to talk of odds, what are the chances of two governors' scholars from Hexham Grammar School rising from nothing to walk our gilded circles?"

"I wouldn't like to think." Christian took her arm and started back to the house. "Regardless, what would you wager that when we learn about Swithin, he, too, will prove to have attended Hexham Grammar School, and that he, too, was a governors' scholar?"

"Regardless of Trowbridge's protestations, his particular bent, no matter how widely recognized, how relatively open and undisguised, still gives him a powerful motive for murder."

Later that night, Christian moved about Letitia's bedchamber; shrugging out of his coat, he laid it over the back of a chair. "For instance, if Randall, who must have known his secret, including numerous details—a gentleman who could claim long acquaintance—were to explicitly expose Trowbridge, then everything he's worked for, his position in the ton, would evaporate overnight. The fact that he and Randall shared another secret wouldn't matter—the secret of their births counts for much less, and affects them both equally."

In light of Trowbridge's "particular bent," they'd had to wait until now, when they were free of both Agnes and Hermione, to discuss the subject.

Standing before the window looking out over the night-shrouded street, Letitia folded her arms. "No lady would be able to allow him to cross her threshold, not if his inclination was public fact."

They'd returned to South Audley Street to find that Tristan had indeed arrived and spent several hours with Dalziel searching through the files and papers. They'd eventually departed, leaving a message with Hermione—chuffed to be a part of their investigation—to the effect that they'd return the following day to continue searching and share any news.

Beyond that, Hermione knew no more, which had done nothing to ease Letitia's growing concern over the Orient Trading Company. She had a gnawing premonition that Randall being a farmer's son might prove the least troubling of the secrets he'd left behind. She leaned against the window frame. "I wish I'd asked Trowbridge about the company— whether he knew anything of it, or whether, indeed, he was another part owner."

On the journey back from Chelsea, they'd speculated as to whether Trowbridge and Swithin might prove to also be part owners in the company, accounting, perhaps, for the other two-thirds.

Unbuttoning his shirt, Christian crossed to stand behind her. "One step at a time. We've established that Randall and Trowbridge were once friends, that they'd known each other for decades, but that for some reason they grew distant with the years . . . or they played down and actively hid their association."

Reaching for her, he drew her back against him; she let him, but remained stiff, spine straight, in his arms. He continued, "If Trowbridge is a part owner of the Orient Trading Company, then claiming he barely knows Randall won't wash—they would have had to meet frequently, and with

Randall leaving him a bequest in a relatively recent will, citing their friendship, then Trowbridge's claim of mere acquaintance isn't believable."

"Which in itself is strange—why hide a friendship if it were there? Trowbridge didn't attend Randall's funeral, yet he must have known of his death. He hasn't called to offer his condolences—he didn't offer any even today."

Settling her against him, he reviewed the short interview. "Trowbridge was taken aback that Randall had named him in his will. It seemed to me his reaction had more to do with Randall acknowledging him at all, rather than that it was via a bequest."

"Hmm." She closed her hands about his at her waist. "What I don't see is how any of this is helping us clear Justin's name."

Secure in the knowledge that she couldn't see, he let his lips curve, then he touched them to her temple, drew them slowly down, barely touching, over the whorl of her ear to press a more definite kiss into the shadowed hollow behind it.

Eliciting an encouraging shiver.

"We're identifying other possible suspects." He murmured the words against the soft skin of her throat. "And once we know more about the Orient Trading Company, we'll doubtless have more. If Randall was managing an enterprise directly engaged in trade, there's always the chance of a disgruntled customer or supplier furious enough, or desperate enough, to commit murder. We now know we can add Trowbridge to our list. And most likely Swithin as well. The more potential suspects we can identify, the weaker the case against Justin."

She eased back against him, into his warmth. "Perhaps, but he's still the prime suspect."

"True." He skated his lips down the long line of her throat, heard her breath catch as she arched her head, allowing him better access. "But once we start winnowing our suspects, the real murderer will emerge." Raising his head, he turned her, met her shadowed eyes. "And once we have him, Justin will be safe. In every way."

She looked into his eyes; he could sense the frown in hers. "You make it sound so . . . straightforward. That it will simply happen, step by step, like that."

"Because it will." He drew her closer. "Because we'll make it happen"—he bent his head—"just . . . like . . . that."

He covered her lips and kissed her—deliberately kissed her to distract her.

To give her something else to think about, to fill her mind with . . .

Him. Them.

And what might be.

He needed to reawaken her dreams again, to convince her to trust that they could come to be. To convince her to put her hand in his again, to be his again.

In his heart he knew it wouldn't be as easy as he'd like, yet when he held her in his arms, when she stepped into him and sank her fingers in his hair and kissed him back with all the pent-up longing in her dramatic soul, he felt like heaven was within his reach.

So close, as he angled his head and deepened the kiss, he could taste it.

She no longer even pretended that she thought he might—or should—leave her each night, that he should go home and allow her to retire alone. Just as well. The single night he'd stayed apart from her had seemed to drag on forever.

Yet as they tussled for direction, wrestled for supremacy, as clothes dropped like so much litter to the floor, as hands grasped and mouths and lips caressed—until he spun her about, bent her forward over a round table and entered her from behind—and she gasped, caught her breath, then sighed, shifted, and took him yet deeper—even then he wasn't sure, couldn't tell whether she was as caught in the moment as he was.

As deeply ensnared by the emotional net that for him, at least, in moments such as this, held him.

All he could do was show her how he felt—let her see, and feel, how possessive of her, with her, he wished— needed—to be.

And hope she understood.

In the end, after they'd both touched glory and he'd carried her, all but staggering, to collapse on her bed, as she curled against him, her head pillowed on his shoulder, the fingers of one hand lazily riffling the hair on his chest, all he could do was hope that she would once again grant him what she'd so freely gifted him with all those years ago.

Hope that with every night, with every day that passed, she would see his unswerving devotion for what it was.

Hope that on this unsettling and unfamiliar battleground, he was advancing his cause, and drawing ever closer to recapturing her heart.

Chapter 13

The following morning, Christian left Letitia sprawled boneless in her bed; returning to Allardyce House, he breakfasted in solitary state, then went to call on Montague. That expert in money matters received him in his office—with a frown.

"I'm having a great deal of difficulty following the trail of Randall's money back in time—which I shouldn't have. It's as if he, as a financial entity, simply came into being, fully funded, twelve years ago." Montague reached across his desk, picked up a sheet and peered at it. "Interestingly, that was the same time—twelve years ago—that the Orient Trading Company first surfaced."

Lowering the sheet, Montague looked over his pince-nez at Christian, seated before the desk. "It's quite remarkable that I can find no trace of any accounts for Randall prior to his establishing the accounts he died with, all of which are with London banks."

"Twelve years ago, Randall was twenty-two years old."

"Indeed. And I can tell you there are few twenty-two-year-olds who could claim the level of capital he had. I've even considered the question of an alias, but there's no sign of that. Much as it shocks me, I'm tending to the theory that when Randall set up his currently held accounts twelve years ago, he deposited the funds in cash. It was a significant amount, yet there's no trace of that money coming from anywhere—meaning any other account or instrument or fund." Montague shook his head. "It *had* to have been moved in cash."

Christian nodded. Given Randall's background, that was perhaps not surprising. Chances were, he hadn't had much to do with banks before coming to London.

"One thing I have made headway with is the estimation of Randall's final estate. I've yet to hear back regarding the estimated worth of the third share in the Orient Trading Company, but even leaving that aside, the figure is quite startling." Montague glanced at a sheet of paper, then handed it across the desk.

Christian took it, read the figure, and raised his brows.

"Indeed." Montague sat back, removing his pince-nez. "While I'm sure it's not what you want to hear, I would have to say that Randall's estate provides an excellent motive for murder, even if the one inheriting is one's sister."

Christian pulled a face. He handed the sheet back. "And the company?"

"The Orient Trading Company appears to be a legitimate enterprise, at least on the surface, with reputable legal representatives. As to the nature of its business, I've sent out inquiries, but have yet to hear more."

"We've found a set of books that Randall kept—they appear to be the accounts, income and expenses, and so on, of the Orient Trading Company, but even though we've only started looking through them, all the entries are in some sort of code—as if they're payments to and from various sources but with only initials identifying the sources, and no indication of what goods were traded."

Montague frowned. "That sounds like an amateurish method of account keeping, but it doesn't preclude what I've said—the company may still be entirely legitimate, just run very privately and secretively."

"Randall was nothing if not secretive, so that's no surprise." Christian thought, then said, "It might be best if you concentrate first on identifying the other owners."

"The beneficial owners." Picking up a pen, Montague made a note.

"Just so. And it would be helpful if you could verify the company's income, at least to the extent of confirming whether it was profitable or not. After that, if we still have no clue as to what the company's business consists of, we'll need you to delve deeper. We'll see what we can learn from the books first, but it might well be that they'll only increase the mystery."

Montague nodded. "Rest assured I'll give these matters my fullest attention."

His enthusiastic tone made Christian smile; as he stood, he remarked, "You seem to enjoy these forays into investigation."

"Oh, I do." Montague pushed back his chair and rose. "Indeed, I will admit I live for the unusual queries you and some of my other clients bring me from time to time. They lend spice to the mundane accounting and investing that otherwise is my bread and butter. While sustaining, bread and butter and nothing else can be rather dull." Smiling, Montague accompanied Christian to the door. "Sadly, good money management often is deathly dull, so I feel rather blessed when you or one of the others looks in."

Christian grinned; he saluted as he went through the door. "Glad to be of service." Walking through the outer office, he headed back to Mayfair.

At midday they all assembled in Randall's study—Letitia, Christian, and Dalziel, with Hermione as lookout. They shut Mellon out and locked the study door, much to his consternation.

Also to Barton's; the runner was still keeping watch from the street. Lounging against the area railings of the house opposite, he'd noted Christian's and Dalziel's arrivals with mounting curiosity. When Letitia drew the study curtains firmly across the windows, then peeked through a tiny gap, she saw Barton frowning. He started across the street; she tugged the curtains closed.

Turning, she glanced at the study door. "Did you leave the key in the lock?"

"Of course," Dalziel replied.

"Good!" She ignored the arrogant look he sent her. "So even if he weasels his way into the house, that pest Barton won't be able to see in."

A heavy knock fell on the front door. Letitia waved dismissively. "Don't bother—it'll only be him." She headed for the window and the catch for the secret door.

"I don't think so." Christian sent her a warning look.

She slowed, halted—and heard deep voices in the front hall.

Christian exchanged a glance with Dalziel. "It sounds like Trentham has brought reinforcements."

Returning to the study door, Christian unlocked and opened it—to admit three gentlemen. Tristan and two other large gentleman Letitia hadn't previously met.

Christian and Dalziel knew them; they exchanged handshakes and greetings, then Tristan brought the newcomers to Letitia and Hermione, who had sidled up to stand beside her. Tristan shook both their hands, then waved to the gentlemen alongside him. "Lady Letitia Randall, Lady Hermione Vaux—Anthony Blake, Viscount Torrington—for his sins, another member of our club—and Jonathon, Lord Hendon, who escaped by being in a slightly different wing of the services."

Anthony Blake grinned and elegantly bowed over Letitia's hand, then Hermione's. "Delighted to make your acquaintance, ladies." The dancing light in his dark eyes suggested it truly was. "Please call me Tony."

Lord Hendon smiled and shook first Hermione's hand, making her blush furiously, and then Letitia's. "A pleasure, ma'am. And please call me Jack—everyone does. I understand you've inherited a share of a trading company."

"Apparently. Unfortunately we've yet to determine just what the company trades in."

Tony glanced around. "Tristan said you had books. . . ?"

Letitia looked across and confirmed that Christian had shut and relocked the study door. "Indeed." Turning to the window frame, she depressed the catch for the secret door. "Come"—turning back to Tony and Jack, she waved beyond them to where Christian was swinging the secret door wide—"and we'll show you."

Jack and Tony were as amazed by the secret room as they'd all been, but they quickly got down to business when Christian showed them one of the ledgers.

"Just from this, it seems certain the Orient Trading Company, whoever they are, are a going concern—a business selling . . . what, we don't yet know." Jack looked up from the ledger. His gaze scanned the rows of packed shelves, taking in the enormity of the task they faced, then, jaw firming, he nodded. "We'll need to get everything down—every box, every file, every ledger. We need to look for the account ledgers—money in, and money out. They could be in separate ledgers—from this one it looks like they will be—and there could well be more than one set of books, too."

Tony nodded, surveying the shelves. "We also need to look for inventory files, documents listing goods, invoices, and any shipping documentation." He exchanged a look with Jack. "If we can get the information on those two areas collected, we'll have somewhere to start."

There were seven of them all told. They buckled down to the task with grim determination. They quickly established a rhythm—Christian, Dalziel, and Tristan reaching and lifting the files and books down from the shelves, then handing them to Letitia or Hermione to ferry to one or other of the two main piles. Tony watched over the pile for inventory and all things to do with goods, while Jack stacked and organized the account ledgers.

Within half an hour they realized they had a problem, but forged on until every box, file, and paper had been considered, and either assigned to a pile or set aside as not immediately relevant.

Surrounded by now empty shelves, they slumped into the chairs or propped against the desk or shelves and took stock. Two hours had passed. From the chair behind the desk, presumably the one in which Randall used to sit, Letitia surveyed what they'd discovered about her late husband's enterprise, glancing from the neatly stacked ledgers, over fifty of them, all fat and plump, surrounding Jack Hendon on one side of the room, to the fourteen thin ledgers by Tony Blake's feet.

Tony looked down at them and shook his head. "Frankly, this is bizarre. These aren't inventory." He picked up one ledger and flicked through it. "It's coded like everything else, but if I had to guess, I'd say it's a property ledger." He stopped flicking pages to scan one leaf. "There's furniture, and furnishings." He turned a few pages. "And what looks like staff rolls and payments, although they don't seem to go on for very long—several months, but not more than a year." He flicked through to the end of the book, closed it, and looked down at the pile, then at the other files and papers they'd set aside. "There's nothing here—no trace at all, either incoming or outgoing, of tradable stock."

"Conversely," Jack Hendon said, an account ledger open in his hands, "we have extremely, even obsessively, detailed accounts going back"—he glanced down at the pile—"for twelve years."

"That's how long the Orient Trading Company has been in existence," Christian supplied. "According to Montague, it first appeared twelve years ago, at much the same time as Randall moved to London."

Tristan pricked up his ears. "Any word on where he came by his money?"

Christian shook his head. "It's Montague's considered

opinion that Randall opened his London bank accounts with cold, hard cash."

Eyebrows were raised.

Christian had already reported Montague's findings to Letitia; she was busy thinking of other things.

"Could he have been renting properties?" She looked around, her gaze coming to rest on Jack Hendon.

He pulled a "could be, might be" face, and stood to start resorting the account ledgers. "Let's take a look at the last year's incomings. That might give us a clue."

Tony forsook his disappointing pile and went to help. Tristan and Christian gravitated in the same direction. Dalziel remained slumped on a straight-backed chair, his hands sunk in his pockets, his long legs stretched before him, his face a mask denoting that he was thinking. Furiously, on many different tracks at once.

They left him to it, crowding around Jack to read over his shoulder as with an "Ah-ha!" he stood, a blue account ledger in his hands, and opened it.

From the chair behind the desk, Letitia, with Hermione perched on the desk beside her, watched.

The four of them scanned the incomings, Jack running his large finger down the relevant column.

"He wasn't renting properties," Christian concluded. "These incoming amounts are simply too large, even if he owned half of Mayfair."

"Not only that," Tony said, pointing to the dates column of the ledger. "These payments are too frequent, especially given their amount, to be rent." He shook his head. "This looks like what you'd expect it to be—the lodgings of business takings, the sort any shop or store that sells things would make."

Dalziel rose and joined the group; picking up another of the account ledgers, he opened it and scanned. "Could it be that the Orient Trading Company has a number of different shops?" He glanced across the room at Tony's deserted pile.

"Fourteen, perhaps? Might that explain the high amounts?"

"Fourteen excellent shops, if that's the case . . ." Reading over Jack's shoulder, Tristan frowned. "But it might be so." He, too, reached for an account ledger. "If there are only fourteen initials, signifying fourteen different payers into the accounts . . . perhaps the Orient Trading Company does have fourteen shops."

"Perhaps," Tony replied. "But if so, what the devil are they selling?"

"Bizarre is indeed the word for it," Dalziel murmured, his attention on the ledger he held. "It's almost as if they're selling something that's not real. . . ."

Slowly he lifted his gaze and met Christian's eyes.

For a moment no one spoke.

Letitia knew what they were thinking, but none of them would say the words "prostitution" or "brothel" in front of her, and even less in front of Hermione, although neither of them would swoon.

Regardless, she felt very real relief when Jack Hendon shook his head. "I don't think it can be that either. Just look at this amount." He pointed to a figure, waited while the others looked, then flicked the page. "And then here again, a week later. Establishments of that sort simply cannot clear those sort of sums in that time. It's simply not physically possible."

There was a general easing of the tension.

"Not that, then." Christian sounded relieved, too.

"No—and here's something else." Tony had picked up a red ledger, presumably one listing expenses. That was confirmed when he said, "Just look at these outgoings. Compare them to the incomings, and it's clear that the incomings outweigh the outgoings by a positively massive margin." He shook his head, poring over more figures. "The Orient Trading Company, whatever the devil it sells, is a cash-generating operation. Whatever they're trading in, it's not just profitable, but wildly, hugely so."

"And," Christian said, a green ledger in his hands, "it looks as if we have three owners." There was a note of triumph in his voice. He looked across the room at Letitia. "They're only identified by their initials—R, T, and S." He smiled intently. "I wonder who . . ."

"Randall, Trowbridge, and Swithin." Letitia sat up. "It has to be Trowbridge and Swithin." She looked at the men. "Have we learned anything about Swithin?"

"I've gathered a little, more or less by accident." Tristan glanced at the others. "Swithin lives very quietly. He's recently married, and a little before that he bought a house in Surrey—I know because it's not far from my principal estate." He grinned at Letitia. "I have aunts, cousins, and female connections—lots of them. A bevy live in my Surrey house, and their primary occupation is keeping an eye on all and sundry in the neighborhood. One came up to town to visit the group who prefer to remain in London—she had all the news about Swithin and his new wife. Apparently he paid above the mark to secure the house, then spent even more redecorating for his new wife, who, so they tell me, is quieter than he—a mouse is how they described her—from one of the minor branches of the Carstairs."

"The Carstairs." Dalziel prowled over to sit again in the straight-backed chair.

"That suggests," Christian said, "that Swithin, too, is accepted within the ton." He raised a brow at Tristan. "Any hint as to his background?"

"None—and given my aunts' propensities for ferreting out everything about everyone, that really means absolutely nothing is known of his background by anyone." Tristan shifted. "As for his standing in the ton, I got the impression that was beyond question. He appears well-entrenched, firmly established with a solid reputation as an exceedingly sound man on the subject of capital raisings. He apparently has a long history in financing this project or that, highly successfully. When I asked around at White's, quite a few of the old guard spoke warmly of him—Lord Lanthorne and Lord Quilley to name two."

"And they're not fools," Dalziel put in. "Certainly I wouldn't describe either as being easily taken in."

"So," Christian said, "Swithin, if he truly is as we suspect and is another ex–Hexham Grammar School governors' scholar, has also managed, in his own quiet way, to succeed to a similar degree as Randall and Trowbridge in becoming a fixture within the ton."

Hands clasped on the desk, Letitia frowned. "Trowbridge is flamboyant—that's his nature. Randall wasn't, yet neither was he quiet or shy." She looked across the room at Christian. "Randall was always, first and last, all business."

Christian nodded. "Against that, Swithin was the quiet one." He looked at Dalziel. "Any word from your contact in Hexham?"

"Not yet." For the benefit of the others, he explained, "After learning about Trowbridge and Swithin, I sent to Hexham again, to see if in fact they, too, were on the Hexham Grammar roll as governors' scholars, as we've surmised. I've also asked after their backgrounds." He looked back at Christian. "With luck, we'll hear tomorrow. However, I would stress that we need to tread warily. We've assumed Trowbridge and Swithin are the Orient Trading Company's T and S, but there are a lot of surnames beginning with T and S. We need to be sure before we press either Trowbridge or Swithin harder."

Christian grimaced; he met Letitia's eyes. "I just realized . . . when we first approached Trowbridge, he was quite happy if not eager to hear what you had to say, even after you made it clear it wasn't about sculpture. But then—"

"I mentioned Randall's murder." Letitia grimaced back.

"And he shut up, took a giant step back and put up all his shields." Christian nodded, remembering. "He thought you'd come to talk about the company—he and Swithin, assuming he's S, must have guessed Randall's share would come to you."

"Yes." Letitia sat up. "He was expecting me to ask him about the company." She looked at Dalziel. "Which means there's no reason we can't go and speak with him about the company now, openly. . . ."

She trailed off, because Dalziel was shaking his head.

"Wait," he cautioned. He glanced at Christian, met his eyes. "Before you question Trowbridge—and Swithin, if the S is he—you need at least to know what type of business the Orient Trading Company conducts. We need to trace at least some of these incoming payments to their source, and find out what the company is selling. Without that knowledge, your position is weak."

He looked again at Letitia. "By your own account, Randall was no fool. I doubt from what we've heard that Trowbridge and Swithin are either. If you try to question them about the company without any idea of what the business actually is, you'll give away your ignorance—you won't know what questions apply and which don't—and then who knows? They could tell you whatever they choose, and you'll have to believe them, at least until you learn more."

"*If* you ever learn more," Tristan put in, "once they realize you don't have the knowledge."

Letitia wrinkled her nose at Dalziel. "Much as it pains me to admit it, you're right." She glanced at Christian. "We need more ammunition to make sure they tell us the truth."

Christian held her gaze and nodded, hoping she didn't notice the grin Dalziel wasn't sufficiently successful at hiding. "Indeed," he replied. "And the only ammunition that will do the trick is learning who's paying the Orient Trading Company, and for what."

Letitia, Christian, Tony, and Jack spent the next few hours poring over the ledgers. Once they'd fixed on an approach they thought would work to identify at least some of the regular customers of the Orient Trading Company, Dalziel and Tristan took their leave, citing other engagements. Hermione hovered, then, finding it all rather dull, went off to report their findings to Agnes.

In the end, their plan was simple. Concentrating on the last month, they listed all the regular payments from the company's coded sources; most made payments weekly, a few twice a week. Those sources they elected to focus on all paid very large amounts.

"Traceable amounts," Christian stressed.

Unexpectedly, and with considerable triumph, they unearthed details of the company's bank accounts. Three accounts, each with a different London bank.

That done, they called it a day.

The next morning, Christian and Letitia set out at nine o'clock to lay their findings before Montague.

That paragon of financial investigation quickly—and eagerly—grasped their direction. "An excellent notion!" He scanned the figures they'd gathered. "Yes, indeed—quite extraordinary. But I should certainly be able to trace these amounts." He paused, a frown slowly replacing his bonhomie. "Except . . ."

Letitia frowned back. "Except what?"

Montague grimaced. He met her gaze. "I've been concentrating on the company itself. I can verify that Trowbridge and Swithin are indeed the other part owners—as with Randall, each owns a third share. Be that as it may, from what you've told me and what I've learned from sources in the banks, it appears that Randall was the primary active partner. He managed all three accounts, at least as far as the banks are concerned. From their perspective, the Orient Trading Company is wildly profitable and has been for some considerable time, more or less since its inception. Well and good, from the financial institutions' point of view. What makes me uneasy is that, like you, I have failed—utterly failed—to find any trace of identifiable goods or cargo, or any real property the company might be trading."

Montague studied the list they'd prepared for him. "Which brings me to my reservation as to tracing any of these 'customers' through the banking system. When I investigated the payments into the company's accounts, I turned up a most surprising finding. All the inward payments—every last one—are in cash. They always have been. And that, to me, is the most curious, and indeed suspicious, aspect of this case."

He tapped their summary with one finger. "As you've noted, the sums are quite often staggeringly large, yet whoever is paying those sums never uses a bank draft or other monetary instrument. Given the regularity of payments, that's very odd."

When he fell silent, studying their list, Letitia asked, "You can't trace cash payments back to whoever pays them in, can you?"

Montague shook his head. "There's no record kept of who pays the money in, only of the money itself—the amount and its destination."

Christian grimaced. "So there's no way forward—"

"No, wait." Letitia spoke over him, still focused on Montague. "These are regular payments." She leaned over the desk to point at one entry. "Look at this one—made into what we've called account number two. This customer, whoever they are, makes a sizable payment into that account every Monday. So every Monday, someone actually goes into a bank somewhere and pays a large amount of cash into that account." She caught Montague's eyes; suppressed excitement lit hers. "Can we learn which branch of which bank?"

Montague blinked. His gaze grew distant. Then, slowly, he nodded. "Yes. I'm certain we can."

"Excellent." Intent and determined, Letitia looked at Christian. "As we need to know why these people are paying huge sums to the Orient Trading Company, might I suggest we simply approach them and ask?"

* * *

They left Montague energized, throwing himself and his people into the task of identifying which particular bank branches were used to pay the largest regular amounts into each of the three company accounts.

"I need to attend an at-home this morning." Letitia glanced at Christian as the hackney picked its way along Piccadilly. "It was recommended that I attend."

He raised his brows. "By whom?"

"Lady Osbaldestone."

"Ah."

"Indeed. So you may drop me in South Audley Street. I'll meet you at the Bastion Club later this afternoon."

Christian nodded. After escorting her up the steps and into Randall's house, he paid off the hackney and walked the short distance to Grosvenor Square. Crossing the square, he entered his own house; he hadn't spent much time there in recent days.

He'd barely settled behind the desk in his study, his accumulated correspondence piled before him, when Percival opened the door to announce, "Lady Cordelia, my lord."

His aunt swept in. Christian inwardly sighed and laid aside his letter opener. He'd long suspected that Cordelia posted a footman to keep watch on his house from hers across the square whenever she wanted to see him; others had difficulty catching him when he didn't want to be caught, but he rarely succeeded in avoiding her.

"Yes, aunt?" he inquired, resigned and mild.

Resplendent in rose-striped figured ivory silk, Cordelia flopped into one of the armchairs before the desk. "I've heard whispers that you and some of your friends are busy investigating Randall's financial concerns." Her gaze grew acute. "So what's going on? You may as well tell me, for I mean to pester you until I receive a reasonable account."

Viewing the firm set of her lips, the determined glint in her eye, Christian rapidly sifted through what they knew and their current tack. "From revelations contained in Randall's will, we discovered that he was engaged in a business of sorts. We're still establishing the details, but it seems likely some disagreement on that front led to his murder."

Cordelia narrowed her eyes, reading between his lines. "*Not* Justin Vaux?"

He raised his brows. "A Vaux involved in business? What a fanciful notion, Aunt."

Cordelia humphed. She sat digesting the little he'd revealed, no doubt wondering if he might reveal more. He picked up an envelope, slit it, extracted the paper from within, glanced at it, then laid it aside and looked at her again. "Was there anything else?"

She studied him for a moment, as if debating whether to speak. "As a matter of fact, there *is* something else. A related issue—namely Letitia Vaux, or Randall as she now is." Cordelia eyed him shrewdly, trying to see past the mask his face had become. "She might be a widow, but you could do very much worse than ask for her hand, as I'm sure you're aware. Very good ton, the Vaux. And, of course, once this nonsense over Justin having murdered Randall blows over, as you and your friends seem bent on ensuring . . . well, once that's resolved, there's nothing in the way of you and Letitia marrying."

When he reacted not at all, simply sat and watched her in stoic silence, Cordelia dropped all pretense and grimaced. "Lord, boy, I know you've been dragging your feet over choosing your bride, but choose you must, and if—as I strongly suspect—it's that old business with Letitia that's behind your reluctance, well, no need to hang back now, is there?"

When, eyes wide, she pointedly waited for some response, Christian merely nodded. "Indeed."

Cordelia snorted. "Damn me if you don't get more like your father every day."

Christian smiled quite genuinely. "Thank you."

Cordelia flapped a hand at him and rose. "You'll go your own road regardless, just as he did, but I wanted to drop a word in your ear. If it's Letitia Vaux you want, then tie her up fast, because once this business is settled and done, and she comes out of mourning, she'll be mobbed."

Christian blinked.

Cordelia saw and smiled intently. "Just so. You're not the only gentleman of your age and relative standing hunting for a mature and capable bride."

True, but he was the only one sharing Letitia's bed.

Christian inclined his head. "Thank you, Aunt. I'll . . . er, take your suggestion under advisement."

Cordelia looked disgusted. "See you do. Heaven knows you need a woman like Letitia Vaux to show you what passion is." With a curt nod, she swept around. "I'll leave you to it."

With more fondness than he'd allowed her to see, Christian watched her march out of the room.

When the door closed behind her, he returned to his letters, but while he sorted through communications from his various agents and stewards, his mind continued to dwell on Cordelia's words, wrestling with what she'd come to tell him, and, more importantly, why.

Cordelia was very well anchored within the ton. She'd been born and bred within it; she knew it and its ways, understood both as instinctively as breathing. Her words were, indeed, a warning.

It didn't take much thinking to concede she was right.

Once Letitia came out of mourning—and given she was a Vaux and not inclined to sit quietly at home, even before then—she would all but instantly become a gazetted prize; she was the sort of woman men fought over.

Although he was sharing her bed, he was well aware he had no guarantee she would, in the end, agree to marry him. To be his again, unreservedly.

A letter opened but unread in his hand, he considered what his life would be like if she decided against him.

Cordelia had also been right in that he needed Letitia to show him what passion was. In that respect, only she would do—only she had ever succeeded.

If he didn't have her . . .

Hearing a crinkling sound, he glanced down. He'd crushed the letter he was holding. Opening his fist, he smoothed the sheet out and laid it on the blotter.

His aunt had been right in all respects.

Tie her up fast.

Wise advice, he felt sure.

Chapter 14

They gathered at the Bastion Club later that afternoon. Christian met Letitia at the gate; they climbed the porch steps to find Gasthorpe receiving a packet from a messenger.

"Ah—here he is." The majordomo bowed to Christian and Letitia, then extended the packet to Christian. "From Mr. Montague, my lord."

"Excellent." Christian took the packet, handed it to Letitia, and hunted in his waistcoat pocket. He tipped the messenger and dismissed him. The boy clattered down the steps just as Dalziel came walking up the path.

Dalziel exchanged nods with them, then waved Letitia and Christian into the house. After a few murmured words with Gasthorpe, he followed them up the stairs and into the library.

Tony, Jack, and Tristan were already there. They got to their feet as Letitia swept in; she smiled and waved them back to their chairs. Appropriating one of the armchairs by the hearth, she sank into it, laying the packet, which she'd retained, on her lap.

Entirely unexpectedly, the door opened again and Justin sauntered in. Although partly disguised in a heavy, nondescript overcoat with a cap pulled low over his face, with his height, build, outrageously handsome features, and distinctive coloring, he remained readily identifiable.

Christian sensed his fellow club members come alert. They exchanged glances with each other and with him; they were all dying to ask Justin where he'd been staying—and more to the point, who his host really was.

Justin flashed a smile around the room, then seeing Letitia's surprise give way to ire, he held up his hands placatingly. "I came in through the back alley—no one saw me."

She humphed, cast him, and then Dalziel, a darkling look, and subsided. She looked down at the package in her lap.

Christian was about to suggest she open it when Dalziel, sinking into one of the deeply padded wing chairs, stated, "I heard from my Hexham contact."

All attention swung his way. He smiled, all teeth. "As we suspected, Swithin was indeed a peer of Randall and Trowbridge at Hexham Grammar School. They entered the school in the same year, and all three were governors' scholars—the only three that year. They banded together from the first, no doubt to ward off the inevitable bullying. Randall as we know was a farmer's son. Trowbridge's father was a goldsmith—quite a talented one by all accounts—and his mother was a potter. His liking for artwork presumably grew from that. Trowbridge's parents are still alive—he visits them occasionally, although the more he's gone up in the world, the more awkward that's become. However, the elder Trowbridges are proud of their son, if a trifle in awe. He's risen far from his humble beginnings—in many ways his life is now beyond their comprehension."

Settling his shoulders in the chair, Dalziel continued, "Which brings us to Swithin. His father was a merchant in the town. He's still alive, but unlike Trowbridge, Swithin has cut all ties. Swithin the elder knows nothing about his son, not even his current address."

"So Randall lost all ties to his past when his parents died," Letitia remarked, "Swithin cut his ties, but Trowbridge didn't." She frowned. "Does that tell us anything?"

No one seemed to know.

"Why don't we see what Montague's sent?" Christian nodded to the packet in her lap.

"Yes, of course."

While she broke the seal and spread out the sheets, Christian explained to the others what tack they were now following to locate the company's customers. "Given that cash payments can't be traced back to the payer, the direct approach is the only one left to us."

Letitia was scanning Montague's communication; from her expression it was clear the news was good. She glanced up, saw them all watching, and beamed. "Montague's a wonder. He's traced three of the large regular payments—all made on Mondays, one to each of the company's three accounts—and all invariably made at the following three banks—Rothchild's in Piccadilly, Child's in Oxford Street, and Barkers in the Strand."

Triumph glowed in her eyes as she lowered the sheet and looked across at Christian.

Tony leaned forward in his chair. "So on Monday, at each of those three banks, someone will come in and go to the teller and make a cash payment into an Orient Trading Company account?"

Letitia nodded. "On Monday, two days from now."

"So"—Jack's voice, too, held a note of anticipation—"if we're there, at each of those three banks keeping watch—"

"And the tellers have been asked to tip us the wink when a particular payment is made to the relevant account"—Tony took up the evolving plan—"we can identify and follow the person making the deposit—"

"And learn what, exactly, their business is." Tristan beamed back at Letitia. "Excellent!"

The sense of building excitement was pervasive; they were all, including Letitia and Justin, constitutionally better suited to action than waiting.

"We don't even need to follow them, at least not far." As ever, Letitia was inclined to directness. "We can simply ask them what they're paying the Orient Trading Company for."

"Damn!"

They all looked around at Justin's muttered oath.

He looked at his sister, disgust in his face. "I can see

where this is leading—while you all get to hunt, I'll have to stay indoors and wait." He glanced at Dalziel, a hopeful expression replacing the disgust. "I don't suppose—"

"No." Letitia uttered the single syllable in a tone that brooked absolutely no argument. "You cannot go out, not even in a much better disguise."

She directed her statement not solely at Justin but at Dalziel as well. He held up his hands in a gesture signifying that he wasn't going to get involved.

Satisfied, Letitia turned her gaze pointedly on her brother.

Justin looked mulish.

Christian caught his eye.

After a moment of inner railing, Justin surrendered. "Oh, all right." He slumped back in the chair. "I'll sit at home, safe by the fire, while you have all the fun."

Entirely satisfied—sufficiently calmed—Letitia glanced at Christian. "So on Monday, how should we proceed?"

They made their plans, eagerness returning in full measure.

"So," Christian summarized, "Tony and Jack will take Barkers in the Strand, Dalziel and Tristan will be at Child's, and Letitia and I will keep watch at Rothchild's. Having two pairs of eyes at each location should ensure we don't miss our quarries."

"It's also easier to remain undetected when following someone if you're walking with another and talking." Tony grinned, and spoke for them all. "It'll be good to be on the street again, rather than leafing through files."

Feeling better—more buoyed and confident—than she'd felt since she learned of Randall's death, Letitia stood. "Well, gentlemen." She cast an appreciative glance around the circle. "On Monday we'll learn what the Orient Trading Company actually does—and then we'll approach Trowbridge, and hopefully learn a great deal more."

* * *

It was Saturday—Monday was two days away.

Bearing that and his aunt Cordelia's warning in mind, Christian saw Letitia home, then repaired to his aunt's house to ask her advice.

Cordelia and Ermina were laid down upon the twin sofas in the drawing room, but when he walked in, were quite content to open their eyes and wave him to a chair.

"What brings you here?" Cordelia inquired, surprise edging her voice.

He outlined his dilemma.

After due discussion and deliberation back and forth between the pair, Cordelia pronounced judgment. "While attending the theater is in general *not done* while in deep mourning, in the case of the Vaux, suffice to say that if Letitia were seen suitably gowned and veiled in a private box at the Theatre Royal, such a sighting would provoke neither excessive surprise nor scandal."

Christian smiled. "Thank you, dear aunts." He rose, inclined his head to them both. "I'll leave you to your . . . musings."

With a salute, he turned and walked from the room; he could hear the buzz of their gossiping before Meadows closed the door behind him.

Later that evening, after an entirely unexpected excursion to the Theatre Royal with Christian, Hermione, and Agnes, where the drama and farce had succeeded in diverting her for more than two hours, Letitia paced restlessly across the library in the house in South Audley Street.

She glanced at Christian as he settled into one of the armchairs, a glass of brandy in his hand. She summoned a grateful, perfectly sincere smile. "Thank you for the evening. I truly appreciated the gesture. And the . . ." She waved.

He smiled and raised his glass. "Distraction?"

"Precisely."

Agnes and Hermione had retired when they'd returned,

yawning and sleepy. She, in contrast, felt far too wide-awake to contemplate her bed.

Even with him in it.

She knew he intended to be there, to sleep beside her tonight—to make love to her first, and probably later as well.

And she had absolutely no intention of dissuading him, much less arguing. That didn't, however, mean she'd made her final decision about letting him back into her life—into her heart and soul, as well as her body.

Her reticence over making that commitment surprised her. Left her a touch uneasy. Emotional caution didn't come naturally; she normally knew exactly what she wanted, yet with him . . . she knew what she wanted, but she still couldn't make herself believe it would be, not with her whole heart and mind and soul. In the deepest recesses of her mind, she hadn't yet accepted that what she truly wanted was still there, that if she embraced him again, totally and completely, admitted him again into her heart as her one and only love, that he would stay.

When it came to him, her reactions were complex and complicated. Difficult to unravel even for her.

Knowing how futile dwelling on that subject would be, especially with him in the same room, she cut off that train of thought and sent her mind in another direction.

Reaching the end of her track, she lifted her head, let her gaze travel the room as she slowly swung around. "I still think of this house as Randall's. I never did consider it mine—which in retrospect was odd. Even now, it's just a house I'm staying in."

Christian was silent for a moment, then murmured, "If you never considered yourself his, then you never accepted what was his as yours."

Looking down, she paced, nodded. "I daresay you're right.

Casting about for another—safer—topic, she remembered the scene she'd witnessed as they were leaving his club. "I had no idea you were *all* so obsessed with learning Dalziel's identity."

On quitting the library, Jack and Tony had cornered Justin at the top of the stairs. Tristan and Christian had gone ahead, flanking Dalziel, talking to him—distracting him and making noise. She'd been descending in their wake when she'd heard, behind her, Jack ask, oh so innocently, "So where exactly does Dalziel live?"

After a moment's hesitation, Justin had replied, "London."

She hadn't needed to look to know that Jack and Tony had been disappointed. But apparently they'd realized Justin had given his word and so wouldn't be swayed. They'd accepted defeat with good grace—and huge sighs.

"It just seems unfair," Christian said, "that he should know so much about us, even things we'd rather he didn't, yet we know absolutely nothing about him, not even his real name."

"You don't need to know his name—you know the man." She hesitated, then added, "I rather think that was his point."

"What point?"

"The reason he uses that name."

Christian snorted and they let that subject fall.

She kept pacing back and forth as the minutes ticked by.

He sighed. "You do realize that the entire purpose of this evening was to distract you?"

"Yes, I know. But I can't get my mind off what, come Monday, we might learn. I have a very bad feeling about the Orient Trading Company's business."

So did Christian.

"I mean," she went on, one arm sweeping wide as she turned, "why *did* Randall—and Trowbridge and Swithin, too—go to such lengths to keep the company so hidden? I can understand not wanting to be openly associated with any mercantile trade—they certainly wouldn't have wanted that if their underlying purpose was to be accepted within the haut ton—but distancing themselves from any legitimate enterprise could easily have been done by appointing an agent, or man-of-business. Lots of others do that—why didn't they? Why did they instead work so hard, with codes no less, to keep the whole enterprise an absolute secret?"

Sweeping up to where he sat, she halted dramatically and fixed him with an uncompromising stare. "The business of the Orient Trading Company has got to be something scandalous. That's the only viable conclusion. You all think so, I know."

He held her gaze. "As Jack pointed out, given the incoming sums are so large, it can't be what we all thought."

Folding her arms, she looked down her aristocratic nose at him. "The sums being so large might also be because whatever scandalous doings Randall and his cohorts were— are—involved in, and have now involved *me* in, is run on a grand scale."

It was pointless to argue, especially when she might well be right. Yet her restless energy was still building; unless it subsided, she'd never sleep.

He'd tried distraction. He'd tried talking.

That left . . .

She humphed and swung away, pacing once again across the room.

Soundlessly, he rose and followed her.

The next time she swung around, she turned into his arms.

He caught her to him, bent his head and kissed her. Given distraction was his aim, he didn't hold back; he parted her lips, surged into her mouth and laid claim.

She was passive for all of two heartbeats, then her hands were in his hair, holding his head while she kissed him back.

Voraciously.

Her mouth was as hungry as he was, her lips pliant and wantonly seductive, flagrantly demanding. She stepped into him, pressed her slender body to his, wordlessly communicated her desire.

In that, at least, they were as one.

Letitia knew why he was kissing her—knew what his stated purpose would be—and even though she suspected he had a deeper motive along the lines of seducing her into loving him again, she didn't in that moment care.

What she cared about was the heat, the instant firing of her blood—just because he was who he was, and he wanted her.

Tonight, for his stated purpose and for her, that was enough.

Enough to let her set aside her reservations and grasp—seize—him with both hands. Enough to have her moving against him, blatantly inviting, with her body demanding his heated attentions.

And more.

Tonight she needed more, as much as he could give her to hold back the tide of her unsettling thoughts, to bury the sense of something dreadful approaching that had burgeoned with each successive discovery about her late husband's business.

Tonight she wanted to forget—to set it all aside and be at peace. And in Christian's arms she knew succor lay.

Not peace, not yet, not while passion and desire, the flames and the fire, were upon them. But tonight they could let them burn, could surrender themselves to the conflagration and be consumed.

So she kissed him back, with her lips and tongue teased and taunted, then reveled as he took control, as his tongue found hers and stroked, then arrogantly explored, reclaimed.

As he deepened the kiss and she surrendered, as she felt the rising heat melt her bones.

His arms tightened about her, crushing her breasts, already peaked and tight and aching, to the hard solid planes of his chest. One large palm swept down her back, pressing her to him, then sliding lower, over her hip, to grasp her bottom and angle her hips to his.

So he could move against her, so he could mold her against the rigid length of his erection, let her feel and anticipate having that hard length inside her. Thrusting into her, filling her, taking her. . . .

Her mind reeled. She broke from the kiss on a gasp. "Upstairs." The word was breathless, weightless. She hauled in a breath and tried again. "We should go up to my room."

He stared down at her, gray eyes dark with passion—the passion she'd stirred, that had turned every muscle in his large body to hard-edged steel.

Then he blinked, focused—and she realized he'd been so caught up in having her, if she hadn't spoken he would have had her there—on the rug before the fire or bent over the desk. A shiver of awareness and something more illicit slithered down her spine.

Before she could rethink, he managed a stiff nod. "Yes. Upstairs." His voice was low and gravelly, already choked with desire. Another shiver threatened, this time one of sheer anticipation.

He had to force his arms to release her. The instant they did, before she could surrender to her baser self she turned and led the way from the room. He followed on her heels, close, close enough when they turned onto the stairs to rest a heavy, possessive hand on her back. Low on her back, on the curve of her bottom. She'd forgotten that—how, in the distant past, when they'd slipped away from balls and parties to be together, he'd always touched her, steered her, like that.

As if he couldn't wait to touch her even more intimately.

As if he couldn't wait to have her naked.

He often hadn't.

But that had been then, when he was younger. Now, as she opened her bedchamber door and led him inside, she was very aware that he, the man at her heels, the male she would give herself to that night, was no callow youth.

Halting in the center of the room, she faced him. Saw

him still by the door, watching her. Heard the click as, his gaze on her, he snibbed the lock.

Then he moved.

He walked toward her slowly, shadows and moonlight dappling his large frame.

When he halted before her, less than a foot away, he was all heat and power in the darkness, his very maleness sliding like a hand over her skin, leaving her nerves flickering. Waiting for his touch.

Moments ticked by as he looked into her face. Although she was tall, he was taller, broad and heavy where she was slender and slight, so much stronger she should have felt fear, yet she never had.

His strength was under his absolute control, and hers to command; she'd always known that.

So it wasn't fear of that sort that sent a tingling lick up her spine.

He seemed to sense it, for he moved. Lifted both large, hard palms and framed her face.

Gently. As if to remind her his strength wasn't to be feared.

But she felt something else in his touch, sensed it in his gaze. An intent she couldn't name, that she hadn't before encountered in him, that she had no experience of to draw on.

His lips curved subtly, as if he could read her sudden wondering in her eyes. He lowered his head—slowly—until his breath washed over her lips.

Making her hungry, making her want—until she tried to stretch up and press her lips to his and take what she needed—

And discovered she couldn't.

That although his touch was gentle, it was enough to restrain her.

She sank back, would have frowned if desire hadn't had her in thrall.

His lips curved a touch more and he bent his head—and gave her what she wanted. He took her lips in an achingly slow, devastatingly thorough kiss.

He drew back, lips supping idly at hers, then lifted his head far enough to meet her eyes. To look into them as he murmured, "Tonight, it'll be my way." His gaze lowered to her lips; he took them again in a heady, flagrantly explicit caress. "All my way."

The words were deep, dark, his voice roughened by desire; she wasn't surprised when he kissed her—even more explicitly, even more suggestively—on their heels.

When next he freed her lips, she breathed back, "I'll think about it."

She could imagine handing him the reins, as she'd recently done, but she couldn't see him taking them from her without her leave, without her explicit consent.

His smile took on an edge. "You might find that difficult."

His eyes, dark with a promise she couldn't—didn't know enough to—read, held hers, then he bent his head and his lips found hers.

In a kiss so scorching it curled her toes. That had her sinking her fingertips into his skull just to hold on to sanity.

His hands released her face, drifted away—for a moment she didn't know to where—long enough to have her senses stretching, searching. . . .

Long enough to have her nerves tight with anticipation when he closed one hand about her breast. Her breath caught, hitched; he kneaded, claimed, possessive beyond question, and her heart started to race.

As she felt his other hand pass across the back of her waist, then slide slowly down, tracing, claiming, to ultimately splay over her bottom and hold her, press her helplessly to him as he once again shifted against her.

A promise explicit both in intent and unscreened desire.

He kneaded her breast, kneaded her bottom, and filled her mouth, the heavy thrust of his tongue mimicking what he intended—and she wanted—to come. His touch wasn't gentle, yet neither was it rough; he was far from untutored, knew just how dominant he could be without awakening her resistance.

He knew her too well; her senses reeling, her wits long gone, sensation her only guide, she reveled nonetheless, amazed and eager to engage with him—this male she'd never before encountered.

Older, wiser, and infinitely more knowing.

More threat to her, and her senses—and she knew it.

But she'd always loved playing with fire.

Christian had a plan. He had no idea if it was wise or not, but now he'd taken the first steps, he couldn't draw back. Couldn't put the genie of his possessiveness back in its bottle, not without first paying its price.

Not without first indulging it to the full.

So he filled his hands and his senses with her. Gorged on the bounty of her mouth, fully yielded, gloried in the knowledge she was under his hands and would do all he wished, everything he wished, yield every last gasp he wished tonight.

They'd never had barriers between them, not long ago. But long ago he hadn't spent years believing she'd betrayed him, only to learn that wasn't the case and he was the one at fault. Only to learn that she wasn't yet ready to forgive him. To welcome him back into her arms, into her body. Into her heart and soul.

The warrior in him had needs, needs his more civilized self held in check. But tonight she needed distraction— tonight she needed something more than his civilized self could, or would, offer.

So he'd dropped the shields he'd learned to employ, and let the genie of his warrior self free.

Now he had to feed it.

She had to appease it.

To be what he needed, give all he needed.

Surrender as needed.

Everything.

He backed her, steered her, not toward the bed but away from it. To the window, uncurtained, where moonlight spilled in. He halted when they stood within the silvery shaft, hauled her even tighter against him, angled his head and deepened the kiss, until she was gasping. Mentally reeling. Too overwhelmed to deny him.

Lifting his head, grasping her waist, he turned her. Set her to face the window, then stepped close behind. Slid his hands around her and filled them with her breasts, closed his hands and felt her sway.

He took a moment to savor her struggle to breathe, to sense the thudding of her heart. Then he bent his head and set his lips to the sensitive hollow beneath her ear.

She shuddered, leaned back against him. He kneaded her breasts, already firm and swollen, already peaked, straining beneath her bodice. He listened to her gasps, orchestrated, sensed when the line where pleasure became pain was approaching.

Releasing the taut mounds, he set his fingers to the buttons of her bodice. Set his lips cruising the long line of her throat, set his teeth to score lightly along the same path.

While he laid her breasts bare.

Opened her bodice, pressed the halves wide, loosened her chemise and lowered it. Exposing the flushed ivory skin to the cool night air.

Smiling at the sight, at her nipples ruched tight, he raised his hands and once again closed them on her, this time skin-to-skin.

When she shuddered, dropping her hands to his thighs clutched, he lowered his head and murmured in her ear, "You're going to stand there and let me love you—let me do whatever I wish to you. Let me have my way with you."

Rubbish, Letitia's rational self scoffed.

Why not? her curiosity prompted.

With the steady beat of passion thrumming in her veins, with the fog of desire clouding her brain, she could find no good answer to the question.

Could summon no resistance when he took her silence as agreement, and eased her gown and chemise down, stopped to unlace her petticoats, then pushed gown, petticoats, and chemise over her hips so they fell with a soft swoosh to the floor.

His hands returned to her skin, but his touch was different, lighter, frankly assessing, exploratory. As if he'd never seen her naked, as if she were a prize, a present he'd unwrapped for the first time.

She dragged in a breath past the constriction in her chest, conscious of her breasts rising, her midriff tightening, aware that he saw and watched. Naked but, once again, for her black lace garters and fine black silk stockings, she could all but feel the silvery touch of the moonlight as it bathed her long limbs, caressed the curves and valleys of her body, and illuminated a self she'd all but forgotten existed.

He moved behind her, a large, dark, powerful figure still fully clothed. She felt the cloth of his coat brush the long planes of her back. His hands caught hers, fingers briefly tangling with hers, then he glided his palms slowly up her arms, closed them for an instant over her shoulders, then slowly slid them, palms to her skin, down.

Over her breasts, hot and aching for more than a simple caress, over her midriff, tight with desire, over her waist and her taut belly, over the curve of her hips and down, around; gripping her bottom, he kneaded.

As he bent his head and set his lips over the pulse point at the base of her throat.

She gasped at the heat of that simple contact. Shivered and closed her eyes—only to have her other senses sharpen. To have her skin grow even more sensitive to his touch.

From behind, one trouser-clad knee pressed between hers, forcing her thighs apart. She sucked in a breath as, releasing her bottom, his hands cruised her hips. One splayed across her stomach and held her captive, pressed her back so she was straddling that hard thigh, the cloth of his trousers abrading the delicate skin of her thighs' inner faces—an unsubtle reminder that he was fully clothed while she was all but naked, impressing a sense of vulnerability heavily on her senses.

His other hand drifted down over her thighs; his fingers briefly flirted with the tiny ribbons securing her garters, then left them for the bare skin above. With cool deliberation, with his fingertips he traced up the inner face of her thigh. Higher, higher . . . then he reached across and traced up the other side.

As if assessing the fineness of her skin, as if fascinated by it.

She tensed, and waited, breathing all but suspended. . . .

Eventually, with a languid authority that in itself was arousing, he let his fingers rise to the next point on his trail of conquest, lightly stroking, then playing with the crinkly dark hair shielding her mons.

He was patently in no hurry; her whole body was taut—she was ready to scream—before he consented to part her curls and reach farther.

To trace, stroke, and caress the already swollen flesh, to slide his fingers through the slickness his earlier caresses had drawn forth.

He chuckled at how wet she was, a dark rumble of male appreciation deep in his chest.

Her hands rose, locked about his hand where it splayed over her belly. He continued to play, as if learning her anew. She was quivering when, after an excruciatingly slow exploration of her tender flesh, he finally pressed one long finger into her sheath.

One slow, smooth, complete penetration.

The sensation brought her onto her toes.

Head back against his shoulder, eyes tightly closed, she gasped.

He held her there, naked before him, her silk stockings sliding against his trousers, her bottom held against his thighs, his erection a heavy rod against her lower back—and made her writhe.

Although her eyes were closed, her mind still saw—saw herself in his arms, held trapped against him, her flushed skin pearlescent in the steady moonlight, her hair tumbling from its pins, long tresses curling over her shoulders as she—her body—responded, helplessly surrendered to the simple blatant act of possession expertly executed.

She no longer had the will to resist. She was captured, not by him but by her fascination with this different side of him, this other lover who was him, yet not the him she'd once known.

The dark lover who held her before him, and pressed pleasure upon exquisite pleasure on her. He was not just older, but more experienced, a scarred warrior who'd lived through battles and had at last come home to claim . . . her.

His due, his reward. His bounty.

His without question.

That seemed to be the case, for he asked no permission, waited for no assent when, once the heat within her built, and the fever threatened to consume her, instead of allowing her to shatter and find relief, he withdrew his hand from between her thighs, set her on her feet, waited only a heartbeat to ensure she was steady, then grasped her hand and towed her toward the bed.

Thank God, was her initial thought. She expected him to lay her down, strip off his clothes and join her.

Instead he led her to the nearest corner of the bed, to where the thick post of the four-poster bed was hung with heavy green damask curtains. He reached for the silk cord that held the curtains back, wrenched it free, with one hand pushed the curtains to either side, exposing the post.

Before she could blink, he had her backed against the post. He caught both her hands in one of his, drew them up, then looped the curtain cord about her wrists and lashed them high above her head.

Stunned, she could only stare. He stepped back, leaving her standing with her spine against the post, her arms raised but not stretched; there was enough play in the loop for her to curve her hands down and hang onto the cord. She did, testing, but his handiwork held; the lashing didn't budge, even under her full weight.

What. . . ? She looked at him, intending to ask.

He met her gaze, his own dark and hard, simply said, "Wait."

He turned away from her and started to undress.

She wriggled, glared, tested her bonds again. Glared at his broad back as he shrugged out of his shirt. Her body was on fire, the flames he'd stoked so deliberately still burning brightly, hungrily, greedily. All she could think about was having him inside her, having the thick rod of his erection moving within her to quench the flames.

But then he turned back, gloriously naked, fully aroused, and expectant relief flooded her. Heightened her readiness, her waiting, her wanting.

She needed him against her, skin-to-skin, more than she needed to breathe.

Then he halted before her—face-to-face, eye-to-eye.

And she suddenly remembered that this wasn't the lover she'd known before, but a hardened warrior intent on claiming his due.

Her.

A shiver raced through her as she looked into his eyes— pure excitement laced with expectation, honed by a sense of dealing with the unknown.

He said nothing, simply raised his hands, framed her face, bent his head and kissed her—as if he would—was fully intending to—devour her.

Her every thought cindered beneath the heat in that kiss.

Her mind was awash with raw scalding need when he lifted his head. He looked down, following his hands as he ran them down her body, heavily, possessively, sculpting her curves, his prize, his reward. He reassessed, caressed, repossessed—then bent his head and set his mouth to her breast.

Treated her swollen flesh, as he had her lips and mouth, to a single-minded ravishment. One that had her hanging in her bonds, the fire within her escalating to an unbearable degree.

She would have writhed but his hands held her steady. She sobbed as he released the nipple he'd tortured to throbbing hardness. Unrelenting, he bent and skated his lips lower, with wet, open-mouthed kisses, with his tongue and his teeth, possessed as he wished.

He went to his knees before her, placed hot kisses over her quivering belly, then set his lips to her curls . . . then he settled back, his knees wide, grasped her thighs, raised them and placed one over each broad shoulder, grasped her hips with both hands and held her, then set his lips to her core.

She swallowed a shriek, tensed against the bonds, spine arching, her thighs pressing down hard against his shoulders.

To no avail. He possessed her there as he had elsewhere, with slow, thorough deliberation. Reduced her to a state of breathless panting need, consumed by the fire he'd so mercilessly stoked.

She was his beyond doubt or question, his to do with as he wished . . . she shrieked as his tongue entered her, screamed as he thrust and her senses imploded.

Letting her legs slide from his shoulders, he surged up, grasped the backs of her thighs, lifted her up and to him, and entered her with one long, hard, relentlessly powerful thrust. Impaling her, filling her.

She screamed again, felt her body clamp hard about him, helplessly clutched her bonds, wound her legs about his hips as he withdrew and thrust heavily again—sobbed as he moved within her and the pleasure rolled on and on.

He possessed her utterly. Thoroughly. Entirely. He refused to let the flames fade, but held her hips and drove steadily into her, almost immediately stoking the blaze again.

Forcing the flames and her higher, then higher.

Then he bent his head and fastened his mouth about the peak of one breast and suckled fiercely.

She shattered into a million shards, so completely fragmented she wasn't, for one bright shining instant in time, sure she'd survived.

Then glory rushed through her, golden and welcome, filling her veins, swamping her nerves, pouring delight through her as he continued to fill her, thrusting long and hard, yet still ruthlessly in control.

She was open to him, completely given over to him.

Surrendered.

His.

Christian's warrior self crowed, gloated, even as he tightened his reins and held himself back from the beckoning edge.

He wasn't finished with her yet. She'd needed distraction; he'd needed her. The exchange was straightforward, but he hadn't yet had his fill.

When the last ripples of her release faded, and she slumped, boneless against the bonds, her body softening deliciously about his, he reached up, yanked the cord free of the bedpost. Leaving it dangling from her wrist, he drew her against him. Lowering her arms, she draped them about his shoulders. His throbbing erection still buried in her scalding sheath, his hands beneath her bottom supporting her, he carried her to the side of the bed.

Juggling her, he drew down the covers, then withdrew from her and tumbled her onto the bed.

Swiftly he arranged her as he wished—stretched out on her stomach down the length of the bed, her head to one side, just off the pillows, her hands level with her head, one on either side. He'd positioned one plump pillow beneath her hips before he'd rolled her over. He drew her long legs down, her ankles only a little apart; she was so boneless she could barely raise her head, much less question his decrees.

He knelt at her feet and considered her, smiled at the sight of her legs still clad in her garters and stockings. Shifting, he caught a garter and worked it down, drawing the stocking off with it. He repeated the exercise on her other leg, stripping garter and stocking away, leaving her totally bare.

Then he stretched himself over her, eased himself down on her, sensed the slight tension that reinvested her limbs as she took his weight, felt it pin her.

Half supported on one arm sunk in the bed beside her shoulder, he reached between her legs, positioned his aching erection at her entrance, and slid slowly home, eyes closing as he thrust slow and deep into the slick scalding haven of her sheath.

He nearly groaned.

She tightened just a little about him, but she didn't have enough energy left to do anything other than lie beneath him and—as he'd warned her she would—let him have his way with her.

Greedily, hungrily, eager for the contact, he let himself fully down upon her, his chest to her back, his shoulders heavy across hers.

He'd taken her from behind before, but never like this. Not with her helpless beneath him, his body spread over hers, trapping her fully under him—giving her no option but to receive him as deeply and for as long as he wished.

Her body was a cushion of feminine curves and hollows against which his rubbed, another delicious friction as he settled to ride her with a slow, steady thrust and retreat.

He'd waited for this. He was going to extract every last ounce of pleasure from it, from her. Expose her to every last facet of his need of her.

And hope she understood. Hope she saw the raw need that drove him to have her as explicitly and as possessively as this for what it was—a symptom of complete and helpless devotion.

A need to have, to possess, that went beyond sinew and bone, that, as his spine flexed in its slow, rigidly controlled rhythm and he felt her instinctively soften, then tighten about him, welled and filled him.

Expanded, then coalesced and tightened within him.

Bending his head, his chest tight, his breath gasping, he pressed his lips gently to her shoulder.

Closed his eyes and let her take him.

Let her have and know all he was. All that he wanted and needed.

Her senses swamped with glorious warmth, Letitia felt his strength all around her, surrounding her, enveloping her, holding her. Rocking her, pressing into her, stroking inside her.

He lay like a cloak over her, possessive unquestionably, yet there was more to it than that. Even with her mind floating in hazed pleasure, in the golden aftermath that courtesy of his body moving on and within hers seemed to be stretching endlessly, she felt the connection—the forging of something new, blending and strengthening what had previously been, what had in the past linked them.

Pleasured to her toes, as his fingers found hers and tangled, and he rode her, unrelentingly slow and deep, to completion, she sensed in her bones that he was giving her more—not just in the physical sense, but more of him. Sharing more of him, aspects of himself he usually kept hidden.

Her cheek pressed to the pillow, she felt her lips curve. Welcomed the escalation as he thrust harder, deeper, nudging her up the bed even though he held her beneath him. The fluctuating pressure of his groin against her bottom, never quite leaving her, a continuous tactile impression mirroring his deeper possession, struck her as frankly erotic.

She'd always loved the sensation of being skin-to-skin with him. Of being naked, no barriers of any sort, with him.

Feeling the telltale rising tension invest and harden his limbs, tighten the steely muscles holding her down even more, her smile deepened and she let her senses expand—to her surprise felt her own body stir, respond, rise again to his beat.

He thrust still harder, once, twice, then a long groan ripped from his chest as his hips slammed hard against her bottom. Pressed in as he pumped into her, his release washing through him—triggering hers.

Amazed—she hadn't thought it possible—she felt the golden tide rise and sweep through her once again, this time gentler, yet longer and more pervasive, an extended moment of exquisite pleasure that had her gasping, struggling for breath. Deep within, she felt her womb contract, felt her body clutch and hold him.

Satiation came in hard and swift, rolling over her, claiming what was left of her mind, disconnecting her senses and setting them free. In the instant before she surrendered to the glorious drugging bliss, she wondered if her body knew more than she.

Tie her up fast.

Lying slumped over Letitia, his head cradled on her breast, her fingers moving slowly, caressingly through his hair, Christian recalled his aunt's words. Hoped he'd managed, over the past hours, to fashion a loop or two with which to reel his elusive lady in.

He'd eventually summoned enough strength to disengage and lift off her. He'd rolled her over and settled them more conventionally in the bed, but had yet to pull the covers over their cooling bodies.

He liked lying on her, their limbs damp and tangled in aftermath, and she didn't seem to mind in the least.

Her fingers slowed. From above him, her voice drifted through the darkness. "What are you doing here, in my bed, in my arms?"

An easy enough question to turn aside with some jocular remark, yet . . . "I'm waiting for you to open your eyes and see me. Here. In your bed, in your arms."

She snorted softly. "I know you're here." She shifted beneath him. "That's no news."

"No." He lifted his head and looked up at her face. "But what you need to see is that I'm not leaving. Not this time."

A long moment passed while she looked into his eyes. Her expression was serene, madonnalike, unreadable, then, her eyes still locked with his, she raised her brows. "Is that so?" Her tone cast the question as rhetorical. After another moment of considering him—studying what she could see— she quietly said, "You don't own me, Christian."

"No." If he'd failed to grasp that before, he knew it now. "I never did."

But as he in turn looked into her green-gold eyes, he had to wonder if, perhaps, he had owned a part of her all along, and simply hadn't understood.

She wasn't sure of his current tack—of him; her uncertainty showed in her eyes. "So . . . what do you want from me?"

The easiest question of all. "The same thing I've wanted from you from the first. You, as my wife."

"Your wife?" She let another moment tick past, then asked, her tone cooler, "And what of your revenge, your strategy to pay me back for not waiting for you and marrying Randall instead?"

"You didn't have a choice. I know that now."

He kept his gaze locked with hers. She searched his eyes, his expression, considered what she saw. Then she quietly said, "Your head knows that. But does your heart?"

The question hung between them.

She did, indeed, know him very well.

He looked inward, found, sensed, the lingering threads of his years-old anger—yet as he looked deeper, as he searched for the truth with which to answer her, he felt those threads wither and crumble. Blow away.

What he saw, what he found . . .

Between them now only the truth would do.

He felt his lips curve in self-deprecating cynicism; he'd been a fool to imagine his heart had ever been, or could ever be, otherwise.

"My heart?" He refocused on her eyes, held her gaze steadily. "My heart only ever had one thought, one want. One need. Despite all, in spite of all." He felt as if he were sinking into the golden depths of her eyes. Let go. "All my heart has ever wanted is you."

The moment stretched, then he asked, "What of yours?"

"Mine?" Her gaze remained unwavering while she debated whether to answer. Eventually she said, "I put my heart aside a long time ago. I locked it in a casket and buried the key."

Her meaning was clear. She'd protected her heart in the only way she could.

And she wasn't yet ready to trust him with it again.

He didn't try to argue. Instead he merely nodded and settled his head once more on her breast. Waited until her fingers returned to stroke his hair before murmuring, "Then I'll have to find the key."

Tie her up fast.

Fast as in quickly, fast as in tightly. Both applied.

She might be stubborn, but he was stubborner. He was in her bed, in her arms. He had her with him again, and he wasn't going to let her go.

Chapter 15

The next day, Sunday, Christian escorted Letitia, Agnes, and Hermione to church—raising untold eyebrows and causing Letitia to send him increasingly narrow-eyed looks.

But as they walked the short distance back along South Audley Street, she saw his curricle waiting, with his chestnuts between the shafts.

Strolling beside her, he leaned nearer and murmured, "I thought you might enjoy a drive to Richmond."

She glanced at him, met his eyes, then looked ahead. "I suppose that will keep me from wearing a track in the carpet."

So they parted from Agnes and Hermione, and he handed her up.

The drive to Richmond was refreshing, oddly peaceful. The day was fine, but a brisk breeze blew beneath the trees, enough of a deterrent to keep many away; the broad swaths of lawn were, if not deserted, then at least not crowded.

Her hand tucked in the crook of his arm, they walked, and talked of events long past. By unspoken agreement they avoided the subject highest in her mind—their plans for tomorrow, and what they might find.

The wind whipped the ribbons of her black bonnet across his chest. In her black gown, with her alabaster skin so pale against the contrast of her dark red hair, she looked even more slender, even more femininely fragile than usual.

She wasn't fragile, at least not physically, yet the hint of vulnerability the black emphasized—that he saw when, while thinking of him she glanced at him—wasn't something she'd possessed long ago.

Now that he recognized it for what it was, his heart constricted and his chest felt tight every time he glimpsed it.

Time, he hoped, would help him eradicate it.

After a brisk ramble under the trees, they repaired to the nearby Star and Garter for lunch. He encouraged her to tell him all she knew of recent ton scandals; the time passed swiftly and easily.

Leaving the hotel, they took one look at the deepening gray of the sky and headed for the curricle. The drive back was uneventful, but instead of taking her to South Audley Street, he drove to Grosvenor Square instead.

Pulling up outside Allardyce House, he tossed the reins to his groom, who came running to the horses' heads, then he stepped down to the pavement, turned and helped Letitia alight.

In response to her questioning look, he waved to the house. "We can have afternoon tea here. I've a pile of correspondence I need to look through."

Because he'd been spending all his time with her. Letitia inclined her head and consented to be led inside.

Christian's butler, Percival, recognized her. His face lit in a most unbutlerish way. He recovered and bowed low. "My lady. Welcome to Allardyce House." He straightened. "If I may take your bonnet . . ."

"Yes, of course." Letitia undid the ribbons, lifted the poke bonnet with its demiveil free of her hair, and laid it in Percival's waiting hands.

"We'll have tea in my study, Percival." Christian took her arm and steered her down a corridor leading from the front hall.

"Indeed, my lord. At once."

She hadn't seen his study before; it had previously been his father's domain. She found herself curious; she didn't lack for distraction while he sat behind the large desk and steadily worked through a stack of letters.

Tea arrived. She poured, sipped, and sampled the scones that had arrived with the pot. They were delicious. As Christian had his head down, tea cup in one hand, she finished three scones, then took pity and called his attention to the last one.

By the time she finished her second cup of tea, he'd polished off the scone and finished with his correspondence.

He rose. "Come—we'll walk back to the house."

Not her house or "Randall's house." She'd noted he rarely uttered Randall's name if he could avoid it, most especially in relation to her.

In the front hall, she reclaimed her bonnet. While securing it, she glanced at Percival, saw he was regarding her with a smile. "Please tell the cook that the scones were superb."

Percival's smile widened as he bowed. "Indeed, my lady. She'll be thrilled to hear you enjoyed them."

She suppressed the impulse to arch one brow. Had Christian said something to his staff? She glanced at his face, as arrogantly austere as ever, and doubted it.

They walked briskly to South Audley Street through the fading day.

Reaching the front steps, she paused—and glared across the street. "He's *still* there!"

Christian grasped her elbow and turned her up the steps. "I warned you he'd be dogged."

"But it's Sunday!" On principle she glowered at Mellon when he opened the door.

Christian followed her in. And stayed.

For dinner, then through a long game of loo with Hermione and Agnes. When at last they were packing up the board and counters, he glanced at Letitia, and was satisfied. She might have thought about their appointment at the banks tomorrow, but at least she hadn't had time to obsess. Like her, he couldn't imagine anything good lying beneath the cloak of Randall's secrecy, yet regardless, they had to lift it off and look.

She was, for the moment, relaxed and at peace. Over the last days, while he'd been intent on distracting her, he'd also been consciously wooing her—for the first time. Before, when they'd first known each other, he hadn't had to exert himself; their mutual attraction had drawn them inexorably together, without any extra effort from him.

Now, however, while he might be sharing her bed, that mutual attraction wouldn't serve to convince her he truly wanted more from her. He hoped the past day had opened her eyes, at least a little, that she'd seen he wanted to share not just a bed but a life, with all the simple pleasures that entailed.

The following morning, they were at the doors of the Piccadilly branch of Rothchild's Bank when it opened at ten o'clock. Christian requested to see the manager; they were shown into an oak-paneled office almost immediately.

Letitia sat back, from behind her veil watched as Christian shamelessly used his rank and title to bend the manager, a Mr. Hambury, to his will.

She wasn't at all surprised that Hambury bent very quickly.

"Indeed, my lord! Of course—I'll instruct the teller to . . . er, look your way and nod when the deposit in question is made."

"While the deposit is in progress would be best."

Letitia gave thanks for her veil; it hid her amusement. Christian's drawl was outrageous, his arrogant pose as he lounged in the chair beside hers the epitome of the powerful, bored aristocrat.

She couldn't complain; the ploy gained them what they wanted.

On returning to the main chamber of the bank and taking up positions along one wall from where they could keep the two tellers in full view, they saw Hambury exit his office by another door and move among the clerks. He spoke first to one teller, then the other—in both cases the tellers looked across at them, then back at Hambury and nodded.

A harassed looking underclerk came hurrying out with a chair for her. He set it down, bowing low; she smiled, murmured her thanks, and sat.

Two minutes later Hambury, who'd disappeared into the depths of the bank, came out again and headed their way, another older clerk with a visor shading his eyes following at his heels.

Frowning slightly, Hambury bowed. "Ah . . . Mr. Wilkes here, our head teller, has some information which might prove useful."

Unlike his master, Wilkes seemed much less obsequious, although he bobbed his head respectfully.

He addressed himself to Christian. "That deposit Mr. Hambury says you're waiting for, my lord. The large one. It always comes in just after one o'clock." He tipped his head back toward the nether regions from which he'd emerged. "I'm back there, counting the money as it comes in, and with a sum like that, the clerks always bring it straight to me. That's how I know—the party who pays that sum in will be here at one o'clock, give or take ten minutes."

Letitia sat transfixed. *One o'clock?*

"Thank you, Wilkes." Christian's voice came from above her. "It was good of you to spare us the wait."

Letitia felt his fingers close about her elbow; inwardly moaning, she surrendered and got to her feet.

Christian nodded to Hambury and Wilkes. "Gentlemen. We'll be back before one o'clock."

Letitia waited until they'd gained the pavement to give voice to her impatience. Christian let her grumble as, her hand anchored on his sleeve, he led her along. When she finally wound down and disgruntledly asked, "What the devil are we to do until one o'clock?" he hailed a hackney.

He took her to the museum.

They wandered around the exhibits, but there was nothing there to catch her eye—or his, for that matter. He was wondering how on earth to keep her occupied for the next two hours when she said, "Tell me about your life as a spy."

He felt his brows rise, but . . . "What do you want to know?"

She made an all-encompassing gesture. "Start at the beginning. I recently learned that Dalziel recruited you to his little band. When was that?"

"Within a month or two of me joining the Guards. He had his pick of the Guards, from any regiment."

She was frowning, looking down as she walked beside him. "But you didn't immediately go to France."

"No. Because I spoke so many languages, at first he had me go in and out of various countries, getting a sense of the lie of the land, and laying down a background as the wealthy bastard of an ex–French nobleman engaged in trade. Later, when I went over and stayed, I was stationed in Lyon. It was the hub for the manufacture of machinery and heavy equipment—such as artillery. Even if it wasn't made there, most of the components came from there. So . . ."

To his surprise, the words flowed easily. She listened, nodded, and asked questions—questions rooted in her knowledge of him and therefore easy to answer, even if sometimes both her questions and his answers surprised him.

Only when he looked up and found they'd wandered all the way back to the museum's door, and the clock above it declared the time to be nearly noon, did he realize just how much he'd talked—and how much he'd revealed.

More than he had to any other living soul, Dalziel included.

He glanced at Letitia; she was still frowning over his last answer—an explanation of how Napoleon's reign had affected the people of Lyon. That she'd even thought to ask it, that he'd answered without reserve, telling her about the resistance and the heartbreak of lost comrades who hadn't even been British . . .

He shouldn't have been surprised. Beneath the blatantly sexual attraction that had always flared between them ran another, deeper bond. One of shared background, of common understanding born of the fact they hailed from the same, very narrow social stratum. They shared the same sensitivities, looked on the world from much the same perspective, held to the same tenets of honor, loyalty, and courage. And stubborn determination, that never-accept-failure arrogance that permeated their class.

Looking at her, her brow furrowed as she digested all he'd said, all he'd revealed of himself along with the facts, all he could think of, all his mind could see, was the rightness of having her as his wife—of seeing her in his houses, surrounded by their children.

It was a vision that stole his breath.

It was a vision his never-accept-failure arrogance would never let him surrender. . . .

And she wouldn't expect him to.

He suddenly knew how St. Paul had felt on the road to Damascus. He wanted to convince her that he truly wanted her as his wife; if he did feel that way, she would expect him to pursue that goal, and her, relentlessly. Stubbornly and doggedly.

She looked up at him, saw the smile on his face, frowned. "What?"

He let his smile widen. "Just . . . this."

With one hand, he tipped up her chin and brought his lips down on hers.

A quick, swift kiss—in the middle of the foyer of the museum in full view of any who might be passing.

He drew back before she could react.

Stunned, she stared up at him. "What was that for?" Then glancing left and right, and realizing they were now the center of attention for a number of other museum patrons, she swore beneath her breath, grabbed his arm and tried to tug him to the door.

He consented to move, a satisfied smile on his lips. "That," he informed her as he held the main door back for her, then followed her through, "was just to confirm that when it comes to you, to my plans for you, I fully intend to succeed."

She looked at him, then snorted. "Naturally."

They had a quick bite to eat at a nearby pastry shop and were back at the bank at a quarter to one. Taking up their previous positions by the wall, they watched the steady stream of customers approach the grilles before the two tellers.

The bank's customers were a mix of well-to-do gentry and prosperous merchants, with one or two less prosperous among them.

At just after one o'clock a striking woman—tall but not young, well dressed but not, to Letitia's discerning eye, expensively enough for the ton—walked into the bank, a lumbering giant at her heels.

The giant was plainly a guard; the way he hovered by the woman, constantly scanning the surrounds even inside the bank, underscored his role. The woman seemed largely oblivious to the stares the giant drew; head high, she waited in line for one of the tellers, then advanced to the counter, drew a large canvas bag from inside the even larger tapestry bag she carried, placed it on the counter and pushed it toward the teller.

Who, as he reached for the bag, glanced at Christian and all but imperceptibly nodded.

Letitia felt her eyes grow wide. She glanced up at Christian.

He took her arm and drew her to her feet. Lowering his head, he murmured, "There's only one door. Let's wait outside."

Letitia cast another glance at the couple at the counter, then let him lead her out.

On the pavement, she shook her head. "Surely Randall didn't keep a *circus*?"

His hand still wrapped about her elbow, Christian steered her a little way along the street. "I don't think that's it."

She looked up at him. "What, then?"

Lips firming, he shook his head. He halted outside the window of an adjacent apothecary's, turned her as if they were looking inside. "We'll follow them when they come out."

"Why can't we simply ask them what they've just paid for?"

His lips thinned even more. "We can ask later. Let's see what business they come from first."

She frowned, but then the door of the bank swung open and the woman came out, followed by the giant. They turned away from the apothecary's and walked off in the opposite direction.

Letitia turned to follow. Christian anchored her hand on his sleeve and strolled, keeping her beside him.

She inwardly frowned at his pace, but she had to assume he knew what he was doing. In his past occupation, he'd no doubt followed people often.

And it was hardly difficult to keep their quarry in sight; the giant towered over everyone. He was wearing a plaid felt cap; even when Christian insisted on dropping half a block behind as they turned up Shaftesbury Avenue, Letitia could track the pair with ease.

Neither the woman nor the giant gave any indication they'd realized they were being followed.

Letitia frowned. "We've followed far enough—they might be trudging for miles. Let's catch up to them and just ask."

"No."

There was a grimness in Christian's voice, mirrored in his face when she glanced up at it, that made her frown even more.

He glanced down briefly. "Not yet."

She sighed; looking ahead, she continued trailing along beside him.

From Shaftesbury Avenue their striking duo turned south into Wardour Street. Letitia glanced narrow-eyed at Christian. "Not yet?"

He didn't even reply.

If she'd thought she could, she would have slipped her hand from beneath his, picked up her skirts and run after their quarry, hailing them and then simply asking directly for the answer they needed. How could that hurt?

But she held no illusions about how Christian would react; for all his size, he could move with startling speed when he wished—she doubted she'd even be able to draw her hand from beneath his before he caught it.

"This is—" She broke off as the pair stopped outside a town house. The area wasn't a bad one, respectable enough; the town house was plain, but reasonably well-kept, with two steps leading up to an emerald green door.

Climbing the steps, the woman paused, hunting in her bag, then she drew out a key, unlocked the door and went inside.

Ducking his head, the giant followed, then the door shut.

On the opposite side of the street, Christian stopped, drawing Letitia to a halt beside him. She regarded the green door. "Well, then, let's go in and speak with her."

Christian clamped his hand about her wrist and remained where he was. He studied the building in question. "It's not a shop—and there's nothing to suggest it's an office of any kind. No sign, no plaque by the door."

Letitia looked at the building, then shrugged. "Perhaps she just lives there. With the giant."

And perhaps it was a high-class brothel, which in this area was perfectly possible. If it was, Christian certainly wasn't going to escort Lady Letitia Randall née Vaux in to speak with the madam. "I think we should go back to South Audley Street."

He tried to draw her on, but she dug in her heels and refused to budge.

She stared at him. "Why? We've followed them here—we know they're in there. Why can't we just go and ask them what they're paying the Orient Trading Company, of which I own a third share, for?"

He set his jaw. "*I'll* come back and ask them—but you can't."

Locking his fingers about her wrist, he tried again to draw her on; this time she pulled back—to the limit of his arm.

"Nonsense!" She glared at him. "I saw that woman—she's perfectly respectable. And if you think I'm going to wait any longer to learn what my devil of a late husband was up to—what he's saddled me with—you're wrong!"

She turned her arm sharply outward and broke his hold—then she streaked away, racing across the street. She reached the door, grabbed the knocker and hammered it down once before he caught her and lifted her from her feet—

A little window in the door flew open.

Gritting his teeth, Christian put her down. She tugged her bodice down, sent him a scorching glance, then turned to the window and smiled.

Whoever was behind the little window rumbled, "The mistress isn't interested in any pamphlets or good works."

Letitia's smile didn't waver. "That's just as well, as I haven't any to offer her. I—" She glanced over her shoulder at Christian, then turned back to the eyes she could see through the little window. "—*we* wish to speak with the lady who entered a few minutes ago. You may tell her Lady Randall requests a few minutes of her time."

The instant she said "Randall," a strange look came into the blue eyes watching her. A moment passed, then the little window shut and they heard bolts being drawn back. The door swung open, held by a large man who appeared to be masquerading as a butler. "Indeed, ma'am," he intoned in a passable imitation of Percival's authority. "If you'll just come this way?"

His bow left something to be desired, but with a regal

inclination of her head, Letitia consented to follow him down the hall, Christian behind her. To her surprise, the man didn't conduct her into any of the rooms to either side; as they passed the open doorways, she glanced in and saw what appeared to be salons, yet there was something not quite right about the furniture, and the curtains were all still drawn.

There was also a curious smell, as if someone had spilled brandy on a rug.

The butler continued into a corridor and all the way to its end; there, he opened a door and bowed them through.

"If you'll wait in here, ma'am—my lady—I'll fetch the mistress. She'll be along in a moment."

Letitia walked in to what appeared to be a cross between a study and an office. A heavy desk sat squarely in the center of the room, with another smaller desk against one wall, a bookcase filled with boxes and files beside it. Two chairs faced the larger desk; glancing around, she moved to one and sat.

Although old and undistinguished, everything was clean and neat.

The butler whisked out of the door, closing it behind him.

She glanced at Christian—and found him surveying the room.

Christian drifted to the bookcase, glanced at the labels on the boxes. Uninformative. He looked at the desk, wondered if he had time to search . . . decided against it.

Letitia shifted on the chair, drawing his attention; she was sitting upright, unusually prim. She caught his eye. "This isn't a brothel, is it?"

He shook his head. "No. I don't think so." But he'd wager the place provided some form of entertainment for wealthy gentlemen; he'd recognized the odors of tobacco and spilled brandy, recognized the decor in the rooms they'd passed.

Footsteps tap-tapped down the corridor—a woman's heels, rapidly approaching. They halted outside the door; a whispered conference ensued, too muted for them to make out any words.

Christian stepped between Letitia and the door.

Abruptly, silence fell, then the door opened.

The woman they'd seen at the bank entered, the giant once again in her train. The butler, Christian noted, hovered by the open door.

The woman came to stand at the front corner of the desk, facing Letitia. Little showed on her handsome face, yet she seemed wary.

Letitia got to her feet. Both she and Christian were taller than the woman, but neither were taller than the giant, who lumbered around to stand behind the woman, openly protective. He'd removed his cap, exposing a balding pate; the face beneath was unprepossessing in the extreme—Christian suspected he'd been a pugilist in earlier years.

Having confirmed Letitia's quality, and his, the woman drew in a breath. Hands clasped before her, she fixed her gaze on Letitia's face. "You're Lady Randall—Mr. Randall's wife, I assume?"

Letitia nodded. "Yes, that's correct."

The woman straightened, her gaze shifting to a point by Letitia's right shoulder. "I understand you wish to speak with me, ma'am."

Letitia inwardly frowned; the woman was behaving like a housekeeper. "Yes." Where to start? "As you may or may not know, Randall died unexpectedly." Brows rising, she amended, "Well, not to put too fine a point on it, he was brutally murdered. Consequently, through his will, I learned I'd inherited a third share of the company he managed, the Orient Trading Company."

The woman clearly knew the name.

Encouraged, glancing at Christian and receiving a tiny nod in reply, Letitia looked back at the woman. "Subsequently, I and"—she waved at Christian—"others acting on my behalf, have been trying to establish just what the business of my late husband's company was. We know that you regularly, every Monday, pay in a large sum to one of the company's accounts. If you would, I'd like you to explain to us what that payment is in relation to."

The woman frowned. "It's the week's takings."

Letitia blinked. "The week's takings from what?"

"From the hell," the woman replied.

"The *hell*?" Feeling suddenly unsteady, Letitia felt behind her for the chair.

Frowning more definitely, the woman looked at Christian. "That's what this place is. Rigby's—one of the most exclusive hells in London, if I do say so myself." She looked from Christian to Letitia. "I'm Mrs. Rigby. I run the place."

Letitia sank into the chair. "And Randall?"

"Owned it."

When Letitia stared blankly and said nothing more, Mrs. Rigby went on, "I came to work for Mr. Randall . . . well, it'd be all of twelve years ago. He was setting this place up and needed someone who knew the ropes to run it. I've been here, running it, ever since."

Letitia blinked. "So I own one of the most exclusive gaming hells in London." Not a question. On the one hand she couldn't believe it; on the other, faced with the evidence, with her evolving premonition, she did.

"Not just one," Mrs. Rigby informed her, effectively reclaiming her attention. "I don't know how many Randall had in his stable—I don't know anything about any other accounts—but I do know of at least three other hells in this neighborhood who pay into the same account we do." She paused, then added, "Not that we're supposed to know about each other—Randall was always very careful, and never let on he had any other properties—but we do talk, those of us who manage the major hells."

Christian thought of the entries they'd found for furniture and decoration, of the fourteen slim ledgers Tony had described as property ledgers.

Letitia continued to stare at Mrs. Rigby. "Not one, but a *stable* of gaming hells." Her voice, weak before, had gained in strength.

Sensing a Vaux storm brewing—entirely understandably—Christian shifted, drawing Mrs. Rigby's attention. "Did you ever meet any of the other partners in the company?"

Mrs. Rigby shook her head. "No. I never knew there *were* any other partners to meet."

Christian nodded. He was starting, finally, to get the lie of Randall's land. He reached into his coat pocket and drew out his card case. "If any others approach you, either saying they're Randall's partners or wishing to take the business over, send word to me at this address." He handed Mrs. Rigby a card.

She took it, read it. Her brows rose. She looked at him. "Grosvenor Square?"

He met her gaze. "I act for Lady Randall." He glanced at Letitia.

She caught his gaze, then looked at Mrs. Rigby and nodded. "Indeed. Please send word if you hear anything at all. We're in the process of sorting out Mr. Randall's affairs, and need to know anything pertinent—including if there's any interest in the business from others."

Consciousness passed behind Mrs. Rigby's eyes. Christian noted it. "Have you heard anything?"

Startled, Mrs. Rigby looked at him, then she grimaced. "Not so much heard as . . . there's been a rumor, the veriest whisper, going around that Randall was thinking of selling. Not just this place but his whole operation. Who to, I—and the other owners I know—never heard, but you may be sure there'd be a lot of interest in the businesses, at least all those I know of."

Given the sums regularly pouring into the company's accounts, Christian could well believe that. He nodded to Mrs. Rigby. "Thank you." He caught Letitia's eye. "We won't take up any more of your time."

Letitia rose. "Indeed." There was an almost feverish light in her eyes as she pulled on her gloves. "We have rather a lot to deal with." She swung around and headed for the door. "Do remember, Mrs. Rigby, to send word if there's any query about the business."

"Yes, ma'am." Mrs. Rigby fell in at Letitia's heels. "I'll send Tiny with a note. That way I'll know it gets to the right place—no one gets in his way."

Letitia glanced back at the giant, and nodded. "Yes—I can see how that might be." She continued her march toward the door.

The butler whisked about and preceded her down the corridor to the front door, there to bow her out with all due deference. Mrs. Rigby came, too, to stand at attention and nod a careful farewell.

Christian followed Letitia down the front steps. When the door shut behind them, she halted on the pavement.

He joined her. She was still rather viciously tugging at her gloves.

Her eyes were narrow slits of fury. "You know, I lied."

"Oh?" He kept his tone mild. "How so?"

"I swore I would never have killed Randall. But if someone hadn't already done the deed, if—when—I found out about this—his secret business—I would *definitely* have murdered him myself!"

Suppressed rage fell from her in waves. She swung around and stormed off, back toward Shaftesbury Avenue. "Let's find a hackney and get back to the club."

Abruptly she halted. Christian nearly ran into her.

He steadied her, his hands on her shoulders.

She stared straight ahead, as if she'd seen an apparition.

"I just realized . . ." Her voice was too calm. *Terribly* calm. ". . . if on this account alone I'm the part owner of four hells, and each regular deposit is a different hell, including for those other two accounts, then . . ."

Her voice faded away.

Fourteen hells, Christian thought. Soothingly, he said, "We don't know that yet." His hand at her back, he urged her on. "Let's get back to the club and see what the others have learned."

"You, it appears, are the part owner of a company running an extensive string of high-class gambling hells throughout London." Dalziel considered Letitia. They'd all returned to the club and gathered in the library to report on what they'd found. Along with Christian and Letitia, Dalziel, Tristan, Tony, and Jack Hendon were all seated in armchairs forming a circle before the empty hearth.

Letitia didn't respond to the startling summation; she appeared to be mentally elsewhere.

"They certainly went to considerable effort to minimize any chance of outsiders learning of their involvement." Tony Blake spoke to the room at large. "Each hell manager knew only one of the partners, and had no idea any other partners existed."

Christian nodded. "The payers into each bank account are answerable to a different partner—Randall handled all the hells paying in at Rothchild's, Trowbridge handles those depositing at Child's, while Swithin oversees those paying in via Barkers."

Dalziel and Tristan had found themselves visiting a hell in Newport Place, not all that far from Rigby's in Wardour Street, while Tony and Jack had been led to an establishment in King Street, not far from Covent Garden.

"If the three hells we've visited are anything to judge by," Christian said, "then it seems the company targeted the very crème de la crème in terms of young gentlemen with money to lose."

Dalziel shifted. "I asked around after we left—the hell in Newport Place is known as an establishment that rash young men with more money than wits simply have to patronize."

"You know," Tristan said, "in terms of making money from the ton, Randall, Trowbridge, and Swithin have demonstrated a fine appreciation of what will work in attracting young gentlemen."

"*That's* what they learned at Hexham Grammar School," Christian dryly remarked.

"Which is all very well," Letitia suddenly said, "but says nothing to my purpose. I don't give a fig for whatever ingenuity my late and unlamented husband and his cronies demonstrated in setting up this enterprise—all I want is to be rid of it!"

She glanced pointedly around the circle, reserving her final near-glare for Dalziel and Christian. "A Vaux," she declared, "cannot be the owner of a string of gambling hells. My father would quite literally have a seizure—and who could blame him?—and I don't even want to *think* of how my aunts would react if ever they heard of it, which I fervently pray they never will."

Her tone made it clear she was not merely troubled by what they'd discovered—she was horrified, aghast, tending toward overset. She was seriously upset, well beyond agitated; they all understood that. They exchanged wary glances, keeping very still.

"Bad enough," she concluded, her voice very nearly wavering, "to discover that Randall was a farmer's son, but now I find he wasn't even an honest one!"

Christian opted for silence.

Dalziel, brave man, tried for rationality. "There's nothing illegal about running a gaming hell, in and of itself. The company isn't breaking any laws per se."

"That may be so"—Letitia's tones were clipped; she clearly wasn't mollified in the least—"but owning a string of gaming hells, no matter how *exclusive*, is breaking every *ton* law ever created." She narrowed her eyes on Dalziel. "You, of all people, know what that means."

Dalziel held her gaze, then, to the utter fascination of his ex-subordinates, inclined his head and retreated.

Letitia looked down at her fingers, clenched in her lap. "The only bright light in all we've uncovered today is that according to Mrs. Rigby, there was talk of someone wanting to buy the hells. If that's so—"

"If that's so," Christian cut in, "you'll need to wait and see who approaches you. Or me as your agent—you should take care not to be involved."

"I have no interest in being involved." She frowned at him. "That's my point—if they wish to buy, then I'll happily sell my share of the company. I want all ties with its enterprises severed and no more, as soon as humanly possible."

"That's understandable," Christian allowed, "but you might want to consider not being quite so open about it."

She frowned harder. "Great heavens, *why*?"

"Because," he replied, jaw firming, "it's entirely possible that the putative sale was in some way behind Randall's murder."

That gave her pause. "How so?"

"I don't know," he admitted, "but until we know more, we need to play our cards very close to our collective chest."

She consider that, then pulled a disgusted face and stopped arguing.

"We should," Dalziel said, breaking into the ensuing silence, "put together all we've learned thus far about Randall, Trowbridge, and Swithin. We need to see how the picture fits together, and what pieces of the puzzle we're still missing. We know all three were governors' scholars, in the same year, at a school with a sizable percentage of boys from ton families and an otherwise solid base of the gentry-born. The three would have been entirely out of their social depth— certainly they wouldn't have been readily welcomed among the other boys—so them banding together makes excellent sense."

"It's also," Christian put in, "not hard to see what might have fired their ambition to become a part of the ton."

"True," Dalziel continued. "But from the time they left school to the time Randall appeared in London—which seems to be much the same time as Trowbridge and Swithin also relocated to the capital and the company was established—we know nothing of their lives. Whatever happened during that interval might be crucial, especially with regard to the motive for Randall's murder."

Tristan was nodding. "However, when they came to town twelve years ago, they immediately set about establishing a string of exclusive gaming hells exquisitely tailored to appeal to the dissolute young gentlemen of the upper echelons of the ton."

Tony snorted. "Well, you can see it, can't you." He glanced around the circle. "They're preying on the very group who, at Hexham Grammar School, would have made their lives hell."

"There is," Christian said, "a certain thread of irony running through all this."

Jack stretched his long legs before him. "Extrapolating from Hexham to how they behaved when they arrived in London, I'd suggest that to fill in those intervening years we look for word of them at Oxford or Cambridge. Who knows? We might find gaming hells—the first they set up—operating there."

Letitia glanced at Dalziel. "Much as I do *not* want to know the answer, I suggest you ask Justin. He would know—at least about Oxford."

Dalziel nodded. "I'll ask him, and send up and ask another who might know if Randall, Trowbridge, and Swithin actually owned a hell or hells in Cambridge." He nodded to Jack. "I agree it seems likely they learned their trade there."

Tristan grimaced wryly. "That would certainly explain their excellent understanding of how to attract their chosen prey—the fattest and easiest of all to pluck—into their establishments."

Looking up to see nods all around, he continued, "While

you're pursuing that, I'll see what I can learn about this rumor of Randall selling. The Newport Place manager seemed to think a deal was in progress."

"I can help with that," Tony said.

"And me," Jack chimed in.

"Meanwhile"—Dalziel looked at Letitia and Christian—"I think we now have sufficient information to make another interview with Trowbridge worthwhile."

"Indeed." Christian rose. "We'll go tomorrow."

He offered Letitia his hand. She took it and rose, too.

All the others came to their feet. Dalziel continued, "Trowbridge's house is in Chelsea." He caught Christian's eye. "You might well find Rupert Honeywell in residence."

Reading the message in Dalziel's dark eyes, Christian raised his brows. "I see."

Letitia, following the exchange, didn't, but before she could ask for clarification, Christian appropriated her hand and anchored it on his sleeve "We'll reconvene here, I presume?" he said.

"We'd better, I think." Dalziel exchanged a glance with the others. "We'll all need to hear what Trowbridge has to say. If we can learn anything else, especially about any suggestion of a sale, then by tomorrow we might have quite a few potential murderers to pursue."

Dalziel's last words set hares racing and chasing through Letitia's mind. That evening, as she stood in Lady Henderson's drawing room and pretended to attend to the conversations around her, all she could think about was what she'd subsequently badgered out of Christian.

The soiree was not one she would have chosen to attend, but there were some invitations that, mourning or not, one did not decline. A summons from Lady Henderson was one such; the old lady was getting on in years, yet remained an institution within the ton. As Letitia was widely viewed as the most senior Vaux lady—with Randall so undistinguished, society had continued to regard her as a Vaux, and as Justin had yet to marry, she was the only female representative of the principal line of age—it fell to her to carry the family flag. The matrons around her would have been thoroughly shocked had she failed to appear.

Not that anyone could conceivably view standing in an ill-lit salon sipping weak orgeat and listening to others, most of whom were twice her age, dwell on the shortcomings of their adult children as at all entertaining.

Which was no doubt why her mind found it much easier to dwell on what Christian had revealed. He'd explained that in the murky world of which gaming hells formed a part, the sale of a valuable set of properties like the company's had the potential to stir all sorts of reactions, any of which might turn violent. Bidders who sensed they might not win and owners of similar establishments were only some of the possible reactees; Christian had hinted that there were other even more shadowy souls within London's underworld who might be moved to take an interest.

The notion of being involved with such persons held absolutely no allure. She was nearly twenty-nine; she'd left unthinking wildness behind her long ago.

Smiling as Lady Washthorne concluded a story about her niece, she wondered how soon she could leave.

"Letitia."

Just the sound of Christian's deep voice sent relief washing through her. She turned to face him and gave him her hand. "My lord. What brings you here?"

He raised her hand; eyes locked with hers, he brushed his lips across the backs of her fingers. "You." He smiled. Instead of releasing her hand, he set it on his sleeve.

The others in the group were delighted to welcome him. He shook hands, exchanged greetings, then, after a few minutes had elapsed, excused them both and drew her out of the circle.

He glanced down at her. "How's your temper?"

"Holding up. Just." She looked around the room. "You know everyone here, do you not?"

"All by name, most by sight, but a potted recent history of the more notable wouldn't go astray."

"I see. In that case, you'll want to know that Lady Framlingham . . ."

Christian steered her around the room in a slow, ambling circuit. A few reckless souls were brave enough to stop them to exchange greetings, but as it was plain they were deep in converse, most simply smiled, nodded, and let them pass by.

Letitia frowned at a gentleman—an aging dandy—across the room. "Did you hear about Findlay-Robinson?"

"What about him?" Christian inwardly smiled as she told him the tale of the faded beau's obsession with one of the more flighty young ladies recently out.

"It will never do, of course, but no one has the heart to tell him."

As they promenaded, she filled his ears with a detailed, colorful, accurate, and often acerbic account of the company and their private lives, their personal foibles. She entertained him while imparting information that, now he was appearing in society again, he needed. While she was frequently cynical, she was never malicious, instead exhibiting an understanding of their world that was both remarkably mature and remarkably well-grounded.

Demonstrating on yet another level why she was the perfect wife for him, and always had been.

Not that *he* needed reminding, let alone convincing.

Deciding they'd both been present long enough to be deemed as having done their respective duties, he turned her toward their hostess. "Come—I'll take you home."

Letitia inclined her head and let him.

Let him take her back to South Audley Street, let him take her upstairs, let him take her to her bed.

Let him take her.

Or, as the case proved, let him let her take him.

It was a distinction she appreciated, yet it was only much later, when she lay in his arms in the rumpled jumble of her bed and listened to his breathing deepen, listened to his heart slow as he slipped into slumber, that she realized.

She didn't need to wake him to ask if he'd done it on purpose; she knew him—of course he had. He'd set the stage, played the part, and she—without thinking, without the slightest warning flicker in her mind—had slipped into the opposing role.

That of his wife.

If her unthinking acceptance hadn't rattled her so much, she would have woken him just to upbraid him.

Damn man! She hadn't seen that coming, not at all.

There was nothing to be done, not now she lay wrapped in his arms, her head pillowed on his chest, still far too physically wrung out to even contemplate moving.

No point in trying to move, either; even in sleep he'd hold her where she was. Over his heart.

All of which led her to contemplate instead the unexpected turn her life had taken. Randall was gone—as Christian had said, removed by fate from her side. And he was there instead, holding her through the night as Randall never had—as she'd never allowed Randall to do, which in itself told the story.

She was besotted with Christian, always had been, and nothing on that front had changed.

And now he wanted to marry her.

She knew he meant it, that this time he intended to stubbornly press his suit until she agreed, but the more cautious and wary, afraid-of-being-hurt-again side of her insisted she had to know why.

Had to know what was truly in his heart before she could decide whether marrying him now, after their years of separation, was the right, safe, and sensible thing to do.

It wasn't being his wife she questioned; she'd always wanted the position, knew it fitted her like a glove and that everyone—simply everyone—agreed. That was not the issue. What she wasn't sure of, what was holding her back, was a sense of not having looked hard enough. Of not yet having gained sufficient assurances to justify taking the risk of loving him again.

Of giving him, as she had long ago, her heart and soul, unconditionally.

Last time she'd done that naïvely, without a second thought—without any idea whatever of the dangers—and when she'd needed him by her side to protect her heart, he hadn't been there. So her heart had been broken and, as she'd told him, she'd put the pieces away, locked them away and buried the key. That was the only way she'd been able to survive, to distance herself from the pain.

She still remembered the pain.

Given that, now he was back, now he was there once again in her arms, before she dug up the key, unlocked the casket, took out her heart, put it back together and handed it to him again, she had to be sure.

Absolutely, beyond all doubt sure that her heart would now be safe with him.

Once bitten, twice shy; in her case the old adage rang true. Regardless, she was going to have to make up her mind, and soon.

With him so intent on pressing his suit, in the next few weeks she would have to decide if what he was offering— all she would gain—was worth facing, accepting, and taking that risk again—this time with full knowledge of the pain she would endure if she agreed and her decision proved wrong.

She lay in his arms, cocooned in his strength, listened to the muffled thud of his heart—and knew in her heart that she was where she belonged.

If only there existed some guarantee.

Or at the very least some sign . . .

She was on the cusp of sleep when clarity shone, a beam sharpened by the prism of her waning conscious.

She knew she loved him—that wasn't, never had been, a part of her dilemma.

The resolution to her dilemma lay in the opposing direction.

She had yet to be convinced that he loved her.

Loved her as she loved him, with her heart, her soul—with everything in her.

She was a Vaux—love was, for her, a grand, burning passion. She needed proof that he loved her in the same way—to the depths of his conqueror's soul—before she again surrendered her heart and gave it into his keeping.

Sleep rolled over her and dragged her down, but the essence of that moment of clarity remained, lodged very firmly in her brain.

Chapter 16

Christian considered it one of life's great ironies that he couldn't take Randall's place as Letitia's husband until he'd uncovered the man's murderer.

He could be her lover—her only lover—but he couldn't press her to accept his suit until she was free of the tangled web of Randall's life. Not because there was any social stricture preventing her from accepting him, but because—he knew her—she wouldn't.

Until they succeeded in divesting her of any association with gaming hells, and freed Justin from all suspicion of Randall's murder by exposing the real culprit, his chances of getting her to agree to a wedding were slim to none.

As he tooled his curricle along the embankment, he hoped that interviewing Trowbridge would advance his cause.

Letitia usually found the river distracting, but not today. When Christian checked his pair and turned into Cheyne Walk, she scanned the houses, then pointed. "That's it."

A short gravel drive led to a set of white-porticoed steps; Christian drew his horses to a halt before them. Leaving the reins with his groom, he descended and rounded the carriage. Handing her down, he arched a brow at her. "Do you think, this time, that I might lead the questioning?"

He was asking in all sincerity. She wrinkled her nose at him. "As interrogation is more your forte than mine, yes, all right. You can do the talking."

She'd already lectured herself on the wisdom of keeping her twin objectives—to rid herself of the gambling hells and clear Justin of suspicion by finding Randall's killer—firmly in the forefront of her mind, to not let herself be distracted by either Christian's agenda or her own sometimes overly dramatic nature. She'd reminded herself that no matter how insistent the compulsion to dwell on Christian and the possibilities he'd placed before her, and on the ultimate question of whether he truly loved her as she loved him, nothing could be decided until her twin objectives had been met and the detritus of her marriage to Randall cleared away.

Placing her hand on Christian's sleeve, she let him lead her up the steps to a lovingly polished wooden door, where a kindly looking butler stood waiting.

Christian smiled his easy social smile. "Lord Dearne and Lady Letitia Randall to see Mr. Trowbridge, if he's in." As it was barely eleven o'clock; chances were that Trowbridge hadn't yet stirred beyond his doors.

The butler bowed low. "Indeed, my lord. If you and Lady Randall will follow me, I'll inform Mr. Trowbridge of your arrival."

He showed them into an airy room, full of light and color. Letitia immediately felt herself relaxing, and reminded herself of their purpose. Still, it was difficult not to respond to the pale lemon-on-white decor, the perfectly balanced arrangement of furniture, art, and beautiful flowers.

The room wasn't overtly sumptuous but seductively comfortable, a haven for the senses.

Noting a painting of the river above the mantelpiece, Letitia crossed to examine it. Deciphering the signature reminded her; she looked at Christian. "Rupert Honeywell's a painter. Why did Dalziel warn you he might be here?"

Christian held her gaze for a moment, then said, "Honeywell was in my year at Eton."

She raised her brows. "How did Dalziel . . . oh, of course. He must have been two years or so ahead of you."

"So I've always assumed, but, of course, I didn't know

him then—I can't recall him. He, however, has a memory that's impossible to overestimate."

She laughed, then turned to the doorway as footsteps approached.

Trowbridge appeared, dressed in much the same fashion as the first time they'd seen him, yet it was instantly apparent that in his own home he was much more at ease.

With a ready smile, he crossed to take Letitia's hand. "Lady Randall." He exchanged nods with Christian. "Dearne." Then he waved. "Please, sit."

Letitia chose the sofa. Christian sat beside her, while Trowbridge sank into one of two armchairs facing them.

Crossing one leg over the other, he regarded them with gentle interest. "Now, how may I help you? I take it this visit isn't about art."

Letitia found herself returning his smile. She was about to reply when Christian's hand closed about hers.

"No," he said, his voice uninflected, "it's not. In the wake of Randall's death, Lady Randall discovered that as Randall's principal heir, she has become part owner of the Orient Trading Company, along with you and Mr. Swithin. We've subsequently learned that you, Randall, and Swithin all attended Hexham Grammar School, in the same year, all as governors' scholars. Presumably the friendship you formed at that time survived through the years, to your arrival in London and the establishment of the company."

Christian paused, reassessing how much of their knowledge to reveal. He'd initially intended to keep a great deal back, but, as before, when Letitia had first approached him, Trowbridge appeared encouraging, almost as if he were eager to talk and was only waiting for the proper, polite moment to do so. "We have, of course, now learned what the business of the Orient Trading Company is, but in the interests of gaining a better understanding, so Lady Randall might decide what to do with her share, we thought to approach you and ask if you would tell us about the company's origins, and how it operates."

Trowbridge beamed. He gestured expansively. "You perceive me only too ready to do so." He looked at Letitia, then at Christian. "I hope you understand that I wasn't prepared to speak the other day, not about Randall and our association, not until I knew you'd learned about the company."

"If I might ask," Christian said, "why was that?"

"Because I much preferred you to learn of the company through Randall's association with it, not directly from me, or, indeed, Swithin. Once you'd had time to assimilate Randall's connection with such an enterprise, as I told Swithin, we then stood in no danger of you exposing Randall's—or our—less than acceptable source of income. Such a revelation would harm Lady Randall as much as myself and Swithin, perhaps more." He inclined his head ruefully to Letitia. "Such is the nature of our world."

"Indeed." Christian waited for Trowbridge's gaze to return to him. "I take it our world is one the three of you set out to join from your days at school?"

"Oh, indeed." Trowbridge sat back, hands folded in his lap. "We had a terrible time of it, our first year. But then Randall discovered how much the other boys—all of whom came from much wealthier families—liked to gamble. But he, and we, quickly learned that if you gamble, you're just as likely to lose as to win, even when you grow skilled. But Randall saw another way to turn their hobby into our career. Indeed, into our future. He started organizing gambling nights in a local barn. He charged admission, and took a small percentage of the winnings. We—Swithin and I— were his lieutenants. We quickly discovered that we'd found a way to make money—a steady stream of it."

Trowbridge paused, then his lips lifted wryly. "Of course, we were still not accepted by the other boys. Out of that— *because* of that, you might say—we came up with our Grand Plan. Our thesis, as it were, was that as people we were all the same, that it was only circumstances that set us apart. Through those other boys, we saw that money, lots of it, combined with the right sort of behavior, the right sort of dress and so on, could see us pass for members of the ton. Not the aristocracy—that was aiming too high—but the higher gentry, members of the upper ten thousand? *That* we could become."

Letitia was fascinated. "So what was your Grand Plan?"

"We studied our peers—those boys, and as we grew older, young gentlemen we wanted to be. Alongside that, we continued to develop our business by providing the right environment, the right inducements, to get those same peers to pay us for the privilege of parting with their cash." Trowbridge smiled. "It was ridiculously easy. As our peers grew older and went to university, so did we—but not as students. Our den in Oxford was our first serious venture into what eventually became the basis of the company's business."

He paused, gaze distant, as if looking back down the years. "It wasn't always plain sailing, but Randall was the primary organizer, I had the flair to grasp what our customers wanted, and Swithin was our cautious, painstaking calculator. He was the one who always ensured we had a position to fall back to if things went wrong. As they inevitably occasionally did in those early years."

"So by the time you came to London . . ." Christian prompted.

"We were entirely confident. We'd worked through all the hurdles in Oxford, and then later when we set up a den in Cambridge."

"Do those still operate?" Christian asked.

Trowbridge nodded. "Oh, yes. Two of our most lucrative venues. London, however, required more care in selecting the right properties and finding the right staff. We were wealthy enough by then to take our time—and if I do say so myself, the years have proved us right in doing so. We've never had to close a hell once it opened, and only twice in all our years have we had to dismiss a manager. The entire network of hells—twelve in London, one each in Oxford and Cambridge—is now very well established." He met Letitia's and Christian's gazes, and smiled. "These days there's precious little for us to do other than keep the books, which Randall always did, and watch the money roll in."

"We've learned," Christian said, "that there are three company bank accounts, each with a group of four hells paying in, and each group was managed by one of you alone. Why was that?"

"Our Grand Plan," Trowbridge said. "It was always our intention to become accepted by the ton—that was the end point of our game, our ultimate aim. We knew that to achieve that we needed to maintain absolute secrecy about the source of our wealth. So from our Oxford days we were very careful to limit any chance of exposure—the fewer people who even knew of our threesome, the better."

"So that was why you, Randall, and Swithin hid your friendship?" Letitia asked.

Trowbridge nodded. "We agreed it was the best way to conceal even the possibility of the existence of the company. If by any chance it became known that one of us owned a gambling hell, there was no reason for anyone to suspect the other two. That's why I was so surprised by Randall mentioning me in his will—he'd always been the most insistent about us not meeting socially, or even greeting each other as anything more than passing acquaintances—but of course he hadn't expected to die when he did."

"Randall's secret room must have been a godsend," Christian remarked.

"Oh, it was! So like Randall, to buy a house with a secret room. No one other than the three of us knew of it, at least as far as I know."

"Did you have keys to the outer doors?" Christian asked.

Trowbridge laughed. "Dear me, no! Randall was positively paranoid about security—I'm quite sure he never gave those keys to anyone. No—when he wanted to see us, he'd send a note via a street urchin. He'd set a time, and the doors would be open so we could simply walk in. He was usually waiting in the office, although if the discussion wasn't about something in the books, we'd often go into his study. More comfortable there." His face clouded. "I heard he was killed there—in his study."

Christian nodded. He waited a beat, then asked, "Have there been any recent developments with the company?"

"Yes, indeed. We'd decided to sell." Trowbridge looked at Letitia. "Of course, that's now on hold, as it were, until you decide what you wish to do. The way the company is set up, we all have to sell, or none of us can—at least not for anything like full value."

Letitia opened her mouth; Christian closed his hand hard about her wrist. Ignoring her resulting stare, he asked, "What prompted your decision to sell?"

Trowbridge opened his eyes wide. "It wasn't anything in particular, but Randall had reached the stage of deciding that continuing to court exposure was no longer necessary, or indeed wise. He had a canny instinct for when to draw back, and indeed, when he approached me I was only too ready to agree. We're all very well established financially, all with significant income from investments and the like— all of us entirely accepted by the ton, as we have been for years—there was simply no reason we needed to continue with the company. I suppose, as Swithin and Randall would say, it had become more an unnecessary liability than a vital asset."

"So you all agreed to sell." Christian watched Trowbridge carefully. "When was this?"

"Quite recently. A few weeks before Randall's death. He suggested it, I agreed, Swithin presumably did, too, and so Randall started the process, whatever that was. I always left that sort of thing to him, and so did Swithin. Business was Randall's forte."

"Did anything come of his . . . process?"

"Yes. He told me he had a buyer, and then, a few days before he was killed, he asked me for a letter stating that I agreed to sell my share at the same time he sold his." Trowbridge met Christian's eyes. "He told me the prospective buyer had requested the assurance, which I was happy to give, of course."

"Did Randall tell you the name of this prospective buyer?"

"No." Trowbridge shrugged. "But that wasn't unusual. He might have told Swithin—because he might have thought to ask. For me it made no difference who bought the company as long as they paid a fair price—and I knew I could trust Randall to secure that." He looked at Letitia. "Have you any idea whether you'll want to sell or not?"

It was all Letitia could do not to leap on the suggestion, but mindful of Christian's eye on her, aware of his fingers braceleting her wrist, she arched her brows regally and prevaricated. "Having only recently learned what my late husband's business entailed, I'll need to take stock and consult with others before making any decision."

Trowbridge smiled easily. "Of course. You must take whatever time you need. Swithin doesn't seem fussed either way, and neither am I. We'll accept whatever decision you make—that was, in some ways, part of our motto, you know—all for one and one for all."

Letitia found herself smiling back. Trowbridge was engaging, yet utterly unthreatening; she could see why so many ladies vied for his time.

"My dear, you've failed to offer your guests some refreshments. It *is* after eleven."

The drawl from the door drew all eyes. A gentleman—he was undoubtedly that despite his rather unusual attire—well-cut breeches and a soft shirt topped by a long, dun-colored coat that hung straight from his shoulders to brush his highly polished boots—stood in the doorway idly observing them through heavy-lidded dark eyes.

Letitia glanced at Trowbridge. His smile had grown warmer.

He made an elegant gesture toward the newcomer. "Allow me to present Lord Rupert Honeywell. Lady Letitia Randall and Lord Dearne."

Honeywell's eyes passed over Letitia and Christian, lingered for an instant on Christian, then he bowed elegantly. "Charmed, my lady." Straightening, he nodded to Christian. "Dearne."

"Be a dear, Rupert, and ring for Cuthbert. Tell him to bring tea." Trowbridge looked back at Letitia. "You will stay and take a cup, won't you?"

Letitia smiled back. "I'd be delighted. Thank you."

Cuthbert was summoned; tea, in an exquisite service, was duly delivered. At Trowbridge's invitation, Letitia poured. When she complimented him on the china, Trowbridge insisted on showing her some of his treasures.

A half hour passed pleasantly. Although initially standoffish, when neither she nor Christian made any comment on what was plainly a ménage, Honeywell thawed. At Trowbridge's suggestion, he took Letitia to view his canvases, set out in a little room off the front hall. As they were of excellent quality, she found no difficulty enthusiastically complimenting him.

At which he thawed even more.

Christian stood in the doorway to the small room. The instant Letitia turned from Honeywell's last painting, he caught her eye. "We need to leave, I'm afraid."

She smiled and made her farewells. He did the same, but with greater reserve.

As he took his leave of Trowbridge, he handed him a card—one inscribed with the Bastion Club's address. "If you think or hear of anything that might bear on Randall's murder, or on the sale of the company, please send word. I'm acting for Lady Randall in this matter."

Trowbridge took the card, cast a questioning glance at Letitia. When she nodded, he smiled and put the card in his pocket. "If I hear anything, I'll let you know."

Outside, Honeywell handed Letitia up. Christian climbed up and took the reins. With a flourish of his whip, he set his horses trotting. Letitia waved, then sat back with a sigh.

After a moment she said, "That was a great deal more entertaining than I'd expected."

He glanced down at her face. "There's one thing you shouldn't forget."

She met his eyes, arched her brows. "What's that?"

He had to look forward to manage his horses. "Trowbridge is an excellent candidate for Randall's murderer."

He took her back to Allardyce House for a late luncheon. He was getting very tired of Randall's house, and of Barton hovering outside.

When he mentioned the man, Letitia snorted. "He has a one-track mind."

"Which, now that I think of it," Christian said, ushering her down his front hall, "does have its benefits—he's stuck to the South Audley Street house like a leech and hasn't been following us."

"True. I suppose that's something in him one can give thanks for."

Percival sat her at the dining table in the chair beside Christian's. As he took his seat, Christian glanced at her and decided that when—when, not if—she sat at this table on a permanent basis, whenever they were alone she would sit beside him, not at the far end of the long table as custom decreed.

Custom was often overrated.

As the dishes appeared, whisked in and out by the everefficient Percival and his minions, they discussed all they'd gleaned from their visit to Chelsea. As Hermione wasn't present, they could speak freely. Letitia commented on the bond between Trowbridge and Honeywell.

"For all that he's a typical, moody, broody painter—and yes"—Letitia raised her fork in acknowledgment—"I do realize I speak as a Vaux—I got the impression that they're both very settled and content."

She paused, staring unseeing across the table, then shook her head. "I really can't see Trowbridge as Randall's murderer. He's . . . serene, content—he's reached that point in life where he has all he wants, and he knows it. He has no ambition for more—doesn't a murderer need ambition? Something to drive him?"

Christian grimaced. "Usually." After a moment he asked, "What of Honeywell?"

Letitia snorted. "He's even less likely." She cocked a brow at him. "You saw his paintings, didn't you?"

"I saw them—I didn't study them."

"Well, you should have. With the . . ." She waved her hand. ". . . intensity and *focus* he pours into his paintings, I'm surprised Honeywell has sufficient energy left to have any connection with anyone. His relationship with Trowbridge must absorb all that he has left in him—murder—any violent emotion—I really don't think he could summon the strength."

Christian knew she wasn't talking of physical strength, and when it came to analyzing emotions, as a Vaux she was particularly well-qualified. Folding his napkin, he set it aside. "Very well. I agree that on an emotional basis neither Trowbridge nor Honeywell measure up well as the murderer, at least not based on what we know at present."

"Hmm." Letitia reached for her glass, took a long sip, then said, "At least Randall had the sense to set up this pending sale of the company. As Trowbridge is willing to sell, and Swithin is as well, there's no reason I can't rid myself of the encumbrance with all speed."

Christian frowned, and checked his memory. "Trowbridge *assumed* Swithin agreed because Randall went ahead with organizing the sale. It didn't sound like Trowbridge knew for certain what Swithin had said."

Letitia frowned. "But Randall wouldn't have gone ahead with organizing the sale if Swithin hadn't agreed."

"He might have." If there was one thing with which Christian was willing to credit her late husband, it was that the bastard had to have been an expert at manipulation. "If Randall wanted to sell—and as he suggested it, we can take that as read—and Trowbridge was very willing—and that, as you've pointed out, is also highly believable—then if Swithin didn't agree, but his disagreement wasn't strong, then yes, I think Randall would have gone ahead and organized the sale, believing that once the deal was imminent, Swithin would fall into line—and *that* explains why Randall needed that letter from Trowbridge. He would also have needed the same from Swithin."

Letitia frowned. "Why?"

"Because the potential buyer—or buyers—were clever enough to suspect that Randall didn't truly have the agreement of both his partners." Christian reassessed all they'd learned, measured it against what he'd just posited. He nodded. "We need to see Swithin and learn what he has to say about this proposed sale before you make any declaration of intent."

Letitia humphed. "Your years as a spy are showing—you're seeing deception and deceit where there is none."

He was unmoved. "Better safe than sorry."

Pushing back from the table, Letitia looked at the clock above the long marble mantelpiece. "In that case—as you insist—let's go and talk to Swithin. Where does he live?"

Christian looked at her, tried to think of some way to distract her.

She frowned and narrowed her eyes at him. "I know you know, and I'm not going to be distracted, so just tell me and save us both the next hour."

He looked into her eyes, saw her determination, inwardly sighed. "Swithin's London house is in Curzon Street—just around the corner from South Audley Street. He's usually in residence during the week."

"Perfect!" Letitia stood. "It's just after two o'clock—a perfectly acceptable time to call."

Mr. Swithin, his butler informed them, was in. The butler showed them into a scrupulously neat drawing room; a minute later he returned to conduct them into his master's study.

From behind a wide, highly polished oak desk half covered beneath stacks of papers, Swithin rose and held out his hand. "Lady Randall?"

Gliding forward, Letitia shook his hand, then waved at Christian. "Allow me to introduce Lord Dearne. He's advising me in the matter of the Orient Trading Company."

"Ah. I see." Swithin shook hands with Christian, then waved them to the comfortable chairs set before the desk.

Letitia sat, mentally cataloging all she could see and sense. Swithin was a very different sort to either Trowbridge or Randall. Both the others had displayed a certain self-confidence Swithin appeared to lack. Where Trowbridge had been watchful, Swithin was wary; he reminded her forcibly of a rabbit, ready to bolt down his hole the instant Christian made a threatening move.

The analogy was so apt—so perfectly described the way Swithin eyed Christian—that she had to sternly suppress a laugh.

"Mr. Swithin," Christian began—they'd again agreed that he should, in the main, handle the interview—"as you no doubt realize, on Mr. Randall's death Lady Randall inherited his share of the Orient Trading Company. Consequently, we've been attempting to learn about the company and how it operates. We now know what the business of the company is, and the mechanics of its day-to-day operation, but we'd like to ask if you can tell us more about the company's history, and its present state."

Swithin didn't immediately reply. He nodded slowly, as if collecting his thoughts. When he spoke, it was in a quiet, collected, largely unemotional tone. "Randall, Trowbridge, and I first met at Hexham Grammar School. There . . ."

For all his reserve, Swithin told much the same story Trowbridge had, confirming the relevant facts—their common history, their Grand Plan, the development of their business and its consequent evolution into the Orient Trading Company. He also described their meetings in Randall's secret room, the notes Randall would send via urchins to summon them, the unlocked doors whose keys only Randall had.

When Christian asked, Swithin revealed that in recent years—the last two, at least—he and Trowbridge hadn't met. Randall had taken to seeing them separately, but, Swithin remarked, there had been nothing in that beyond Randall's obsession with secrecy.

In addressing the present state of the company, and its proposed sale, Swithin's account differed in only one respect from Trowbridge's.

When Christian questioned the point, Swithin shook his head. "No, indeed. Randall approached me about the sale several weeks before his death, and for much the same reasons as no doubt drove him and Trowbridge, I agreed. After that, I heard nothing more from Randall—he sent no message to set up a meeting—although I'm sure he would have once he had anything further to report."

Christian pressed. "So Randall didn't ask you for a written statement that you would sell your share at the same time he did?"

His expression bland, Swithin met Christian's gaze directly. "No. I didn't hear back from him at all."

Christian fell silent.

After a moment Swithin added, a faint frown forming, "As I didn't hear back from Randall, I have no idea who his prospective buyer was—it's a pity Trowbridge didn't think to ask, but that's typical of him. It seems that Randall was killed before he could see me and ask for the written statement."

Swithin switched his gaze to Letitia. "If I may ask, Lady Randall, what are your feelings regarding the sale of the company? As I'm sure Trowbridge mentioned, it was our policy to stick together, so if you wish to retain the company, we will, of course, not pursue the sale."

Letitia waved airily. "I fear I'm not ready to even consider such matters. Lord Dearne is collecting the relevant information and I'm sure will eventually advise me of how the company stands vis-à-vis Randall's estate, and how I stand in relation to both." She added a vague smile for good measure; Swithin, she suspected, was the sort of man who expected women to be vague and flighty, especially about money and business. "I suspect it will be some little time before I can form any opinion on a sale."

Swithin held his hands wide, paternalistically soothing. "There's absolutely no reason for any rush."

Politely inquiring, he looked at Christian. "Is there anything else?"

There wasn't. Christian rose, assisted Letitia to her feet, and they took their leave.

They walked back to Randall's house, summoned Letitia's carriage, and directed the driver to the Bastion Club.

Leaning back against the squabs, oddly comforted by the large, warm body beside her, Letitia considered her impressions of Trowbridge and Swithin, contrasted that with her memories of Randall. "You know, while in retrospect there were some very telling oddities in Randall's makeup, I would never have suspected him of being a farmer's son. He'd . . . I suppose you might say 'lost the roughness,' long ago—he was certainly polished enough to pass muster. As for Trowbridge, he's so flamboyantly at ease in the ton, no one would suspect him of being a tradesman's brat. But Swithin . . . he's so quiet, so retiring, so patently avoiding notice, that that would, I think, if I didn't know his background, make me wonder."

She thought, then grimaced. "I might have wondered why he was so retiring, but I seriously doubt I would have questioned his antecedents." After a moment she said, "I would have thought him—do think him—a trifle out of his social depth."

"It's the way he watches people," Christian said.

She nodded. "Yes—as if he fears getting caught out. As if he knows he'll need to think before he reacts, and so has to watch carefully so he doesn't make a mistake. Neither Randall nor Trowbridge were like that. If one were assessing how well each had performed in their Grand Plan, while all three succeeded in being accepted by the ton, Randall and Trowbridge were completely at ease, entirely confident of their place, but Swithin still doesn't feel secure in his." She glanced at Christian. "Is that how he struck you?"

He nodded. "Not entirely comfortable, not assured, but no one would ever guess why."

"True. Most would simply think him a quieter, more nervous sort—which he is."

The carriage drew to a halt before the club's gate. Christian alighted and helped Letitia down. Inside, they discovered Justin in the library, along with Dalziel, Tristan, and Tony.

"Jack sends his regrets," Tony informed them.

But Letitia's gaze had fixed, fulminating, on her brother. "What are you doing here?"

Her tone suggested there was no answer she would find acceptable.

Justin merely raised his brows. "Better I come here than get eaten by boredom to the extent I slip my leash and go on the town."

Christian watched as Letitia narrowed her eyes, but an inability to bear boredom was something she understood. In the end she sniffed and turned away—fixing Dalziel with a look dark enough to have him defending himself with, "He's safe enough."

Letitia's expression said he'd better be. She consented to sit; with, Christian suspected, identical inward sighs of relief, all the men sank into armchairs.

"We spoke with Trowbridge, and then later with Swithin." He seized the stage and outlined what they'd learned, especially the concept of the men's Grand Plan, which made sense of many things.

"I heard back from Oxford and Cambridge," Dalziel said. "I can confirm those hells of theirs are still operating, and are known to rake in large sums from the more well-heeled students. Both hells are tolerated because they don't encourage *excessive* drinking, actively discourage womanizing, and by and large keep the students off the streets."

"So both Trowbridge and Swithin told exactly the same story," Christian concluded, "which suggests that, at least in what they told us, they were telling the truth."

A knock on the door heralded Gasthorpe. He bore his silver salver, which he presented to Christian. "From Mr. Montague, my lord."

"Thank you, Gasthorpe." Christian opened the missive with the small knife on Gasthorpe's salver; while the majordomo retreated, he unfolded the note and read, then looked up. "I sent to Montague earlier to ask how many different regular payments were made into the company's accounts. The answer is fourteen, which matches the number of hells."

"Twelve hells in London, and one each in Cambridge and Oxford." Tristan raised his brows. "Anything else?"

Christian nodded. "Montague confirms that those fourteen regular payments—the profits from the hells—account for the entire income of the Orient Trading Company. It appears that once established, as all the hells now are, each hell runs its own books for upkeep and all day-to-day running costs. What appeared in the fourteen property ledgers we found were the initial costs to set up each hell—the furniture, decorating, salaries, and so on for a time, until the hell could pay its way. Subsequently, all profits were paid into the three company accounts. Those fourteen hells form the sum total of the company's assets—there's nothing else within the company we need consider."

"Nothing else?" Letitia muttered. "I would have thought fourteen gambling hells was quite enough." She looked around the group. "Did anyone learn anything about this sale Randall was organizing?"

"I heard rumors, whispers, and so did Jack," Tony reported. "But neither of us could unearth anything definite."

Tristan nodded. "I found much the same—the prospect of a sale of fourteen highly profitable hells has naturally caused ripples in the murky pond of the underworld, but while my contacts had caught whispers, including some names, none move in the right circles to have heard anything certain."

The London underworld was Christian's arena, as all his colleagues knew. He thought, then said, "There are only so many operators who could aspire to buy such a portfolio of properties. I doubt any of the others would band together, so that leaves us with Edson, Plummer, Netherwell, Gammon, Curtin, Croxton, and of course Roscoe."

Tony's, Jack's, and Tristan's contacts had mentioned all the above except for Gammon and Croxton.

"No hint who the leading bidder might be?" Dalziel asked.

Tristan shook his head. "No one even seemed sure that a sale had as yet been agreed upon."

Christian glanced at Dalziel. "There's a wealth of suspects in that list alone. Together with the others—Trowbridge, Swithin, any disgruntled managers, employees, or patrons— we have a plethora of potential murderers."

"All of which suggests," Letitia acerbically said, "that selling the holdings of the Orient Trading Company with all possible speed, so I can wash my hands of this entire business, is the most sensible thing to do."

All the men looked at her.

Leaving it to Christian to, very mildly, say, "Actually, no. All we've learned argues for extreme caution, and that you should avoid any mention, however slight, of any intention to sell until we catch Randall's murderer."

She looked at him, harassed frustration plain in her face. *"Why?"* She delivered the single word with a level of dramatic force only a Vaux could command.

"Because," he replied, clinging to his mild, unchallenging tone, "as things stand, it remains very likely that Randall's move to sell was what provided the motive for his murder."

For a long moment she held his gaze, then she pulled a face. "Very well." Her tension left her. "So what now?"

"Now," Dalziel said, "we need to learn, definitively and absolutely, if Randall had chosen a buyer. If his negotiations had proceeded to the point where he'd made a decision, and even perhaps taken the first steps toward formalizing the sale."

"Trowbridge and Swithin both made it clear Randall was the primary active agent when it came to running the company, and Montague confirmed that," Christian reminded them. "So the fact they don't know any details about a pending sale doesn't mean it hadn't progressed to the point that Randall had shaken hands on a deal."

"If he had," Tony said, "then given the hells and their profits, I'd place the bidder who missed out at the top of my suspect list."

"Possibly," Christian replied. "But I know who to ask for definite information, at least as to who the interested parties were and how far the sale had progressed."

Dalziel cocked a brow at him. "Gallagher?"

Christian nodded.

"If you're going to visit Gallagher," Tristan said, "you'll need someone to watch your back. I'll come, too."

"And as two is always better than one," Tony quipped, "so will I."

Letitia frowned and tried to catch Christian's eye.

But he was looking at Tony and nodding. "Tonight, then. Let's meet here at eight."

Tristan and Tony agreed. "Eight," Tony said as the men all stood. "Ready for an evening in the stews."

"What did Torrington mean—an evening in the stews?"

Swiveled on the seat of her carriage, Letitia looked into Christian's face.

He waved. "Just a figure of speech. A joke of sorts."

She frowned direfully. "I *know* you're not planning an evening of dissipation. What I wish to confirm is that you are, indeed, planning on going into some dangerous, far from salubrious area of the slums, there to meet with some man named Gallagher, who's the sort of acquaintance with whom both Trentham *and* Torrington judged you need physical support." She glared at him. "*That's* what I'm asking—as you damned well know!"

Christian's lips lifted; he tried to straighten them. Reaching out, he closed a hand around one of hers. "Sssh. You'll scare your coachman."

"He's been with me for years. I could scream and he—and his horses—would simply plod on. Don't change the subject."

"Which subject was that?"

"The subject of you swanning off on some dangerous enterprise at the first opportunity." She wasn't sure why the point so exercised her; it simply did. "Bad enough you were gone for twelve years plunging into God knows what dire situations, but there's no reason—none whatever—that you need do so now, and certainly not on my account." Perhaps that was it? Yes, obviously. "I don't want you on my conscience. All very well to have Torrington and Trentham at your back—who's going to be protecting your front? You men never think. I want you to promise me you won't—absolutely will not—take any unnecessary risks. Any undue risks—for that matter I think this whole excursion qualifies as an undue risk. Learning about the likely buyer might be important—especially as I wish to pursue the sale—but I'm sure if we just wait, he'll contact us, or Trowbridge or Swithin. *You* don't have to go and consult some nefarious underworld figure—I assume from the fact that Torrington and Trentham both knew his reputation that he's some sort of criminal magnate—who knows what he'll demand in return?"

Her voice was rising, growing suspiciously unsteady. Christian squeezed her hand. "Meeting Gallagher's price won't be a problem."

"He'll have a *price*? Great heavens—he should help you for the honor of it, in repayment of his debts. You're a damned war hero, and I'm quite sure he—whoever he is—has never bestirred himself in the service of his country." She barely paused for breath. "I'm really not happy about *any* of this."

"Yes. I know." Raising her hand, Christian placed a kiss on her fingers just as the carriage rocked to a halt outside the house. He'd always wondered how she'd viewed his secret service; now he knew—she thought him a hero. He'd always wondered if she'd worried about him while he'd been on the Contintent; apparently she had. To now hear her so agitated over him perversely left a warm glow about his heart.

Releasing her, he opened the door, stepped down, then helped her to alight. Meeting her gaze levelly, he calmly stated, "Regardless, I'll be meeting with Gallagher tonight."

She made a frustrated sound like steam escaping. She went to wave her arms, but he'd kept hold of her hand.

Smiling, he raised it and kissed her fingers again. "I'll see you tomorrow, and tell you what I learn."

She blinked at him. "*Tomorrow*? What about tonight?"

Releasing her, he stepped back and saluted, battling a grin. "No telling what time I'll get back. I'll see you in the morning."

Turning, he sauntered off up South Audley Street. He could feel her dagger gaze boring into his back, but he didn't glance back.

He didn't whistle, but he felt like it.

Seeing Barton's carroty head peeking over the edge of another set of area steps, he waved and, surprisingly content, continued on his way home.

Chapter 17

At ten o'clock that night Christian, with Tristan at his heels and Tony a few paces behind, walked down a narrow alley in the labyrinth of lanes between Cannon Street and the Thames. In Mayfair's wide streets the moon shone down, but here the tenements and warehouses hemmed the lanes in; it was nearly pitch-dark. This close to the river, fog had already thickened, wisps wreathing about their greatcoated shoulders, clinging as they passed. Their boots fell softly on ancient cobbles.

"I'm glad you know where you're going." Tristan's voice came in a whisper from behind. "I just hope you know the way back."

Christian's lips quirked.

Five yards farther on he halted and faced a plain wooden door. Raising a fist, he knocked once, waited a heartbeat, then knocked twice.

A moment passed, then a small screened window in the door slid open. There was no light within. Another silent moment ticked past, then a hoarse voice demanded, "Who is it?"

"Grantham."

The window slid shut.

Tristan tapped his arm. Christian glanced his way, saw Tristan's raised brows, whispered, "Previous title."

"Ah."

They waited, patiently, for several minutes, then they heard heavy bolts sliding back.

A huge bruiser hauled open the door. He nodded to Christian. "The master'll see you."

Christian's lips twitched. "Good evening to you, too, Cullen." He stepped over the threshold.

Cullen snorted. "Yeah, yeah. Here—who's these two with you?"

Christian glanced back at Tristan and Tony. "They're just that—'with me.' Gallagher won't mind. Incidentally, how's his mood?"

Cullen scowled at Tristan and Tony, but allowed them inside, then shut the door and bolted it. He turned back to Christian. "He's prepared to be entertained—which I'm thinking is just as well for you."

Christian inclined his head. "We'll see. I know the way." He strolled down a barely lit corridor, then, ducking his head, stepped through an open doorway into a room that never failed to surprise.

It was Gallagher's domain, and he'd set it up as a gentleman's study, glaringly incongruous given what lay beyond the polished oak door, yet although no expense had been spared and the room was indeed luxurious, someone— Christian had always suspected Gallagher himself—had exercised restrained good taste.

Straightening, he walked farther in, nodding to the gargantuan presence behind the massive mahogany desk. "Gallagher."

"Major." Gallagher dipped his head a fraction—the best he could do by way of a nod. He had some condition that made his body store excessive amounts of fat, making the simplest movement difficult. But there was nothing wrong with his brain. He studied Tristan and Tony through small, bright blue eyes almost lost in rolls of fat, then looked at Christian and tipped his head toward the others. "Friends of yours?"

"Indeed. This is an insalubrious neighborhood, especially after dark."

Gallagher emitted a cackle. "At any time of day." Evincing no further interest in Tristan and Tony, he fixed his gaze on Christian. "So what can I do fer you?"

Christian kept his smile easy. "You can tell me all you know about the proposed sale of the Orient Trading Company."

Gallagher's eyes widened a fraction. "You have an interest there?"

"I'm acting for one of the part owners."

Gallagher wasn't slow. "The heir, heh? Or should I say heiress? Heard tell it was Randall's widow got the whole of his share."

Christian nodded. Gallagher's price was information; if you wanted some, you gave some in return.

"So has she decided to sell?"

"Until we know more, she can't decide one way or the other."

Gallagher raised his brows. "Not the sort of business a lady like I hear tell she is would want to sully her dainty fingers with, I'm thinking."

"True. She doesn't. But her brother knows the value of a cash-generating asset."

"Ah-ha." Gallagher took a moment to digest that, then offered, "Last I heard, before Randall got himself murdered, he'd come to an agreement of sorts with Neville Roscoe. Not a binding one—an agreement in principle, as it were. I heard tell Roscoe had some stipulations, some conditions he wanted Randall to meet before they shook on the deal."

"But Roscoe's price was right?"

"So I heard. Randall was right chuffed when he left Roscoe."

Christian raised his brows. "You have a watcher inside Roscoe's?"

Gallagher snorted. "Nah—not inside. What I wouldn't

give for that. But a body's got to learn what he can howsoever he can—I've got someone keeping an eye peeled outside."

Christian nodded. "Do you know who else was looking to buy?"

"The usual suspects—Edson, Plummer, and I heard tell Gammon was making overtures, too. But once Roscoe raised his hand, there weren't much competition."

"Unsurprising—Roscoe's hells are probably even more profitable than the Orient Trading Company's."

"Aye." Gallagher nodded. "So I'd think." He studied Christian for a long moment, as if deciding whether to speak, then said, "I don't know exactly why you're asking, howsoever, if you're thinking Randall's murder had anything to do with the sale, I'd say you're barking up the wrong tree. For certain Edson, Plummer, and Gammon weren't best pleased when Roscoe butted in and snatched the prize, but unless there's some bad blood there no one knows about, there's no benefit to any of them in killing Randall. All that's done— all it could ever do—is delay the inevitable."

Gallagher settled on his massive chair. "From the business side of things, given the company was on the sale block anyway, Randall's death hasn't changed anything—unless the new owner decides to hold onto the company, and that, in effect, changes even less."

"Perhaps," Christian suggested, "there's some reason that, for someone, a delay in the sale was desirable."

Gallagher shrugged, a faint movement of his massive shoulders. "Could be, but if that's the case, I ain't heard nothing about it."

Christian hesitated, then asked, "Do you know anything more that's pertinent to this subject?"

Gallagher thought, then shook his head. "Can't say as I do. Randall wasn't one of us. He was on the upper end of things, like Roscoe. Never anything actually illegal, but they're both on our fringes, which is why we keep a weather eye on them and their doings." Gallagher smiled, not a pretty sight. "Just in case. But I'm thinking that when it comes to Randall, Roscoe would know more."

"Very possibly." Christian glanced at the others, collecting them. "We'll leave you, then. Thank you for your time."

"And me knowledge." Gallagher's eyes sharpened. "If you want to keep me sweet, you send word when you learn who killed Randall, and even more important, if the widow and those other two agree to sell. If Roscoe's going to grow twice as big, twice as powerful, I want to know."

Christian nodded as he ducked through the doorway. "I'll send word when I know for certain."

It was after midnight when Christian let himself into his house. The large mansion was quiet, peaceful and serene; moonlight pooled on the tiles of the front hall, falling through the multifaceted skylight far above.

Aware of the quiet luxury of his home, yet even more aware of what it lacked, Christian snuffed the candle Percival had left burning and in the moonlit dark slowly climbed the stairs, wondering if he'd made a tactical error.

If he shouldn't, instead, be climbing a set of stairs in South Audley Street.

Yet he wanted Letitia to realize that he wanted more than the merely physical from her, with her . . . and if he were honest, he'd wanted her to feel a tiny portion of the need, the driving compulsive need, he felt for her. So he'd grasped the chance of a night apart in the hope it would spur her to think more of him and her, and of becoming his wife.

The marquess's apartments were on the first floor, opposite the head of the stairs. Walking around the gallery, he opened the door that led directly into his bedroom.

Despite the fact that the room was huge, he instantly knew someone else was there—in the same heartbeat knew who it was.

Almost disbelieving, wishing he'd brought the candle up after all, he stepped into the room and silently shut the door.

His night vision was excellent but he didn't need it to locate her; all his senses seemed to lock on her, helplessly drawn.

She lay in his bed, sleeping.

On silent feet he crossed the large room, shrugging off his greatcoat and laying it on a chair along the way.

Drawing near the bed, he slowed. Halting at one corner, he looked down at her.

She lay sprawled under the covers, her dark hair splayed in a silken wave across his pillows.

Exactly where he wanted her to be.

Where he wanted her to sleep for the rest of her life.

His gaze was drawn by a glimmer across the room—silk shimmering in a stray beam of moonlight. Through the darkness he saw, laid on a chair, a black gown the color of night, a froth of ivory petticoats, two black garters, two neatly folded black stockings, and the gossamer-fine drape of her silk chemise.

Not only was she lying in his bed, she was lying in his bed naked.

The realization had its inevitable effect, yet for long moments he stood silently and watched her, simply because he could. Savoring that he could.

Eventually he turned away and quietly undressed. He didn't hurry, deeply aware—to his bones aware—that he didn't need to; she was there—he had all night to absorb the simple pleasure of having her in his bed.

His bed.

That was something quite different—and he couldn't believe she wouldn't have realized that. Wouldn't have known how finding her as she was, waiting for him, would affect him.

She might have come to his house because she was impatient to learn what he'd discovered, but that wouldn't have placed her naked in his bed. Being there . . . consciously or not so terribly consciously, she was, in her own Vaux way, telling him something.

But tonight he didn't want to dwell too much on that, on what decision if any she'd actually made.

Tonight was for embracing the simple fact that he would have her in his bed, in his arms all night. That for at least that long, his dream would be reality.

Lifting the covers, he slid in beside her. The mattress bowed beneath his weight; instinctively she turned toward him, her arms, her body, reaching for him, holding him, embracing him.

Loving him in the dark.

Letitia dreamt, not that the years had fallen away, but that she'd trod a different path. That somehow her feet had found their way not just onto the path of her long ago dreams, but to the end of that road and beyond.

Beyond to a time and place where he and she were the lovers they'd once been, but older, wiser, more mature. Where their love, given voice through long slow caresses, through rich, drugging kisses, through an acceptance of possessiveness that went soul deep, was more intense, richer, a broad river instead of a burbling stream, one that could carry more passion, more powerful emotions, infinitely deeper meaning.

His hands sculpted her body, reverently possessive, as if he couldn't, still, quite believe she was his. That element of uncertainty in a man who could and did command all aspects of his life—wordless confirmation that her power as a woman over him still lived—quietly thrilled; she moved beneath his caresses, sensuously languid, taking her time to savor, to absorb, to let the pleasure of his loving sink to her bones.

To let it seep into her soul and fill it as he moved over her, parted her long legs with his hard muscled thighs and, with one slow powerful thrust, filled her.

She arched beneath him, the veil between reality and dreams flickering, as it had throughout. Some part of her knew that all she felt was real, yet this reality lay so close to, not simply her long ago dreams but the natural evolution that should have come from them, that the two effortlessly merged.

Dreams and reality became one as she rode with him through the night, wrapped in his strength, cushioned within his bed, cradled within the warmth of his loving. She embraced him, clung, took him into her heart, drew him deeper into her body, let her soul reach for his and wrap around it.

Merge with it.

That's how it felt as they raced toward the peak, stretched, reached it, hung suspended for one bright, glittering, scintillating moment . . . then together they shattered, let go and fell, let release claim them, let the void have them, let glory fill their veins with incandescent pleasure, golden and glowing.

When it was over, and he'd disengaged and drawn her to him, she lay safe in his arms, cocooned in his bed.

It was easier, so much easier, to communicate this way, in the dark, through lingering kisses, intimate caresses. To show him, let him see . . . what in the stark light of day she still found hard to put into words, to declare.

In the dark, in his arms, it was easy to ignore the risk.

To ignore her underlying, perhaps irrational fear.

To simply love him.

Turning her head, she gently kissed his chest, then snuggled her head on his shoulder and let her dreams take her.

Sated, replete, so deeply satisfied on so many levels he couldn't raise a thought, Christian held her close, closed his eyes—felt an emotion, familiar and strong, well and pour though him.

More intense than ever before. More certain.

Feeling her body stretched out along his, feminine curves pressed to his chest, her long legs tangled with his, her skin soft and flushed beneath his hands, he felt his lips curve as he surrendered to sleep.

Christian stirred her as dawn approached. Faint pearly light washed into his room, gliding ephemeral fingers over the bed as within it she cried out as passion crested and broke, and a long glorious wave of satiation washed through her.

Through them.

Holding the moment, and him, close, she wrapped herself in its warmth and, with a smile on her lips, sank back into slumber.

"Letitia?"

She sensed him shaking her, but refused to respond.

"I know I said I'd see you in the morning"—his voice was a gravelly rumble in her ear—"but I hadn't envisaged it would be quite so early."

She felt moved to complain. "Why is it so damned early?"

"Because you have a decision to make."

"Oh?" She felt him shift in the bed so he was lying back against the pillows, his arms crossed behind his head. She considered, decided she had to know. "What decision would that be?"

"About what you want to do." She felt his gaze on her face, then he went on, "Whether you want to make my staff very happy, or slip back to South Audley Street before anyone sees."

She groaned. She'd known there'd be a price for sleeping in his bed, but the bother of having to get up, dressed, and out before the tweenies were about hadn't registered. "Damn!"

Wrestling aside the covers, she glanced at the window, and groaned again. She was torn, but . . .

He chuckled, then sat up, throwing off the covers. "Come on—I'll walk you home."

He helped her lace up her gown, then led her silently down the stairs and out of the front door—just in time; they could hear the maids' voices approaching from behind the green baize door as they slipped outside. He drew the front door closed, then took her arm, wound it with his, and they set off to walk the short distance to . . . the house where she was staying.

That's how she'd always thought of Randall's house; it had never been hers.

She glanced at Christian, strolling beside her. When he'd joined her in his bed last night, the very first thing she'd done was run her hands over him, confirming he wasn't in any way hurt. Even half asleep, some part of her mind had been on full alert on that score, ready to take charge if it had proved necessary. Scanning his face in the pale morning light—devoid of even the faintest hint of a bruise, as was the hand—his right—that lay over hers on his sleeve, she concluded that his meeting with Gallagher had passed civilly enough.

Looking ahead, she asked, "So what did you learn from your excursion last night?"

Christian told her, seeing no reason to hold anything back. Unsurprisingly, she asked about Roscoe; he related what he knew of the man; he'd run into him a few times in his professional capacity in his early years of working for Dalziel.

"So," Letitia said, as they neared Randall's house, "I take it our next move is to go and see this Roscoe person and find out what he knows."

"Indeed." Christian halted before the steps. "I'll go and see him as soon as we can arrange a meeting."

"I'll come, too." Letitia halted beside him.

As she faced him, he took in the determined light in her eyes, the stubborn set of her chin. Inwardly sighed. "Unfortunately, in the same way you couldn't go with me to speak with Gallagher, you can't come with me when I visit Roscoe."

She narrowed her eyes on his. "Nonsense. Gallagher's an underworld czar—a known criminal—but you told me yourself Roscoe's another Randall."

"I meant in terms of his business interests. Otherwise, Roscoe's nothing like Randall. He's ten times—a hundred times—more dangerous."

Her lips thinned; her eyes couldn't get any narrower . . .

then her expression cleared and she smiled. Too sweetly. "If Roscoe's as clever and as canny as you say"—turning, she started up the steps—"then he's not going to tell you the details of a business agreement he struck with Randall."

Halting on the top step, she plied the knocker, then faced him as he joined her. She smiled again, this time more assured. "Roscoe won't divulge those details to anyone but me—the one who, businesswise, now stands in Randall's shoes."

She waited a heartbeat—no doubt to allow him to grasp the incontestability of her reasoning—then briskly said, "I've an at-home I must attend, then a luncheon. I assume we're all to meet later at the club?"

When, after a moment's hesitation, his face expressionless, he nodded curtly, she informed him, "I'll join you there."

With a regal inclination of her head, she moved forward as Mellon opened the door.

Raising a hand in mute farewell, Christian turned and walked down the steps. Gaining the pavement, he paused, then set off, striding back to his house.

While she was spending her day swanning around the ton, he would spend at least a part of his arranging to ensure she didn't accompany him to see Neville Roscoe.

She would understand once she'd thought it through; she knew him—understood men like him. She couldn't possibly expect to spend the night in his bed, to acknowledge him—them—at least that far, and then expect him to take her, to stand back and allow her, to do something so reckless as to visit Neville Roscoe.

Letitia arrived at the Bastion Club a minute before Dalziel—two minutes before Justin slipped in via the back lane. She frowned at her brother as he sank into a chair in the library, but he merely smiled back.

She inwardly sniffed, and gave her attention to Christian as, for Dalziel's and Justin's benefit, he recounted what he'd learned from Gallagher.

"Roscoe." Dalziel shook his head. "Correct me if I'm wrong, but our list of suspects already includes Trowbridge, Swithin, fourteen hell managers, countless possible disgruntled staff, business rivals—and to that we must now add all those who might have very good reasons to stop the deal with Roscoe going ahead. As that last crew include many who would consider murder an acceptable deterrent in such circumstances, we can't discount them."

"Actually," Christian said, "Gallagher thought that last scenario unlikely. It seems everyone in that group is resigned to Roscoe growing more powerful. And as he keeps very much to himself and takes care not to impinge on their turf, then their motivation for not wanting to exchange Roscoe-plus-Randall for just Roscoe is hard to see."

He paused, then added, "From my own observations, if Randall's chosen buyer was Roscoe, then I'm inclined to think Gallagher is right—the others will back away and let him have that bone."

Dalziel looked steadily at Christian for a long moment, then nodded. "That's your area of expertise—if you think it unlikely, then by all means let's erase them from our list. Even then, the list is too long, and we've made precious little headway in defining which of the available suspects we should pursue. Apropos of that, I'll go with you to see Roscoe. I've heard about the man for years, but we've never met. See if you can set the meeting for tomorrow morning. I've other appointments, but for that I'll make time."

Christian nodded. He glanced at Letitia.

Before he could lay his tongue to adequate words with which to broach the subject, Dalziel did.

Like Christian, he'd looked at Letitia, but then his dark gaze moved on to Justin. "We'll take Justin with us as Letitia's representative." His gaze returned to Letitia. "I doubt Roscoe will talk openly about any deal without some assurance, albeit by proxy, from you."

"No." Letitia all but visibly bristled; the air about her

seemed to sharpen and crackle. "There's no reason for Justin to risk exposure. I'll accompany you."

Dalziel's dark gaze didn't waver. "You can't meet with Roscoe."

A bald statement of what all the males in the room knew to be absolute fact.

She heard, not just the words but the nuance, that in no circumstances would they take her with them, would they allow her to go.

She drew in a quick breath and looked at Christian. The question—the plea—in her eyes was plain to see.

He read it—for one instant considered—but it simply could not be. He shook his head. "You can't accompany us."

Her eyes flared—not just with anger but with hurt, too, and something else he couldn't define.

Before he could look deeper, she lowered her lids. An uncomfortable, heavily charged moment ensued; more familiar with her than the others, both he and Justin knew her emotions had erupted—that that was what was roiling through the air, rippling across everyone's nerves, the projection of her temper.

The herald of an almighty explosion.

Justin uncrossed his legs and sat up—slowly. Christian looked at him; they exchanged a glance, but before either could react—could even think of how to—she reined the unruly passions in.

Not completely, but enough to let them all realize they'd been holding their breaths.

Before anyone could say or do anything, she seized her reticule and—without looking at any of them—inclined her head. "If you'll excuse me, gentlemen, I'll leave you to your plans."

She stood, swinging around so fast none of them caught sight of her face. Leaving them scrambling to their feet, head high she swept to the door, opened it and went through.

They heard her heels clattering—quickly—down the stairs, then the front door opened—and shut.

Feeling horribly awkward, and out of their depth, the five men stared at the open library door, then Justin sighed, walked forward and shut it.

The sound of the latch released them from the spell; they glanced at each other, then Dalziel looked at Christian and grimaced apologetically. "I take it I metaphorically stepped on her toes."

Justin shook his head. "By the reaction, I'd say it was the ones with bunions."

Christian drew in a breath; his chest felt tight, as if he were the cause of her distress. He caught Justin's eye. "Just how"—he waved at the door—"upset is she?"

Justin grimaced and waggled his head from side to side. "She might throw a Vaux tantrum, she might be truly angry—or she might be in a rage. The last you never want to see, and unless I miss my guess, she was on the brink of that, but drew back from wreaking havoc on us—and while I thank God she did, I've never seen her do that. I didn't know she could."

Justin frowned; he met Christian's eyes. "What worries me is that I'm not sure, if she is in a rage, that she'll even be able to see straight."

Christian felt an icy hand clutch his heart. "I'll go after her." He turned to the door. "I'll arrange the meeting with Roscoe and send word." Hand on the doorknob, he looked back at Dalziel. "Where will you be?"

"For my sins, at the office. If I'm to accompany you to-morrow, I'll be there until late."

Christian nodded and went out, closing the door behind him. Going down the stairs, he saw Gasthorpe hovering, un-characteristically uncertain, by the front door. Without pre-amble he asked, "Which way did she go?"

"Toward Mayfair, my lord. On foot. I would have sum-moned a hackney, but she'd already . . ."

Stormed off. "That's quite all right, Gasthorpe. I'll see she gets home."

Gasthorpe hurried to open the front door; Christian went out, went quickly down the steps, strode down the path, turned right into Montrose Place, then lengthened his stride.

He caught up to her just beyond the corner of Green Park. Head still high, reticule clutched in both hands, she was striding along—entirely forgetting her customary glide. He doubted she was paying any attention to her surroundings; people walking in the opposite direction took care to get out of her way.

Knowing well enough not to try to take her arm, he fell into step alongside her. He glanced at her face; her expression was far too stony for his liking.

She knew he was there, but she gave no sign.

Eventually, he asked, his tone the epitome of mild, "Why are you so set on seeing Roscoe?"

That was, apparently, the right question to ask to break the hold she was keeping on her temper.

She stopped walking, rounded on him; eyes blazing, she locked them on his. "It's not *Roscoe*, you dolt! I couldn't care less if I never set eyes on the man in my entire life!"

He searched her eyes, a frown in his; he was now entirely at sea.

She saw, and flung up her hands. "It's *you*, you fool!" She thumped him on the chest with her reticule. "I don't—can't . . ."

He recalled—belatedly—her agitation over him seeing Gallagher.

She drew in a shuddering breath. Eyes still locked on his, she spoke through clenched teeth; although she didn't actually stamp her feet, she managed to convey that impression. "I *can't* handle not knowing what's happening to you. Knowing you're going into danger—*and* on my account. Knowing you like it, that you find it exciting—that you might do God knows *what* if the mood strikes you!"

Waving her hands, she continued to rail at him—in the middle of Piccadilly in the middle of the afternoon, with total disregard for the interested—nay, *fascinated*—onlookers.

He stood there and let her, while understanding slowly seeped into his brain.

"Didn't you notice the damned track I wore in your rug last night? I'm a *Vaux*, for heaven's sake—I can't *not know*!"

He suddenly—in another road-to-Damascus revelation—saw the light. Just in time to stop himself from pointing out that he'd spent the past twelve years behind enemy lines doing supremely dangerous things. That wasn't, he now realized, her point.

He suddenly realized, fully and completely, just what that was.

He would have beamed delightedly had he not also comprehended how strung up she was, how brittlely tense.

Finally comprehended that that was a measure of how much he now meant to her.

He trapped her gaze. "About Roscoe."

She blinked, her tirade momentarily derailed.

Moving slowly, holding her gaze, he gently took her arm. "There is no physical danger of any sort involved in meeting with him."

She frowned, but let him turn her and guide her onto the path behind her, one leading into Green Park. "So I can go?"

He steered her on, under the leafy trees. "Let me explain. While going to see Gallagher was dangerous, that danger stemmed from the area in which he lives, not from him. He might be an underworld czar, but he's not about to attack anyone, at least not directly." He glanced at her; she was looking ahead, as yet unmollified, but at least she was listening. "Regardless, even if Gallagher had lived in Chelsea, you still couldn't have gone to meet him because of the risk of someone seeing you and speaking of it, ultimately resulting in a serious scandal. That—the threat to your reputation—was the reason, all physical danger aside, that you couldn't go with me to meet Gallagher.

"The reason you can't go to the meeting with Roscoe is the same—if anything, even more so. If you were seen entering or leaving his house, regardless of the circumstances, your reputation would be shredded irretrievably." That caused her frown—the quality of it—to change. His eyes on her face, what he could see of it, he strolled slowly on. "Roscoe lives in Pimlico, in well-to-do affluence. If Gallagher was unlikely to pose a physical threat, Roscoe is even less likely—that would be totally and comprehensively uncharacteristic. Roscoe would think it beneath him to resort to violence of any sort."

He drew breath, then quietly said, "So you don't need to worry about me when I go to see him."

She didn't say anything, simply kept walking by his side. Then she glanced at him, quickly read his eyes, then once more looked ahead. And sighed—tightly, but a little of her dangerous tension slipped away. "I know it's irrational—you don't have to tell me, I *know*. I didn't feel this way—well, not so strongly—before, when you went away to war, but now . . ." She gestured helplessly. "I can't help how I feel. And what I feel—and when I feel. . . ."

"It affects you strongly." Raising her hand, he kissed her fingers. "I know. I understand." She wouldn't feel so powerfully unless she loved him even more powerfully.

He knew those feeling irrational fears couldn't simply stop. And in her case, before, his "going into danger" had indeed been the prelude to something disastrous happening in her life; small wonder that she reacted badly to any such situation now.

"Tomorrow, I'll go to see Roscoe with Dalziel and Justin in the morning, then I'll come back—directly back—and tell you what happens, what he says, what we learn—what the status is regarding the sale of the company."

The telltale tension that had kept her ramrod stiff beside him ebbed step by step. Eventually she glanced at him, met his eyes. "You promise you'll come directly back?"

He smiled slightly, turned her around and started them back toward Piccadilly. "Word of an Allardyce."

She nodded and looked ahead. "Good." After a moment she added, "I'll be waiting."

But that was for the morrow. That night they met at his aunt Cordelia's house, first in her drawing room, then later they sat side by side at her long table while a highly select company dined.

It was primarily a political gathering, a renewal of contacts before the autumn session got under way; discussions ranged widely. Now he was Dearne, and fixed once more at home, Christian knew he would need to take a more active interest. Somewhat to his surprise, he discovered Letitia was more than qualified to advise him.

When he cocked a brow at her—Randall had held no seat in either the Commons or the Lords—she shrugged. "I act as Papa's surrogate of sorts. I keep an eye on events, and if I tell him his vote is needed, he'll grumble but come down to cast it. These days Justin could do the job, but with their falling out, the task has remained with me." She glanced around the table. The ladies had yet to retire, primarily because they were, one and all, too deeply involved in the discussions going on. "It's at events such as this that one hears the true story. Not just what the news sheets say, not just what the Prime Minister might decree, but the true nature of affairs underlying the decisions, or forming the basis for those yet to come."

She looked back at him. "Do you plan to be active in Parliament?"

He met her gaze. "Until I know more, I can't say, but . . . if one holds a seat in the Lords by virtue of one's birth, it seems incumbent on one to do what the job requires—just like any other part of the duties of a marquess."

She considered him for a moment, then nodded. Looking about the table, she murmured, "In that case, you might want to consider . . ."

Over the next twenty minutes, she gave him a concise political history of those about the table, the ladies included.

With the discussions still raging, Cordelia dispensed with the customary separation and the whole company rose and adjourned to the drawing room.

They circulated, then Cordelia swooped, captured Letitia and bore her off to clarify some point with two other ladies—leaving Christian to fall victim to Lady Osbaldestone.

Watching Letitia's back—wondering if, once they left, he could persuade her to walk across the square rather than around the corner into South Audley Street—he didn't even know that terrifying dame had him in her sights until he felt something strike his foot. Glancing down, he discovered it was her cane; he looked up and met her eyes, blacker than night, sharp and shrewd.

"You could do much worse," she regally informed him, "than to follow what is clearly your inclination. Indeed, there are many of us who view Letitia's previous marriage as a regrettable if unavoidable aberration, one that should be wiped from the collective conscious of the ton." Her eyes bored into his. "We're counting on you to accomplish that task. See you don't let us down."

With that, she inclined her head and moved on to her next target.

Letitia reappeared moments later. "Lady Osbaldestone said you were looking for me."

He'd never been one to look a gift horse in the mouth. "Indeed. I think we should leave. There's something I should tell you, but not here."

She agreed readily enough. They took their leave of Cordelia—who to Christian's alerted eyes looked far too satisfied—then walked out into the night.

Once they'd gained the pavement, Letitia wrapped her shawl more snugly about her shoulders. "What did you want to tell me?"

Christian took her hand and drew her to walk beside him. He crossed the street and headed around the deserted square; the gates to the park in the center were locked at sunset. "Did you know that some of the ladies—who exactly, I don't know, but Lady Osbaldestone at least—suspect you had some . . . for want of a better word, ulterior motive for marrying Randall?"

He glanced at her, saw the face she pulled. "I always worried they might—they're so sharp-eyed, nothing much escapes them—but while Randall was alive, they kept their suspicions to themselves. I'd hoped they would continue to do so."

"They are, they will . . . I think." They would as long as he did as they wished.

"I gather she spoke to you—what did she say?"

"In her usual inimitable fashion she was cryptic, but I gathered she and they, whoever 'they' encompasses, were not at all happy about you marrying Randall."

"They weren't. But now he's dead, so . . ." She shrugged. Frowning, eyes down, she kept pace beside him.

They'd reached the other side of the square. He led her up his steps, fishing in his waistcoat pocket for his latch key.

Only when they halted before the door did she look up and realize.

"This is your house." Letitia looked at Christian.

He shrugged. "My bed's bigger than yours."

An unarguable point.

When he simply held her gaze, and waited, she inwardly shrugged. She waved to the door. "All right. Just as long as you remember to wake me up in time to walk me home."

He smiled and opened the door. The truth was, she felt more comfortable there, in his house, than she ever had in Randall's. And she had far greater faith in Percival's discretion than she had in Mellon's.

As it transpired, Percival wasn't there to greet them.

Christian noticed her looking down the front hall. "I told Percival not to wait up."

Of course he had. She caught his gaze as he drew her to the stairs. "You planned this—bringing me here."

"Of course." He looked ahead as they started climbing. "I told you there was something I wanted to tell you, and I can only tell you that here. Upstairs."

She arched her brows, but he didn't meet her gaze again, didn't add anything as he led her to his bedroom.

He didn't, in fact, say another word. Not for a very long time.

Instead he spoke with actions, more persuasive than any words could ever be. Both in the way his hands drifted over her body, reverently, worshipfully, in the way he reined in his desire enough to let her take the lead, for her to take her time stripping the clothes from his large frame, unwrapping him—discovering anew the heavy muscles, the strength, the hardness, the heat.

The solid reality of him, a male of her kind, in his prime—and he wanted her.

He'd never made any secret of that, yet that night when he reached for her, she sensed there was more. That this was what he'd wanted to tell her, as his lips moved on hers, as his tongue filled her mouth, as skin to naked skin his body claimed hers and his hands grasped, held while she clung.

I love you.

I need you.

Please be mine.

The litany replayed over and over in Christian's mind. Love was a word that long ago had come very easily to them both. Now . . . now he knew what the word meant in all its pain and glory, he couldn't simply say it—couldn't let it fall from his lips like any other word.

Powerful, dominant, all-consuming. Love now burned, a strong, steady flame within him, and using a single, simple four-letter word to encompass all it was wouldn't do.

Love had to be seen, felt, experienced.

To be fully expressed, love had to be let free, had to be allowed to burn, to claim and consume, to rack and then, in benediction, suffuse them with its gold and silver glory.

Love required surrender to be fully realized.

So he surrendered.

And let her see.

Love ruled him in the here and now, and into his future,

just as it had for the past countless years, ever since he'd first laid eyes on her. Love between them was a reality that wouldn't be denied, not by years of separation, not by Randall and his machinations.

That night, he told her. Told her he loved her with all his being—his heart, his body, his soul.

And when at last they lay in a tangled heap, racked, unable to move, satiation a heavy blanket weighing them down, he knew she'd heard, knew she understood.

Chapter 18

The next morning, as he'd promised, Christian woke Letitia in plenty of time to walk her back to South Audley Street before their respective households stirred. As they strolled arm in arm through the pearly predawn light, she wondered at the serenity, the tranquility, that held her.

The certainty. The blissful conviction.

Yesterday . . . rather than dismiss her fears for his safety as irrational, and therefore inconsequential, he'd accepted them. Even though he hadn't stated it, unlike most men of their class he'd acknowledged her feelings as a consequence of her regard for him, and dealt with her and them on that basis.

Although she hadn't intended it, that moment had been a test—one he'd passed with flying colors. If they were to have a future together, then him accepting her and her love as it was—fears and all—was crucial.

That moment in Green Park, she felt, had been a sign.

As for what followed . . . from the moment he'd joined her in his aunt's drawing room to now, the past night had possessed an almost dreamlike quality. Standing by his side at an event like the dinner, then leaving with him and returning to his house, his bed—all of it had been just as she'd imagined, just as she'd dreamed long ago.

Not one moment, not one word, had marred the match between expectation and reality.

But this was now, no long-ago dream.

No turning back of the clocks, but a stepping forward onto the right path at last.

She now possessed the conviction she'd earlier lacked. Now she believed—in their future, in the resurrection of their dreams.

Glancing at him as, assured, at ease, he strolled beside her, she wondered when she'd find the courage, and the right moment, to broach the matter—their future—in words. She knew he was waiting, giving her time and space to find her own feet, to come to her own determination while simultaneously giving her ample, unstinting evidence of his regard for her.

He might not have said the words—not verbally—but given the sort of gentleman he was—a nobleman for whom vulnerability was a sin—expecting a declaration was unrealistic—and anyway, actions spoke much louder, much more surely and convincingly than any words.

Over the past twenty hours he'd convinced her.

She was the expert at setting a stage; she knew he'd been doing essentially that—constructing the position he wanted her to fill, and placing her in the role, presumably hoping she'd notice how well she fitted.

Her lips quirked. Last night had been all about that—and more. But what he perhaps hadn't realized was that in setting his stage and playing his part, he'd naturally filled the opposing role.

And that, more than any other thing, had convinced her of how he felt for her—that in his own more reserved, more controlled way, he loved her as she loved him. He hadn't been acting, not at any time; despite his past career, she wasn't sure emotional subterfuge had any place among his talents. As a Vaux, she would know; she was the ultimate judge of emotional sincerity, and he hadn't feigned a moment, not one word, not one response.

They were almost at Randall's house. She mentally shook herself into the immediate present. "I won't go out today." Looking up, she caught Christian's eyes. "You said you'd come and tell me all once you leave Roscoe's."

His hand closed over hers on his sleeve; he smiled reassuringly. "I will. You said you'd be waiting."

She frowned as the situation with the company resurfaced fully in her mind. "I want to sell those gaming hells—at the very least sell my share of the company—as soon as possible. Quite aside from any threat of scandal—and what a scandal that would be, Lady Letitia Randall née Vaux as the owner of such properties—it's—" She gestured with her free hand. "—*offensive* to me, deeply disturbing, to know that I own a share in an enterprise that exists to lead young men of the ton astray. I've seen too many ton families brought to grief over gambling debts. That *I* should be associated with a company that preys on others' weaknesses . . ." She glanced up, met his eyes. "I want to divest myself of my inheritance from Randall as soon as it can be arranged."

When she put it like that . . . Christian nodded. "I'll make sure Roscoe understands that the sale is still on."

"Good."

They'd reached the steps to Randall's door.

She halted, looked at him, then to his surprise she stretched up and lightly kissed him.

He responded, touched—caught—by the sweetness, the warmth.

She drew back. Her eyes searched his briefly—as if checking to see that he understood—then she smiled, softly mysterious, and stepped back. "Take care."

Summoning every bit of sangfroid he possessed, he smiled in reply, squeezed her hand, then reluctantly let her go. He watched as she climbed the steps, opened the door and went in.

The instant the door closed, his smile spontaneously widened into a grin—one he couldn't contain. Turning, he started back to his house.

Spying Barton's red head, he waved—plunging the runner into a quandary over whether to respond, and if so, how.

Christian laughed at the consternation on Barton's face. He picked up his pace, striding along jauntily. He was closing in on Randall's killer—all his instincts said so—and Letitia would be waiting for him to return, safely at home under Barton's unimaginative yet unwavering eye.

And she'd made her decision—the right decision.

Matters were definitely looking up. Triumph beckoned. Victory would soon be his.

Christian alighted from the hackney he, Dalziel, and Justin had taken from the Bastion Club, joining the other two on the pavement in Chichester Street, Pimlico. As the hackney rattled away, they all stood and surveyed the large white-painted mansion that was Neville Roscoe's residence; over-looking Dolphin Square, it was an imposing sight.

Yet there was nothing overdone about it. The house was a simple statement of solid wealth and permanence, a description that fitted the owner as well.

They trooped up the steps and rang the bell.

The butler was expecting them; he led them through halls and corridors that could very easily have graced any of their houses. Opening a door at the end of one wing, he announced them, then stepped back, allowing them to enter an airy, excellently proportioned room, well-lit by long windows and elegantly furnished as a gentleman's study.

Tall bookcases were built into one wall. Pedestals bearing a set of superb busts stood between the windows. A large mahogany desk, its lines clean and precise, dominated the room. Various furniture polished to a lustrous gleam, green leather upholstery, brass lamps and two spindle-legged side tables completed the decor.

That the gentleman who rose from the chair behind the wide expanse of the desk belonged in such refined surrounds no one could doubt.

Neville Roscoe was an enigma. He was rumored to be the scion of a minor branch of one of the major ton houses, although no one had ever identified which. Roscoe almost certainly wasn't the surname he'd been born with. Tall, with the same aristocratic features that marked all of them as descended from one or another of William's nobles, long limbed and rangy, blessed with an athletic physique and the muscles to match, after a cursory glance at Christian, who he'd met before, and a curious glance for Justin, who he hadn't, Roscoe fixed his dark gaze on Dalziel.

The only obvious difference between the two men was that Roscoe wore his dark hair in a close crop, while Dalziel's sat in elegant waves about his head.

Watching the pair take stock of each other, Christian hid a wry grin. "I believe you haven't previously met. Dalziel. Neville Roscoe."

After an instant's hesitation, both inclined their heads, the action eerily similar.

Roscoe transferred his attention to Justin. "And this, I take it, is Lord Justin Vaux."

Justin politely inclined his head.

Roscoe didn't offer to shake hands; he waved them to the three substantial chairs set before the desk.

Christian knew Roscoe's history. He'd appeared in London about a decade earlier, and had made his fortune much as Randall had, although in Roscoe's case he'd had no truck with secrecy—that wasn't his style. The other difference was that, while Randall had worked to come up in the world, Roscoe had patently, and very deliberately, stepped down from whatever his base within the aristocracy was to run a string of select gambling hells. He was a superb card player, was known to have won fortunes, yet rarely lost more than modest amounts. Even by the ton's jaded standards, he was a gamester extraordinaire. Yet although he was now very wealthy, rather than attempt to rejoin the ton—something he most likely could do with reasonable ease—he continued to eschew society. Indeed, he lived a very private life.

One of the few concessions he made to his true station was his surroundings; he lived in luxury, and the way he moved within the elegance of his house verified beyond doubt that that was, indeed, the milieu to which he'd been born.

He sat as they did, then arched his brows. "And how may I help you, gentlemen?"

"At this stage," Christian replied, "we're interested in information about the proposed sale of the Orient Trading Company. We've been led to believe you were hoping to be the buyer."

Roscoe's eyes were watchful. "And what's your interest in the sale?"

"I'm acting for Lady Letitia Randall née Vaux, Randall's widow." Christian waved at Justin. "Lord Vaux is here as her surrogate."

Roscoe's gaze flicked to Justin. "The one with a warrant sworn against him for Randall's murder?" His gaze shifted to Dalziel. "But of course, you'd know that."

"Indeed," Dalziel replied. "We also know someone else murdered Randall."

Roscoe's brows rose. That was news to him.

"We're currently pursuing the avenue," Christian smoothly went on, "that Randall was murdered because of the proposed sale."

Roscoe met his eyes, then dropped all pretense of nonchalance; leaning his forearms on the desk, eyes narrowing, he was suddenly all business. "If that's the case, obviously the murderer wasn't me."

Christian inclined his head. "Just so. But we need to learn all we can about the proposed sale in order to identify those most affected—at present there's possibilities aplenty as to who might actually have done the deed."

Roscoe's gaze turned inward.

They waited.

"First," he eventually said, his gaze lowering to fix on his hands, clasped on the desk, "I should clarify that, as matters stand, at some point I would, almost certainly, have made an offer for the Orient Trading Company—an offer Randall and his partners wouldn't have been able to refuse." Lifting his gaze, Roscoe met Dalziel's eyes, then looked at Christian. "Randall and the others had worked diligently to establish themselves. They'd come a long way."

"All the way from Hexham," Christian said.

Roscoe smiled; that had indeed been the information he'd been probing for. "You discovered that, did you?"

"Indeed. And you?" Christian asked.

"Only recently." Roscoe met Dalziel's eyes. "I make it a point of learning all I can about those I propose to do business with."

"So you approached Randall?" Dalziel continued the interrogation.

Roscoe shook his head. "I would have eventually—there's many who'll tell you that. But I didn't have to make overtures. Randall came to me—or rather, he let it be known in the right quarters that he and his partners were interested in selling the Orient Trading Company, lock, stock, and barrel."

"There were other potential buyers," Dalziel remarked.

"True, but none with pockets as deep as mine. And I was prepared to pay well—acquiring the company was always a part of my long-term strategy."

Christian could well imagine it. And there were few who would or could effectively stand in Roscoe's way. Although the acquisition and the merging of the company's gaming hells with his own would make him extremely powerful, as Gallagher had intimated, even the underworld czars would nod and let him be. Roscoe was regarded as a stabilizing influence at the interface between legal and illegal activities. He refused to allow any underhanded practices in his establishments, and by and large, all was kept strictly aboveboard.

He held no truck with crime, and with his views so widely known—and so rigidly enforced—even the czars preferred the devil they knew, even if he marched to a beat not their own.

"Apropos of which"—Roscoe's dark eyes turned to

Christian—"I'm willing to tell you all I know about Randall's proposed sale in return for an agreement to be presented, at the appropriate time, to the new owner and the other two partners, as Randall's chosen buyer."

Christian held his gaze for a moment, then nodded. "We're prepared to give you an assurance to that effect."

Roscoe inclined his head. "Very well. On that basis . . . in response to Randall's fishing for buyers, I contacted him by letter. He came here . . ." Roscoe paused, then went on, "It was two days before his death. We discussed the sale— he'd had offers from others, Edson, Plummer, and Gammon, that I'm sure of, but none of them would take all the properties. They each wanted only certain ones, and there was overlap, so, quite aside from the price, if Randall went with any of them, things were going to get messy. So he and I sat and talked—we worked out an offer that satisfied us both. I agreed to take the entire company for a price he thought reasonable. Once the others heard I wanted the whole company, they would back off. Any further interest from them would only result in Randall making more, and while there's no love lost between them and me, there was even less goodwill for Randall—essentially because he pretended to be something he wasn't."

"We've heard you had conditions," Christian said, "and that you and he hadn't yet shaken on the deal."

Roscoe nodded. "I had two conditions Randall had to meet before I was prepared to do more than talk. The first is an obvious one—I wanted to see the books from each of the hells. I'm sure that wouldn't have been a problem. The other condition was one peculiar to the situation." Roscoe met Christian's eyes. "As I'm sure you've discovered, Randall was the active partner of the three. Because of that . . ." Roscoe paused as if considering, then continued. ". . . and because of another piece of information which I suspect I was one of the few privy to, I asked Randall to provide a signed written statement from each of his partners to the effect that they were willing to sell their shares at this time."

Trowbridge's written statement. "Why insist on that," Christian asked, "and what was the piece of information?"

Roscoe tapped a finger on his blotter. "I insisted primarily because I don't have partners. I don't have time for them—having any sort of partner would slow me down and generally get in my way. Although the Orient Trading Company is structured so it's supposedly all or none for any sale to proceed, there's ways around that, namely for the buyer—me—to take on one of their partners as my partner in a new company. That wasn't going to happen. I made it clear I was only interested in acquiring the Orient Trading Company if I could buy it outright."

"So it was all the shares in one deal, or no deal?" Dalziel asked.

"Just so." Roscoe paused, then went on, "Obviously I would have asked Randall for those declarations anyway, but the reason I haven't bothered to make any appointment with my bankers regarding the deal is because . . . well, frankly, I had serious doubts it would proceed."

Justin's eyes had narrowed. "You thought one of the other two wouldn't sell?"

Roscoe nodded. "I made my offer for the company primarily to ensure it wasn't sold to anyone else." He paused, then went on, "That piece of information I mentioned came to me in a roundabout way. I was approached about an investment—it sounded an excellent prospect, but instinct reared its head and at the last I didn't buy in. Naturally I kept an eye on what happened. The investment was a swindle, a very sophisticated one but a swindle just the same. Everyone who'd invested lost every penny they'd put in."

"Swithin," Christian guessed.

Roscoe met his gaze. "He was mentioned as one of the principal investors. The gentlemen behind the scheme specifically targeted the knowledgeable investors—they courted us, pandered to our vanity. That was what made me suspicious, but in Swithin's case it apparently played into his hubris. His reputation went to his head, and he risked . . . a very great deal."

"So, he's what?" Justin asked. "Ruined?"

"No, but my sources suggest he's very close to it, and he's taking extreme care to hide the fact. He knows money, how to move it around, how to practice sleight of hand with it to conceal his state. But he's already liquidated most of his other investments, and even his new wife's portion is gone. He still owns two houses, one in London and one in Surrey, but when it comes to cash, he'd be lucky to lay his hands on two pennies to rub together."

"But," Dalziel said, "if he needs money so desperately, wouldn't that make him more likely to sell, rather than less?"

Roscoe shook his head. "You're forgetting what the Orient Trading Company is—it's a cash-generating machine. Swithin has liquidated all the assets he can that don't show. He desperately needs more cash, but he can't sell his houses without people knowing—and if it becomes common knowledge that he—the canny, wily investor—was ruined by some smooth-talking swindlers, his reputation as a man to go to for investment deals will evaporate. His standing in the ton will be gone."

Glancing at their faces, Roscoe went on, "My guess is that Swithin is counting on—banking on, if you will—the steady income from the Orient Trading Company to keep him afloat. If the company is sold and he gets his third share, it won't be enough to cover his debts *and* generate any future income. But the company has always been a gold mine, and with that steady income behind him, he can go to a bank and take out a loan to cover his shortfall—the bank will look at the company's income and happily agree."

Roscoe leaned back in his chair. "What I suspect, gentlemen, is that Swithin is down to his last penny and was preparing make that trip to the bank when Randall proposed selling the company. My understanding is that the three partners weren't close, so Randall's tack might well have come as a complete shock to Swithin, and given Randall was sitting in my office discussing the sale, it seemed Swithin hadn't shared his situation with his partners. My request for a written statement from Trowbridge and Swithin would, I reasoned, force Swithin to tell Randall and Trowbridge of his difficulties, and that would be the last we'd hear of any sale, at least in the short term."

He met Christian's eyes. "All that said, I have no idea if Swithin killed Randall. I honestly can't see why he would have—Randall and Trowbridge couldn't have forced him to sell. However, I know he had a very good reason for not wanting to sell his share of the Orient Trading Company."

Christian exchanged a glance with Dalziel and Justin, then looked back at Roscoe. "You've been a great help."

They all got to their feet. Christian held out a hand. After a fractional hesitation—one induced by surprise—Roscoe gripped it.

Dalziel's lips quirked; he nodded to Roscoe. Justin opted to shake the man's hand.

Roscoe remained standing behind his desk while they walked to the door. As they reached it, he said, "Dearne, Vaux—you will remember our agreement. When all this is over, I'll still want to buy." His lips lifted slightly. "And I daresay the lady will want to sell."

Justin nodded. Christian raised a hand in salute and followed Dalziel out of the door.

In South Audley Street, Letitia tried to keep her mind occupied, without much success. Hermione had been invited to a morning tea at Lady Hamilton's town house, to meet with her ladyship's daughters; Agnes had gone with her, leaving the house unhelpfully quiet.

Too restless to sit, Letitia drifted about her front parlor, repositioning ornaments, straightening curtains.

When Mellon entered to announce that Swithin had called to see her, she all but fell on his neck. "Yes—please show him in here, Mellon."

She walked to one of the sofas and stood before it. When Swithin entered, she smiled. "Mr. Swithin."

He came forward, politely grave. Taking the hand she offered, he bowed. "Lady Randall. I hope I see you well and that this time is convenient. Albeit belatedly, I wanted to pay my respects and convey my most sincere condolences on poor Randall's death."

"Thank you, Mr. Swithin." With a wave, Letitia invited him to sit on the opposing sofa, and sank onto its mate. "Will you take tea?"

Swithin assented. Letitia rose, tugged the bellpull, then returned to the sofa. Mellon appeared almost instantly; while they waited for him to return with the tea tray, Swithin and she exchanged idle comments on the weather.

Once Mellon had reappeared with the tray and Letitia had poured and handed Swithin his cup, she raised her own, sipped, then said, "If you will, I would appreciate hearing any memories of my late husband you feel able to share. It seems I didn't know him well." Quite aside from being a distraction, it was possible Swithin might let fall some clue.

He nodded, set his cup gently on its saucer. "He, Trowbridge, and I were all born in Hexham. We grew up there, but we didn't know each other until we met at the grammar school. Once we had . . ."

She listened while he gave her what was plainly a heavily edited account of Randall's life, with more personal color than he'd imparted before, yet still carefully avoiding any mention of their lowly origins.

Eventually he came to the present. "I quite understand, of course, why Randall wanted to sell. Now that the company has served its purpose for all of us, there's really no point retaining our interest, especially given the concomitant risk of exposure."

Letitia nodded. "Indeed."

Swithin looked slightly conscious. "Not, of course, that I wish to pressure you to sell. I agreed with Randall, and I believe Trowbridge did, too, but perhaps you have reasons to want to hold onto the company."

It wasn't quite a question; she didn't need to answer, yet if he agreed, and Trowbridge did, too . . . "On the contrary." Letitia set aside her empty cup. "I'm absolutely determined to dissociate myself from the company with all possible speed." She glanced at Swithin, realized she couldn't read his expression at all well. Remembered he was known as a canny investor; presumably a poker face was something he'd cultivated. "As we all three agree that we want to sell, I'm hoping the matter can be arranged without delay."

"Yes, indeed." Swithin looked down, then leaned forward to hand her his empty cup. "In pursuit of that aim, I wonder if I might ask if I may take a look in Randall's desk. In your presence, of course. When he suggested selling, I worked up some summaries of the latest profits. They will be useful to have when we're deciding on a price—that's why I gave them to him."

Letitia frowned. "I can't recall seeing any such papers." She'd watched Barton's search with an eagle eye.

"It might not be instantly obvious what they are." Swithin stood.

Letitia rose, too. "Of course I wasn't aware of the company at that time, so it's possible I overlooked them."

She led the way from the room, then diagonally down the hall to the study. She went straight to the desk. As her fingers brushed the edge, she heard the click of the door lock. Surprised, she glanced back.

Swithin stood just inside the door, his gaze locked on her. "We don't want to be disturbed."

She frowned; his manner had changed. *He* was now disturbing her.

His hand dipped into his coat pocket; he withdrew it— her eyes widened as she saw the small pistol he'd retrieved.

He leveled it at her. "No histrionics, please, or I'll be forced to shoot you and flee."

No histrionics? Eyes locked on the pistol, Letitia swallowed an impulse to ask if he knew who she was. She blinked instead—and felt a most peculiar calm descend on her. "I've had people react to my temper before, but never with a weapon."

Where the words, let alone her even diction, came from, she had no idea, but Swithin didn't smile, didn't react at all—which chilled her all the more.

"If you would open the door." He waved with the pistol toward the secret door. "Please don't pretend you can't—it's obvious you and Dearne found Randall's room."

She tried to think what to do—how to seize control—but her brain had stalled. Moving slowly, her attention helplessly locked on the pistol, she went to the window and depressed the catch hidden in the frame.

The bookcase popped ajar.

"Good. Now fetch the keys from Randall's drawer—I know they're there."

She did, still moving with slow deliberation, while inside, panic of a degree she'd never felt before welled and swelled.

When she lifted the keys free, Swithin nodded. "Excellent. Now go down the steps and into the room."

She hesitated, considering the pistol; its aim hadn't wavered. If she screamed . . . given she'd screamed in this very room so often before, would Mellon react? Even if she screamed for help?

Regardless, searching Swithin's face, she didn't doubt he would do as he said; he'd shoot her and flee. There was something beyond desperate lurking behind his pale eyes.

An expression of impatience lent brief animation to his otherwise bland features. "If you would? We don't have all day."

His voice hardened on the last words; she'd dallied as long as she dared. She walked to the secret door, opened it wider, then went through and down, into the hidden room.

Swithin followed, dragging the panel closed behind him. Halting in the center of the room, she faced him.

Swithin held out one hand, palm upward. With the other, he kept the pistol trained on her breast. "The keys."

Drawing in a breath, trying desperately to think, she dropped them into his palm, fixed her gaze on his face. "You killed Randall."

He met her gaze, his own unwavering. "Yes, I did."

"Why?"

"Because he wanted to sell the company."

"But you would have got your share." The longer she could keep him there, talking, the closer Christian would be.

"Indeed." Swithin's face tightened. "Much good would that have done me. I would have lost the steady, all but guaranteed income, which is what I currently desperately need."

"But you're wealthy—hugely wealthy."

He sucked in a tight, tight breath; in a rigidly controlled voice he replied, "No. I'm not. I won't bore you with the details, but thanks to two unscrupulous blackguards, almost all my capital is gone. Vanished."

His teeth had clenched.

"But . . ." It took no effort to project confusion. "Why not simply tell Randall it didn't suit you to sell? Neither he nor Trowbridge were in any great hurry, and as I understand it, they wouldn't have—couldn't have—forced you to sell."

"No—but then they would have known."

"Known what?"

"Known that I'd *failed*!" His hand fisted about the keys; for one instant his expressionless mask dissolved and twisted fury looked back at her. His lips curled; he spoke in a near hiss. "There they were, sitting pretty, Trowbridge with his art and Randall with you—they'd succeeded at our Grand Plan so much better than I. All I had was my money and my reputation—and now the money's gone, my reputation is all I have left. If I'd told them, that would have gone, too."

Frowning, truly puzzled, she shook her head. "But they

wouldn't have told anyone—you could have sworn them to secrecy, especially considering your shared pasts."

He looked at her as if she hadn't understood a word he'd said. Then in a voice eerily devoid of emotion, stated, "*They* would have known."

Pride. With a jolt of comprehension, she realized it was that—that *that*, a desperate clinging to pride in the face of fate, was what lay behind Randall's death.

Juggling the keys, Swithin backed to the outer door, his expressionless gaze never leaving her. He glanced briefly at the lock—far too briefly for her to make the slightest move— then slid in the key. He unlocked the door, opened it, with the pistol motioned her through.

As she went past him, he murmured, "Remember—no sound, no fuss, and I won't have to shoot you."

If he wasn't going to shoot her, what did he have planned?

Letitia walked the few paces to the lane door; as he moved past her to unlock it, she evaluated her options. She strained her ears, but could hear no maids in the lower yard, yet even if she could bring them running, Swithin would have shot her and fled long before anyone could reach her. The street outside—her nemesis Barton who was always there, keeping watch—was her best and only bet.

It was time Barton earned his salary.

And damned if he hadn't been right—the murderer had, indeed, returned to the scene of the crime.

Swinging the laneway gate open, Swithin all but pushed her through, crowding close by her shoulder in the narrow lane. His fingers clamped about her elbow; the muzzle of the pistol dug into her side.

A chill slid through her at the touch of cold metal through her silk gown.

"See the carriage?" Swithin hissed, urging her forward.

She could hardly miss it; a black traveling carriage, it was drawn up across the mouth of the lane.

There had to be a coachman on the box, but doubtless

he was Swithin's man. But Barton would be just across the street.

She let Swithin propel her forward. As they neared the carriage, he spoke into her ear. "Be quiet and get in."

She managed not to humph derisively.

The instant she stepped out of the laneway, she wrenched back from him, twisting her elbow, pulling away from the cold metal of the pistol's muzzle—praying he wouldn't shoot her in the open street. "Help! *Ow!* You're hurting me! Let go!" Desperate, she glanced around—there was no one in sight. She redoubled her volume. *"Help!"*

Swithin snarled—then something like a rock hit her on the head.

She swayed as the world turned gray.

"Damn you, damn you!" Swithin muttered under his breath.

For a moment she knew nothing, then felt herself being lifted and bundled—into the carriage.

Swithin shoved her onto a seat; her head pounded as it fell against padded leather.

From a great distance she heard Swithin say something to his coachman.

Then the light from outside was cut off. Swithin had shut the door. The carriage lurched sickeningly, then rumbled off.

Swithin was inside the carriage with her. She could sense him moving around, but couldn't open her eyes, couldn't focus her swooning senses well enough to guess what he was doing.

Then he muttered from quite close, "I'd hoped this wouldn't prove necessary, but clearly you're a Vaux to your toes and therefore totally untrustworthy when it comes to scenes."

A waft of sweetness reached her, then got closer, intensifying to a horrible cloying smell—a cloth clamped over her nose and mouth.

She struggled, tried desperately to shift her head away

from the smell, but Swithin held the cloth in place so she had to breathe through it.

Blackness closed in.

Her last thought before darkness engulfed her was that she was alone. At the last, at the end, all alone. Christian wasn't there, he hadn't come for her, and even Barton hadn't been there.

Everyone had deserted her.

And left her in the hands of a murderer.

Chapter 19

"Why can't we just go to his house and put it to him?" Justin looked from Christian to Dalziel.

Christian reined in his own impatience. "Because it might not be him. And if it is, we need an approach that's going to advance our position, gain us some ground, not simply serve to advise him of our suspicions."

"You heard Roscoe." From his corner of the carriage, Dalziel gazed out at the familiar streets. "Swithin didn't need to kill Randall—it's difficult to see why he would."

"Swithin is quiet, cautious. Of the three of them, he's the last one you'd imagine had the intestinal fortitude to commit murder." Christian added, "Far easier to imagine Roscoe was our man, except he's far too clever."

Dalziel humphed in agreement.

The carriage drew up outside Allardyce House. They couldn't go to Randall's house because of Barton's dogged watch, so Christian had suggested they call in there to take stock and plan their next move—almost certainly a call on Swithin, but exactly how . . .

They'd alighted and were climbing his front steps when a messenger—one of those Gasthorpe used—came pounding up the pavement.

They all halted, turning to face him.

"My lord!" The youth offered Christian a folded note, then caught the railing, almost doubling over as he worked to catch his breath.

Christian unfolded the missive; the others watched his face as he read. "Trowbridge has been attacked at his home and left for dead."

"Randall's murderer strikes again." His face hardening, Dalziel stepped down to the pavement, reclaiming the hackney that hadn't yet moved off. He glanced back at Christian. "Chelsea?"

Christian nodded. "Cheyne Walk." He went down the steps, but then halted. "I promised I'd go and see Letitia and let her know what Roscoe said." He held up the note. "She'll want to come."

Dalziel looked at him, a species of disbelief in his eyes.

Christian hesitated; he glanced at Justin as he joined them. "And if Randall's murderer is attacking the owners of the Orient Trading Company, she's now on his list."

Justin humphed. "She's sitting in a house full of servants, and you told me she said she'd wait there. She usually does what she says she will, and Barton's there, too, keeping watch over her and the house—she couldn't be anywhere safer."

"Exactly." Dalziel opened the door of the hackney. "And while we debate the issue, the murderer's trail is growing cold."

Christian hesitated. Why, he didn't know, yet reluctance dragged at him as he forced himself to nod. "All right. When we've finished in Chelsea, we'll come back to South Audley Street."

Following the others into the carriage, he shut the door.

The scene that met their eyes when they walked into the house in Cheyne Walk—through the wide open, unmanned front door—could only be described as chaotic. Christian caught a rushing footman, relieved him of the fruit bowl he was ferrying and directed him to announce their arrival. After staring at Christian, then at Dalziel and Justin, the footman turned tail and went.

Christian walked into the drawing room and set down the

bowl. The three of them stood in the middle of the fabulous room with its wonderful light and white-and-lemon decor, and waited.

Eventually they heard heavy footsteps raggedly descending the stairs.

Rupert Honeywell came in. He looked haggard and distraught even though he was making a herculean effort to bear up. Any doubt of the depth of his regard for Trowbridge would have been banished by one look into his tortured eyes.

"Thank you for coming. I didn't know who else to send for." He looked at Christian. "I remembered the card you gave Russell—he still had it in his pocket."

Christian nodded. "What happened?"

Honeywell dragged in a huge breath, held it for a moment, then said, "He went out for his morning walk as he always did, along the bottom of the garden—there's a path that follows the boundary wall along the river." He hauled in another breath. "When he didn't come back for breakfast, I sent a footman to look for him, then decided to go myself. Sometimes he sat on a bench looking out over the river and forgot the time."

He paused, then, gaze distant, continued, "I got to the bench, but he wasn't there. Then I heard the footman call out and strode over. Russell was sprawled on the path—from a distance I thought he'd swooned, but then I got closer and saw the blood on the footman's hand . . . and on Russell's head."

Honeywell's voice broke, but he swallowed and went on, "He'd been hit—*bashed*—with a rock. It was lying nearby. The footman thought he was dead—he kept saying he was— but I found a weak pulse. We got him back to the house and summoned the doctor—he's with him now."

"He's alive?" Christian asked.

Honeywell nodded. He pulled out a handkerchief and blew his nose. "The doctor says he thinks he'll live. He's regained consciousness." Honeywell paused, then added, "It was he who insisted I send for you, and as I couldn't think of anyone else, I did."

"We'll go and see him in a moment, but first, did the staff see anyone they didn't expect to see this morning?"

Honeywell shook his head. "I asked. No one saw anything, and they're all devoted to us, so they would say if they had."

Christian nodded. "This walk Trowbridge took—you said he walked every morning. Always the same route?"

"Yes. It was his way of clearing his head for the day. That's why I didn't walk with him."

"What about the walls?" Dalziel asked. "Are they high, glass on top—or low? Could someone have climbed over without coming through or past the house?"

Thrusting his handkerchief back into his pocket, Honeywell nodded. "Easily. The wall at the back is the boundary of the river walk—it's chest height for a man, easy to look over. Not difficult to climb over. It's the same for the properties on either side, so anyone could have gone down through any of the gardens along this stretch—and early morning, who would see them?—or someone could have walked up along the river path."

"So every morning Trowbridge walked alone along a path that anyone could reach." Dalziel grimaced.

"Anyone who knew about his habit." Christian considered Honeywell, but elected to go to the source. "We need to speak with Trowbridge."

Honeywell was clearly not happy in a purely protective way. However, he equally clearly knew Trowbridge wouldn't thank him for such solicitude; tight-lipped, he turned to the door. "If you'll come this way, we'll see what the doctor says."

The doctor agreed they could speak with his patient. "He's groggy, but he won't settle otherwise."

In a room hung with exquisite Chinese silks, Trowbridge lay propped up on a bank of pristine white pillows in a massive four-poster bed. An even whiter bandage circled his skull; his skin was very nearly the same color. His eyes were closed, his arms lying on the covers on either side of his body.

Honeywell went around the bed and took one limp hand between both of his. "Dearne's here."

Trowbridge's lashes flickered, then his lids lifted. After a moment of vagueness, his gaze sharpened. Christian was relieved to see the man's usual acuity swimming beneath the haze of pain.

Then Trowbridge's lids fell. "I didn't see him." His voice was a thin thread, but clear enough. "Coward—the bastard sneaked up on me." Opening his eyes, Trowbridge glanced at Honeywell. "I was thinking about that latest canvas of yours, so I was far away." Slowly, he brought his gaze back to Christian. "I didn't get so much as a glimpse."

Christian nodded. "Have you done anything—spoken to anyone at all—regarding the company? Or done anything else that might connect with Randall's murder?"

Trowbridge pursed his lips, a line between his brows. "No. I haven't discussed the company with anyone—not since I spoke with you."

Honeywell frowned. "What about Swithin? You spoke with him when he called."

"Oh. Yes." Trowbridge smiled vaguely at Christian. "Forgot about him."

Trowbridge was too dazed to notice the instant awareness, a primal tensing of muscles, that affected his three visitors at the mention of Swithin. Honeywell did; it was he who gently asked, "What did you talk to Swithin about? He doesn't often call."

Eyes again closed, Trowbridge carefully nodded. "About the company. About the sale and when we might go ahead with it. About how much we stood to make—because it's such a risky business, that's not as much as one might think given the high income. The income could end tomorrow if any number of things happened." He moistened his lips, then went on, "I suggested that I'd be quite happy to settle for a third of the total income for a year—I vaguely recall Randall mentioning that—the income for a year—as the figure he hoped to secure."

Trowbridge lifted his shoulders in a light shrug. "Reasonable when you think about it. Swithin agreed. That was more or less all we discussed. All perfectly innocent."

"Not so innocent," Christian quietly said, steel infusing his voice, "once you learn that Swithin is neck deep in debt and desperate for income to qualify for a massive loan."

Trowbridge opened his eyes. "He's in debt?" He frowned. "Good God. *How?* He was wealthy—the wealthiest of the three of us."

"Never mind how—we don't have time."

Dalziel caught Christian's arm, holding him back as, with a muttered oath, he turned for the door. Letitia was definitely in Swithin's sights.

"One thing in all this I don't understand." Dalziel spoke quickly. "Why didn't Swithin simply *tell* you and Randall about his need for income, and that therefore he didn't want to sell the company?"

Christian looked back to see Trowbridge blink.

Twice. Then he shook his head. "Oh, but he wouldn't. Indeed, Randall and I are the very last people he'd ever tell. He'd never tell us, never let on, that he'd failed with our Grand Plan."

Seeing their incomprehension, Trowbridge struggled to sit up; Honeywell helped him. "What you have to understand about our Grand Plan was that for Randall and me it was us against them—us against society as a whole. But for Swithin, it was us against each other. He . . . simply couldn't see the wider picture—for him it was always a competition." Trowbridge searched their faces for some sign they understood. "That's what I meant about his wealth—he took great pride in having amassed more than Randall or I had. Money was the one issue on which he could trump us—and we let him, because that—who was more wealthy among us—wasn't important to us. . . ."

Trowbridge's face suddenly fell, all animation leaching away. "It was he who struck me, wasn't it? After all these years, he tried to kill me, because in his mind he'd failed, and he couldn't bear that. Couldn't bear me knowing . . . and he killed Randall, too."

Christian nodded curtly. "Yes, and if you'll excuse us, we need to make sure he doesn't kill anyone else."

Trowbridge grasped his point. "Yes, of course."

Christian strode for the door. Behind him, he heard Dalziel speak to Trowbridge.

"He almost certainly thinks you're dead. We'll send word when we have him—until then . . ."

At the door, Christian glanced back and saw Dalziel looking at Honeywell.

"Make sure there's someone with him at all times."

Mentally nodding, Christian strode out. Justin was on his heels.

Dalziel caught up with them as they bundled into the hackney, Christian having instructed the jarvey to drive hell-for-leather for South Audley Street.

The man took him at his word. They rattled through the streets, taking corners at speed; grim-faced and silent, the three of them braced themselves, each absorbed, thinking ahead.

Christian told himself that Barton was there, watching from outside—but that wouldn't stop Swithin going in. He'd told Letitia that Swithin was a suspect, but none of them had seriously thought him the murderer—not until today.

As they raced into Mayfair, leaving curses in their wake, he prayed they'd be in time.

They arrived at South Audley Street. Leaving Dalziel to deal with the jarvey, Christian strode up the front steps, threw open the door—and stepped into outright uproar.

A cacophany of myriad feminine voices all raised, all exclaiming—all at once—assailed him. Behind him, he heard Justin mutter, "Good Lord! They're *all* here."

"Christian!" Letitia's aunt Amarantha spotted him as he stood rooted just inside the door. "Just the man—Letitia's disappeared."

They came at him from all sides, more pouring from the parlor to add their voices to the din. It appeared to be an assembly of all the Vaux females, close and distant; all Letitia's aunts and female cousins seemed to be there.

He tried to make sense of what they were telling him, but there was so much dross camouflaging the facts it was hopeless. Eventually he spotted Agnes in the parlor doorway, Hermione beside her, but he couldn't reach them short of mowing through the crowd.

Grim-faced, he held up his hands. *"Quiet!"*

A sudden silence fell, if anything even more painful than the preceding cacophany. Stunned, they all looked at him with wide eyes.

Stepping farther into the hall so Dalziel could come in and close the door, he focused on Agnes. "I need one of you—*only one*—to tell me what's happened. Agnes?"

She nodded. "Letitia was here—she stayed in this morning. Hermione and I went to a morning tea." Her voice wavered but she dragged in a breath—glowered at Constance, who had opened her mouth—and went on, "She's obviously had visitors—there's a tea tray." She waved into the parlor. "But when we came home, she wasn't in there. We thought perhaps she'd gone up to her room, but then the others arrived and Hermione went up to fetch her—but she wasn't there either. She's not in the house. And she hasn't left any message, which she would have if she'd been called away, or gone to Bond Street, or . . ."

Letitia had said she'd be waiting for him to come back to her; while he wasn't insensible to the echoes of their past, Christian knew absolutely that this time she wouldn't have gone anywhere—not willingly.

While Agnes had talked, he'd made his way through the crowd to her. Justin had followed; Hermione grabbed his hand.

Looking past Agnes, Christian saw the tea tray set on a low table between the sofas. Only two cups. He'd hoped . . .

He turned back to the hovering horde. "Where's Mellon?"

The butler was nowhere in sight. One bright cousin slipped into the parlor and tugged the bellpull.

A moment later the baize door at the rear of the hall swung open and Mellon marched through.

Over the heads of the ladies, Christian beckoned; the ladies parted, allowing Mellon to make his way to him.

Which he did with a supercilious air. "Yes, my lord?"

Christian looked down at him. "Who called on your mistress?"

Mellon arched his brows. "A good friend of the master's called to offer his condolences, as was proper."

Justin made a frustrated sound. He stepped around Christian, grabbed Mellon by the throat, lifted him off his feet and slammed him up against the hall wall; the pictures hanging on it bounced. "*Who* called on my sister?"

Mellon goggled, hands ineffectually scrabbling at Justin's.

Far from fainting or being scandalized by the violence, all the Vaux ladies looked on eagerly. Even encouragingly. When Mellon didn't immediately divulge the name, Agnes pointed imperiously to the tea tray. "*Who* did she have tea with?"

"Come on, man—spit it out," Constance said. "Dearne hasn't got all day."

"It was a Mr. Swithin," Mellon gasped. "From what I heard, he was the master's great friend."

Justin's lip curled. "Mr. Swithin—your master's murderer."

Mellon's face turned ashen. "*He* killed Mr. Randall?"

"So we believe." Dalziel joined them by the parlor door. "What happened after you served the tea?"

With Justin, Christian, and Dalziel facing him, Mellon looked as if he would like to faint but was too scared to. "I . . . ah, listened at the door for a time. Mr. Swithin was telling the mistress about Mr. Randall at school. Then I was called away to the pantry. When I came back, the parlor was empty. I thought the mistress must have gone upstairs. It seemed odd she'd seen Mr. Swithin out herself, but—"

"Did you hear the front door open and shut?" Christian asked.

Mellon shook his head. He frowned, looked back down the hall. "I should have—I was only on the other side of the door."

Christian looked down the hall, too, past the stairs. "The study."

Once again the sea of ladies parted, letting them through. Christian grasped the handle, tried it. "Locked."

The door was thick, solid oak. He exchanged a glance with Dalziel, then they both stepped back, balanced on one leg, then together kicked the door hard, level with the lock.

It gave with a crack. Christian used his shoulder to force the door open, then strode in. He was relieved to find the room empty, devoid of bodies. Going straight to the window, he released the secret panel.

Crowding the doorway, the ladies looked in, oohed as Dalziel caught the hidden door and hauled it wide.

Christian followed Dalziel down into the hidden room. It was the work of a moment to verify that the door to the little yard and the lane door were both unlocked.

"Just as they were when Randall was murdered." Dalziel stood in the lane looking toward the street. "He couldn't come in this way—he had to come in via the front door. But he left this way, just as he did before."

"But this time he took Letitia with him." Christian looked the other way along the lane; it ended in a wall a few houses along. He looked back toward the street. "But the only way he could have gone was back into South Audley Street."

Frowning, he turned and strode back into the house. "Where the devil is Barton? He was keeping watch as usual this morning—Letitia knew he'd be there. She would have tried to attract his attention." He eased his way through the mass of females thronging the hidden room and the study to regain the now relatively free space of the front hall. Justin came up with him as he made for the door; Dalziel was close behind.

Throwing open the door, Christian halted on the front step and looked across the street—to see Barton paying off a jarvey.

"What the hell?" Justin muttered.

Barton saw them. Lifting his head, squaring his shoulders, he marched toward them.

"Where the devil have you been?" Christian demanded as the wiry runner approached the steps.

Barton halted, blinked.

Christian reined in his temper, ruthlessly squelched his panic, and ground out through clenched teeth, "Lady Letitia was kidnapped this morning—she was taken from here, almost certainly in a carriage. She would have called out, struggled—you *must* have seen . . ." The little runner had lost all color. A chill clutched Christian's chest. "You weren't here, were you?"

Statement more than question.

Barton shook his head. "I . . ." He cleared his throat, then spoke more firmly. "I was following you. I didn't see anyone nab her ladyship."

Christian swore—colorfully, inventively, at length.

Justin eyed him with approbation. "You were always destined to marry a Vaux."

"I'll have to find her first." And he would.

Apparently judging the worst had passed, Barton reached into his coat pocket, produced his warrant card, held it up for them to see. "Lord Justin Vaux, I'm arresting you on suspicion of murdering your brother-in-law, Mr. George Randall."

"Lord, you're not still on about that, are you?" Justin frowned down at him. "You can do that later, if you've a mind to after we've found my sister and got her out of the hands of Randall's real murderer."

Barton's lips thinned. "Be that as it may, I've found you—Lord Justin Vaux, as is my quarry—and I'm taking you into custody, as is my duty, and I'm calling on you two gents"—he indicated Christian and Dalziel—"to bear witness. I followed him in your presences to Mr. Trowbridge's, where I heard there's been a spot of bother. It's clear as the day there's something afoot, and Lord Vaux here is in the thick of it."

"The day," Dalziel pointed out caustically, "is cloudy. And yes, Lord Vaux is assisting in investigating Randall's murder and exposing the real killer, and now we know who he is, you can continue to follow us and do your duty when we corner him." He eyed Barton coldly. "At present, however, you're in our way."

With that, Dalziel moved down the steps. Christian fell in behind him, Justin in the rear.

Barton had to give way; he backed across the pavement, watching, faintly stupefied, as Dalziel swung off the steps and strode off toward Curzon Street. Lengthening his stride, Christian caught up; his and Dalziel's long legs ate the distance.

Justin strode close behind. Christian heard Barton's footsteps following, at first hesitantly, then more definitely.

Eventually the runner dared to draw level with his "quarry." As they turned the corner into Curzon Street, Christian saw Barton tweak Justin's sleeve. "What's going on?"

Justin glanced down at him, faintly exasperated. "Just follow along and you'll see."

Barton didn't have much option.

"Which house?" Dalziel slowed.

His face like stone, Christian pointed it out.

Dalziel halted before the front steps. He looked at Christian. "How do you want to handle this?"

Christian eyed the front door, then marched up the steps and pounded on it.

Swithin's butler quickly opened the door.

"Where's Swithin?" Christian demanded. He stepped forward.

Startled, the butler backed. "Ah . . . I'm not sure I know, my lord."

Christian pinned him with a glare. "Think carefully."

"And quickly," Dalziel advised.

"Ah . . ." The butler stared at them, his gaze moving from one to the other.

Then Justin ranged alongside Dalziel in the doorway. "Believe me, this is not the time to hesitate—we have a Bow Street runner with us, and he's keen to make an arrest."

The butler goggled.

"Did your master leave in his carriage, perhaps?" Christian took another step forward so he was looming over the hapless man.

The butler looked up, into his eyes; what he saw there had him swallowing, nodding. "Yes. That's right." The man's head kept bobbing. "He called for his carriage well over an hour ago—he said he was picking up one of the mistress's friends and was taking her to visit the mistress in Surrey."

"Surrey?" Lifting his head, Christian stared unseeing across the hall for a moment, then glanced at Dalziel. "He would, wouldn't he?"

Dalziel nodded. "Much easier to hide a body in the country—that's how he'd think."

The butler paled. "Body?"

Christian ignored him, turned and strode back out of the door. Dalziel and Justin joined him; Barton hovered.

Christian felt as if his heart was being slowly fed through a mangle. He forced himself to think past the pain, to ignore the incipient panic. "We'll have to follow as fast as we can, and pray she can slow him down enough for us to reach them."

Dalziel said nothing, simply nodded.

"At least he's in a carriage," Justin said. "In curricles, we'll close the distance."

But not fast enough. Surrey wasn't that far away.

"Hey!"

They all turned to see Tristan and Tony striding along the pavement.

"We called at Randall's house to take another look at the books and walked into a madhouse," Tony said. "Hermione told us Swithin has kidnapped Letitia and you'd come this way." He raised his brows. "What's afoot?"

In a few brief words, Christian told them.

"We can catch him, or come very close." Tristan caught Christian's eyes. "With God's help, close enough to save her."

"He's got what sounds like nearly an hour's head start," Justin pointed out.

"True, but he's new to the area. I'm not." Tristan smiled intently. "There's shortcuts he won't know about—with luck we can make up half an hour just getting out of town." He glanced at Christian. "We need curricles and fast horses. I'm close enough to fetch mine."

Justin slanted a glance at Dalziel. "I can get mine."

Dalziel nodded. "Go. I'll travel with Dearne."

"We'll meet back here—at the corner," Christian declared.

They scattered, Tony striding off with Tristan, Justin disappearing along Curzon Street with Barton trotting at his heels, Dalziel accompanying Christian back to Grosvenor Square.

She was alone—but *this time* Christian would come for her.

Letitia lay on her side on the seat of Swithin's carriage and kept her eyes closed. The horrible stuff he'd used to drug her had left her nauseated, but the sensation was slowly ebbing.

Her faculties were slowly returning.

They were traveling southward; the direction from which sunlight fell through the carriage windows told her that. She recalled hearing that Swithin had a country house in Surrey; presumably he was taking her there.

Or perhaps he intended putting her on a boat to who knew where?

A possibility, but she didn't think it likely.

She thought he meant to kill her; how, she didn't know, exactly where, she didn't know, but if his aim was to halt the sale of the company without saying anything—without letting anyone who knew of his descent into poverty live . . . then he was going to have to kill her.

Telling her he'd killed Randall, telling her why, even if it didn't make all that much sense to her, showed very clearly what he planned for her.

Therefore her only goal until this was over was to avoid being killed.

She had to slow him down until Christian came.

Her confidence that he would was, somewhat to her surprise, rock solid. Unshakable, unwavering. He might not have come to save her years ago, but then he hadn't known she'd needed saving. This time he would know; this time he would come.

She examined that certainty and what fed it. In her heart, locked away though it was, she no longer doubted his devotion to her. Circumstances or fate might part them, yes, but he never would.

And nor would she.

But she hadn't yet told him that. Hadn't found the courage or the moment . . . No. In light of her heart's certainty, given her predicament, she might as well be brutally honest—she hadn't found the backbone to set aside her pride, to relinquish the one prop she'd had left to her and openly embrace him and their love again.

To, in the eyes of their world, claim it, and him, for her own again.

Damn!

Pride had twisted Swithin into a murderer. She wasn't, she vowed, going to let that less than admirable trait deprive her of the one thing she most wanted in life—Christian, and through him, the resurrection of their dreams.

She wasn't going to die, and she wasn't going to let pride retain any further hold on her.

And she certainly wasn't going to let a sad case like Swithin take their future—the future they'd waited twelve long years for—from them.

Determined, she carefully cracked open her lids and peered through her lashes. Swithin sat dozing on the opposite seat.

Very carefully, she straightened her legs, seeking to ease her cramped muscles. Only to detect, then confirm, that he'd hobbled her. Her ankles weren't lashed tight, but they were joined—she could part them only a few inches, not even a foot.

Faintly horrified, she tried to move her hands—and discovered her wrists were tied together. Without moving too much, she squinted down at the knots—and cursed long and vividly, if silently.

Her hands were lashed palm-to-palm with the knots on the outside of her wrists. She wouldn't be able to ease the knots undone with her teeth; she couldn't reach them well enough to do so.

More silent cursing ensued; she let herself indulge—temper buoyed her. Gave her untold courage, false though it might be.

At that moment she would willingly embrace anything that gave her strength. If she was going to foil Swithin's plans long enough for Christian to rescue her, she was going to need all she could get.

Chapter 20

Christian sent his whip snaking out to flick his leader's ear. The horse responded with a surge of power, drawing his curricle closer to Tristan's, just ahead.

Behind, Justin kept two horses' lengths back. He'd taken Barton up beside him; when Christian had glanced back, he'd seen the runner, pale, eyes staring, hanging onto the rail for dear life.

All their passengers were holding the rails, even Dalziel beside him. At the pace they were traveling, it was too dangerous not to; it was just as well Tristan knew the roads better than the backs of his hands.

He'd led them surprisingly swiftly out of London. As soon as they hit more open country, he'd lowered his hands and let his horses have their heads. Christian had been on his heels, with Justin's blacks breathing down his neck all but literally.

They were rattling along too rapidly to talk. Regardless, he and Dalziel had nothing they needed to say. They both knew the odds, knew that time was ticking away—knew that without some help—not discounting divine intervention—they were unlikely to reach Swithin's house in time.

Always assuming they'd guessed aright and Swithin hadn't headed somewhere else entirely.

The paralyzing fear that flashed through him at the thought had him sucking in a breath.

He pushed the debilitating reaction away, bundled it out

of his mind; for one of the few times in his dangerous life he began to pray.

Divine intervention wasn't to be sneezed at.

He hadn't saved Letitia years before; he'd be damned—literally—if he let her down again.

They swept into the drive of Swithin's house, all six horses in a lather. Tristan pulled up before the front steps; Christian drew his horses to a stamping halt right behind.

Justin swept past, with a flourish of his whip indicating he was heading around to the stables.

"Good move." Dalziel stepped down and followed Christian to the door.

As he had in Curzon Street, Christian hammered on the front door until it swung open. A butler stood in the doorway, all but frozen in shock at the sight of the four large and menacing men crowding the front porch.

"Where's your master?" Christian's growl suggested—accurately—that he wished to rend said master limb from limb.

The butler swallowed and found his voice. "He's not here. He lives in London for much of the time—in Curzon Street."

"We've just come from Curzon Street—he left there, apparently for here."

The butler had caught sight of their steaming horses. "Perhaps he's still on the road?" He lifted his gaze to Christian's face. "He doesn't like rattling along—it makes him ill."

That was the best bit of news Christian had had all day. Yet even traveling slowly, Swithin should have been there. He glanced at Dalziel, who met his gaze. Neither of them thought the butler was lying.

"All that means"—Dalziel swung back to the forecourt—"is that he hasn't come through his front door."

"And if he had a struggling prisoner in tow, he wouldn't." Tristan went back down the shallow steps. The others followed; the butler, puzzled, came out in their wake.

Justin came striding around the side of the house, great-coat flapping, Barton at his heels. A bevy of stableboys rushed past, racing to take the high-stepping horses in charge.

"He's here," Justin bellowed as soon as he was in earshot. Halting, he beckoned. "The stableman says he arrived about five minutes ago—with a lady."

Moments later they all stood in the stableyard, where two carriage horses were being watered.

"The lady wasn't well," the stableman said. "Fainting and weak—she could barely stand. The master had to half carry her up to the house."

"He didn't go in through the front door." With the others, Christian turned to look at the house. "The butler hasn't seen him."

The stableman frowned. "That's odd. The state the lady was in, I'd've thought he'd have her inside right away."

From where they stood, the side door of the house was visible. Dalziel pointed. "Did you see him go through that door?"

The stableman shook his head. "Saw him head off in that direction, but . . ." He waved to the wide vistas rolling away to either side, then at the horses nearby. "I was busy with these—he could have gone anywhere, for all I know."

"Could any of your boys have seen which way he went?" Justin asked.

The stableman shook his head. "They were inside, mucking out."

Frustrated, ridden by a sense of time running out, of being near yet not near enough, Christian strode back out of the stableyard. Just beyond the arch, he halted and looked about. The others ranged around.

"So he's here, with her." And she was still alive. "I'll check to see if he went in through the door." Christian glanced at Dalziel.

Who nodded. "The rest of us will scout outside. Whoever sights him, yell."

Christian left them to sort out who would look where. He

jogged to the house, scanning the ground along the way for any signs of a struggle or fresh footsteps.

He reached the door. There might have been a scuffle just outside it, but the grass was thick; he couldn't tell who might have stood there or how long ago it had been.

Opening the door—unlocked, as most doors in the country were—he stepped inside, into a shallow hall with two corridors leading off, one to the left, one to the right. He debated for an instant, then turned left, away from the front of the house. The other corridor almost certainly led to the front rooms the butler watched over, and presumably Mrs. Swithin would be somewhere in that region, too.

If Swithin had brought Letitia inside, he would have gone somewhere else—somewhere away from all others.

It wasn't that large a house, but a modest, relatively modern manor in the Palladian style. The first stretch of floor beyond the hall was covered by a runner, but beyond the runner's end, bare floorboard stretched.

Noting a darker mark on the wood, Christian crouched, touched a finger to it; his fingertip came away damp, slightly green.

The grass outside the door had been damp.

Moving faster, he went on—and found an even clearer set of footprints around the corner, at the base of a set of bare wooden stairs—servants' stairs, leading up. There were two sets of footprints, the larger clear and well-defined, the smaller smudged and muddled, as if Letitia had been tripping over her own toes.

Christian swore beneath his breath and started up the stairs. The blackguard must have drugged her.

He didn't yell for the others; they almost certainly wouldn't hear him, but the servants would—and so would Swithin.

Reaching the first floor landing, he forced himself to search for footprints to show him the way—along the corridor or up the next flight of stairs. His inner clock told him time was running out; panic threatened—but now more than ever he couldn't afford to go the wrong way.

But there were runners all about, even on the stairs. "Swithin!"

The hail came from outside.

Two strides took Christian to the landing window. Looking out, he saw Dalziel, hands on his hips, looking up and shouting—at the roof.

Christian swore and bolted up the stairs. If Swithin had taken Letitia onto the roof . . . there was only one possible reason he would.

And she was drugged.

On a narrow ledge a bare yard wide, just behind the low parapet encircling the roof, Letitia struggled—wrestled—for her life.

Her wrists were still tied—she hadn't been able to do anything about that—but by pretending she couldn't get up the stairs, she'd forced Swithin to unhobble her ankles.

So she could balance well enough to counter his shoves, pull back enough when he tried to yank her forward. But bit by bit, his jaw set, his fingers biting into her arms, he maneuvered her closer to the edge.

She'd pretended to be drugged as long as she could, used her slumping weight, her inability to walk, to slow them.

He might not be anywhere near Christian's size, but Swithin was still heavier and stronger than she; fighting him in the carriage wouldn't have worked—she'd been afraid he might simply have drugged her again. But Swithin had managed her exit from his carriage well, making sure she was out of sight and too distant from his stablemen for there to be any chance of escape. Not with his pistol pressed to her side.

So she'd worked and worked, forcing her panicking wits to find ways to slow them as much as possible.

But now she had to fight to keep him from flinging her over the edge.

Screaming hadn't been an option, not with that pistol digging into her ribs and no one nearby, but he'd had to put the pistol away so he could use both hands to seize her.

Now she could scream.

"No!" She didn't want to die—not when everything in her life had at last come right. "Stop it—*let me go!*"

What right did Swithin have to take her life from her—and for such a nonsensical reason?

Temper, as ever, was her strength. She used it, drew on it, worked to keep it stoked.

Desperate, she wrestled, fought as well as she could with her hands tied—would have kicked but she had to keep her balance.

Swithin pushed—she pushed back.

But she couldn't keep going forever.

She was weakening; just as she started to wonder if Christian would be too late, yells came from below.

She recognized Dalziel's voice. If he was there, Christian was close.

Swithin knew; his face empurpled, then contorted in a snarl. He steeled himself, locked his fingers even more tightly on her arms.

Letitia felt him gather himself, muscles bunching, prayed she'd have strength enough to counter his shove when it came—

Heavy footsteps pounded up the stairs beyond the half-open roof door.

Smothering a roar, Swithin wrenched back from her. Holding her at arm's length with one hand, with the other he scrabbled at his coat pocket.

He pulled out his pistol.

Aimed it at the door.

Just as Christian thrust it wide.

"No!" Letitia's heart clogged her throat.

Time stopped.

Christian took in the scene in one glance. He saw the pistol aimed at his heart, saw Swithin—no longer the quiet, reserved, cautious gentleman-investor, but a disheveled merchant's son with a crazed light in his eyes.

His gaze found Letitia, fixed on her. She'd largely thrown

off the effects of the drug. She'd been fighting Swithin. Her green-gold eyes showed healthy fear, but no panic.

They also glowed with temper, and a determination not to be killed.

He would have closed his eyes and given thanks, but she wasn't safe yet.

Locking his gaze with Swithin's, he slowly stepped onto the narrow parapet walk, letting the door swing half closed behind him.

"Get back," Swithin shouted. "Or I'll shoot!"

Christian halted. Looked puzzled. "You don't want to shoot me."

The unexpected reply confused Swithin. He frowned.

Christian couldn't risk looking at Letitia—he wanted Swithin's full attention on him. All he could do was will her to stillness, and silence.

From the corner of his eye, on the ground far below he could see Justin haring back to the stables. He'd be after the long-barreled pistols they all carried beneath their box seats. Justin had been a crack shot since his childhood, and, Christian suspected, so was Dalziel.

From where they were, they'd have a clear view of Swithin.

All he and Letitia had to do was wait.

And keep Swithin occupied.

"There's no sense to any of this, Swithin." He spoke calmly, matter-of-factly. "Letitia won't sell her share of the company if you don't want her to."

Swithin sneered. Jeered. "Of course she'll want to sell— no lady like her would want to have anything to do with such an enterprise. And Trowbridge wanted to sell, too—he told me so. And then I'd have to sell, no matter that I don't want to, because how can I not without admitting—"

Abruptly he closed his lips. Eyes distinctly feverish, he shook his head. "No, no—I'm not going to say. I'm never going to tell anyone. Can't. It's *my* secret. We kept a lot of secrets, but that one's mine alone." His lips lifted in a parody of a smile. "No one else gets to know that one."

Christian inclined his head in acceptance. "But why kill people?" Justin had returned, pistols in hand. Christian could see the others moving about below. Keeping his gaze locked with Swithin's, he frowned. "I don't understand. Killing people never helps."

Swithin's expression turned superior. "In this case, it will—it does. It stops them from selling the company without me having to admit . . . anything. Without me having to beg them not to."

"But being convicted of murder's not going to help. You don't want that."

Swithin smiled slyly. "It won't happen—*I* won't be convicted. No one can prove I killed Randall and Trowbridge. It was surprisingly easy. Just a knock on the back of the head and they were gone. Quick and neat. But there's no proof I killed them—I made sure of that. No—now I just have to pitch this bitch off the roof and everything will work out."

He shifted, turning toward Letitia as if to do just that.

Christian seized the moment to glance down; the others were repositioning, trying to get a bead on Swithin without Letitia or he anywhere close. Dalziel saw him looking and waved, beckoning—they wanted Swithin closer to the edge. Christian hurriedly asked, "But why from the roof? Why not just knock her on the head like the others?"

It was the only thing he could think of to ask.

Swithin looked back at him, a strange smile curving his lips; beyond him, Christian saw Letitia gathering herself—she'd used the time he'd bought them to regroup.

"I can't do that," Swithin told him. "She's Randall's and Trowbridge's murderer—*she's* the one who knocks people on the head. Not me. Never me. She was making far too many inquiries—or you were on her behalf. I know you spoke with Gallagher, and then you went to see Roscoe. I couldn't allow that—couldn't allow you, and her, to learn too much. But it doesn't matter now. Once she goes over the edge, you won't be able to help her anymore. And everyone will see that she killed the other two, then came after me, and when she couldn't kill me, she rushed up here and threw herself off." His smile widened. "It's obvious."

Christian didn't know what to say, how to respond to such foolishness.

But it seemed they'd run out of time.

That quantity slowed as Swithin turned to Letitia. Christian saw him tighten the grip he had on her arm.

He was going to half throw, half swing her over the edge—he'd only need to make her topple. He could do it without stepping closer to the parapet. There was only one thing Christian could do—one risk, one gamble, he had to take.

"Swithin." He poured every ounce of command he possessed into his voice. "Look down."

Startled, Swithin glanced back at him; he still had his pistol in a firm grip. Christian didn't move so much as an eyelash.

Puzzlement growing, unable to read anything in Christian's face, Swithin shifted; bracing his arm, anchoring Letitia at arm's length, he edged closer to the parapet, looked over and down.

Two shots rang out, virtually inseparable.

Swithin jerked, then stumbled backward, crumpling to the ground.

Slinging Letitia forward as he fell, his descending weight acting as a fulcrum propelling her over the edge.

Christian shot forward, leapt over Swithin, dove for the edge, grabbed—but her body had already cleared the parapet.

He couldn't reach her—but her bound hands, desperately reaching out to him as she twisted and fell, brushed, clutched at his sleeves.

He seized her wrists, hung on with both hands as her falling weight yanked him to the edge. Going down on his knees, he braced his body behind the low parapet, his hands locked viselike about hers.

Her fingers clenched convulsively, gripping, clinging.

Then came the jerk as he took her weight.

The muscles in his arms screamed; pain shot across his shoulders. He heard her cry out in pain and shock.

But he had her. Mentally giving thanks, he closed his eyes for a second, savored the feel of her hands still in his.

Still alive in his.

She gasped, gulped in air as her swinging weight steadied.

After a moment she looked up; he felt the shift in her weight.

Spreading his knees, lowering his body, he leaned into the parapet, and opening his eyes, looked down.

Into her face.

He smiled. "I've got you."

The concern—the fear—in her eyes didn't fade.

She studied his face, then he saw her gaze lower.

"You can't hold me forever."

"Believe me, I can—or at least for long enough now to be able to manage forever."

She smiled faintly; something in her face changed. Her eyes, when she lifted them to his again, were filled with an emotion he hadn't seen in them before—one she'd never let him see.

"I love you." Letitia knew that, no matter what he said, she was going to fall and die. The muscles of his neck, shoulders, and chest were under horrendous strain, the veins in his throat starkly corded. Even now the muscles in his arms were starting to quiver.

So she had to say now what she hadn't yet. "I've loved you from the first moment I saw you. I've always loved you, every day through all the years. I never stopped loving you. Even when I lay with Randall, it was you I was with in my heart." She smiled softly. "That was yours from the first, and will be yours to the last."

"I love you, too." He continued to look into her eyes. "I always have. I never stopped loving you—I never will." His hands tightened on hers. "Now hold on."

Her smile faded. "It's hopeless."

"Nothing's ever hopeless—just look at us. And in this case, we have friends who are running hither and yon as we speak."

He glanced past her. "Apparently there's refurbishing still going on around the house—they've found a large oilcloth. And there's bales of hay, too. They're arranging them beneath you." His gaze switched back to her face. "You can't possibly be so gauche as to fall before they're ready to catch you—they're going to so much trouble."

Hope sprang to life within her. A bright burning flame, it caught and flared—so quickly, so strongly, she felt giddy. She nearly laughed.

If there was hope, she'd cling to it—cling to life, and him.

He was looking down past her again. "They're almost ready—they've stretched out the oilcloth. There's only four of them—no, Barton has joined them. Good man. You'll have to stop hounding the poor beggar now—very bad ton to hound a man who was instrumental in saving your life."

The thought of Barton finally being helpful was too much; she humphed.

But then his expression sobered and he looked back at her.

"Now comes the difficult part." He held her gaze. "You have to trust me. When I say let go, you have to let go. Believe me, that won't be as easy as it sounds. You'll be falling. But the straw bales are beneath you—you won't hit the ground. And the oilcloth will slow you—which is why you have to let go *exactly* when I tell you, because they're going to have to pull the cloth taut at the right moment."

She nodded her understanding. "Yes, all right." She trusted him implicitly, more than enough to trump all fear.

"Good." He looked down, raised his voice. "On the count of three." His gaze returned to her face. His hands shifted on hers, easing his grip but not yet releasing her. "One, two . . ." His eyes held hers. "Let go."

Wrapped in his gray gaze, she opened her fingers.

Felt his warm grasp slip away as gravity took hold and she started to fall.

Heard him call from above, "Three!"

And then she was falling.

Falling.

Onto the taut oilcloth. As she landed, she saw the other men hauling back hard, hands locked on the edge of the cloth, their weight fully back.

She bounced once, then settled onto the bales of hay as the men released the tension on the cloth. Sitting up, she flicked her black skirts down, then frowned at her bound wrists.

Justin grabbed her, hauled her to the edge of the bales and hugged her wildly. "Are you all right?"

"Yes. Perfectly." And she was. She thumped his side with her hands. "Here—untie my wrists."

Without meeting her eyes, Justin bent his head to pick at the knots.

Dalziel, as cool as ever, came up. "Here—let me." He had a wicked-looking dagger in his hand.

Justin straightened. Letitia held out her hands and Dalziel expertly sliced through the cords.

She couldn't quite believe she was alive.

Determined to hang onto her composure, she glanced regally around the circle of her rescuers, inclining her head and bestowing a smile on each of them—even Barton. "Thank you, gentlemen. That was . . . quite an experience."

Beyond Dalziel she saw Christian come out of a door.

"Now, if you'll excuse me . . ." She stood, discovered her legs were fully functional. She started to walk along the facade to where Christian had halted, just beyond the door.

Then her Vaux heritage got the better of her; she picked up her skirts and ran.

Straight into his arms.

He opened them as she neared, closed them tightly about

her as she landed against his chest, wrapped her arms around him and hugged him hard.

She closed her eyes, felt the tears leak out.

She was safe. She was where she'd always wanted to be. This time he'd come for her. This time he'd saved her.

Christian knew beyond doubt what she was thinking. He buried his face in her hair, breathed in her scent—that elusive, unforgettable scent of jasmine—murmured, "I'm here," in her ear.

She hugged him harder.

For one moment they simply stood, wrapped in each other, and let the past go, let it fade. Knew they stood on the cusp of their future—the future they'd dreamed of so long ago.

Eventually she drew back. Looked up into his eyes. Smiled one of her seductive smiles. "I've already thanked the others. I'll have to thank you appropriately . . . but later."

He smiled back. "Later." Releasing her, he took her hand. "Now"—expression hardening, he looked up as Dalziel and the others neared—"we have to deal with the aftermath of Swithin's Grand Plan."

Inside the house, they located Swithin's wife. A pale blonde of good but minor family, she was a mild, gentle, quiet female; with his extensive experience in dealing with such ladies, Tristan took on the task of explaining what had occurred without reducing the poor woman to hysterics. Letitia sat beside Mrs. Swithin, lending wordless support, but wisely leaving the talking to Tristan.

Tony meanwhile organized butler and footmen to fetch Swithin, not dead but wounded, and definitely incapacitated, from the roof. Barton assisted; he no longer had his eye on Justin, but on Swithin.

Swithin wasn't unconscious. He babbled incessantly, the pain and shock of his wounds having unhinged what little rationality he'd possessed.

When he was carried, still babbling, into the drawing room, Christian, who had more experience of gunshot wounds than the others, took one look at his injuries and ordered the butler to summon a doctor, then examined the wounds more closely. The bullet lodged in Swithin's right shoulder he attributed to Justin; at twenty-six and unbloodied in war, he still possessed the naïveté to shoot to incapacitate rather than kill. The other bullet—just a fraction too high to put an end to Swithin's life—would have come from Dalziel, a man far too experienced to court the slightest risk.

As it transpired, they were all soon sorry Dalziel's bullet hadn't found its mark; it would have saved everyone a great deal of bother, and freed Swithin from a life of misery as well.

Luckily, Mrs. Swithin proved to have rather more backbone and nous than her meek demeanor had suggested. She accepted the tale of her husband's villainy without protest or argument. "He's always been quiet and strangely secretive for as long as I've known him, but over the last weeks he's been acting *most* peculiarly."

Swithin's continued bleating in the background, fragments of sentences jumbling together in an incomprehensible ramble, verified that he'd deteriorated even further.

Tristan exchanged a look with Christian and Dalziel, then turned back to Mrs. Swithin and gently suggested, "Given the circumstances, it might be best for everyone concerned if we apply to have Swithin certified."

Mrs. Swithin frowned. "What circumstances, and what would having him certified entail?"

Christian listed the number of people who would be harmed if Swithin and his secrets were put on public show via a sensational murder trial. Mrs. Swithin herself was at the top of the list; she nodded her understanding as he added Trowbridge, Honeywell, the elder Trowbridges, Letitia, Justin, the Earl of Nunchance, and the Vaux family in general.

When he fell silent, she stated, "There's surely no need for all of us to suffer more."

"No." Tristan looked at Barton, who was frowning. "And if we manage it carefully, no one but the authorities needs to know the full story."

Barton brightened considerably; he hadn't wanted to end with no quarry to show his superiors.

"If everyone agrees?" Tristan looked around. Most nodded. No one protested. He looked at the butler, who had returned after sending for the doctor. "Who's the nearest magistrate?"

As it turned out, Tristan, a magistrate himself in the neighboring area, knew Lord Keating well. His lordship arrived promptly; shown into the drawing room where they'd all remained, he was at first shocked by the bare bones of the story Tristan related, but then quickly got down to business.

Settling in a chair with a traveling writing desk balanced on his knees, his lordship decreed, "I'll want statements— perhaps from the representative of Bow Street first, and then you, Trentham"—he inclined his head to Tristan— "and perhaps one of you others?" He cast a vague glance at Tony, Christian, and Dalziel, then beckoned Barton forward. "Now, then."

Under cover of Barton explaining what he knew, Tony glanced at Christian and Dalziel, and grinned. "One of you outranks me, and I suspect the other does, too. It should be one of you two."

So saying, he wandered off to join Justin, who was sitting beside Swithin, listening, curiously intent, to his ramblings.

Christian glanced at Dalziel. He'd always wondered . . .

Dalziel's lips lifted slightly. "No, I don't outrank you. We could toss a coin, but all things considered, I suspect it had better be you Keating speaks with."

Christian raised his brows but nodded. "All right."

Dalziel drifted away to settle in a chair by the windows, attempting to be as inconspicuous as possible. Not an easy task, especially as Lord Keating, regardless of that earlier vague look, was very aware of his presence.

Letitia noted the exchange between Dalziel and Christian. While Tristan, and then Christian, gave their version of the affair and answered Keating's questions, riveting the attention of most in the room, she patted Mrs. Swithin's hand, rose, and glided to the windows. She sank into the chair alongside the one Dalziel occupied.

He acknowledged her presence with a sound suspiciously like a grunt. "At least," he said, his gaze fixed across the room, "I now know why you married that upstart. I never could understand it—I'd always regarded you as one of the saner of our females. Nice to know my judgment wasn't at fault."

Letitia smiled, not the least offended. That was a typical enough comment from him.

They chatted—bantered—for some minutes, about the likely reaction of the ton once they learned it was Swithin who'd killed Randall, not Justin.

"He'll have to be extra careful." She considered her brother, still listening, a frown on his face, to Swithin's all but continual blather. "He'll not only be eligible again, he'll be famous to boot."

"I don't think you need to worry about him," Dalziel dryly replied. "Not unless the matchmaking mamas and their charges have taken to hunting in libraries. He's barely stirred from mine except in pursuit of our investigation."

Letitia smiled fondly. After a moment she more quietly said, "Speaking of hiding, your time for hiding—for being in exile, as it were—will soon be at an end."

She glanced at Royce, but he didn't meet her gaze; his remained fixed broodingly on the tableau before them, although she would have sworn it wasn't Christian and the others he was seeing.

A long moment ticked past, then he softly sighed. "If you want to know the truth, I'm not sure it will ever end."

"It will. It must. You are, after all, his only son."

"That, if you'll recall"—Dalziel straightened in his seat—"didn't stop him before."

There was no answer to that. Letitia looked across the

room and saw that Lord Keating had shifted to sit beside Swithin. He attempted to question Swithin, raising his voice to cut through the constant babbling.

Swithin paused. For a moment it seemed he might respond rationally, but then his gaze found Letitia and he grinned. "I even helped Randall organize his bride. Now *that* was plotting to a high degree. And then there was . . ." He went off on another, unconnected subject.

Justin, sitting close on his other side, had paled. He leaned closer, tried to catch Swithin's eye. "How did you help Randall organize his bride?"

Swithin's silly grin grew broader. "Investments are my forte, you know. The old man . . ." His voice trailed off, then he said loudly, "The grammar master was always unfair, you know. He liked Randall and Trowbridge better than me."

From that, he switched to buying a house. His mind seemed unable to remain on one subject for more than two short sentences.

Lord Keating sat back, defeated. After a moment Justin did the same. Then he looked across the room and met Letitia's eyes.

Justin rose. Leaving Lord Keating consulting with Tristan, Christian, and Mrs. Swithin, he came to stand beside Letitia's chair; he pretended to look out at the garden.

"So it was as I suspected," he murmured. "It wasn't Papa's fault."

"Apparently not." Her marriage to Randall no longer held any power to disturb her; it was all in the past—a past that no longer mattered.

Lord Keating cleared his throat portentiously. "Very well—it seems we're all agreed. Given the circumstances, and the testimonies I've received today, I cannot but conclude that Mr. Henry Joshua Swithin, for reasons of his own advancement, killed Mr. George Martin Randall of South Audley Street in London, and this morning attempted to kill a Mr. Trowbridge of Cheyne Walk in Chelsea, then later today attempted to kill Lady Letitia Randall, also of London, by flinging her, bound, from the roof of this house."

His lordship glanced around. "It is my judgment that Mr. Swithin is incapable of standing trial by virtue of his transparent insanity. I therefore order that he be confined within this house for the foreseeable future." He turned to Mrs. Swithin. "My dear lady, I realize this is an onerous burden to place on your fair shoulders, but I must ask for a declaration that you are prepared to ensure that your husband never leaves these premises."

Mrs. Swithin nodded decisively. "Yes. The staff and I are prepared to give our assurance that Mr. Swithin will remain confined within doors."

"Thank you." Lord Keating turned to Tristan. "That's all we can do, I believe."

"Indeed." Tristan stood, holding out his hand to assist his lordship to his feet. "The last duty I believe we need to attend to is to compose a report for the authorities, to be conveyed back to London by Barton here." Gathering the grateful runner with a look, Tristan turned his lordship to the door. "I assume there must be a study here somewhere?"

"Indeed." Mrs. Swithin waved at her butler. "Please show their lordships to the master's study, Pascoe."

"Of course, ma'am."

While the butler led Tristan, Keating, and Barton out, Mrs. Swithin looked, somewhat uncertainly, around at the company. "I realize this is a trifle awkward, but I do think tea would be appropriate before you all start your journeys back to London."

They all exchanged glances. It had been a long day.

"Thank you." With a bow, Christian accepted for them all. "Tea would be much appreciated."

They set out in their curricles an hour later.

Dalziel gave up his seat in Christian's curricle to Letitia, handing her up with a bow.

She looked down her nose at him, but her lips quirked.

Christian flourished his whip and they set off.

Dalziel walked back to where Justin waited in his curricle, the reins of his restive blacks in his hands. Tristan and Tony had already set off. Swinging up to the seat beside Justin, Dalziel nodded ahead. "Home, James, and don't spare your horses."

Justin laughed and flicked his whip.

Barton, hanging on behind, mumbled, "Just as long as you don't drive as fast as you did coming down."

"I promise not to lose you," Justin called back. "Aside from all else, you hold my freedom in your hands—I'm counting on you to explain all to your masters in Bow Street."

"Aye, I will. They'll be pleased to close the case."

"Indeed, they should be." Sitting back, arms crossed, Dalziel's gaze was fixed on the road ahead. "It occurs to me that you should receive a commendation—not least for saving your masters the unfortunate embarrassment of wrongfully arresting the future head of one of the oldest aristocratic houses. Just think how unpopular that would have made them."

"That's undoubtedly true," Justin chimed in. "You really should work on how to present this result in the best possible light, Barton—so it reflects most favorably on you."

After a moment's hesitation, Barton asked, "So how should I do that?"

Justin grinned, and with helpful advice from Dalziel, proceeded to tutor the runner in how best to gild his triumph.

All three quite enjoyed their journey back to town.

Chapter 21

Twilight had taken hold by the time Christian drew his horses to a halt outside the house in South Audley Street. Every window was ablaze. Leaving his curricle in the care of an urchin—the horses were too tired to be difficult—he escorted Letitia up the steps and into the house.

Into chaos of a different sort to that earlier in the day.

Hermione spotted them first. With a shriek she flew across the parlor to wildly hug Letitia.

The assembled ladies—many having left, then returned despite the hour—surged in her wake; they enfolded Letitia in a welcome full of exclamations and relief.

They embraced him as if he were a conquering hero.

"An excellent outcome all around." Amarantha stretched up to kiss his cheek. "Thank you for bringing her back to us, dear."

"And in such spirits." Constance bussed his other cheek. "Although," she said, drawing back, "I do wonder why that is."

She and Amarantha fixed him with identical inquiring looks—in response to which he merely smiled.

He knew better than to even hint of what was in the wind in such company; the faintest suggestion that he and Letitia might be planning a wedding would be all over the ton before midnight.

Agnes eventually won through to his side. "You did very

well, Dearne." She looked at Letitia, surrounded on all sides by the females of her family. "It's been a long time since I've seen dear Letitia so . . . animated." She cocked a brow at him. "I do hope you won't disappoint us."

He looked into Agnes's eyes, realized that in her he now had a firm supporter. "Actually . . ." He took her arm; after a quick glance over the sea of heads, he steered her toward the front hall. "Along those lines, there is something you might help me with."

He quickly outlined what he proposed. Agnes was delighted. They found Mellon and gave the necessary orders, then, sharing pleased, conspiratorial smiles, they returned to the fray in the parlor.

Two minutes later Justin walked in. The ladies fell on him—the future head of their house—with unbounded enthusiasm.

Standing to one side, Christian smiled as he watched Justin play to his appreciative audience. He told his tale with verve and flair; there was no doubt he was a Vaux.

Letitia appeared beside Christian, sliding her arm into his. "Never before have I been so glad to be upstaged by my little brother." But she was smiling fondly as she surveyed the crowd, now all hanging on Justin's every word.

"Not so little, these days."

"No, indeed. He'll have to take care to avoid the matchmakers' snares now he's become so famous."

Christian glanced at her. "So Dalziel's a marquess."

Her lips curved. "He let that slip, did he?"

"In a manner of speaking." He waited a moment, then asked, "Is it a courtesy title, or. . . ?"

Her smile grew. "Now that would be telling." Turning to him, she laughed. "You're just going to have to wait, like the others. Trust me—you'll learn the truth soon enough."

He would prefer to learn it sooner, but . . . looking into her eyes, he set the mystery of Dalziel aside. There was something much more important he had to say. "I meant what I said on the roof."

She searched his eyes. Her gaze remained steady as she arched her brows. "So did I."

His chest suddenly felt unaccountably tight. "So . . . when can we marry?"

Her brows rose higher; her expression, her eyes, told him she was considering. "I'm honestly not sure of the possibilities in our particular case. As it now seems clear Randall contrived the reason that forced me to marry him—a fact guaranteed to set the ton's social arbiters firmly against him, and therefore in our camp—even if I only whisper the truth into a few select ears, those of ladies I can trust not to spread the details but only their conclusions . . . once I have their backing, I doubt we'll need to wait out the year. Not even six months."

"Good. How about next week?"

Her lips twitched. "Hmm. Well, that's certainly a goal to aim for, but it might be a trifle ambitious." She met his eyes, love glowing in hers. "Let's say the week after. A quiet wedding at Nunchance."

He looked at her, looked beyond her, and laughed.

She frowned. "What?"

He smiled down at her, then, ignoring the eyes that had strayed their way, bent his head and kissed her. Still grinning, he drew back and met her eyes. "A quiet Vaux wedding? That would have to be the archetypal contradiction in terms."

To Letitia's surprise, when she finally closed the door on the last of her female relatives, neither Agnes nor Hermione were anywhere in sight.

Puzzled, she glanced up the stairs. "Are we having dinner, or have they gone up to change?"

"Both, in a way." Christian took the shawl Mellon had fetched and draped it over her shoulders. "We are having dinner, but not here."

"Oh?" Settling the shawl, she faced him. "Where, then?"

At Allardyce House was the answer, not that he told her. If she could keep Dalziel's secret, he could keep one of his own. He put her in his curricle and drove the short distance to Grosvenor Square, where one of his grooms was waiting to lead the tired horses to the mews.

Handing Letitia down, ignoring her quizzical look, he led her up the steps to the front door. It swung open just before they reached it. Percival stood beaming in the doorway.

"Welcome, my lady." He bowed low—too low for an earl's daughter, but just right for a marchioness.

Letitia, always alive to social nuance, sent Christian a look, but smiled graciously on Percival and greeted him with her customary collected air.

As Christian led her on, she leaned close and whispered, "What have you done?"

He smiled. "I haven't said anything, I swear."

It was simply that Percival and the rest of his staff could read between his lines.

He led her into the drawing room where Agnes and Hermione were waiting. After he'd answered several questions for Agnes over his mother's collection of Sevres figurines, they adjourned to the dining room, where his staff outdid themselves in presenting an elegant but cozy family meal.

Christian sat at the head of the table, with Letitia on his right and Agnes and Hermione on his left, and couldn't stop smiling. This was what his house needed—females, and family.

In stylish comfort they ambled through courses while Letitia filled in all sorts of feminine details for her aunt and sister, then she turned to interrogate him on his meeting with Roscoe, showing equal interest in Roscoe's decor and style as in the words exchanged. Nevertheless . . .

"So he's still definite about wanting to buy the company?"

He nodded. "He insisted I present him as Randall's chosen buyer in exchange for his information."

"Well"—she waved the spoon she was using to demolish

a delicate *crème anglaise*—"as it seems I can't visit him in Dolphin Square, he'll have to come to me. I'm sure Mrs. Swithin and Trowbridge will be only too happy to sell, so there's no reason we can't settle the business of the Orient Trading Company as soon as may be."

When she turned limpid eyes on him, Christian inwardly sighed. "I'll contact him and make arrangements for him to call on you—perhaps here might be best. Late at night."

She waved. "Whatever you think best."

Just as long as she had her way and divested herself of her share in the company. As he strongly suspected she would want to do so before any wedding, he nodded. "I'll send a message to Roscoe in the morning."

Eventually, replete and happy, they returned to the drawing room. Noticing the piano in one corner, Hermione sat herself before it. "I haven't been practicing much of late. I suppose I should if I'm to make my come-out next year." She proceeded to entertain them with a sonata.

Relaxed on the sofa beside Letitia, Christian smiled all the more. This was how his evenings would henceforth be, with Agnes sitting by the hearth, he and Letitia comfortably ensconced, and music floating through the room. Simple family pleasures, something he'd known and taken for granted as a child and youth, but had missed throughout his adult life.

With Letitia, he would have those family pleasures again.

With her, he would have the life he'd always dreamed of.

An hour later, after the tea trolley had come and gone, Agnes rose, collected a sleepily content Hermione, then bade Letitia and Christian a good-night.

Letitia smiled and nodded, then realized where they were. "Oh. I'll—"

"No need to disturb yourself." A gleam of mischief in her old eyes, Agnes gathered her shawl. "We're staying here. Dearne and I thought it more appropriate—no need to live in that man's house any longer. We know our way upstairs."

She fluttered her fingers at them as she turned to the door. "We'll see you in the morning, my dears."

Letitia stared after her, and at Hermione, who, with a smug smile and a wave, followed Agnes out of the door. "They're staying here," she repeated. Turning, she stared at Christian.

He smiled, even more smugly content than Hermione. "Your Esme is upstairs—I gather she's been furiously busy hanging all your gowns in the marchioness's apartments. I suggested, however, that she needn't wait up for you tonight."

He studied her eyes, then leaned closer, gently framed her face with one hand. Lowered his head and brushed her lips with his. "Welcome to my house. Welcome to my home. I hope you'll make it yours."

Tears—tears of a happiness she'd never thought to feel—filled her eyes. The same emotion swelled in her chest, filled her heart to overflowing. She raised her hand and laid it over his, felt the gentle strength, savored it. "Nothing would make me happier, my lord."

He smiled, slowly, the gray of his eyes peaceful and calm, then he kissed her again—a longer kiss, one that stirred the flames between them to life.

When he eventually drew back, they were both breathing more rapidly. "Let's go upstairs."

She rose as he did. "Indeed. No need to shock Percival. At least not yet."

Christian glanced at her as he led her to the door. "Actually, quite aside from any shock, I suspect he'd be thrilled. He and the rest of the staff have been waiting for over a decade to serve you, you know."

But they did go up the wide stairs, to the marquess's suite, to his bedroom. To his bed.

There, under the soft radiance of a waxing moon, they celebrated all they now had, all they'd reclaimed. All the heat and passion—all the life.

All the indefinable gifts love had to offer, even love itself they claimed anew.

With hands, lips, mouths, with every inch of their bodies, every particle of their souls.

In harmony, attuned, they scaled the peak; gasping, clinging, they loved wildly and let go, celebrating the beginning of a new life, celebrating the fact they were both still alive, that with the past behind them, buried and gone, they would, now, at last, have a chance to live their dreams of long ago.

Love drove them, racked them, enfolded them in its grace.

When, at the last, as they lay slumped, long limbs tangled in the jumbled billows of his bed, the warmth of satiation heavy in their veins, their hearts slowly slowing, as their new reality closed around them Christian shifted his head and pressed a kiss to her temple. "This is where we were always supposed to be."

Letitia didn't answer, but he felt her lips curve against his chest.

Felt her fingers gently riffling through his hair.

Smelled her elusive scent, of jasmine heavy in the night, wreath about him.

And knew they'd finally secured their dreams.

"Mr. Roscoe, my lord. My lady."

Letitia rose from the chaise in the smaller drawing room of Allardyce House, Christian beside her. Her gaze fixed on the doorway as Percival stepped back; she would own to considerable curiosity over Neville Roscoe. Quite aside from the fact that she expected to divest herself of the troublesome business of the Orient Trading Company, everything Christian had told her of the mysterious Roscoe had only whetted her appetite.

Four days had passed since Swithin had tried to push her to her death; somewhat to her surprise, her fear-filled memories had all but immediately been overlaid by feelings of relief, and then happiness.

Christian had been responsible for both.

He'd also contacted Roscoe. She in turn had visited the house in Cheyne Walk, to tell Trowbridge and Honeywell all that had transpired, and to get from Trowbridge his written agreement to sell his share of the company if and when she did.

She'd also sent one of Christian's grooms into Surrey with a letter for Mrs. Swithin confirming the business of the Orient Trading Company and the desirability of a sale, and the consequent need for a written agreement. She had received by reply the requested agreement, along with a declaration from Swithin's solicitor, who had, most fortuitously, been in Surrey dealing with Swithin's affairs.

So all was in readiness to effect the sale.

Roscoe appeared; he literally darkened the doorway. With his close-cropped dark hair, dark clothes, and cynical, dark blue eyes, he looked the epitome of a dangerous character. With an inclination of his head, he moved past Percival and approached them; he walked with the same, arrogant, faintly menacing stride Dalziel employed. Not so much an intentional affectation as an expression of what, underneath the sophisticated glamour, they really were.

As he neared, she saw that Roscoe was as tall as Christian, but not quite as large, as heavy, his build more rangy, but in no way less lethal for that.

Christian extended his hand.

Roscoe quirked a brow—apparently at being accorded the courtesy—but gripped and shook nonetheless. "Good evening."

It was after ten o'clock.

Christian inclined his head. "Thank you for coming." He turned to her. "Allow me to present Lady Letitia." He left out the Randall, she was quite sure deliberately.

Letitia gave Roscoe her hand, smiled as she looked into his face . . . and barely felt his fingers close about hers.

Barely heard his proper, "Lady Randall," barely registered the rumble of his deep voice or his perfectly executed bow.

She knew, looking into his eyes, that she'd met him before—long ago, when they'd been in their teens.

She let her smile widen, and sensed his wariness grow. "I believe we've met before, Mr. Roscoe, although I can't at the moment recall where. But then I expect you would rather I didn't recall at all, so perhaps"—retrieving her hand from his suddenly slack grasp, she waved to the armchair opposite the chaise—"we should get down to business before I do."

Roscoe cast Christian a look, then moved to comply.

Still smiling delightedly, Letitia sat and promptly took charge of the negotiations.

Much to Roscoe's disquiet.

Realizing that the threat of her knowledge of his identity, plus the inherent difficulty a man like Roscoe faced in negotiating business with a female of Letitia's class, played heavily into her hands—and that she was supremely well-qualified to capitalize on the fact—Christian sat back and left her to it.

She did well, extracting both a higher price and more favorable payment terms than Roscoe had expected to have to concede; that much was clear from the irritation that briefly shone in his dark eyes.

But he took it well.

When, all the details thrashed out and agreed upon, the written agreements from Trowbridge and Mrs. Swithin tendered and accepted, they all rose and Roscoe shook Letitia's hand, there was a reluctantly admiring glint in his eyes. "I'll have my man of business draw up the contract in conjunction with . . ." Roscoe cocked a brow at Christian. ". . . Montague?"

Christian nodded. "He's under instruction to take over the management of Lady Letitia's affairs."

Roscoe's lips quirked. "Naturally." He looked at Letitia, hesitated, then said, "I understand felicitations are in order." He bowed, inherently graceful. "Please accept mine."

Letitia glowed. "Thank you."

Straightening, Roscoe met her eyes. "And don't try too hard to remember our previous meeting."

She waved airily. "I doubt I'll have time, what with all else that's going on."

"Good." With that dry comment, Roscoe turned to Christian; this time he spontaneously held out his hand. "Dearne."

Christian gripped his hand, entirely content with how the meeting had gone. "Come—I'll walk you out."

Roscoe bowed again to Letitia, then fell into step beside Christian as he headed for the door. While Christian opened it, Roscoe glanced back—at Letitia settling on the chaise to await Christian's return.

Then he turned and went through the door.

As they passed down the corridors and into the front hall, Christian was aware of Roscoe glancing about—not so much taking note as breathing in the ambience. "Do you ever think you'll return to"—he gestured about them—"tonnish life?"

Roscoe didn't immediately reply. When they reached the front door, he turned and faced Christian. "Much as I might envy you the life you now have, I long ago realized it wasn't in the cards for me."

There was a finality in his tone that closed the subject.

Roscoe accepted his cane from Percival, then, when that worthy opened the door, nodded to Christian and went out into the night.

Christian watched him go, saw him disappear into the gloom before Percival shut the door. He stared unseeing at the panels for a minute more, then recalling all that awaited him in the smaller drawing room, he smiled, turned, and strolled back to embrace it.

And her. The love of his life and, God willing, the mother of his children.

Letitia's second marriage was in no way the travesty her first had been. Consequently, their wedding was every bit as massive, noisy, and full of life as Christian had foreseen.

He didn't mind in the least. Looking around the huge ballroom of Nunchance Priory, noting the sheer exuberance that held sway, he gave thanks that he and Letitia had won through to this, that the years and fate hadn't bound them, chained them, to lesser existences.

To an existence apart.

He glanced at her, radiant and so vitally vibrant beside him, her dark hair gleaming, the Allardyce diamonds glittering about her throat and depending from her ears, the simple gold band he'd placed on her finger mere hours ago the only ornament she wore on her slim digits. Her long, slender frame was encased in silk the color of the palest pink rose; the scent of jasmine rose from her alabaster skin.

There was, however, an incipient frown in her eyes, a slight line between her brows.

Before he could ask, she volunteered, "That wretch Dalziel isn't here."

"He's never attended any of our weddings. Didn't the other ladies tell you?"

"They did, but given the timing, his absence today is, in my opinion, taking the whole thing simply too far."

He hesitated, then asked, "What thing?"

She looked at him, then shook her head. "Never mind. You'll learn all about it soon enough—any day, as it happens."

Any day?

Christian knew well enough that he would get no more from her. Jack Warnefleet had confirmed that his wife, Lady Clarice, also knew exactly who Dalziel was. The others, including Jack Hendon, who like the rest of them had become obsessed with learning Dalziel's true identity, had grumbled and admitted they now believed all their wives knew the truth—and none of them would say. Regardless of the persuasion, the interrogation tactics employed.

That they'd worked so closely with the man for the past decade and more yet still didn't know his identity irked. Yet it appeared that all the ladies of the ton had colluded in keeping Dalziel's secret.

"Which is frankly amazing," Tony later remarked, when Christian, having left Letitia chatting with her cousins, joined the other club members. "There are so many inveterate gossips, you'd swear at least *one* would be unable to resist whispering his name, but no. On that one subject, total silence reigns."

The others all grumped, and sipped their wine. They'd gathered just like this at each successive wedding, to toast the man fallen and fix their sights on the next one to go. This time, however, there were no more club members left unwed; consequently their thoughts turned to their ex-commander, who had become an all but formally declared ex-officio member.

But Dalziel wasn't there to prod.

Justin detached himself from the throng, charmingly disengaging from two young ladies who would happily have continued to monopolize his time—and sought refuge with them. Christian cocked a brow at him.

He grimaced. "I'm seriously contemplating becoming a recluse."

Deverell grunted. "Won't do you any good. The more determined will still hunt you down."

Justin didn't look thrilled.

"You know who Dalziel is," Christian murmured. "I don't suppose, given all is now over and done, that you'd like to share the information?"

Justin hesitated.

They all held their breaths.

Then he shook his head. "I can't." He met Christian's gaze. "The punishment is too dire. But anyway, you'll know soon enough."

"Everyone keeps saying that," Jack Warnefleet complained. "'Soon enough.' When is 'soon enough' going to be?"

Justin frowned at him. "Well, obviously, any day now."

"It's not obvious to us," Charles replied, his tone threatening all manner of violence.

Justin looked at him, then at the others. "It *is* obvious. You'll learn who he is when he resigns his commission and returns to civilian life. And by all accounts that's any day now."

That gave them all something to think about. Leaving them to it, Justin slipped away. There was something he needed to do.

He knew the corridors like the back of his hand; avoiding the guests—so many of them female—flitting about, he made his way into the other wing, to the library.

In the wake of Swithin's babbling revelations, Justin had visited Trowbridge, who had confirmed that the huge investment loss incurred by the earl eight years before, leading to Letitia's marriage to Randall, had indeed been arranged by Randall, the scheme itself engineered by Swithin.

There was no proof to be had, or ever likely to be found, yet the simple knowledge had cured the malaise that had for years eaten at Justin's heart.

He entered the library on silent feet. As he'd expected, his father was there, seated in his favorite armchair, a book open on his lap.

The earl had dutifully walked Letitia down the aisle, given her away, then attended the wedding breakfast and made a short speech—surprising everyone by being no more than mildly blunt. Then he'd disappeared.

Justin quietly walked to the chair opposite the earl's. Halting beside it, he looked down on his sire. "It wasn't your fault."

The earl grunted; he didn't look up. "I know. I just couldn't prove it. And you . . . you and Letitia both seemed so ready to believe I'd risk such a lot—your lives, in effect." One long finger marking his place, the earl lifted his gaze, staring across the room. "But I didn't. I never would have."

"No," Justin said. "We know that now."

The earl finally looked up, through shrewd hazel eyes scanned his son's features, then he nodded. "Good."

With that, he returned to his book.

Justin looked down on his sire's white head, then his lips curved in a slow smile.

Surveying the nearby shelves, he crossed to one, pulled out a book, glanced inside it.

Then returning to the armchair opposite his father's, he sat, opened the book on his knee, and started to read.

Back in the ballroom, Letitia swept up to Christian's side where he stood with his fellow Bastion Club members. They were toasting the last man to fall into wedlock—Christian; she linked her arm with his, smiled graciously, and allowed them to toast her as well.

Christian looked down at her. "One point you can clarify—Dalziel, Royce Whoever-he-is, isn't married, is he?"

She looked at him, then at them all, eagerly waiting on her answer; she clearly debated whether that information could be shared, then said, "No. He's not."

"But," Charles put in, "he's the sort of gentleman who has to marry, isn't he? If he's a marquess, then that follows as night follows day."

"So," Tony suggested, "there's really one more wedding to come." He caught Letitia's eye. "Isn't there?"

She returned Tony's gaze; anticipation bloomed, then grew until it gleamed in her eyes. "Yes, indeed." She smiled ecstatically. "He'll have to marry. And quite soon—at least if he wants any peace."

"Once he ends his commission . . . ?" Jack Warnefleet prompted.

She nodded. "Once he goes back to being who he really is, there won't be a matchmaking mama in London, or indeed the country, who won't have him squarely in her sights."

The members of the Bastion Club exchanged a communal glance.

"Now *that*," Tristan said, "is a toast we can make with alacrity."

"Indeed." Charles, their unofficial toastmaster, raised his glass high. "To the end of Dalziel's commission. It can't come too *soon*."

With a cheer, they all raised their glasses high and drank.

"And to Dalziel's bride," Christian added. "Whoever and wherever she might be."

Epilogue

Standing in the center of the study in his elegant town house, Royce dropped the last of the files he'd cleared from his desk into a storage trunk. Chances were he'd never look at them again, but they were, in effect, all that remained as proof of his existence over the past sixteen years.

He stood looking down at the trunk. Felt the full weight of all he'd done, all he'd ordered to be done, over those sixteen years. Knew the price—exacted on so many different levels—he'd paid that it all should be so.

Faced with the same choice, he would pay that price again, regardless.

He'd been barely twenty-two when he'd been approached and asked—all but begged—to take on a very particular commission with His Majesty's Secret Service. Despite his lack of years, there were few others with connections in Europe the equal of his, still fewer with his talents, with his inherent ability to command, along with the zeal to inspire others with similar background and skills, to willingly go into extreme danger, trusting in him to be their anchor, their only contact, their sole lifeline to safety.

Few who could have, as he had done, readily recruited the best, brightest, and most able of a generation of Guards.

Especially when they hadn't, quite, known who he was.

Memories threatened to claim him; abruptly shaking free, he stalked back to his desk. Rounding it, he dropped into the leather-covered chair behind it. Once again his thoughts circled; he would have preferred not to indulge them, yet the hour was, it seemed, one for taking stock.

He'd never lost an agent, not one solely under his command. That, he felt, was his greatest triumph.

His greatest failure was equally easy to define; he'd never succeeded in identifying his "last traitor," a fiend he and his ex-colleagues now knew to be flesh and blood, a man they'd come within a whisker of catching a month ago, but, as always, he'd slipped through their—his—fingers.

Although it went very much against his grain, he'd accepted that he would have to let that failure lie; he'd run out of time.

But as for all the rest—all the years of keeping strictly to himself, a social pariah of his own making, while ruthlessly and relentlessly managing the reins of the agents he'd deployed far and wide across the Continent—he was more than satisfied with what he'd achieved, the contribution he and those men had made to England's safety over the last fraught decade.

They'd been good men all; some—the seven members of the Bastion Club—he would now consider friends. They'd consistently included him in the adventures that had befallen each of them in returning to civilian life.

Now he faced the same prospect, although he seriously doubted there would be any interesting adventure attached.

Fate, in his experience, was rarely that kind.

His resignation from his commission was effective from that day. He'd spent the last weeks tidying up, writing and delivering the inevitable reports to various ministers and government functionaries.

Many had requested a briefing, seeking to remind him that they existed, to establish a connection with his alter ego—his real self. He'd viewed such requests with due cynicism, but in the main hadn't denied them, knowing he'd have to make the transition to his other self sooner rather than later.

That as of today, the individual known as Dalziel had ceased to exist.

He snorted softly. Steepling his fingers, he set them before his face. Relaxed in the chair, he stared across the room. And consciously tried to bring his other self to mind. To life.

But sixteen years was a long time.

And a name changed nothing of what a man truly was.

Distantly, beyond the solid walls, he heard a horse clatter up and come to a stamping halt in the street outside; although his mind recognized and identified the sound, sunk in a survey of the past he didn't register its import.

The front door knocker was another matter; plied with considerable force, it jerked him from recollections—some painful—of his distant past.

Hauled from his reverie, he focused on the door. Ears straining, he heard his butler, Hamilton, cross the front hall. An instant later, muffled by doors and walls, came the sound of men's voices—Hamilton's and one other's. Presumably the rider's.

The cadence of the unknown rider's accent unexpectedly kicked premonition to life.

Had his heart pumping just a tad faster, had him steeling himself against what was coming.

His mind raced, imagining what the message might be, what latest hurdle was to be erected in his path.

What else his father might think to throw at him.

He was waiting, tense inside but outwardly at ease, his hands, long fingers relaxed, draped over the end of each chair arm, when Hamilton approached the study door, knocked briefly, and entered.

Royce's gaze went to his butler's hands, expecting to see his silver salver with a missive lying upon it.

But Hamilton's hands were empty.

Raising his gaze to Hamilton's face, Royce read his expression with the barest glance.

Felt like he'd been kicked in the chest.

His features grave, Hamilton bowed—lower than usual. "Your grace. A rider has arrived from Wolverstone."

No further explanation was necessary; the title said it all.

It could only be his if . . .

Somehow he gathered enough wit to speak. "Thank you, Hamilton. Please see to the comfort of whoever it is. I'll speak with him shortly."

Once he'd absorbed the latest blow.

Once he had the rage roaring through him contained.

Hamilton bowed. "Indeed, your grace." He silently withdrew.

Leaving Royce to face a prospect he hadn't, despite all his experience of dicing with fate, ever contemplated.

His father had been a constant in his life—over the last decade a constant foe. One to whom he'd owed filial obedience, but filial obedience had stretched only so far.

Paternal command hadn't stopped him from serving his country in the way his country had needed, in the way he was so uniquely qualified to do.

Paternal denunciation—one step short of outright disinheritance, but socially even more damning—had seen him adopt a name from a distant branch of his mother's family tree.

His father had drawn his line short of disinheritance purely because he'd had only one son.

So he'd had to make do with Royce, a son who openly chose to live by his own creed, by an interpretation of loyalty, honor, courage, and service to his country that was significantly different from that of the generation of noblemen to which his father belonged.

Had belonged.

It was from his mother's family he'd inherited that finer,

more selfless creed; they'd always been warriors. His father's family had been the money-makers, the power brokers, the kingmakers; serving their country had, for them, had a different meaning.

Brought up beneath his father's heavy hand, but with his mother, strong and vibrant, an equal influence, he'd always been aware of the distinction.

When his father had learned of the exact nature of his commission, he'd been forced to choose between his father's creed or that other. Forced to make a choice between his father's approval and his country.

He'd chosen, and his father had made his stand—in the main room of White's, of all places. Carefully chosen to be a bastion of his generation, a perfect setting to support him in bringing his errant son to heel.

Only the encounter hadn't gone as his father had expected.

He'd never expected Royce to take all his fury, then, with a face carved from stone, simply turn and walk out.

Out of society, out of his father's life.

His reentry into both had been imminent for the last month. He'd been putting off the moment, finding reasons to delay resigning his commission, which, while overdue, his superiors had been in no hurry to receive.

He'd chosen the Monday after Christian Allardyce's wedding as the first day of his return to his past life, the first day of becoming once again the Marquess of Winchelsea, the courtesy title bestowed upon the first son and heir of the Duke of Wolverstone.

It had seemed appropriate to choose the first weekday after the last of his seven ex-colleagues of the Bastion Club had wed. He'd assumed he would drive north, walk into his father's presence and see what came next.

Instead . . .

There wasn't going to be any "next." No reconciliation, no understanding.

Certainly no apology.

Given the events of the past decade, let alone the commendations, royal and otherwise, he and his men had earned, even his father would have been hard-pressed to deny him the latter.

Except he, and fate, had, in the one way Royce had no power to control.

Staring across his study, he all but snarled as, fingers now locked white about the chair's arms, he sat up. *"Damn you!"*

Whether he was addressing fate or his dead father wasn't entirely clear.

"It wasn't supposed to be like this." Biting off the words, he surged to his feet. Swinging around, he stalked to the wall and tugged the bellpull.

When Hamilton appeared, he delivered his orders in a crisp, even tone, one that brooked no question, much less invited any. "Have my curricle brought around—I'll want the blacks. Tell Henry I won't need him with me—he's to follow with the luggage." Henry was his personal groom who'd followed him from Wolverstone, disregarding his father's edict against anyone in his households giving his errant son succor.

"Tell Trevor to pack everything and travel up to Wolverstone with Henry as soon as he can. For now, all I'll need is a small bag—he'll know what to pack." Trevor was his valet—another hangover from his father's days, but one he'd never had the heart to dismiss. And Trevor was useful in more ways than the purely sartorial. With both Henry and Trevor behind the scenes, he'd be well placed to handle whatever waited for him at Wolverstone.

He hadn't set foot on the property—on any of his father's diverse and numerous holdings—since that scene in White's sixteen years ago; he had absolutely no idea who was managing what, or if they were competent. While he could have asked any number of people for information—which they would have given him, conflict of interest or not—he'd been too nice, and too proud, to drag others into the firing line between himself and his father.

"Tell Handley when he comes in that I'll need him at Wolverstone, too. As soon as he can arrange it." Handley was his amanuensis, another he could rely on to see his orders carried out to the letter.

"And I suppose I'd better check that someone has remembered to notify Collier, Collier and Whiticombe." His father's solicitors. "I'll write a letter before I go, and there'll be another I'll want delivered to Montague in the city."

"Yes, my l—" Hamilton caught himself. "Your grace."

Royce's lips twisted. "Indeed. We're both going to have to get used to that."

Mentally reviewing his preparations, he could think of only one thing he'd missed. "And if anyone calls, you may tell them I've gone north, and that I have no notion of when I'll be back."

The Last Volume of the Bastion Club Novels

brings the unresolved mysteries to a close. This volume tells of Royce, now Duke of Wolverstone, and his return to his ancestral home, now his principal seat. In taking up the reins of his real life, he unexpectedly discovers the lady he cannot live without, then even more unexpectedly discovers that, while he is willing to resign his quest to unmask the last traitor, the last traitor is not of a mind to let him—and his—be.

FALL 2009

in the meantime . . .

Stephanie Laurens's Cynster Novels

continue with

Where the Heart Leads

JANUARY 2009

Following is an excerpt from *Where the Heart Leads*, which is the story of Barnaby Adair and the lady who captures his interest, his attention, and ultimately his heart.

THE NEXT CYNSTER NOVEL,

Temptation and Surrender

WILL BE RELEASED
FEBRUARY 2009

November 1835
London

"𝕿hank you, Mostyn." Slumped at ease in an armchair before the fire in the parlor of his fashionable lodgings in Jermyn Street, Barnaby Adair, third son of the Earl of Cothelstone, lifted the crystal tumbler from the salver his man offered. "I won't need anything further."

"Very good, sir. I'll wish you a good night." The epitome of his calling, Mostyn bowed and silently withdrew.

Straining his ears, Barnaby heard the door shut. He smiled, sipped. Mostyn had been foisted on him by his mother when he'd first come up to town in the fond hope that the man would instil some degree of tractability into a son who, as she frequently declared, was ungovernable. Yet despite Mostyn's rigid adherence to the mores of class distinction and his belief in the deference due to the son of an earl, master and man had quickly reached an accommodation. Barnaby could no longer imagine being in London without the succor Mostyn provided, largely, as with the glass of fine brandy in his hand, without prompting.

Over the years, Mostyn had mellowed. Or perhaps both of them had. Regardless, theirs was now a very comfortable household.

Stretching his long legs toward the hearth, crossing his ankles, sinking his chin on his cravat, Barnaby studied the polished toes of his boots, bathed in the light of the crackling flames. All *should* have been well in his world, but. . . .

He was comfortable yet . . . restless.

At peace—no, *wrapped* in blessed peace—yet dissatisfied.

It wasn't as if the last months hadn't been successful. After more than nine months of careful sleuthing he'd exposed a cadre of young gentlemen, all from ton families, who, not content with using dens of inquity had thought it a lark to run them. He'd delivered enough proof to charge and convict them despite their station. It had been a difficult, long-drawn and arduous case; its successful conclusion had earned him grateful accolades from the peers who oversaw London's Metropolitan Police Force.

On hearing the news his mother would no doubt have primmed her lips, perhaps evinced an acid wish that he would develop as much interest in fox-hunting as in villain-hunting, but she wouldn't—couldn't—say more, not with his father being one of the aforementioned peers.

In any modern society, justice needed to be seen to be served even-handedly, without fear or favor, despite those among the ton who refused to believe that Parliament's laws applied to them. The Prime Minister himself had been moved to compliment him over this latest triumph.

Raising his glass, Barnaby sipped. The success had been sweet, yet had left him strangely hollow. Unfulfilled in some unexpected way. Certainly he'd anticipated feeling happier, rather than empty and peculiarly rudderless, aimlessly drifting now he no longer had a case to absorb him, to challenge his ingenuity and fill his time.

Perhaps his mood was simply a reflection of the season—the closing phases of another year, the time when cold fogs descended and polite society fled to the warmth of ancestral hearths, there to prepare for the coming festive season and the attendant revels. For him this time of year had always been difficult—difficult to find any viable excuse to avoid his mother's artfully engineered social gatherings.

She'd married both his elder brothers and his sister, Melissa, far too easily; in him, she'd met her Waterloo, yet she continued more doggedly and indefatigably than Napoleon. She was determined to see him, the last of her brood, suitably wed, and was fully prepared to bring to bear whatever weapons were necessary to achieve that goal.

Despite being at loose ends, he didn't want to deliver himself up at the Cothelstone Castle gates, a candidate for his mother's matrimonial machinations. What if it snowed and he couldn't escape?

Unfortunately, even villains tended to hibernate over winter.

A sharp *rat-a-tat-tat* shattered the comfortable silence.

Glancing at the parlor door, Barnaby realized he'd heard a carriage on the cobbles. The rattle of wheels had ceased outside his residence. He listened as Mostyn's measured tread passed the parlor on the way to the front door. Who could be calling at such an hour—a quick glance at the mantelpiece clock confirmed it was after eleven—and on such a night? Beyond the heavily curtained windows the night was bleak, a dense chill fog wreathing the streets, swallowing houses and converting familiar streetscapes into ghostly gothic realms.

No one would venture out on such a night without good reason.

Voices, muted, reached him. It appeared Mostyn was engaged in dissuading whoever was attempting to disrupt his master's peace.

Abruptly the voices fell silent.

A moment later the door opened and Mostyn entered, carefully closing the door behind him. One glance at Mostyn's tight lips and studiously blank expression informed Barnaby that Mostyn did not approve of whomever had called. Even more interesting was the transparent implication that Mostyn had been routed—efficiently and comprehensively—in his attempt to deny the visitor.

"A . . . lady to see you, sir. A Miss—"

"Penelope Ashford."

The crisp, determined tones had both Barnaby and Mostyn looking to the door—which now stood open, swung wide to admit a lady in a dark, severe yet fashionable pelisse. A sable-lined muff dangled from one wrist and her hands were encased in fur-edged leather gloves.

Lustrous mahogany hair, pulled into a knot at the back of her head, gleamed as she crossed the room with a grace and self-confidence that screamed her station even more than her delicate, quintessentially aristocratic features. Features that were animated by so much determination, so much sheer will, that the force of her personality seemed to roll like a wave before her.

Mostyn stepped back as she neared.

His eyes never leaving her, Barnaby unhurriedly uncrossed his legs and rose. "Miss Ashford."

An exceptional pair of dark brown eyes framed by finely wrought gold-rimmed spectacles fixed on his face. "Mr. Adair. We met nearly two years ago, at Morwellan Park in the ballroom at Charlie and Sarah's wedding." Halting two paces away, she studied him, as if estimating the quality of his memory. "We spoke briefly if you recall."

She didn't offer her hand. Barnaby looked down into her uptilted face—her head barely cleared his shoulder—and found he remembered her surprisingly well. "You asked if I was the one who investigates crimes."

She smiled—brilliantly. "Yes. That's right."

Barnaby blinked; he felt a trifle winded. He could, he realized, recall how, all those months ago, her small fingers had felt in his. They'd merely shaken hands, yet he could remember it perfectly; even now, his fingers tingled with tactile memory.

She'd obviously made an impression on him even if he hadn't been so aware of it at the time. At the time he'd been focused on another case, and had been more intent on deflecting her interest than on her.

Since he'd last seen her, she'd grown. Not taller. Indeed,

he wasn't sure she'd gained inches anywhere; she was as neatly rounded as his memory painted her. Yet she'd gained in stature, in self-assurance and confidence; although he doubted she'd ever been lacking in the latter, she was now the sort of lady any fool would recognize as a natural force of nature, to be crossed at one's peril.

Little wonder she'd rolled up Mostyn.

Her smile had faded. She'd been examining him openly; in most others he would have termed it brazenly, but she seemed to be evaluating him intellectually rather than physically.

Rosy lips, distractingly lush, firmed, as if she'd made some decision.

Curious, he tilted his head. "To what do I owe this visit?"

This highly irregular, not to say potentially scandalous visit. She was a gently bred lady of marriageable age, calling on a single gentleman who was in no way related very late at night. Alone. Entirely unchaperoned.

He should protest and send her away. Mostyn certainly thought so.

Her fine dark eyes met his. Squarely, without the slightest hint of guile or trepidation. "I want you to help me solve a crime."

He held her gaze.

She returned the favor.

A pregnant moment passed, then he gestured elegantly to the other armchair. "Please sit. Perhaps you'd like some refreshment?"

Her smile—it transformed her face from vividly attractive to stunning—flashed as she moved to the chair facing his. "Thank you, but no. I require nothing but your time." She waved Mostyn away. "You may go."

Mostyn stiffened. He cast an outraged glance at Barnaby.

Battling a grin, Barnaby endorsed the order with a nod. Mostyn didn't like it, but departed, bowing himself out, but leaving the door ajar. Barnaby noted it, but said nothing. Mostyn knew he was hunted, often quite inventively, by young ladies; he clearly believed Miss Ashford might be such a schemer. Barnaby knew better. Penelope Ashford might scheme with the best of them, but marriage would not be her goal.

While she arranged her muff on her lap, he sank back into his armchair and studied her anew.

She was the most unusual young lady he'd ever encountered.

He'd decided that even before she said, "Mr. Adair, I need your help to find four missing boys, and stop any more being kidnapped."

Penelope raised her eyes and locked them on Barnaby Adair's face. And tried her damnedest not to see. When she'd determined to call on him, she hadn't imagined he—his appearance—would have the slightest effect on her. Why would she? No man had ever made her feel breathless, so why should he? It was distinctly annoying.

Golden hair clustering in wavy curls about a well-shaped head, strong, aquiline features and cerulean blue eyes that held a piercing intelligence were doubtless interesting enough, yet quite aside from his features there was something about him, about his presence, that was playing on her nerves in a disconcerting way.

Why he should affect her at all was a mystery. He was tall, with a long-limbed, rangy build, yet he was no taller than her brother Luc, and while his shoulders were broad, they were no broader than her brother-in-law Simon's. And he was certainly not prettier than either Luc or Simon, although he could easily hold his own in the handsome stakes; she'd heard Barnaby Adair described as an Adonis and had to concede the point.

All of which was entirely by the by and she had no clue why she was even noticing.

She focused instead on the numerous questions she could see forming behind his blue eyes. "The reason I am here, and not a host of outraged parents, is because the boys in question are paupers and foundlings."

He frowned.

Stripping off her gloves, she grimaced lightly. "I'd better start at the beginning."

He nodded. "That would probably facilitate matters—namely my understanding—significantly."

She laid her gloves on top of her muff. She wasn't sure she appreciated his tone, but decided to ignore it. "I don't know if you're aware of it, but my sister Portia—she's now married to Simon Cynster—three other ladies of the ton, and I, established the Foundling House opposite the Foundling Hospital in Bloomsbury. That was back in '30. The House has been in operation ever since, taking in foundlings, mostly from the East End, and training them as maids, footmen, and more recently in various trades."

"You were asking Sarah about her orphanage's training programs when we last met."

"Indeed." She hadn't known he'd overheard that. "My older sister Anne, now Anne Carmarthen, is also involved, but since their marriages, with their own households to run, both Anne and lately Portia have had to curtail the time they spend at the Foundling House. The other three ladies likewise have many calls on their time. Consequently, at present I am in charge of overseeing the day-to-day administration of the place. It's in that capacity that I'm here tonight."

Folding her hands over her gloves, she met his eyes, held his steady gaze. "The normal procedure is for children to be formally placed in the care of the Foundling House by the authorities, or by their last surviving guardian.

"The latter is quite common. What usually occurs is that a dying relative, recognizing that their ward will soon be alone in the world, contacts us and we visit and make arrangements. The child usually stays with their guardian until the last, then, on the guardian's death, we're informed, usually by helpful neighbors, and we return and fetch the orphan and take him or her to the Foundling House."

He nodded, signifying all to that point was clear.

Drawing breath, she went on, feeling her lungs tighten, her diction growing crisp as anger resurged, "Over the last month, on four separate occasions we've arrived to fetch away a boy, only to discover some man has been before us. He told the neighbors he was a local official, but there is no central authority that collects orphans. If there were, we'd know."

Adair's blue gaze had grown razor-sharp. "Is it always the same man?"

"From all I've heard, it could be. But equally, it might not be."

She waited while he mulled over that. She bit her tongue, forced herself to sit still and not fidget, and instead watch the concentration in his face.

Her inclination was to forge ahead, to demand he act and tell him how. She was used to directing, to taking charge and ordering all as she deemed fit. She was usually right in her thinking, and generally people were a great deal better off if they simply did as she said. But . . . she needed Barnaby Adair's help, and instinct was warning her, stridently, to tread carefully. To guide rather than push.

To persuade rather than dictate.

His gaze had grown distant, but now abruptly refocused on her face. "You take boys and girls. Is it only boys who've gone missing?"

"Yes." She nodded for emphasis. "We've accepted more girls than boys in recent months, but it's only boys this man has taken."

A moment passed. "He's taken four—tell me about each. Start from the first—everything you know, every detail, no matter how apparently inconsequential."

Barnaby watched as she delved into her memory; her dark gaze turned inward, her features smoothed, losing some of their characteristic vitality.

She drew breath; her gaze fixed on the fire as if she were reading from the flames. "The first was from Chicksand

Street in Spitalfields, off Brick Lane north of the White-chapel Road. He was eight years old, or so his uncle told us. He, the uncle, was dying, and . . ."

Barnaby listened as she, not entirely to his surprise, did precisely as he'd requested and recited the details of each occurrence, chapter and verse. Other than an occasional minor query, he didn't have to prod her or her memory.

He was accustomed to dealing with ladies of the ton, to interrogating young ladies whose minds skittered and wandered around subjects, and flitted and danced around facts, so that it took the wisdom of Solomon and the patience of Job to gain any understanding of what they actually knew.

Penelope Ashford was a different breed. He'd heard that she was something of a firebrand, one who paid scant attention to social restraints if said restraints stood in her way. He'd heard her described as too intelligent for her own good, and direct and forthright to a fault, that combination of traits being popularly held to account for her unmarried state.

As she was remarkably attractive in an unusual way—not pretty or beautiful but so vividly alive she effortlessly drew men's eyes—as well as being extremely well-connected, the daughter of a viscount, and with her brother Luc, the current title holder, eminently wealthy and able to dower her more than appropriately, that popular judgment might well be correct. Yet her sister Portia had recently married Simon Cynster, and while Portia might perhaps be more subtle in her dealings, Barnaby recalled that the Cynster ladies, judges he trusted in such matters, saw little difference between Portia and Penelope beyond Penelope's directness.

And, if he was remembering aright, her utterly implacable will.

From what little he'd seen of the sisters, he, too, would have said that Portia would bend, or at least agree to negotiate, far earlier than Penelope.

"And just as with the others, when we went to Herb Lane to fetch Dick this morning, he was gone. He'd been collected by this mystery man at seven o'clock, barely after dawn."

Her story concluded, she shifted her dark, compelling eyes from the flames to his face.

Barnaby held her gaze for a moment, then slowly nodded. "So somehow these people—let's assume it's one group collecting these boys—"

"I can't see it being more than one group. We've never had this happen before, and now four instances in less than a month, and all with the same modus operandi." Brows raised, she met his eyes.

Somewhat tersely, he nodded. "Precisely. As I was saying, these people, whoever they are, seem to know of your potential charges—"

"Before you suggest that they might be learning of the boys through someone at the Foundling House, let me assure you that's highly unlikely. If you knew the people involved, you'd understand why I'm so sure of that. And indeed, although I've come to you with our four cases, there's nothing to say other newly orphaned boys in the East End aren't also disappearing. Most orphans aren't brought to our attention. There may be many more vanishing, but who is there who would sound any alarm?"

Barnaby stared at her while the scenario she was describing took shape in his mind.

"I had hoped," she said, the light glinting off her spectacles as she glanced down and smoothed her gloves, "that you might agree to look into this latest disappearance, seeing as Dick was whisked away only this morning. I do realize that you generally investigate crimes involving the ton, but I wondered, as it is November and most of us have upped stakes for the country, whether you might have time to consider our problem." Looking up, she met his gaze; there was nothing remotely diffident in her eyes. "I could, of course, pursue the matter myself—"

Barnaby only just stopped himself from reacting.

"But I thought enlisting someone with more experience in such matters might lead to a more rapid resolution."

Penelope held his gaze and hoped he was as quick-witted as he was purported to be. Then again, in her experience, it rarely hurt to be blunt. "To be perfectly clear, Mr. Adair, I am here seeking aid in pursuing our lost charges, rather than merely wishing to inform someone of their disappearance and thereafter wash my hands of them. I fully intend to search for Dick and the other three boys until I find them. Not being a simpleton, I would prefer to have beside me someone with experience of crime and the necessary investigative methods. Moreover, while through our work we naturally have contacts in the East End, few if any of those move among the criminal elements, so my ability to gain information in that arena is limited."

Halting, she searched his face. His expression gave little away; his broad brow, straight brown brows, the strong, well-delineated cheekbones, the rather austere lines of cheek and jaw, remained set and unrevealing.

She spread her hands. "I've described our situation—will you help us?"

To her irritation, he didn't immediately reply. Didn't leap in, goaded to action by the notion of her tramping through the East End by herself.

He didn't, however, refuse. For a long moment, he studied her, his expression unreadable—long enough for her to wonder if he'd seen through her ploy—then he shifted, resettling his shoulders against the chair, and gestured to her in invitation. "How do you imagine our investigation would proceed?"

She hid her smile. "I thought, if you were free, you might visit the Foundling House tomorrow, to get some idea of the way we work and the type of children we take in. Then . . ."

Barnaby listened while she outlined an eminently rational strategy that would expose him to the basic facts, enough to ascertain where an investigation might lead, and consequently how best to proceed.

Watching the sensible, logical words fall from her ruby lips—still lush and ripe, still distracting—only confirmed that Penelope Ashford was dangerous. Every bit as dangerous as her reputation suggested, possibly more.

In his case undoubtedly more, given his fascination with her lips.

In addition, she was offering him something no other young lady had ever thought to wave before his nose.

A case. Just when he was in dire need of one.

"Once we've talked to the neighbors who saw Dick taken away, I'm hoping you'll be able to suggest some way forward from there."

Her lips stopped moving. He raised his gaze to her eyes. "Indeed." He hesitated; it was patently obvious that she had every intention of playing an active role in the ensuing investigation. Given he knew her family, he was unquestionably honor-bound to dissuade her from such a reckless endeavor, yet equally unquestionably any suggestion she retreat to the hearth and leave him to chase the villains would meet with stiff opposition. He inclined his head. "As it happens I'm free tomorrow. Perhaps I could meet you at the Foundling House in the morning?"

He'd steer her out of the investigation after he had all the facts, after he'd learned everything she knew about this strange business.

She smiled brilliantly, once again disrupting his thoughts.

"Excellent!" Penelope gathered her gloves and muff, and stood. She'd gained what she wanted; it was time to leave. Before he could say anything she didn't want to hear. Best not to get into any argument now. Not yet.

He rose and waved her to the door. She led the way, pulling on her gloves. He had the loveliest hands she'd ever seen on a man, long-fingered, elegant and utterly distracting. She'd remembered them from before, which was why she hadn't offered to shake his hand.

He walked beside her across his front hall. "Is your carriage outside?"

"Yes." Halting before the front door, she glanced up at him. "It's waiting outside the house next door."

His lips twitched. "I see." His man was hovering; he waved him back and reached for the doorknob. "I'll walk you to it."

She inclined her head. When he opened the door, she walked out onto the narrow front porch. Her nerves flickered as he joined her; large and rather overpoweringly male, he escorted her down the three steps to the pavement, then along to where her brother's town carriage stood, the coachman patient and resigned on the box.

Adair reached for the carriage door, opened it and offered his hand. Holding her breath, she gave him her fingers—and tried hard not to register the sensation of her slender digits being engulfed by his much larger ones, tried not to notice the warmth of his firm clasp as he helped her up into the carriage.

And failed.

She didn't—couldn't—breathe until he released her hand. She sank onto the leather seat, managed a smile and a nod. "Thank you, Mr. Adair. I'll see you tomorrow morning."

Through the enveloping gloom he studied her, then he raised his hand in salute, stepped back and closed the door.

The coachman jigged his reins and the carriage jerked forward, then settled to a steady roll. With a sigh, Penelope sat back, and smiled into the darkness. Satisfied, and a trifle smug. She'd recruited Barnaby Adair to her cause, and despite her unprecedented attack of sensibility had managed the encounter without revealing her affliction.

All in all, her night had been a success.

Barnaby stood in the street, in the wreathing fog, and watched the carriage roll away. Once the rattle of its wheels had faded, he grinned and turned back to this door.

Climbing his front steps, he realized his mood had lifted. His earlier despondency had vanished, replaced with a keen anticipation for what the morrow would bring.

And for that he had Penelope Ashford to thank.

Not only had she brought him a case, one outside his normal arena and therefore likely to challenge him and expand his knowledge, but even more importantly that case was one not even his mother would disapprove of him pursuing.

Mentally composing the letter he would pen to his parent first thing the next morning, he entered his house whistling beneath his breath, and let Mostyn bolt the door behind him.